D0500159

THE COMMANDER

Also by Patrick A. Davis

- ★ The General
- ★ The Passenger
- ★ The Colonel

THE COMMANDER

PATRICK A. DAVIS

G. P. PUTNAM'S SONS
NEW YORK

This is a work of fiction. Names, characters, places, and incidents either are the product of the author's imagination or are used fictitiously, and any resemblance to actual persons, living or dead, business establishments, events, or locales is entirely coincidental.

G. P. Putnam's Sons
Publishers Since 1838
a member of
Penguin Putnam Inc.
375 Hudson Street
New York, NY 10014

Published simultaneously in Canada

Library of Congress Cataloging-in-Publication Data

Davis, Patrick A.
The commander / Patrick A. Davis.
p. cm.
ISBN 0-399-14002-5
1. Americans—Korea (South)—Fiction. 2. Korea (South)—Fiction. I. Title.
PS3554.A937617C66 2002 2002022708
813'.54—dc21

Printed in the United States of America
10 9 8 7 6 5 4 3 2 1

This book is printed on acid-free paper. ♾

Book design by Stephanie Huntwork

To Colonel Dennis (Gumby) Hilley,
friend, LCWB classmate, and the
most courageous person I know.

ACKNOWLEDGMENTS

★ As always, I have many people to thank for their selfless efforts in helping me mold this book into something readable.

My heartfelt gratitude to Bob and Katie Sessler, who are exceptional editors, wise counselors, and even better friends. Thanks also to my informal reading team for having the courage to be honest even when I didn't want to listen: Nate and Linda Green, Doug and Ann Anderson, Dave and Catherine Mark, Michael and Lori Roche, Cecil and Barb Fuqua, and Delores and David Olson.

A deep and abiding thanks to Kathy and Bobby Baker, Martha Jones, Andrew Hobbs, Carolyn Grieser, and Kevin Esselstrom and Becky Stefanski of WaldenBooks, for their support and friendship over the years, and to Mark and Dana Johnson of Barnes & Noble, for their efforts to publicize a new author.

I'd also like to express my appreciation to Vina Houck, Karen Poe, Pu-cha Choe, and Che Choe, for patiently answering my questions on Korean customs and laboring through the initial translations. Thanks also to SSgt Melissa Prince USAF and Kyeong-seon West, linguists extraordinaire, for keeping me straight on the Korean spelling; to Dr. Bill Burke, M.D., for sharing his medical and forensic wisdom; to Chris Pepe and Lily Chin at Putnam, for their careful nurturing of this novel; and to my agent, Karen Solem, for continuing to aspire and believe.

Finally I would like to thank my wife, Helen, whose love and faith still inspires me; my parents Bill and Betty Davis, who made everything possible; and my niece Charlotte Steiner, who'll one day write the novel that I never could.

1

TUESDAY

It was another muggy summer evening in Song-tan, South Korea, an industrial city roughly sixty miles south of Seoul, and I was playing salesman in my wife's jewelry store located in the Ville, the GI term for the ten square blocks of shops, bars, and whorehouses outside the main gate of Osan Air Base. A vaguely familiar young airman in a green Battle Dress Utility uniform stood before me at the counter, intently looking over a diamond engagement ring. He glanced up and asked nervously, "How much is it, Major Webber?"

"Eleven hundred dollars," I answered, finally placing him as the personnel clerk who had processed my separation paperwork from the Air Force last month. I added, "And you can relax, Tanner. I'm not a major or a cop anymore. Call me Burt."

Airman Tanner quickly diverted his eyes back to the ring. "Sure, Maj—uh, Burt."

I had to smile at his reaction. Like most of the base personnel who came into the store, Tanner treated me as if I were still Major Burton Webber, the chief of the Osan Air Base Office of Special Investigations. Frankly, I saw myself that way, too. I'd planned on being a military criminal investigator until I could have retired at twenty years. Instead, I'd abruptly resigned from the Air Force after fifteen, forgoing any chance of a pension. A lot of people thought I was crazy not to stick out the extra time, but in light of the circumstances, I really had no choice. Besides, it's not like my wife, Chung-hee, and I are hurting for money. Even though her jewelry store, which Chung-hee's father left to her when he died, is fairly modest compared to those back home, it does pretty well. Last year we cleared almost two hundred grand, give or take.

Not that I saw myself running a jewelry store in Korea for the rest of my life. But until Chung-hee and I could figure out our next move, maybe sell out and move back to the States, it's not a bad gig.

Airman Tanner sighed dejectedly and handed me the ring. "It's sure pretty, but—"

"Too much, huh?" I said, knowing it was. As a two-striper, Tanner barely made that much money in a month. To me, it's a crime how little military enlisted were paid, but don't get me started.

Tanner nodded.

I said, "You could make payments—no?" He was shaking his head.

"I'm heading home to Iowa in a couple of weeks. I was going to give it to my girl then."

"How much can you afford?"

"Maybe seven, eight hundred."

"A ring like this will run you a couple of grand back in the States. Maybe more."

"I know . . ." He drifted off with a shrug. "Guess I'd better go with something smaller—"

"Not so fast. Maybe we can still work something out."

"Oh?"

Before knocking that much off the sticker, I'd wanted to clear it with my wife. Even though she's always gone along with my altruism, it bugs her when I let items go below cost.

At the moment, Chung-hee was at the far end of the counter, haggling over the price of Korean Rolex knockoffs with a couple of fighter pilots in flight suits. I settled on a stool, waiting for her to finish. Watching her, I kept thinking I was one lucky man.

By any standard, Chung-hee was a beautiful woman. At five-seven, she's tall for a Korean, with shiny, waist-length black hair and delicate, almost fragile, features. She's pushing thirty, looks twenty, and has the kind of willowy figure made for magazine covers. We'd met shortly after I arrived in Korea, when I'd popped in to buy something for my sister's birthday. While I'd definitely noticed her looks, what really heightened my interest was her accent. Chung-hee speaks English with a soft southern drawl, like she'd been raised in the Deep South. Later, after I finally wore her down and she agreed to go out with me, she explained that she'd received her undergraduate degree at the University of Alabama and earned her master's in economics at Auburn. She'd planned on a career as a Wall Street analyst but, upon her father's sudden death, had to return to run the store and look after her mother.

We had a whirlwind courtship that caught us both by surprise and became engaged within a month. In hindsight, I probably should have kept our relationship quiet until my tour was up and married Chung-hee when I returned to the States. But when you're in love, you don't really stop to think. My biggest mistake was misjudging my superiors' resistance to the marriage. Once I announced our engagement, they acted as if I'd suddenly lost my senses. Next thing I knew, I was summoned before a very annoyed Lieutenant General Harry Muller, the 7th Air Force commander.

General Muller started off by reminding me that the military had an informal policy of discouraging marriages between servicemen and Korean nationals. He rehashed what I already knew, that most of these unions were shams, where some naive kid was enticed, hooked, reeled in, then dumped once he brought the woman to the States. Muller stated that, in my position as a commander and the base's top cop, I had a responsibility to set an example for the troops.

"For chrissakes, Burt," General Muller had said, "fucking these women is one thing, but marrying them. You gotta be shitting me."

I almost lost it then, but didn't feel like going to Leavenworth for punching out a three-star. I tried to explain that Chung-hee wasn't just some hooker I'd picked up, but Muller wasn't in any mood to listen. He cut me off with a not-so-subtle threat about what the marriage could do to my career. After a heated exchange, I bluntly told him my mind was made up, saluted smartly, and left.

Two weeks later, Chung-hee and I got married in a traditional Korean ceremony. Only a few people from the base bothered to attend. My primary promotion board for lieutenant colonel met the following year. I had a fistful of outstanding ratings and should have been a shoo-in.

I was passed over.

"I tried to warn you" was all General Muller had said, when he gave me the news.

That episode occurred two months ago. The next day I handed in my resignation and—

I glanced out the front window at the sound of a car door slamming. It was dusk now, and the streetlights had come on. I saw a tall, black colonel in Air Force blues emerge from a staff car, a cell phone to his ear. He paused on the curb, continuing his conversation.

My jaw tightened. *Him? Coming here?*

"You need something, hon?"

When I faced Chung-hee, she was giving me a quizzical look as she rang up a sale for the fighter jocks. As they left, I went over and made my pitch about giving Tanner a break on the ring.

Chung-hee rolled her eyes in exasperation. "Burt, this is a business. We can't keep—"

She broke off, stiffening visibly. I grimaced, turning toward the front door. The bell above it tinkled as the colonel entered, tucking his cell phone into his jacket. In his late thirties, he was young for a full bull, athletically built and with prominent cheekbones that tapered to a square jaw. Decked out in his uniform, with the rows of fruit salad on his chest, he cut an imposing figure. He slowly removed his wheel cap, took a few tentative steps, then stopped, eyes on us. He flashed a friendly smile.

"Hello, Chung-hee," he said.

"Hello, Raymond."

He nodded to me. "Burt."

I glowered back at Colonel Raymond Johnson, General Muller's executive officer and chief dog walker, not trusting myself to speak. I noticed Airman Tanner had automatically popped to attention, eyes riveted to the silver eagles on Raymond's shoulders. In Tanner's world, the only things higher than a colonel were generals and God, not necessarily in that order.

We all stood in an awkward silence, listening to the rattle of the ancient window air conditioner. Rock music pulsed faintly from the bar next door.

"It really is good to see you, Raymond," Chung-hee said, sounding as if she meant it.

I shot her a look of annoyance. But then she'd always liked him.

Raymond nodded. "Look, I'm sorry I haven't come around recently—"

I cut him off. "Save the excuses, Ray. What are you doing here?"

He shrugged. "Just wanted to drop by and say hello."

"That's the only reason, huh?"

"That's it." He tossed out another smile.

"You're lying," I said.

Ray blinked in surprise.

"Burt . . . ," Chung-hee said, her voice rising in warning.

I ignored her, my eyes boring into Ray's, whose face was now a mask. "Two months. We haven't heard from you for two months. Not even a goddamn phone call. What's the matter? Too busy playing lapdog for General Muller . . ."

"Burt, please . . . ," Chung-hee said.

". . . or maybe screwing over another buddy?"

"*Fuck* you, Burt," Ray snarled, suddenly stepping toward me. He planted his feet wide, glaring at me.

I waved a hand toward him in disgust. At six-three, Ray was big, but I was bigger. I had him by forty pounds and two inches. Out of the corner of my eye, I caught Airman Tanner staring at us in shock. In his mind it didn't compute, an ex-major chewing out a full bird.

Chung-hee grabbed my arm hard, letting me have it with a stream of rapid-fire Korean. She stuck her face up to my chin, saying, "That's enough, Burton. Raymond made the effort to come by. The least you can do is—"

"He drove up in General Muller's staff car," I interrupted.

Her pretty brow furrowed.

I pointed at the curb, where the car was parked, its three-star placard visible under the glow of the streetlights. "Ask him, honey," I said. "Ask Ray when he suddenly began using the general's car for social calls."

Chung-hee looked at Ray.

He sighed, his anger fading into something approaching embarrassment. "Guilty as charged. I was sent here by General Muller. He has a . . . proposal for Burt." Noting Chung-hee's disappointment, he added, "Look, I've been meaning to talk things out. Clear the air. But it never seemed the right time . . ." He lapsed into silence, realizing Chung-hee had tuned him out.

No one spoke for a moment.

I spotted Tanner, sneaking toward the door. I said, "Tanner, wait. The ring—"

By then, Tanner had flung the door open and was motoring down the sidewalk.

I shook my head. To Ray, I said, "Tell General Muller the answer is no."

"Burt, at least hear me out—"

"No point. I'm not interested." For emphasis, I pivoted, heading for the stairs at the back, which led up to the office on the second floor.

Ray said, "Dammit, this is important. We need your help."

I kept walking. "Talk to Captain Sorenson."

"Sorenson is in Pusan, working a case with the Navy. Besides, this thing is out of her league."

I was almost to the staircase. I swung around and squinted at Ray. The desperation in his voice confirmed the obvious, that something damned serious had occurred to bring him here. His dig against Captain Melissa Sorenson, my former deputy who'd run the base OSI office, suggested what that probably was.

The cop in me wanted to give in, hear him out. And if it had just been my anger toward General Muller holding me back, maybe I would have. But I couldn't get past my deeper resentment toward the institutional racism that existed on Osan and its effect on Chung-hee.

After our marriage, I'd tried to prepare Chung-hee for the bias she would face, but she wouldn't listen. She was determined to fit into my world, become the ideal officer's wife. With her education and fluency in English, she was convinced her assimilation into the country-club world of the military spouse wouldn't be a problem.

She was mistaken.

From the beginning, wherever we went on base there were disapproving glances and whispered comments. When Chung-hee tried to reach out to the other wives, she was not-so-politely rebuffed. In social gatherings, the women went out of their way to avoid her. After a month, Chung-hee finally got the painful message that no one would ever care about her degrees or accomplishments. In their eyes, she was judged to be no different from the hundreds of women who plied their trade in the Ville's seedy bars.

I gazed into Chung-hee's beautiful face, to see how she wanted me to play this. She gave me a nod, which I anticipated. She'd always had a capacity for forgiveness that went way beyond mine.

I shifted my attention to Ray. "We talking about a murder?"

He hesitated. "I'm not allowed to say anything until you agree to help."

"Fine. Have it your way."

I turned my back on him and went up the stairs.

★ The colorful flower-print wallpaper in the upstairs office projected a sense of cheerfulness that contrasted with my mood. An ornately carved rosewood desk sat across from the door, and a six-foot-high steel safe was tucked in the back corner. In between were four metal file cabinets, a wooden table topped by a computer and fax machine, and two straight-backed rattan chairs. Dozens of grainy black-and-white photographs of Chung-hee's family covered one wall. Most depicted relatives who had been trapped in North Korea when the armistice was signed. Chung-hee's father had hoped to live long enough to see a reunified Korea, but hadn't made it.

I slumped down heavily in the worn leather chair behind the cluttered desk, surprised at the turmoil I felt. I tried to convince myself that I wasn't a cop anymore, that I had no obligation to help. Still the guilt tugged at me. I swore.

I'd left the office door open and could hear Ray and Chung-hee conversing downstairs. Ray seemed to do most of the talking. From the bits and pieces floating up, I realized he was trying to talk Chung-hee into approaching me, to see if she could get me to change my mind.

She would go along, of course. In spite of the recent problems between Ray and me, she still considered him my closest friend.

And for almost twenty years, he had been.

Ray and I went back to our days as freshman cadets at the Citadel, the military college in Charleston, South Carolina. We'd been recruited for football; I was an offensive tackle from upstate New York, and he was a highly regarded quarterback out of Virginia. We became friends early on because we were both initially regarded with indifference by our classmates, most of whom hailed from prominent southern families. My sin was to be from New York, and his was being black. During our four years together, Ray and I grew extremely close, despite sharing few interests outside football. My approach to school was to have fun and get by with as little effort as possible. Ray, on the other hand, was always striving. Whether it was academics, athletics, or playing soldier, he always had to be the best. He got pretty close, too, graduating number three in our class.

But for Ray, close wasn't good enough. I remembered going with him to a bar a few days after the final class standings were announced. Ray wasn't much of a drinker, so when he inhaled his third bourbon, I knew something was wrong.

Ray had never been one to share his feelings, and I had to ask a half dozen times before he got drunk enough to tell me. He said he'd called his father, a retired Navy captain, and told him his graduation order.

"And you know what the son of a bitch said," Ray said bitterly.

I shook my head.

"Said if I'd worked harder, I coulda been the first black man to graduate number one."

At that moment, I remembered feeling truly sorry for him.

Ray got an odd look in his eyes as he drained his drink. "I'm gonna show him, Burt. I'm gonna show that bastard. You'll see."

The raw emotion in his voice unnerved me. There wasn't anything I could say, so I just nodded.

In the ensuing years, Ray had kept that promise. By continuing to work and achieve, he'd risen spectacularly up the Air Force pecking order, pinning on full colonel years ahead of his contemporaries, like me. Still, that only put him even in his personal competition and Ray wanted more.

Frankly, that's what started our rift: his ambition to make general and surpass his father, no matter the cost. Even if that meant abandoning a friend.

I frowned, realizing the voices had stopped. Moments later I heard footsteps coming up the stairs. Heavy steps.

I looked toward the door.

2

Ray appeared in the doorway. "Chung-hee thinks we should talk," he said quietly.

I shrugged.

"Mind if I come in?"

I hesitated, then waved him to a chair.

After he sat, he gave me a long look. "For the last time, I didn't know General Muller screwed you on your OPR."

OPR stood for the annual officer performance report. I'd been passed over for lieutenant colonel because, in my most recent one, General Muller had marked "nonconcur" in the promotion block.

"Ray," I said wearily, "we've been through this. You're his exec. You processed the evaluation—"

"Damn right. And when I passed it to him, Muller said he *would* recommend promotion. How was I supposed to know the son of a bitch was lying? I was as surprised as you were when you didn't get picked up for light bird."

"Uh-huh," I said dryly.

"Cut me some slack, huh? If I'd known, don't you think I would have told you?"

"Maybe. Unless you were ordered not to."

His face hardened. "You're way out of line, Burt. You know I'd never have gone along with something like—"

"What about my wedding?"

Ray grimaced, but said nothing. He had no response, and we both knew it. Ray had promised to come to the ceremony but never showed. Later, he'd called to apologize, explaining that General Muller had suggested it wouldn't look good for his executive officer to attend.

"Jesus, Burt, what was I supposed to do?" Ray had said. "The son of a bitch practically ordered me not to go."

I'd told him I understood, that it was okay. But of course it wasn't okay. I was hurt. From then on, I knew our friendship would only go so far.

Ray eased back in his chair with an apologetic smile. "We've been friends for a long time. Let's not let it end like this."

I appraised him, trying to determine whether he was sincere or just talking. Because with Ray, I couldn't tell anymore.

"Aw, hell," he said, rubbing a hand over his face. "You're right. I know I push too hard, trying to make rank. Over the years, I must have told myself a hundred times to ease up, but it's not that easy to . . . to just turn things off. And it's cost me big-time. First Linda and the kids . . ." He focused on me. "And now maybe you."

Linda was his ex-wife. She'd gamely hung on for five years, trying to get Ray to put her and their twin sons, Michael and James, somewhere on his list of priorities. I remembered her phone call to me, a week before she left him. They'd had a fight about his working another weekend, and Linda was crying. She said she couldn't take the neglect anymore and asked me whether I thought he would ever change. I was torn about how to respond, but figured I owed her the truth. Besides, I wasn't telling her anything she didn't already know.

"He won't," I'd said.

Their divorce became final a year later, shortly before Ray came to Korea. In the past fourteen months, he's flown back twice to see his sons. He'd planned another visit recently, but had abruptly canceled it without explanation.

Ray was staring at me, his expression subdued. As if he sensed my thoughts, he said, "She recently got remarried, you know."

"Linda?"

A nod. "A college professor. That's why I didn't fly out to see the kids. I couldn't have handled seeing him there. With them."

"I'm sorry, Ray."

"Yeah . . ." He stared at his hands.

Seeing his pain, I felt a wave of sympathy. Even though he hadn't been much of a husband or father, he'd loved Linda and his boys deeply.

Looking up, he said, "Burt, I'd really like to square things between us—"

"We're square."

"You sure?"

"Like a box." I gave him a faint smile. "Anyway, Chung-hee thinks I overreacted. Maybe she's right. I always knew getting passed over was a possibility, but when it actually happened—" I stopped. The cell phone in Ray's jacket was chirping.

He answered it, listened for perhaps ten seconds, then said curtly, "I'll call you back in five minutes, sir." He eyed me uneasily as he hung up. "That concerned you . . . whether you'd agreed to help."

I shook my head. "Tell General Muller—"

"That was Ambassador Gregson."

I frowned, my curiosity rising. I had gotten to know Ambassador Gregson from a case I'd worked on last year, involving an Air Force major assigned to the American embassy in Seoul. It turned out the guy was a junkie who had been selling classified information to North Korean operatives to support his drug habit. I asked, "Why would Gregson care whether I'm involved—"

Ray abruptly stood and went to the door.

After he shut it, he returned, speaking quickly. "Burt, what I can tell you is this thing is damned serious. The Korean government, the State Department, the American military, everyone is jumping through hoops, trying to figure out how to handle the situation. The current plan is to keep the particulars out of the press until an investigation can be conducted to determine who is responsible. The Koreans will have the lead, but Ambassador Gregson wants an American to monitor the investigation and protect U.S. interests. You must have impressed Gregson on that embassy investigation, because he personally called General Muller and ordered him to assign you to this thing. When Muller told him you'd resigned from the service, Gregson went ballistic. He calmed down when I told him you still lived in the area and might be available. Officially, you'll be a contract civilian assigned to the embassy security detail. Gregson's already having the paperwork ginned up for your signature." Ray stepped toward me with an expectant look. "So how about it?"

"Jesus," I murmured. Ray had spit everything out so fast that I was having trouble taking it all in. "We're not talking a murder investigation, are we?" Because with all the high-level interest, I was thinking it had to be something with a major political connection, possibly another espionage case involving a high-ranking diplomat or—

"First things first. You in?"

I paused, uncomfortable with rushing into a decision before knowing the facts. But I knew Ray wouldn't give me anything more. "I'm in."

Ray grinned and asked for my fax number as he thumbed the redial on his cell phone. After a brief conversation with Ambassador Gregson, he made a second call to General Muller. By the time he hung up, my fax machine on the table was clicking away. I went over to it, and Ray joined me.

"Your contract with the embassy," he said to me.

I nodded. "Let's hear the rest of it."

"It's a murder."

"Okay . . ."

"A bar girl from one of the clubs. Her body was found a couple of hours ago in her apartment after someone anonymously called the Osan security police emergency line to report an injured woman. The Security Police dispatcher said the voice was heavily muffled, but was definitely made by a man." He paused. "An American."

I felt a chill. No wonder the State Department and the Korean government were running scared. This would be the third major PR hit against the U.S. military in less than a year. The first, the shocking revelation that during the Korean War, American GIs had intentionally gunned down fleeing civilians, generated a swell of anti-American sentiment among the Korean public. The U.S. government tried to temper the outrage by calling for a full inquiry and promising restitution to the victims. For almost six months, the policy seemed to work. The protests died away, and the clamor for an American troop withdrawal faded.

Then three GIs got liquored up and gang-raped a fourteen-year-old girl.

In the ensuing riots, a block of Seoul was burned to the ground and forty-two protesters, mostly college students, were killed by the Korean military. With emotions still raw, there would be no telling the extent of the carnage when the word got out that an American soldier had now murdered a Korean.

"Son of a bitch," I murmured.

Ray nodded grimly. "And that's not the worst of it. The brutality of the killing is particularly scary. If that aspect ever became public—"

"How brutal?"

The fax machine had gone silent, and Ray was plucking the pages from the tray. After a quick look, he passed them over. "Sign the last page and fax it back. Then we'll run over to the murder scene." He frowned at my head shake. "There a problem?"

I told him I needed to go home and change first, explaining that Korean detectives always wore suits and I was going to be out of place in a pullover shirt and khaki slacks. He was gazing at me skeptically when I finished.

"It's important, Ray. They might take my dress as a sign of disrespect."

"You're actually serious?"

I nodded. Ray's ignorance of Korean customs didn't surprise me. Other than an occasional shopping trip to the Ville, he rarely left the confines of the base.

Ray checked his watch. "There's no time, Burt. Investigation's already started. General Muller ordered me to get you there ASAP."

The lapdog image popped into my head again, but I refrained from comment. I quickly read through the contract.

It was for thirty days and listed my job title as a security consultant. I'd be paid a little over seven thousand dollars, the monthly salary of a GS-13—the Civil Service–rank equivalent to a lieutenant colonel. There wasn't anything in the fine print that I couldn't live with, so I grabbed a pen when I got to the last page.

"By the way," Ray said, "the girl was disemboweled."

I froze, holding the pen over the signature block. Seconds passed. I didn't move.

"I know," Ray said. "That really shook me, too."

But the horror of the crime didn't disturb me as much as what it suggested about my role. I slowly straightened, setting down the pen. "Why does Ambassador Gregson really want me on this case?"

Ray seemed puzzled. "I told you. You'd impressed him."

"Bullshit. The case against the major was cut-and-dried."

He shrugged. "Well, that's what Gregson told— What are you doing now?"

I'd stepped around him and was reaching for the phone on my desk. I said, "Gregson needs to understand I won't cover anything up. If an American turns out to be the killer, then I'm obligated to—"

"Oh, come on, Burt. Don't you think Gregson knows that? His concern . . . the State Department's concern . . . is that the ROKs don't pin this on some American without cause." ROK stood for Republic of Korea; it was a common term used to describe the South Koreans.

I gave Ray a dubious look. He was suggesting a possible frame job. To me that was the last thing the Koreans would do, because of all the turmoil it would cause.

"You're forgetting," Ray went on, "the push for reunification. A lot of ROK officials would love to see Uncle Sam tossed out because they think it will speed up the process."

I paused, holding the phone. Ray had a point, but I still thought I should—

"Trust me on this, Burt," Ray said. "You're wasting your time calling. Ambassador Gregson personally assured me he's only after the truth."

I couldn't help but wonder if maybe Ray had a reason for not wanting me to talk to Gregson. But that's crazy. Why should Ray mind if—

"Anyway," Ray added, "Ambassador Gregson won't be in now. He's already left for a meeting with President Rhee and the ROK cabinet. How about I call Gregson at home tonight? Express your concerns? Okay?"

I nodded, hanging up the phone. "A couple of things I'll need. I don't have a military ID to get on base."

"Way ahead of you. General Muller has instructed the security police to allow you entry."

"Fine. I'd also like someone from the OSI office assisting me."

"It's being arranged. That woman investigator you're so high on, Lieutenant Torres, will meet you at the scene."

I nodded my approval. Despite her relative inexperience, I considered Susan Torres the most competent investigator on the OSI staff.

"Anything else?" Ray asked.

I thought, then shook my head. It took me another minute to sign and fax the acceptance page to the embassy. I grabbed a notepad, my dog-eared Korean-English dictionary, and a couple of pens from the desk and went over to a small storage closet by the safe. Next to Chung-hee's raincoat hung a blue corduroy sports jacket that had seen better days. I slipped it on and joined Ray, who was holding open the door.

Following him out into a short hallway, I said, "I assume I'll report my findings to Ambassador Gregson."

"Nope. To me."

"Oh?"

He pulled up at the staircase and faced me. "Both Gregson and General Muller feel it will be more efficient for me to act as liaison. Not that I agree. Hell, I think it'd be easier for you to talk to them directly."

So did I. But at least this explained why Ray hadn't wanted me to call.

He gave a suggestive cough as he eyed my coat. "Uh, Burt, about your jacket. You might reconsider wearing something—"

"Don't go there, Ray."

He grinned, about-faced, and we went down the steps.

3

"So you're not angry with me?" Chung-hee asked.

She and I were huddled over the display counter while a couple of giggling blondes in matching *NSYNC T-shirts tried on gold chains nearby. When Ray and I had come downstairs, he'd continued out to the car and I'd peeled off to inform Chung-hee that I'd agreed to help on an investigation. I didn't go into any specifics, but I would later, and not just because she was my wife. A lot of the locals will tell her things that they would never reveal to a *Mi-guk-in*—an American. Since our marriage, she's twice come across information that has proved useful on a case. I asked her, "Why would I be angry with you?"

She seemed surprised. "Ray didn't say anything?"

"Such as . . ."

"It's . . . nothing." She glanced toward the staff car where Ray was now cinching the vinyl cover over the three-star placard, so we'd be a little less conspicuous cruising around. "You'd better go."

As if I were going to leave now. "Honey . . ."

She sighed, her eyes crawling up to me. "Promise you won't be mad."

"Scout's honor."

She took a deep breath. "I told Ray the disagreement was mostly your fault."

I stared at her. "My fault? How could you say—" Her finger went to my lips. She told me to calm down.

I pulled away and lowered my voice. "I am calm. But, Jesus, why would you—" Again I got the finger. By now the two women were watching us with amused smiles.

Chung-hee dropped her hand, speaking into my ear. "I only told him that so he'd feel more comfortable approaching you."

I shook my head, both mystified and annoyed by her logic. "I gotta tell you that sounds damn silly to me. How in the world would—" I noticed the sudden coldness in her eyes. "Look, I didn't mean you were—"

"Silly?" Chung-hee breathed. "You think I'm silly, Burt."

Christ. "No. Of course not." I reached for her hand. She yanked it away.

I said, "Honey. Please. You know I'd never—"

She pushed past me and went over to the two women, who were no longer smiling. Instead, they glared at me as if I were the biggest jerk in the world.

I felt my face redden. I waited a few seconds, hoping Chung-hee would look my way. Not a chance. I made my way to the door and turned the handle, looking back. "I'll call when I know what time I'll be home."

Silence.

I sighed and stepped out into the night.

★ At night, the Ville resembled a seedy version of the old Las Vegas strip or a glitzy Mexican border town, with maybe a little Sodom and Gomorrah thrown in. Everywhere you looked along the main drag there was movement and color and noise. Gaudy neon signs on run-down buildings pulsed out the names of the seventy-odd bars and discos. Throngs of people, mostly base personnel, strolled the narrow sidewalks, disappearing into alleys or doorways as they went. On each street corner, the pimps—usually middle-aged former prostitutes decades past their prime—were busy shouting or tugging at GIs, trying to drum up business.

As I closed the jewelry-store door, I watched Chung-hee through the window, wondering if someone from the base had recently said something hurtful to her. Because that's what usually brought on these bouts of insecurity, where the slightest thing could set her off. I've told her she shouldn't let the comments get to her, but of course they do. And the more she hears them, the more she questions her own self-worth. That's what constant belittling does to a person. After a while, you start to believe that you are somehow inadequate or—

A car horn blared.

Ray's silhouette motioned impatiently from the staff car. I had to wait for a knot of GIs to stagger past me into the bar next door. The bouncer, a thick-necked guy in a red muscle shirt, shouted my name and pointed to an approaching black limo. I squinted, then nodded that I understood.

I went over to the staff car and rapped on the passenger window. When it whirred down, I told Ray I'd be a few more minutes.

"Dammit, Burt. We need to get—"

But I was already walking toward the limo, which had rolled to a stop in front of the bar. Moments later, a uniformed chauffeur the size of a small house popped out and hustled around to open the right rear door. A dapper-looking man with slicked-back gray hair emerged, wearing a white linen suit and smoking a cigarette. I got within ten feet of him before the chauffeur noticed me. He must've had a hard-on for burly white guys, because he immediately pivoted to me, a hand rising to the bulge under his jacket. The older man grunted something, and the chauffeur's face registered surprise. He dipped his head and meekly drifted back.

The older man came toward me with a smile. "*An-nyeong-ha-se-yo*, Burton." He spoke with a smoker's rasp and pronounced my name "button."

I gave a little bow. "Mr. Chun, *jal-ji-naet-sseo-yo*." I acknowledged Mr. Chun's greeting with the standard response that I was doing well.

Chun looked disappointed. "*Geu-nyang sam-chon-ira-go bul-leo-yo.*"

It took my brain a second to translate. He was telling me to call him uncle. "*Joe-song-hae-yo, sam-chon.*" My apologies, Uncle.

He smiled again, switching to English. "Your Korean is getting better, Burton."

"I'm trying."

He puffed on the cigarette, his eyes drifting past me to the jewelry store. "Tell my niece she should visit more often. My wife and I miss her." Even though he said it casually, I knew it wasn't a request.

"I'll tell her, Uncle."

As he dropped the cigarette to the curb, he glanced to the covered placard on the staff car. He returned to me, his face puzzled. "Is that General Muller's car?"

"His aide is an old friend."

A nod. Then curtly: "*Jo-ka-ttal-e-ge hal-mal it-chi-ma.*" Reminding me not to forget to speak with his niece.

"*A-rat-sseo-yo.*" I bowed.

"Good-bye, Burton."

"Good-bye, Uncle." As I stepped aside to let him by, I thought, *What the hell,* and gave the chauffeur a wave. "Later, Odd Job."

His fleshy face stared back blankly, but Chun laughed.

They continued into the bar, and I walked over to the staff car.

★ As I crawled into the passenger seat, Ray had the engine running and the air conditioner going full blast. He glowered at me. "Mind telling me what the hell that was all about?"

When I did, his eyebrows curled up. "Chun? That the guy who owns about a dozen businesses in the Ville?"

"Closer to twenty. He also chairs the Song-tan Business Council."

"Isn't he supposed to be tied to some crime syndicate in Seoul?"

"That's only a rumor." I didn't mention that Chung-hee told me it was true, which was why she avoided him.

Ray focused on the driver-side mirror, waiting for a base taxi to pass. "What do the local police say about him?"

"To me, nothing. That would be impolite."

"Impolite?"

"They don't want to tell me anything derogatory because I'm related to him." I clicked on my seat belt and added, "One cop did advise me to always treat Chun with *chon-gyong*. Respect."

Ray pulled a tire-squealing U-turn and tucked in behind the taxi. He glanced over. "Meaning don't piss off the old man?"

I nodded.

"So you don't?"

"What's the point?"

He grinned. "Sounds to me like you're a little afraid of him."

I let the comment go because it was basically true. Chun projected a quiet sense of violence that gave me the willies. And it didn't help that Chung-hee told me her uncle hadn't been exactly thrilled when he learned she was going to marry an American.

For the next few minutes Ray focused on the traffic, which crawled along because the cars constantly had to brake for people darting across the road. As we approached the end of the strip, the Osan Air Base main gate came into view. Instead of the normal complement of two guards manning the gatehouse, I spotted six, all wearing flak jackets and armed with M-16 rifles. Concrete berms had also been spaced in a Z pattern out front, so no vehicle bent on mayhem could blow through the checkpoint. The enhanced security was understandable but grossly inadequate. If the murder became public, Korean protesters would descend here en masse and the ROK government would be forced to send in the Army, essentially turning the area into a war zone.

At the three-way intersection, I expected Ray to hang a right down Arrogon Alley, toward the shabby buildings where most of the bar girls lived.

Instead, he continued on the main road, heading into downtown Songtan. I asked where we were going.

"The victim lived on Sochon Road."

This surprised me. I was familiar with the area because one of Chung-hee's cousins lived there. "You sure? That's a high-end residential section. Apartments go for at least a grand a month."

In response, Ray fished into his jacket and handed me a folded page. On it were neatly typed directions to a Sochon address. I passed the paper back thoughtfully.

Ray said, "Maybe she was splitting the rent with a couple of roommates. Why not?"

I was shaking my head. "Because she still couldn't afford it. Hustling drinks, a girl who busts her ass might make maybe five hundred bucks a month. After the bar owner takes his cut, she keeps maybe two hundred—"

He gave a low whistle. "The owner takes that much?"

"Sixty percent is standard until the girls pay back the bar owner for his investment." I shifted to face him. "You familiar with the process of how the owners get the girls to work for them?" I knew he probably wasn't, since this was a dirty little secret that the Koreans tried to keep quiet.

We stopped at a red light in an industrial part of town about a mile from the glitter of the Ville. Ray shrugged. "Never thought much about it."

So I rehashed what I'd learned from Chung-hee, that the owners lure the girls from the poorest villages with promises of high-paying factory jobs. When they show up, the women are told the original jobs are filled, but they can work as dancers in bars. Desperate for money, most take the offer. Once they begin dancing, they become trapped. The girls get charged big bucks with interest up-front for their costumes and rooms and anything else the owner could tack on. It often took years for them to work off their debt.

I finished my spiel as the light turned green. Ray came on the gas, murmuring, "Hell, you're talking slavery."

"Pretty much. And that's not even the worst part. Chung-hee says most of the girls are abandoned by their families because of the shame. So even if they manage to pay off their debts, there's nowhere for them to go. For most it's really a life sentence."

Ray was quiet, but I could tell he was troubled by what I'd said. A curious reaction, since he rarely displayed much compassion about anything.

At the next corner, we made a right past an abandoned Daewoo auto plant, another victim of the ongoing Asian recession. I settled back and watched the light poles flicker by, waiting for Ray to bring up the obvious explanation of how the girl could've paid for the apartment. When he didn't, I had a nagging suspicion why. I cleared my throat. "My guess is the girl had an American boyfriend. Probably an officer, since he could afford to pay—"

That's as far as I got because Ray's head snapped around, his face as angry as I'd ever seen it. "How the fuck can you know that?" he demanded.

"Now hold on a minute—"

"God*dammit*, Burt. You're supposed to be objective. I told Gregson you'd be objective. If you're going to assume that just because an American made the phone call—"

"Ray! Look out!"

We'd drifted into oncoming traffic. Ray jammed on the brakes and turned the wheel hard. We fishtailed wildly back into our lane, barely missing a small pickup.

Neither one of us spoke for a few moments.

I broke the silence, more disappointed than angry. "You lied to me."

He flashed a look of annoyance. "What's that supposed to mean?"

"Your reaction," I said dryly, "makes it clear that Ambassador Gregson has no interest in the truth. He wants a Korean tagged with this thing."

"Hell yes, he does. So does the ROK president. But if you're suggesting that either of them would cover up for an American, you're flat wrong." He saw I was about to respond. "I'm not finished."

I bit my tongue, shaking my head.

"As for my reaction," he went on, "I got pissed because it sounded like you'd already decided that an officer might be involved. We both know that if the girl had a sugar daddy, the guy could just as easily be a wealthy Korean or maybe even—"

Just then his cell phone rang. Ray answered it, listened intently, then said, "Aw, Christ. You must be kidding. When?" He swore. "We'll be there in ten minutes. What's that? Got it. I'll tell him." He hung up, eyeing me. "The shit just hit the fan. That was Lieutenant Torres calling from the dead girl's apartment. It seems the Korean cops are talking to the local press about the murder."

"I thought you said they were going to keep it quiet."

"That was the arrangement between the ROK government and the KNP."

The KNP was Korea's national police force, which operated almost like a fourth branch of the military. I suggested that maybe the cops down at the province level hadn't gotten the word that they were supposed to keep their mouths shut.

"Uh-uh. The bastards *knew,* Burt. We were assured the Province Police chief was on board. The only thing I can figure is that the ROKs have decided to pull a double cross and screw Uncle Sam." He paused, thinking. "Or maybe the detective in charge has a hard-on for Americans and is acting on his own."

His latter suggestion would never happen, but I didn't feel like explaining the Korean mentality toward obedience. I asked Ray if he knew the name of the detective.

"Torres said it was a guy named Lieutenant Son-yon Sam."

I eased back into my seat. "Relax. We're okay. I know him. He won't accuse an American without evidence."

"How the hell do you know that?"

I shrugged. "He likes Americans."

Ray shot me a dubious look as the car picked up speed.

★ Sochon Road was in the middle of a residential section in the southwestern part of Song-tan, not far from the soccer stadium. Because it was almost 8 P.M., traffic was fairly light. As we drove by a narrow cross street I recognized, I told Ray he'd missed a turn.

"This way's quicker," he said.

"You were here earlier?" A given because he'd never once stopped to look at the directions in his pocket.

He hesitated, then shook his head. "But I'm familiar with the area. I've come here with General Muller a couple of times to visit General Pak. A retired Korean four-star who lives nearby."

We made a left onto a winding street lined with small apartment houses and modest one-story homes. Two quick rights brought us onto Sochon Road. Here, the buildings were newer and more upscale, most having been built during the economic boom of the early nineties to cater to business types. After a few blocks Ray pointed to a charcoal gray, six-story job on the opposite corner. I dimly recalled that it had been under construction the last time I was here.

"Looks like Torres was right about the press," he said gloomily.

I nodded. In the circular driveway, I counted three satellite trucks, two vans, and a nest of black police cruisers. Men in suits and uniformed officers conversed under a green awning out front, most puffing on cigarettes.

Ray eased over to the curb. "Better drop you off here. Torres says to avoid the lobby because the reporters are there. Go around to the service entrance at the back and give her a call. She'll come down and let you in. You know her number?"

I nodded and held out my hand. "I'll need your cell phone."

Ray sighed and reluctantly handed it over, along with a spare battery he dug out from the glove compartment.

I said, "You want me to call you at home or the office?"

"The office until eleven."

I tucked the phone and battery in my jacket and reached for the door handle.

"Uh, Burt . . ."

When I glanced over, Ray was gazing at me apologetically. "I was out of line earlier. You handle this thing any way you want. Whatever you find out, I'll back you up all the way."

He sounded and looked sincere. Still, I was cautious because I knew if push came to shove, Ray would probably—

"I mean it," Ray said. "You're the quarterback on this thing. My job will be to keep the bastards off you."

His comment took me back to our days at school, when I used to tell him the same thing before each game. I smiled to let him know I appreciated the gesture, then climbed from the car. Before closing the door, I said, "If you change your mind about supporting me, I'll understand."

He frowned.

"There isn't any Korean sugar daddy, Ray. A wealthy Korean would never have a mistress who made her living fucking Americans."

Before he could reply, I closed the door and walked away.

★ In Korea, when you're six-five and blond, it's tough to go around unnoticed. Since a few of the reporters would probably recognize me from earlier investigations, I continued past the apartment building until I reached the cross street, then jogged across the intersection toward the fenced-in parking area at the rear.

If this were five years earlier, odds would be I wouldn't be going through these gyrations. Back then, the South Korean government still exercised considerable influence over the press and I could have waltzed in through the front door, knowing the reporters could be pressured to keep their mouths shut. When the current president, a Nelson Mandela–like dissident who'd been jailed by his predecessors, came to power, he actually followed through on the democratic reforms he'd promised. At the top of his list was ensuring complete freedom for the press.

Looking up at the seven-foot-high steel-mesh fence, I shook my head, thinking maybe dictatorships weren't all bad. I hunted down the gate that opened into an alley that smelled of rotting garbage. The gate was padlocked, so I went over to a shadowed area in a corner, waited for a car to pass, then pulled and grunted until I finally struggled over.

I was still breathing hard by the time I got to the service entrance. I squeegeed sweat from my forehead, tested the door with a yank, then took out the cell phone. It took four rings before a woman answered. Her voice sounded strained, and for a moment I thought I'd misdialed.

"Susan?"

"It's me, Burt. You downstairs?"

"Yes. Something wrong?"

A pause. "I'm looking at the body."

4

The service door opened and I stepped into a dank concrete corridor that smelled of fresh paint, blinking against the harshness of the fluorescent light. Lieutenant Susan Torres closed the door, then turned to me, her pretty face ashen. A small woman in her late twenties, she had curly dark hair and a killer figure that made men look more than once. Instead of a uniform, she wore a tan suit because the OSI brass had been smart enough to figure out that wearing one's rank hindered criminal investigations. Officers understandably resented being grilled by someone they outranked, while enlisted men felt intimidated when questioned by an officer.

I gave her a sympathetic smile. "You going to be okay?"

She leaned against a wall and pushed her hair from her eyes. "I'll survive. You heard how the victim died?"

I nodded.

"Nobody told me. When I walked in and saw the way she was, lying there . . . I . . . I almost lost it. Right in front of the ROKs." She grimaced, upset with herself.

"It could happen to anybody."

"Yeah, well . . ." She abruptly pushed away from the wall.

"Take another minute," I said.

She batted back my suggestion with an annoyed look and headed down the corridor.

I trailed after her, shaking my head. As usual, Susan was determined to prove how tough she was. When we first began working together, I thought her Joan Wayne attitude was a persona she'd created to prove herself in a man's world. My impression lasted for almost a month, until we went to the Officers' Club and she confided in me about her past over a beer. It turned out she hadn't been acting at all.

As Susan tells it, she'd grown up in a broken home in a rough section of East L.A. By the time she was seventeen, she had a half-dozen juvenile arrests on her record and an infant son. After dropping out of high school, she spent a year on welfare when she learned her younger brother had been killed in a drug deal. They'd been close, and his death made Susan realize that the only chance she and her son had for a future was for her to turn her life around. Taking classes at night, she got her GED, then impulsively joined the Air Force when she caught a commercial touting the educational benefits. She found it ironic that, considering her past, the Air Force assigned her to become a Security Policeman. She'd intended to transfer to another career field at the first opportunity, but never did because she discovered she liked law enforcement and was good at it. Over the next seven years, between her job and caring for her child, she somehow found the time to earn a bachelor's degree and eventually a commission as an officer.

That same determination with which Susan had transformed her life made her a good investigator. Once she began working a case, she stubbornly plugged away until she resolved it. It was a quality I'd wished more of my investigators had possessed.

Now don't get me wrong. She had more than her share of faults. She could be abrasive and a pain in the ass. But the bottom line was Susan got results.

We came to another door. She pushed through, and we entered a stairwell. I said, "Did Sammy mention why he decided to talk to the reporters?"

"Sammy?"

I explained that's what Lieutenant Son-yon Sam went by.

She made a face like she'd eaten something sour and started up the stairs. "What's his story, anyway?"

I sidled up next to her. "What do you mean?"

"Guy looks like a pimp. Talks like one, too."

I smiled. She was exaggerating, but Sammy did wear loud suits and was comfortable using American slang. South Korea still had a draft, and I told her that Sammy was a medic who had served his two-year hitch as a KATUSA, which was an acronym for Korean Assigned To United States Army. I added, "Sammy learned a lot of his English from the grunts in his unit. The rest he picked up from watching American TV. Mostly MTV and action movies."

"Figures," she grunted. "And he's never spent time in the States, huh?"

"Not that he's ever mentioned. Why?"

"Thought I noticed an accent. New York maybe."

I grinned. "His favorite actor is Sylvester Stallone."

She rolled her eyes like that said it all. I repeated my press conference question.

She shrugged. "Lieutenant Sam said he had no choice because the reporters showed up and began asking questions."

We reached the third-floor landing and continued up. "Who tipped them off?" I asked.

"Someone made an anonymous call. Probably a neighbor who heard the commotion. Lieutenant Sam said he gave the reporters what he had to, that a girl had been murdered and there were no suspects. He told me he didn't pass on that she worked in the Ville, but figures they'll find out the connection pretty quick."

"You know the victim's name?"

"Soon-ri Kim."

"That her real one?" Because bar girls changed names like their hairstyles, in an effort to shield their profession from their families.

"Hard to say. Someone went through the victim's purse and removed all her ID. My guess is the name's probably legit, since Lieutenant Sam—"

"He prefers Sammy."

She nodded. "Since Sammy got it from the lease."

I asked if robbery could be a motive.

"Not damn likely. There's still some cash in the purse, and nothing of value seems to be missing." She hesitated. "Besides, a thief wouldn't kill like that."

"Witnesses?"

"ROK cops are checking with the neighbors, but nothing yet. Part of the problem is the place has been opened only a few months and most of the apartments are still vacant. Only four people even live on her floor, and they were at work during the murder." She paused, then added, "Lieutenant Sam . . . Sammy . . . did say something about an old woman. I don't think it's anything though."

"Old woman?"

"When the cops showed, she was standing out on the curb. Apparently she was pretty distraught. And when the cops came back down to talk to her, she was gone."

"The victim have a maid?"

"No."

We'd passed the fifth floor, heading up to the sixth. I was getting winded again. "Is Sammy aware of the phone call to the base?"

"Yeah. But he said that doesn't prove squat. His take is it could have been a Korean who spoke English and made the call to throw off the investigation."

I nodded. An unlikely possibility, but one I hadn't considered.

We finally reached the sixth floor. Susan was going toward the fire door when she abruptly stopped to gaze up at me. Sounding uncharacteristically awkward, she said, "Burt, I want you to know that the unit . . . everyone . . . thinks you got screwed."

"Thanks."

"Anyway, you left before we had a chance . . . we all pitched in . . ." She reached into her pocket and took out a gold Rolex knockoff.

She gave it to me, saying, "It's engraved on the back."

I turned the watch over. On the back it said simply, "To Our Commander."

Something seemed to catch in my throat. "This means a great deal," I said.

She grinned and threw open the door to reveal a Provincial cop in a crisp black uniform. He squinted at us before drifting back to let us pass. As he did so, he gave Susan a condescending smile that suggested to me he'd heard about her reaction to seeing the body.

Susan obviously saw it that way, too, because without missing a beat, she looked right at the guy and said pleasantly, "Screw you, buddy."

The cop gazed back blankly, the smile frozen on his face. We scooted by him into a carpeted hallway that teed right to left, rooms on either side. A few doors down, two more uniforms were interviewing a man in a green silk robe. Past the elevator, another policeman was talking to a bookish-looking man in a brown suit.

The cops fell silent, their eyes never leaving Susan as she led me to an apartment at the far end of the hallway. An expected reaction in a male-dominated society like Korea, where a female detective was considered an amusing curiosity. Of course the fact that she was a looker didn't hurt.

The apartment door was open, and as we approached, we could see a forensics team in their baby blue jumpsuits going over the room. Behind them, a photographer darted around, snapping pictures. Susan paused to point out a second set of fire doors, just to the left of the apartment.

"That stairwell exits on the south side of the building, Burt. Might explain how the killer got in and out without anyone noticing."

"To enter from the outside, would he need a key?"

She nodded.

"Any security in the lobby entrance?"

"A key-card entry system. Visitors can be buzzed in. No guard or surveillance cameras."

"Did the victim have any roommates?"

"Nope. Lived alone."

Which suggested that the victim either let in her killer or knew him well enough to have given him a key.

At the door, Susan stepped aside. "Think I'll hang out here and call the Security Police. Let them know we'll drop by later tonight to listen to the tape."

It was her way of saying she needed a few minutes to gather herself. I said, "I'll also want to interview the dispatcher who took the call."

A nod. "Better put on these." She held out a pair of latex gloves.

As I slipped them on, I gave her a questioning look.

"She's in the bedroom."

5

I took a moment to study the lock on the door, which was sturdy and showed no signs of having been forced. I continued inside, careful to avoid the forensics men as I looked over the apartment. The apartment was larger than I had expected, with a separate living-and-dining area to the right and a kitchen to the left. The drapes along the back wall were half open, and I could see a small balcony and the silhouette of an enormous flowerpot. The floor was a dark polished wood and tastefully accented with brightly colored throw rugs. The furnishings consisted of a black lacquer dining table with four chairs and a wicker sofa with two matching armchairs spaced around a short Korean chest that served as a coffee table. In a corner by a floor lamp sat a television on a pedestal and a curio cabinet topped by celadon figurines. Everything gleamed as if new and projected an understated elegance that I wouldn't have expected from a girl who worked in a bar. The only clutter came from a couple of magazines on the chair and a string purse that appeared to have been tossed to the floor, its contents strewn nearby. Compared with the dives most of the dancers lived in, this place was practically a palace.

One of the forensics men squinted at me as he dusted the phone on an end table. I vaguely remembered him from a burglary case last year. In my kindergarten Korean, I asked where Sammy was, and he jabbed a gloved thumb at an area behind the kitchen wall.

As I walked over, I spotted a partially closed door and a man in a white jumpsuit standing outside, peering in. White meant the coroner's office.

I approached and tapped the guy on the shoulder. He frowned but moved aside.

I entered a spacious bedroom that held a four-poster queen-sized bed, a bureau with an attached mirror, and two formidable dressers, each topped with a few framed photographs. Again, the furniture struck me as new. Glancing to the right, I saw a closet and a white-tiled bathroom. Two men in suits stood at the foot of the bed, their backs to me, talking quietly. Even though they blocked my view, I could tell they were looking down at the victim on the bed. I eased to the right to get a better look.

I'd mentally prepared myself for what I would see, but still recoiled in horror. The girl was lying faceup, her hands and feet spread-eagled and secured with white rope to each corner of the bed. Even though her head was angled away from me and long dark hair obscured much of her face, I could tell she was young. For an instant, I focused on the bright red fabric jammed in her mouth. Panties, I realized. She wore a short, pale-pink blouse pushed up below her breasts and was nude from the waist down.

And that's where I forced myself to look now, at the gaping, football-sized wound that began at her crotch and ended a few inches below her blouse. Raw flesh and portions of her intestines were visible through a crusted layer of matted blood, much of which had soaked into the sheets.

"Jesus . . ." I shivered involuntarily at the pain she must have felt.

The men turned as if startled. The guy on the left was middle forties, round, and balding. The second man was at least ten years younger, thin to the point of being gaunt, with boyish good looks. His face lit up as he casually shot the cuffs of his garishly gold Armani-style suit and stepped toward me, hand extended.

"Hey, hey, my man, Burt," Detective Lieutenant Son-yon Sam of the Provincial Police said. "About time you got here. I thought you'd decided to sit this one out. Spend time with that beautiful wife. Nice jacket. Where'd you get it? Salvation Army?" He grinned at his joke.

I managed a smile as we shook hands. In the three times we'd teamed up together, Sammy always seemed to be in constant motion, a walking and talking Energizer Bunny. His quick smile and engaging manner masked a ruthless efficiency that made him one of the top homicide cops in Korea. Blessed with a remarkable intellect that he regularly downplayed, Sammy also possessed an almost computerlike ability to constantly sift through scenarios until he hit the one that seemed most likely. It wasn't a conscious thing. You'd be having a drink or maybe driving somewhere, and out of the blue, he would toss out a suggestion. More often than not, that turned out to be key to unraveling the case. From Sammy's perspective, the one tangible benefit of his "hunches" was being allowed to dress the way he did. While his flashy clothes annoyed his conservative superiors, he was too successful for them to screw with.

After Sammy introduced the second man as Dr. Yee, the Song-tan deputy coroner, he stepped back to look me over. "It's good to see you, Burt. How long's it been? Three, four months?"

He was referring to the suicide we'd worked, where a very inebriated young airman had done a half gainer from his Korean fiancée's fourth-story apartment after he found out she was dumping him for another guy. "About."

His face turned serious. "I heard about what happened. I'm real sorry, man. General Muller is a *gae-ja-sik*. You understand what it means?"

I nodded. "He's an asshole."

He thumped his chest. "Damn right. If you want to get drunk sometime, give me a call. We'll have fun. I guarantee you'll forget your problems."

"Thanks, Sammy." I glanced at the doctor, whose lost expression told me he didn't understand English. Returning to Sammy, I dug out my notepad and asked him how long the girl had been dead.

"The doctor here guesses about four to five hours."

I scribbled. "So she was killed between one and two this afternoon?"

"Around then. He'll narrow down the time after the autopsy." Sammy said something to the doctor. The guy nodded, then motioned to his assistant by the door, who entered, carrying a large leather case. The two stepped around the bed, and while the doc bent over the wound, the assistant opened the case and handed him surgical forceps and a small flashlight. As the doctor gently probed the girl's wound, the assistant rose and carefully began taping a plastic bag over one of the girl's hands to preserve trace evidence.

Watching all this, I shook my head. "Doesn't make sense. Why the hell would someone kill her this way?"

Sammy popped a piece of gum into his mouth. "No clue. It wasn't a quick killing, that's for sure."

"What do you mean?"

"Her main blood vessels weren't cut. No major arteries in the stomach area. She died slowly. The doc says it could have taken twenty, thirty minutes for her to bleed to death. Maybe even longer."

I felt a chill as I noted this. "So they were going for pain? Wanted to torture her—*no?*" I'd glanced up from writing to see Sammy doing a slow head shake.

"If they'd wanted to hurt her, why did they cut her only once?"

"Once?" I immediately looked at the body. Because of the caked blood, it was hard to tell much. There did seem to be only one deep incision below her stomach—

Sammy said, "Doc said it was like gutting a fish. One big slice to open her up. He thinks he's got a theory why. He's checking it out now."

"Checking what out now?"

But Sammy was focused on the coroner's assistant, who was starting to untie the girl's right hand. He barked out angrily, and the guy's head snapped up. Sammy immediately went over and inspected the knot on the girl's wrist. I understood his concern. Knots were evidence to be preserved. Sammy straightened and lit into the bowing and scraping assistant. In the past, I'd seen other senior investigators viciously slap down subordinates who'd screwed up, but getting physical wasn't Sammy's style. He pointed to the case and said a word I understood. *Kal.* Knife. He wanted him to cut the ropes free.

As the assistant reached into the black bag, Sammy motioned me over. When I approached, he pointed to the knot, which was slightly loosened but intact. The skin around the wrist area was rubbed raw from the girl's desperate attempts to break free. Sammy said, "This one isn't tied like the others, Burt."

"Oh?"

"It's a square knot. The rest are like this." He indicated the other end of the rope, which was tied around a corner post. I studied the knot and shook my head. My scouting career had begun and ended in Cub Scouts. All I could tell was the knot was a lot more complicated than a square knot.

"Both on her feet and her other hand, too. Those are all tied all the same." He gave me a meaningful look.

I understood. "Two knots suggest at least two killers."

"And the rope is old and dirty. You probably noticed."

I had. The rope appeared to be made of a natural fiber, possibly hemp. It was frayed from use and portions were stained a light rust color, as if someone had handled them with soiled hands.

"It seems to me," a voice said from behind, "that would suggest the killers weren't American military. Someone from the base wouldn't normally be carrying around an old rope."

Sammy and I looked toward the door, as did the doc and his assistant. Susan walked in, slipping her cell phone into her jacket, showing no signs of her earlier discomfort.

Sammy gave her a sympathetic smile. "Are you feeling better now?"

Wrong thing to say. Susan thrust out her chin and glowered at him.

Before she could fire off a comeback, I said to her, "The mobile aeroport squadron uses rope. So does maintenance. Could be the stains aren't dirt, but oil or hydraulic fluid."

"But aren't those ropes usually nylon or parachute cord?"

I shrugged; point taken.

"We'll test the stains," Sammy said, still appearing puzzled by Susan's reaction. He tried another smile. No reaction.

I asked Sammy if he'd found any similar rope in the apartment; he hadn't. I didn't voice the obvious: that the killers must have brought the rope with them, which meant they had planned to kill the girl in this fashion.

Sammy gazed into the dead girl's face. Her sightless eyes peered back through strands of tousled hair. As I took my first good look at her, it struck me she didn't appear completely Korean. Her features were too sharply defined and her hair was actually a dark brown and not completely black—

"Damn shame," Sammy murmured. "Such a pretty girl. Sweet thing, too. I always liked her."

My eyes widened. Susan said, "You *knew* her?"

Sammy glanced back at us. "Sure. She was very popular. Everyone in the Ville knew her. You knew her, Burt. At the club she went by Si-re Pak, not Soon-ri Kim." He gave me an expectant look.

In the course of my investigations, I'd gotten to know a number of the girls, but neither of the names rang any bells. I studied the girl's face. The hair made it difficult to tell whether—

"Anyway," Sammy went on, "I had the same problem. I didn't recognize her until a few minutes ago. When I saw this."

As he spoke, he reached into his jacket and removed a gold-framed photograph similar to those on the dressers. He passed it to me as Susan swung around to see.

A young girl of maybe fourteen standing with a Korean woman in a white *han-bok*, the billowing dress similar to a kimono. Their faces were somber and unsmiling, and I sensed a deep sadness. Behind them we saw a valley and the lush greenery of rice fields, mountains visible in the distance.

I focused on the girl. Even though the picture was slightly blurred and taken from a distance, I was struck by her beauty. As I stared, it dawned on me who she was.

"I'll be damned," Susan breathed, as she made the connection.

I nodded. The names we'd been given hadn't meant anything because we knew her by what the GIs called her. Her unofficial stage name.

Sammy carefully removed the hair from the girl's face. He stepped aside so we could see.

"She's the Tiger Lady," I said.

6

The most popular bar in the Ville was the Studio 99 Club, a shimmering Studio 54–like monstrosity of mirrored ceilings and red-felt walls. While the GIs were attracted by the club's glitz, what really packed them in was the headline dancer, a beautiful Amerasian girl with a killer bod and a baby-doll face.

Over the past two years, I'd seen her dance at least a half dozen times. Her act was simple, but devastatingly erotic. Wearing her trademark tiger-print thong bikini, she did an increasingly frenzied bump-and-grind number to the pulse of a hard-driving rap tune, and for a finale, whipped off her top and spewed champagne over her bare breasts.

I shook my head at Sammy. "We don't have much time. The reporters will have her ID'd by tonight. And when they do—"

"Chill, Burt," he said. "I bought us a couple of days."

I frowned.

"Once I figured out who she was, I knew we had a big problem. So I sent Sergeant Ko to give the reporters another name. To confuse them a little."

Ko was Sammy's quietly precise assistant. I asked, "What name?"

He winked. "One I made up. Said she just came from Cheju-do."

I had to smile, but Susan didn't react at all, suggesting she was still annoyed with him. Cheju-do was the large resort island off the southern tip of the Korean peninsula. It would eat up a couple of days for the press to fly down and sniff around long enough to figure out they'd been had.

As Sammy returned the photo to his jacket, Susan said, "You guys do know she doesn't dance at the Studio 99 anymore."

I looked at her in surprise. But then I'd been out of the base gossip loop since resigning.

Sammy nodded. "She quit about two months ago. It was big news around town. The word was she got a new boyfriend to buy out her contract with the club." He abruptly motioned to the coroner's assistant, who sprang forward to cut the rope from the girl's wrist. As we moved out of his way, Sammy went on, "It caused a stink between her and the owner. He didn't want to let her go. He came up with a price he didn't think she could pay, but she did."

I said, "Someone must have known who the boyfriend was. Spotted them together."

"You'd think," Sammy said. "But that was part of the mystery. Soon-ri was very hush-hush about him. She wouldn't even confirm that she had a boyfriend."

"The apartment manager," I said. "Susan said you spoke to him . . ."

"Right. He only dealt with her."

"How much did it cost for Soon-ri to buy out her contract?" Susan asked.

Sammy shrugged. "I'm not sure. I heard around a hundred million won. Maybe more."

I started crunching the numbers. Susan rang up the cash register first, saying, "Hell, you're talking over seventy-five thousand dollars."

I shook my head, thinking maybe Ray had been right after all.

"Problem, Burt?" Susan asked.

I waved a hand at nothing in particular. "What do you think it cost to set up the girl in this place?"

A shrug.

I said, "Maybe five grand?"

"Try double," Sammy said, holding up two fingers. "If you look in her closet, there're plenty of nice clothes. Mostly new. Her shoes, too. I counted six pairs still in boxes."

"Call it ten thousand, then," I said. "Tack on another fifteen hundred a month for rent and living expenses, and you're talking an eventual outlay of close to a hundred grand. My initial feeling was her boyfriend had to be someone from the base. But it's damned unlikely a military member could swing that kind of money."

Susan nodded her agreement while Sammy gave me that vaguely unsettled look of his, the one that usually meant he disagreed.

I sighed. "What am I missing?"

"The tags."

"What tags?"

But Sammy was already stepping around the bed toward the closet.

★ The closet was a small walk-in, roughly four feet deep, and smelled of flowers. Women's clothing hung neatly from racks on either side, with more piled on the shelves above, many items still wrapped in plastic. Susan and I stood by the door as Sammy removed two summer dresses. He turned and handed them to me.

I focused on the price tags still attached to the collars. I could explain away the dollar signs because a number of Korean vendors dealt in U.S. currency. But the tricky part was getting around the three words printed on the very bottom.

OSAN BASE EXCHANGE.

"They could be black-market items," I said.

Sammy immediately began plucking more items from the rack. After he had collected an armful, I said, "Those all have BX tags?"

A nod. He held out the pile.

"Never mind," I said, taking out my phone. "You made your point. We're probably looking for an American from the base."

"Maybe more than one," Sammy corrected.

"Who you calling, Burt?" Susan asked.

★ Ray was still in his office. His voice sounded a little slurred, which told me he'd been drinking. He was obviously feeling the stress, and I wasn't going to help matters by my call.

I gave Ray the bad news about the girl first. The Tiger Lady tag meant nothing to him, which was mildly surprising considering her notoriety. But as a boy-colonel bucking for general, Ray was conscious of his image and never set foot in the bars.

"Jesus, this stripper was that popular?"

"If you'd seen her, you'd understand."

Then I went into our theory that her boyfriend might be someone from the base. As I spoke, I kept expecting him to interrupt. That he didn't meant he was either too far in the bag to care or was sincerely trying to follow through on his promise to back me.

"That it?" he said when I finished.

"So far."

"General Muller and Ambassador Gregson aren't going to be happy."

I was silent. Ice tinkled in a glass.

"How long until you ID the boyfriend?"

"Depends. Odds are one of the victim's neighbors would have noticed an American hanging around. If we get a detailed description, maybe in a day or two. Otherwise, we'll have to run a fingerprint check."

"So you have his fingerprints, huh?"

"We will. The guy must have spent a lot of time in the apartment."

Silence again. More tinkling.

"I need a favor, Ray."

An audible sigh. "What?"

"Contact the unit commanders. Find out if any of their personnel has family money or has recently cashed in a large amount of savings or investments. I'll also need a list of anyone they know who might have a girlfriend in the Ville."

Ray sounded both weary and irritated. "All right. I'll call first thing in the morning—"

"Tonight, Ray. I want the names by morning."

I heard him swallow and cough. "Fine," he grunted. "I'll do it fucking tonight. But remember one goddamn thing, Burt. Just because the girl might have had an American boyfriend doesn't mean the guy was the killer."

I was struck by the conviction in his voice. "Ray, do you know anything—"

A dial tone.

★ Sammy and Dr. Yee, were again conversing at the foot of the bed. The coroner's assistant knelt beside them, carefully cutting away the rope attached to the girl's left leg. Susan stood at the mirrored bureau, digging through a drawer. Two more men in white coveralls appeared at the door and set down a stretcher with a black neoprene body bag.

As I watched all this, I fought the urge to call Ray back. Ask him flat out if he knew—

"Burt . . ."

Susan was motioning from the bureau, her brow furrowed. Walking over, I had to squeeze by Dr. Yee, who had shifted around to point out something in the wound to Sammy. I risked a glance and immediately looked away.

"What's up?" I asked Susan.

She opened the top drawer of the bureau. "Look."

I saw a woman's folded knit shirts. I had no clue why I should care. "Okay . . ."

She threw open the remaining two drawers. Panties and bras in one. Shorts and colored T-shirts in the other.

I said, "I'm not sure I understand—"

"What's missing, Burt?"

"Missing?"

A sigh of exasperation. "Her boyfriend. Unless the guy was a monk, he must have slept over, right?"

"Yeah . . ." Then I made the connection and glanced at the nearer of the two dressers.

"I already searched them both," Susan said. "Only a woman's stuff. Nothing belonging to a man. Not even undies or a robe. Doesn't figure. What kind of guy shells out a hundred grand for a bar girl and doesn't sleep with her?"

I thought. "Maybe he never actually stayed the night."

She gazed back dubiously.

"Yeah, I don't buy that either. You check out the bathroom?"

"Not yet."

★ Susan poked through the medicine cabinet over the sink while I took the tub and the commode, which was Western style and not the squat-and-drop hole found in older Korean homes. The tub was dry and the dark hairs stuck to the drain were all at least a foot long, confirming they were probably the girl's. I shifted my attention to the toilet. The seat was down, which told me it had last been used by a woman or a maybe a polite guy. I flipped it up with my foot.

The dried yellow droplets stood out against the white-enamel rim.

"Lover boy's a little sloppy," Susan said.

I nodded, resisting the temptation to say that most men were. I glanced at Susan as she shut the cabinet door. "Anything?"

A head shake. She pointed to the wall-mounted toothbrush holder, which held a single red toothbrush. "But this might be something."

Her finger hovered over one of the empty holes. I bent down. At an angle, I could make out scummy smudges around the edge.

"Could be residue from a toothbrush," I said, rising.

She eyed me. "Only one logical reason the guy would have removed it."

I nodded. "If he killed her."

"That explains why none of the guy's stuff is here. And why the place is so damn clean."

She was suggesting the boyfriend had also removed anything linking him to the girl. I asked her if any of the dresser drawers were empty.

"Two."

Good enough. As we turned to leave, Susan murmured, "Wonder how they knew?"

"Knew what?"

But Susan was already striding out the door. I trailed her to the closet and watched her flip through the clothes on the hangers. She studied the folded items on the shelves, then stepped back and made a slow 360-degree turn, finally settling on me.

"Her costumes aren't in here, Burt."

"Okay . . ."

"They weren't in the dressers, either. And none of the pictures show Soon-ri as a dancer. With her ID missing and probably stolen, there's nothing in the apartment that indicates she even worked in a bar." She gave me a knowing look.

I was still lost and told her to get to the point.

"My point," she said, "is that Sammy only ID'd the girl maybe what? Twenty minutes ago . . ."

I nodded.

". . . yet when I was called out tonight, I was told the victim was a *bar* girl. How could someone have known that before a positive identification was—"

I wasn't listening any longer, because I'd pivoted to ask Sammy.

★ I'd taken two paces from the closet when I stopped so suddenly, Susan bumped into me. "Jeez," she murmured. "What's gotten into him?"

She was referring to Sammy, who seemed on the verge of losing it. He was by the bed, angrily shaking his head as he listened to Dr. Yee. He interrupted Yee with a sudden, almost violent, gesture at the corpse. He began spitting out Korean that was too rapid for me to decipher. Then I caught a word that sounded familiar.

My stomach knotted as I fumbled in my jacket for the dictionary. I pawed through the pages. I stopped, my eyes flying down the column.

The horror sank in. I slowly shook my head, hoping I was mistaken. That I'd heard the word incorrectly.

"What is it?" Susan asked. "You know what they're talking about?"

I nodded and pointed out the definition.

Susan's face went pale. "My God . . ."

★ Sammy continued to vent his anger. Susan watched him, trembling with both shock and rage. I closed my eyes and visualized how it must have happened. How the victim Soon-ri lay there, racked with unimaginable pain, struggling against the ropes as they ripped out her—

I opened my eyes, my heart pounding. I put the dictionary away and took a few ragged breaths, trying to calm down. But Sammy's earlier words kept playing in my head like a tape on an endless loop.

They gutted her like a fish.

Only one slice to open her up.

The doctor has a theory why.

And Dr. Yee did. The brutality of the crime made sense now. The killers cut her because that was the only way to get what they wanted.

The word was *a-gi*.

It meant baby.

7

Sammy abruptly fell silent. Stepping away from Dr. Yee, he came over to Susan and me and grimly confirmed that the victim, Soon-ri Kim, had been pregnant.

"Dr. Yee," he said, "thinks she wasn't very far along. Maybe only a couple of months."

I swallowed. "So the fetus . . ."

"Removed." He rubbed his face hard in disgust. "They sliced through her uterus to get it. Yee figures they must have tried to drug her first."

"Drug her?" I said.

"The cut's pretty clean, Burt. That wouldn't be possible if she'd been struggling. Yee thinks they must have knocked her out with something and didn't use enough. Sometime during the process she became conscious, which explains the marks on her wrists."

Susan and I slowly nodded, taking this in. Getting drugs for anyone, even an American, would be simple since Korean pharmacies didn't require prescriptions. Susan asked Sammy, "Would the person who cut out the fetus have to have medical training?"

"Not necessarily. Could have looked it up in books. Fetus was about this big." He circled his fingers to a tennis-ball size.

"Dr. Yee have any idea of the drug?" I asked.

A head shake. Eyeing me, Sammy went on, "Now we have the motive. The boyfriend must have been someone important. Someone who couldn't afford for the word to get out that Soon-ri was going to have his baby."

"An officer," I said, automatically.

"Career?" Susan said. "You think someone killed Soon-ri to protect his career?" Her tone indicated she was having trouble believing this.

"Why not? People kill for less." Sammy punctuated the comment with a glance at me, as if reminding Susan of how the military had drop-kicked me because of my relationship with Chung-hee.

"But why did he have to kill her at all?" Susan said. "Why not arrange for her to have an abortion?"

Sammy snorted. "Soon-ri would never have gone along; she couldn't. For a girl like her, the baby was her way out, a chance for a better life."

He was painting a picture of blackmail, which bothered me a little. I said, "If the guy planned to kill her, why go to the expense of buying out her contract? Fork over the bucks to put her up in here?"

Sammy shrugged. "Who the hell knows, Burt? Could be the boyfriend was going to keep Soon-ri as a mistress. Then something happened, and he changed his mind. Decided she had to go."

Susan said, "And he removed the fetus to prevent—"

"Sure," Sammy interrupted. "The boyfriend was trying to stop us from getting a DNA match so we couldn't prove paternity. Doctor Yee says that's where he made a mistake."

"Oh?" Susan said.

A nod. "Yee says forensics can test the tissue in the womb and get a genetic fingerprint from the fluid in—" He broke off, as if something had suddenly occurred to him.

"What is it?" I said.

No response. He was lost in thought for a few moments. He sighed unhappily, his eyes seeking out Susan. "My mistake. You were right about the killing. It doesn't fit. The boyfriend couldn't be that stupid. He has to know we will identify him and he will be the prime suspect. But he kills her anyway. Why?"

He had me. I shook my head.

Susan said, "Didn't we just cover this? You said he was trying to prevent anyone from knowing—"

"That's what's bothering me," Sammy said. "We're assuming he killed her to prevent his relationship with her from becoming public. If true, why not kill her and dump her body where it wouldn't be found? At least try to hide it. Why make it easy for us? *Why kill her in an apartment that can be connected to him?*"

By "connected," Sammy meant possible witnesses, fingerprints, phone records, and any forensic evidence that might tie the guy to Soon-ri.

Susan wasn't ready to concede to his logic. She countered by bringing up the missing toothbrush and empty dresser drawers. "Maybe the guy's not as bright as you think. He obviously cleaned out his stuff for a reason. Could be he killed her in here because he thought he could get away with it."

"Then," Sammy said, "why didn't he wipe down the apartment?"

Susan started visibly. I was also caught off guard by the statement. Like her, I'd assumed there would have been an attempt to obliterate fingerprints. That it would prove unsuccessful was a given, since it's virtually impossible to wipe down an entire apartment.

Susan tried to come up with a response and couldn't. She surrendered with a head shake.

To Sammy, I said, "Are you telling me you *don't* believe the boyfriend is the killer now?"

He hesitated. "All I'm saying is it's a possibility."

I thought. "That would explain the phone call to the Security Police. Maybe the boyfriend found her, called it in."

"Hold on a sec," Susan said. "If the boyfriend wasn't the killer, why cut out the fetus?"

One answer came to mind. Sammy started to respond, but I spoke first.

"Somebody else could be the father," I said.

"Including," Sammy added, "a Korean."

★ We all stood in silence, considering this new wrinkle. A deep thinker I'm not, so I made notes to organize my thoughts. It occurred to me that Ray might be proved right after all, since the girl's boyfriend might not turn out to be the killer. But if he was innocent, why didn't he wait for the cops to show? And why go to the trouble of removing all his stuff from the apartment? The obvious answer was he was married or trying to protect his career. Possibly both.

As I closed the notepad, Susan asked Sammy the question that had bugged her earlier.

He frowned. "When did *I* know Soon-ri worked in a bar?"

Susan nodded.

"I told you. When I saw the photograph."

"I don't mean *who* she was specifically. I want to know when you were told the victim was a bar girl."

"From the beginning. When I was assigned the case—"

"So your superiors knew?"

"Yes. Of course." Sammy still seemed confused by Susan's interest.

So I joined in, saying, "What's bothering us is that everyone has known from the beginning that the victim was a girl from the Ville. The military. Your government and mine. How could they have known that before you did?"

"The phone call, Burt," Sammy said. "The person who called the SPs must have mentioned— No?"

I was gazing at him skeptically. "Even if the caller had said something to that effect, you know damn well no one would have started jumping through hoops without confirmation."

Sammy considered this, then shrugged. "All I can tell you is it wasn't my men."

"Well," Susan said, "someone sure as hell told them."

I took out my phone to ask the one person who would know. As I thumbed the redial, I noticed Susan appraising Sammy.

"Nice suit," she said to him. "I like it."

Sammy reddened slightly. "Uh, thank you."

She focused on his jacket. "Silk?"

Sammy nodded.

Susan smiled coolly, flipped open her notepad, and casually jotted something down.

Sammy's eyes went to me. I shook my head. But whatever was behind Susan's interest, it wasn't his suit.

The phone began ringing in my ear.

★ "Colonel Raymond Johnson is unavailable," the metallic voice said. "Leave a message at the tone . . ."

I did, then tried Ray's home number. Another recording. I ended the call with a thoughtful frown. But maybe Ray had decided to leave his office early and was en route to his quarters.

As I put away the phone, Susan tossed out a suggestion. I glanced at the coroner's assistant, who was bagging the last piece of rope. After clearing it with Sammy, I told Susan to go ahead.

As she went over to the assistant, Sammy reached past me to another photo on the dresser and held it out so we both could see. Like the earlier one, this was also an image of the woman and Soon-ri, as a child. This time, they were standing side by side on a gravel street, dilapidated stores with Korean lettering in the background. I concentrated on their faces, finally detecting a resemblance. Particularly around the eyes and the slope of their mouths. Mother and daughter. Again they gazed out with an almost haunting sadness. Soon-ri looked about ten or eleven. She wore a faded blue dress, and she didn't have on shoes. I glanced at the remaining photographs on the two dressers. All were of Soon-ri and her mother, together or alone. I never saw them smile.

"Life," I said, "must have been difficult for them."

"It was," Sammy said, looking up from the picture. "And not only because they were poor. An unmarried woman with a child fathered by a foreigner is a *wang-tta*. An outcast. Someone to be despised because she has dishonored her family and village. It's a life without hope."

I nodded. I knew all this because, in my capacity as the OSI commander, I'd often dropped off donations collected by my unit to the two local orphanages sponsored by Osan Air Base. One of the tragic legacies of the U.S. presence in Korea were the hundreds of Amerasian children who'd been abandoned by their mothers after their GI fathers had been reassigned back home.

And it was Chung-hee who made me realize that the children weren't the only victims. In fact, this was one of her main concerns when we began dating. How she'd react if I knocked her up and walked away.

"At least her mother kept her," I said softly.

"She was a brave woman. Soon-ri said for many years her mother struggled to make them a life. But in the end, she couldn't take it anymore. The abuse and the shame." He sighed. "Maybe it was for the best. At least she will be spared learning of Soon-ri's death."

It took a moment for his comment to register. "Her mother killed herself?"

Sammy didn't reply. He was again staring at the image. This was a side of him he rarely displayed, the quiet, reflective Sammy. But I'd worked with him long enough to know that he was someone with a lot of emotional layers.

When he spoke, he sounded almost wistful, as if he were talking to himself rather than to me. "Before Soon-ri left the club, I used to drop by once, twice a month. Talk to her. Buy her a few drinks. It's not what you think, Burt. It was her idea. She wanted me to help her practice English. She had a dream of going to America someday. To try to find her father. And now . . ."

He almost reverently returned the photo to the bureau. Looking at me, he said, "Soon-ri grew up in Chun-ye, a farming village to the east. It's in a small valley near the mountains. Not more than forty-five minutes away. Soon-ri and her mother lived with her mother's sister and her sister's husband. The husband, Soon-ri's uncle, was supposed to be a real son of a bitch. Worked them like dogs. Five, six years ago, Soon-ri's mother got up one morning and went off to work in the rice fields. Only she didn't come home. People remembered seeing her walking up a hill. A few months later, the uncle came across her remains at the bottom of a cliff."

"She killed herself?" I asked again.

He shrugged.

Since bar girls rarely spoke of their past, I told Sammy that Soon-ri must have trusted him a great deal to tell him all this.

"Not really, Burt. Soon-ri told everyone she was from Chun-ye. She *wanted* people to know. When she became popular, she called the Song-tan paper, got them to do a story. She sent copies of the article to people in her village. She even sent a large poster of herself onstage to her uncle."

"To embarrass him."

Sammy nodded. "That's why she became a bar girl. It was the only way she could pay them back—her uncle and the village for the way they had treated her and her mother."

"If the conditions in the village were that bad, why didn't the mother take Soon-ri and just leave? Why stay and suffer the abuse?"

"It's not that easy. I doubt a Westerner would understand."

"Why not?"

He gave me a tired smile. "Where would she go, Burt?"

★ Susan returned a minute later, pocketing the glassine bag containing a rope remnant we'd try to match against the stockpile on base. Dr. Yee motioned to the two men by the door, who entered with the body bag.

Sammy spun toward me, his face very red. He hissed angrily through his teeth. *"Jo-ka-ttal-e-ge hal-mal it-chi-ma."*

It took me a second to translate. "What's changed?"

"Everything. I want the killer now."

"Now?" Susan said. "You mean you didn't before?"

Sammy remained focused on me, his voice clipped, anxious. "You understand what I'm telling you, Burt?"

"I think so."

"Then you know it won't be easy. There will be trouble. Problems."

I nodded.

"What kind of trouble?" Susan said.

Sammy's eyes flicked cautiously to her, then back to me. "She doesn't know?"

"No."

"Know what?" Susan asked. "What are you two guys talking about?"

Sammy spoke to me in Korean. Overpronouncing, so I could follow him. I finally realized what he was asking. I nodded to let him know she could be trusted.

He stepped forward and took Susan by the elbow, saying, "I need a smoke. How about we talk outside—"

She yanked away from him as if she'd been scalded. "Don't *touch* me."

Sammy stared at her in shock. So did I. Susan's reaction was beyond rude. The intensity suggested a deep resentment. That made little sense, because she barely knew the guy.

Sammy recovered with an embarrassed smile. He bowed in the formal Korean way and murmured an apology.

Susan glowered back.

Sammy tried to save face by acting as if nothing had happened. He calmly adjusted his tie and smoothed his suit. He looked at me. "I'll be on the balcony."

As he left, I tapped Susan's arm harder than necessary. I wanted her to know I was angry. "That was way out of line."

Her face darkened. “He touched me. He had no damn right to—”

“Bullshit. You humiliated him, and I want to know why.”

Her jaw clamped tight. I became aware of Dr. Yee and his assistants watching us. I was torn between making a scene and wanting to know. I lowered my voice. “Look, Susan—”

“Sammy knows,” she snapped.

And in dramatic fashion, she turned and walked out.

8

Susan stewed in the living room while I joined Sammy on the balcony. He was leaning over the railing, smoking a cigarette. The night air was sticky, and we could hear the sounds of traffic. I bent down beside him and gazed at the darkened parking area below. For almost a minute, neither one of us spoke.

"One tough girl, huh?" Sammy said.

When I glanced over, he had a wry smile on his face. I said, "Susan can be difficult—"

He waved the cigarette. "Forget it, Burt. Besides, I think attitude in a woman is okay. It shows she's got *bu-ral*. Good thing for a cop."

I gave him a blank look.

He winked, making a fist. "You know. Balls."

I thought it odd, hearing a Korean male say this. Even someone as Americanized as Sammy. "Mind if I ask you something?"

"Shoot." He took a last drag and flipped the butt over the railing.

"You hit on her earlier?" Because this was a very real possibility, and not solely based on Susan's comment. Sammy was something of a ladies' man and was known to have a thing for Western women. He'd even dated a few women from the base.

He appeared stunned. "Hit on—shit no, Burt. I swear."

"Okay, Sammy . . ."

"Hell, I never saw her until tonight."

"Fine. I believe—"

"She *said* I hit on her?"

"Not exactly."

"Don't screw with me, Burt. Why would you ask me if—"

He broke off at the sound of the sliding glass door opening. We turned and saw Susan standing in the doorway. Her expression was more indifferent than angry now.

"You two done talking about me?" she asked.

I didn't even try to deny it. I nodded.

"Good." She stepped onto the balcony and closed the door. She placed her hands on her hips and appraised us coolly. "Now who wants to tell me what kind of trouble we might get into pursuing this case?"

I was surprised when Sammy volunteered.

★ In a soft monotone, Sammy explained that when he'd been assigned the case, the Provincial chief of police had lectured him for almost an hour on the political sensitivities. The chief had emphasized the need for complete discretion and stated that Sammy was to concentrate on Korean suspects. Should the evidence indicate an American's involvement in the murder, Sammy was ordered to take no action without the chief's approval.

To Sammy, this meant only one thing: Regardless of the evidence, an American would not be held responsible.

Sammy shrugged. "At first, I didn't have a problem with that. I figured if the chief wants me to cover something up, it's not my place to ask questions. My job . . . my duty . . . is to obey. But now, I feel different." He tapped his chest. "In here."

"Because you knew her?" Susan said.

"Sure," he said simply. "It's personal." Up to this moment, he'd avoided looking directly at her as if worried that might set her off. But now he seemed to study her, and I knew he was trying to decide if they'd met before.

She said, "You could get in serious trouble. Lose your job."

He shrugged, but kept looking at her.

I cleared my throat. When Susan shifted to me, I said, "You do realize you're in a similar situation."

Her brow knitted.

"I should have said something earlier. We're playing under similar ground rules." I related my conversations with Ray, emphasizing my concerns that we, like Sammy, would never be allowed to charge an American with murder. I added, "If we keep pushing, it could get ugly. You have a son to consider. I'll understand if you withdraw—"

"You trying to scare me, Burt?"

"No. I just want you to know how things stand."

"Well, save it. I'm staying."

"You're sure?"

She swallowed hard, her voice becoming hollow. "The bastard could have removed the fetus after he killed her, but he didn't. He butchered her while she was alive. You and I know damn well it was no mistake that she regained consciousness after being drugged. That's what the sick son of a bitch wanted. He wanted her to wake up. He wanted her to know that she was dying and why. When I think about how she must have suffered . . ." Her voice trailed off into a grim silence.

A car horn blared, and a breeze touched my face. Unlike Susan, I still felt conflicted by my decision. I couldn't completely discount the consequences of arresting an American. I tried to tell myself that we were doing the right thing. That someone had to be held accountable.

When I looked at Sammy, he was giving Susan a faint smile of approval. While she didn't acknowledge it, at least she didn't look at him like he was scum.

I checked my watch. Almost nine. There wasn't much that Susan and I could do here. The important thing now was to get to the base and check out the tape. Find out if the caller sounded like an American and determine whether he had mentioned Soon-ri's occupation—

The sharp rap on the glass door broke the quiet. Looking over, I saw a squat, round-faced man in a dark suit peering out.

Sammy opened the door for Detective Sergeant Ko. They conversed briefly. Ko did most of the talking and seemed unusually tense. Abruptly, Sammy faced Susan and me.

"Ko found a witness."

9

We left the apartment, heading down the hallway toward a door where one of the uniformed cops we'd seen earlier was waiting. Sergeant Ko and Sammy were in the lead, Susan and I trailing.

Susan leaned over to me. "You trust him?"

She meant Sammy. I nodded. "He's a good cop."

We went a few more steps. Susan's pace slowed, and we dropped back a few yards.

"Even if he lied to us," she said quietly.

Christ. "Give it a rest, Susan. You've obviously got something against him—"

"This involves the photograph, Burt."

"What about it?"

"You can see the outline in Sammy's jacket."

"So what?"

"When I showed up here, I remembered noticing it. The outline. At the time I didn't think much about it."

I caught on a step later and stared at her.

She nodded suggestively. "Yeah. Sammy's known who Soon-ri was for at least an hour. He obviously lied to us, and I'm wondering if—"

She stopped when she realized we were almost at the apartment. The cop bowed respectfully to Sammy and Sergeant Ko, then quickly stepped around to open the door.

We filed inside to interview the witness who had described an American.

★ It was a large, airy apartment with a distinct modern/European feel. The carpeting was white and very thick, and the furniture was imported Danish teak, with too many angles to be considered comfortable. An assortment of large Art-Deco paintings hung on the walls, providing a dramatic splash of color. A single place setting of dirty dishes sat on the dining table, next to an opened bottle of German wine. In the living room, a flat-screen Hitachi TV played an Asian music video, the sound turned down.

Susan and I hung back by the edge of the living area, our attention on the same bookish-looking little man we'd noticed in the hallway. He was perched on the edge of a chair, back straight, hands on his knees. His eyes flicked nervously through thick Clark Kent glasses as Sammy and Sergeant Ko sat across from him on a couch.

Sammy handed the man his card as he went through the standard introductions. The guy's name surprised me a little. Mr. Yata. He said he was a Japanese businessman. He spoke Korean fluently, but with an accent that threw me off. Even though he kept glancing at Susan and me, Sammy never explained our presence.

Once Sammy began the interview, the conversation became too rapid for me to keep up. A couple of times, Yata appeared confused by Soon-ri's name, as if uncertain he'd recognized it. He called her *ye-ppeun yeo-ja*. Pretty girl. Sammy spoke in soothing tones, and Yata gradually relaxed. Twice he grimaced and made a show of being upset. Then he said the word I was waiting for: *Mi-guk-in*. American.

Sammy jotted down the man's description. I picked up most of the particulars because Sammy had Yata repeat them twice. Two meters tall and around seventy kilograms in weight. Short blond hair. Thirty to thirty-five. I didn't hear Yata mention the man's name.

Sammy appeared satisfied, but I wasn't. The description easily fit a couple of hundred guys on Osan Air Base. Sammy switched subjects and, in the rapid back-and-forth, lost me again. After a few minutes, he murmured something to Ko, then rose and came over to Susan and me.

He briefed us without consulting his notes. Yata had first met the girl when she'd moved in two months earlier, not long after the building had opened. It had been on a Saturday. Yata remembered seeing the big truck with all the new furniture and thinking she must be from a wealthy family. He'd gone by her apartment, to offer any assistance. She'd declined politely, telling him she already had someone to help.

That's when he saw the young man coming from the bedroom. Yata assumed he was an American, because he spoke English to the girl. Yata didn't know the man's name, since he was never introduced. He mentioned that the girl never gave him her name either. Yata considered this odd and a little rude. But he said it fit the pattern of her lifestyle. During her time in the building, she'd kept to herself and avoided the rest of the residents.

Since that first day, Yata had seen the man on only two other occasions. The second time had been the previous week, when he'd returned from work and noticed the man and the girl getting into her car.

I said, "Her car?" Because I'd never known a bar girl who knew how to drive much less owned a car.

"Yata," Sammy said, "assumed it was hers because it was parked in her space. But he never actually saw her drive it. Ko checked the lot earlier, but it's missing. According to Yata, this wasn't unusual. He recalled a number of occasions when the car had been gone for long periods while the girl was in her apartment."

"The boyfriend," Susan said, glancing at me. "It had to be his. He could have driven the car back to Osan when he left."

I considered this a remote possibility, since the guy had to know the base would be the first place we would look. Still, the vehicle had to be somewhere, and I asked Sammy for a description.

When he described a late-model gold Hyundai sedan, I felt encouraged. On Osan, most people didn't go to the expense of owning cars. With everything within walking distance, there wasn't any real need. Among the drab military vehicles, I tried to recall if I'd seen a shiny gold sedan; I hadn't. "No dice, Sammy."

But he wasn't looking at me. Instead, he was staring at Susan, who had gone completely still. She was so focused, she seemed to be barely breathing.

Sammy said, "Yes, Susan?"

She didn't react. I gave her a few seconds, then reached out to tap her—

"Did it have a sunroof?" she asked suddenly.

Sammy relayed the question to Yata, who nodded emphatically. I felt a buzz of excitement.

Susan said, "Now, I'm not sure about the year—"

"Doesn't matter," I interrupted. "When did you see it?"

"I . . . within the past week."

"Where?"

"In the parking area by the BOQs."

BOQ stood for Bachelor Officers' Quarters. Now we knew we were looking for an officer.

Sammy said, "And the owner . . ."

Susan was already taking out her phone to find out.

★ Two minutes later, Susan cupped her phone as she spoke with Sergeant Barnette at the Security Police duty desk. "Burt, the car's registered to Major Sean Wilson at the Thirty-sixth FS. Barnette is looking up his phone number and BOQ room—" She jammed the phone under her chin and began writing furiously on her notepad. "Got it, Sergeant. Thanks." She ended the call and looked up.

The 36th was one of the two F-16 fighter squadrons. Even though Osan had a population of fewer than four thousand, I couldn't recall running into Major Wilson. Neither could Susan when I asked. On military bases, people tended to be cliquish, and as cops, we didn't have the pedigree to hang out with fighter jocks.

"See if he's in," I said.

She did; he wasn't.

I cautioned, "He still might not be the guy."

"Easy way to find out," she said, eyeing Yata.

Sammy asked Yata if he would be available later this evening to make a visual identification. Yata responded with another head bob.

Ray would be upset that I didn't run this by him first, but the last thing I wanted was General Muller interfering and possibly preventing us from contacting Major Wilson. Whether he would or not, I didn't know. One thing I'd learned in the military was if you can't stand the answer, don't ask the question.

After passing on Ray's cell-phone number and telling Sammy I'd call once we located Wilson, I was almost to the door before I realized Susan wasn't with me. When I looked back, she was contemplating her car keys.

I sighed. "I take it you parked out front."

"Yeah. Press wasn't here then."

Sammy offered up a solution, then explained it to Ko, who immediately rose and took the keys from Susan. She flashed him a smile of thanks, and as she turned to leave, she reached up and casually tucked a few curly locks behind an ear. At that instant, I saw Sammy look at her in astonishment. He recovered quickly, clearing his expression to neutral. As Susan walked away, he continued to stare at her back, his face reddening.

A possibility occurred to me. Just maybe . . .

When Susan approached me, I took my time opening the door. I was hoping that Sammy would say something and clear the air between them. But as she went by me into the hallway, he never said a word.

10

I went out of the building the way I'd come in. The fence was even more of a struggle the second time around. Susan, of course, scampered over easily.

Afterward, she rubbed it in by saying, "Hell, Burt. You should have said you needed help. I could have given you a boost."

If I could have caught my breath, I'd have fired off a caustic remark. We were hidden in the darkened alley twenty yards from the cross street. Something skittered in the shadows nearby, and Susan didn't even flinch; she wouldn't.

As we watched through the chain-link fence for Ko, I caught Susan glancing over a few times. After the third look, I asked what was on her mind.

"Just wondering when you're going to ask Sammy why he lied to us."

"I'm not sure I am."

Her head swiveled around. "You serious?"

"Sammy must have a good reason. I figure he'll tell me when he's ready."

She snorted, but refrained from comment.

I decided to take my shot now. "Want to tell me about it?" I asked casually.

"Tell you what?"

"What you've got against Sammy."

"Didn't you ask him?" She sounded surprised.

"Yeah. He said he doesn't have a clue." Which was still the truth. Sort of.

She was silent, her face frosting over.

I said, "So you have met him before?"

She drew in a breath, nodded.

"Where?"

Another pause. "A party."

"What party?"

"I really don't want to talk about it, Burt."

"C'mon, Susan. If there's something between you two—"

She froze me with a look.

I gave up. She wasn't about to tell me.

"Ko's coming," she said, changing the subject.

I glanced at a green Chrysler Sebring coming up the street. To the right, I noticed another vehicle slow and pull up to the curb alongside the fence, maybe fifty yards away.

For an instant, what I was seeing didn't register. I pressed up against the fence, thinking I had to be mistaken. Why would he—

When the light came on, I felt slow. I should have considered this possibility.

Moments later, the Sebring swung into the alley and the headlights went out. As Susan walked over, I kept staring at the vehicle by the curb. I wanted to be absolutely certain.

But the doors never opened.

★ "We'll stay here," I told Susan. "Leave the engine and lights off."

We were sitting in her car, which was actually an unmarked Air Force OSI vehicle. Susan had been about to crank the ignition when I'd waved her off. Sergeant Ko had hopped out seconds earlier and was hurrying up the sidewalk toward the apartment building.

"Any particular reason?" Susan asked.

We were partially shielded by the cars in the parking lot, but still had a view of the limo. I jabbed a thumb at it and explained. Afterward, she asked, "Why would your wife's uncle be here?"

"Chun owns a number of businesses in the Ville."

It took her a sec. "Including the Studio 99 Club?"

"I don't know. But that would explain his presence here and why he's apparently reluctant to enter the building."

"You lost me on the second part, Burt."

I twisted around to her. I could barely make out her facial features in the dark. I said, "If you were the owner of the Studio 99 Club, would you want the press to start asking questions? Possibly connect you to the murder?"

"Huh? Why would the press—" She jerked upright, talking fast. "*Shit.* Of course. The owner's got a motive. He had to be plenty pissed off at Soon-ri when she quit. Maybe saw it as a pride thing. Thought she'd embarrassed him, made him look foolish . . ."

"Possibly—"

"'Possibly'? He's *Korean.* By definition, those guys are sexist as hell. No way the owner could accept some girl . . . some stripper standing up to him. The only question is, was he angry enough to have had her killed?" She paused, thinking hard. "Even the removal of the fetus makes sense. He could have been doing Soon-ri on the side. Gotten her pregnant." She eased against the seat back, shaking her head. "Son of a *bitch.*"

"There's more."

"Oh?"

"Chun," I said, "reportedly has ties to organized crime."

"You serious?"

I nodded. "His presence here is also suggestive as hell. It means he must know about the murder. But how? It can't be from the press, since they haven't even identified Soon-ri."

She digested this in silence. I became aware that she was staring at me, and I had a pretty good idea why. She coughed. "Uh, Burt, I have to ask . . ."

"Relax, Susan. Neither Chung-hee nor I have any loyalty toward Chun. Family or not, if he's involved in the murder, we take him out."

She nodded. "No offense?"

"Not at all." And I meant it. She had a right to know if I could be objective.

By now, Sergeant Ko's bulk was almost to the limo. He continued past and disappeared into the apartment building. At the intersection, one of the press vans made a right and drove away. A minute later, we watched two young men stagger down the sidewalk toward us, arm in arm in the typical Korean display of friendship. They were sharing a bottle. At the entrance to the alley, they stopped and went up to the fence. I frowned until I realized what they were doing. One turned toward the other, who yelped and scurried out of range.

Susan sighed disgustedly. "What is it with guys anyway? You treat the world like one big outhouse."

"It's a physical thing."

She glanced over.

"Small bladders."

Not even the hint of a smile. I guess it wasn't that funny.

The men finally shuffled off. More minutes passed, and the limo continued to sit. The air hung in the car, and I was beginning to perspire. Susan turned the ignition key so we could lower the windows for air.

Checking her watch, she said, "The limo could be here for a while."

"I doubt it. They're obviously waiting for someone."

Susan was in the middle of a yawn when she thrust out a finger. "Movement."

A man had appeared in the service door, framed in light. The door closed, and the figure began striding purposefully toward the street side of the fence. It became apparent he was heading toward the limo.

"Wonder who he is," Susan said.

★ The man continued to the fence, keeping to the shadows. All we could tell was he had an average height and build. I shifted my gaze to the limo as a second man emerged from the passenger door. Even partially illuminated by a streetlight, he was still too far away for me to make out his face. But I recognized the white linen suit.

"Chun?" Susan murmured.

"Yes."

Chun slowly looked around, to check if anyone was watching. Satisfied, he headed toward the darkened section of the fence where the first man was now waiting. Their silhouettes merged.

The sudden flare of a lighter startled us. Susan gave a little gasp, while I shot forward in my seat. Even though the man's face had been visible only for an instant, there was no mistaking his identity.

It was Sammy.

11

We watched as Sammy and Chun continued their conversation. At the moment, they appeared to be scrutinizing something under a small flashlight. My head was spinning as I tried to understand.

Susan said tersely, "You still trust the double-crossing son of a bitch?"

I hesitated. "For now."

She was incredulous. "*Jesus*, Burt. What's it going to take? Sammy lied about the picture. He didn't tell you he was meeting Chun—"

"He may not have known Chun was going to show."

"Oh, *right*. What about Sammy's relationship to the girl, Soon-ri?"

"What about it?"

"C'mon. I heard you two talking about her. Whatever Sammy had going with her, it sure as hell wasn't English lessons. And now he turns up running her murder investigation. That doesn't strike you as a little too damned coincidental?"

"Susan, he's willing to risk his career to solve—"

"How do we know that? Maybe he's just feeding us a line so we'll let down our guard."

"Why would he do that?"

"Like I know? He's obviously got something going with Chun. Could be Sammy's getting a payoff to sit on the investigation."

I had no response, because payments were a common and legal practice in Korean business and politics. And while Sammy occasionally accepted "gifts" to overlook minor transgressions, I knew in my heart that he'd never take a bribe to cover for a killer.

"Meeting's breaking up," Susan announced.

Chun was returning to the limo. This time the big chauffeur appeared and opened the door. Sammy remained by the fence, the glow of a cigarette visible in his hand. He stretched, fired the cigarette to the ground, and immediately lit another. He began to pace slowly. He obviously wasn't in a hurry to leave, and it gradually dawned on me why.

"Seen enough?" Susan asked.

"We'll wait a little longer."

"What for?"

I gave her a smile. "Sammy. My guess is he's waiting for the limo to leave so he can come over here."

Her eyes shot past me. "You're wrong, Burt."

I sighed, thinking she was being stubborn. But when I looked over, it was clear I was the one who was mistaken.

The limo hadn't moved, and Sammy was already walking over.

★ The limo slowly rolled up to the red light at the intersection. Sammy was almost to the fence. He waved at us, and I opened the passenger door.

"I'll pass," Susan said. "I want to give David a call before he goes to bed."

Maybe this was an excuse to avoid Sammy, but I didn't think so. Susan's life centered on her son, David. That's the main reason she had volunteered for an extended three-year tour in Korea, so she could afford a live-in maid to look after him while she was away. I asked, "Doesn't David have a birthday coming up?"

A tiny, appreciative smile. "He'll be eight on Saturday."

I only knew this because Chung-hee had marked the birthdays of everyone in my unit on the kitchen calendar, including the children. It was one of the many little projects she'd undertaken, trying to prove she could be a supportive commander's wife. "Wish him happy birthday," I said.

"Sure. And Burt . . ."

I glanced back.

Her voice was soft, hesitant. "Despite what you think, I'm not out to get Sammy. I know he's a friend of yours, so don't take this the wrong way. . . ."

"Go on."

She gave me a long look. "Remember, he knew Soon-ri."

A tactful reminder that anyone connected to the girl had to be considered a suspect. Even a cop.

"I'll remember," I said.

★ "Asshole," Sammy grunted, sucking hard on his cigarette.

He and I were standing across from each other at the fence, watching the limo's taillights disappear around the corner. I said, "So Chun owns the Studio 99 Club?"

Sammy squinted at me through a cloud of smoke. "Yeah. You really didn't know, huh?"

His tone was casual, but I caught the inference. "If I had," I said dryly, "don't you think I'd have mentioned it?"

"Sure, Burt. But, hey, I figured maybe you had a reason." He dropped the cigarette and stepped on it.

I shook my head, curious about why he would say such a thing. Susan querying me about Chun was understandable, but Sammy knew I couldn't stand the guy. I asked irritably, "Why the hell were you meeting with him, anyway?"

"Orders." And then he explained that shortly after Susan and I had left, he'd received a call from the Provincial Police chief, who'd informed him that Chun was on the way. Sammy was bluntly told to brief Chun on the details of the investigation.

While I knew Chun had influence, horning in on a murder investigation with this level of political interest took real clout. I asked Sammy how Chun had managed it.

Sammy shrugged. "It's no secret, Burt. Chun has a reputation for being a tough guy. His specialty is scaring people into doing what he wants. He had the mayor pressure my superiors into cooperating."

"So Chun is *kkang-pae?*" *Kkang-pae* is the generic term for the Korean gangsters who control the crime rackets in a number of the major cities. They are loosely associated with the Japanese *Yakuza* and have a reputation for being well connected and extremely violent.

Sammy hesitated. Even now, he seemed unwilling to make the accusation to my face. I had to ask a second time before he reluctantly nodded.

I studied him. "You're aware that Chun had a motive to kill Soon-ri?"

"Sure. That's the problem. Soon-ri got around, had a lot of boyfriends. There was talk that she had something going with Chun and one of the club managers. Soon-ri told me it was all a big lie. She said the other girls started the rumors because they were jealous. They wanted people to think she'd fucked her way to the top." Sammy's face was pinched and angry as he spoke. Watching him, I knew there was more he wasn't telling me.

Up to this moment, I'd given him the benefit of the doubt because he'd always been straight with me in the past. But now I wanted to know. I said, "What the hell's the matter with you, Sammy?"

He squinted, puzzled. "What do you mean?"

"You're holding out on me. Why?"

"What are you talking about, Burt? Why would I hold out on you?"

"Sammy—"

"You're thinking crazy. We're friends. Shit, you're the only one I trust now."

"Sammy, I know about the photograph."

His head jerked. He looked at me as if he didn't understand.

"*Soon-ri's* photograph," I said, pointing to his coat. "Susan saw its outline in your pocket when she arrived."

A long silence. Twice he seemed on the verge of saying something, but didn't. Finally, he nodded in acceptance, avoiding my gaze. "This is awkward, Burt."

I folded my arms. Waiting.

Sammy sighed dejectedly and tugged on a cheek. "It's not what you think. You have to believe me. All the pressure was coming down on me. I had to take time to . . . to figure things out. I was going to tell you when I was sure."

"Sure about what?"

He didn't answer. He removed another cigarette and lit it. He took a few puffs and seemed to be stalling. When he finally spoke, he sounded embarrassed. "You, Burt."

My jaw turned hard. "Dammit, Sammy. Just because Chun is my—"

"No. You don't understand. It wasn't *only* Chun. It was the other investigator that confused me. The one who was assigned to the case before you."

"What other investigator? What are you talking about?"

After he told me, it took me a few seconds to grasp the significance. When I did, I felt both disappointed and betrayed. Not by Sammy, but by Ray.

He'd lied to me again.

12

Lieutenant Colonel Jimmy J. Brannigan was the head of the Army's Criminal Investigation Division, headquartered at the Yongsan Garrison in Seoul. He was brash, overbearing, and egotistical, but as the son-in-law of a three-star, he could afford to be. A marginally competent investigator, Brannigan had a reputation for skirting the legal niceties required by the Uniformed Code of Military Justice in order to pad the CID arrest record. Twice in the past year, his unit had been accused of evidence tampering. As the commander, Brannigan normally should have been canned after the first charge, and certainly by the second. In the end, the Army Inspector General's Office quietly dropped their investigation for lack of evidence. No one was really surprised. After all, that's how things worked in the military.

The brass takes care of their own.

Having worked with the Army CID in the past, Sammy was familiar with Brannigan's style. He knew if anyone could be counted on to salute smartly and go along with a cover-up, it was Jimmy J. Brannigan. When the word came down that I was coming on board as a last-minute replacement, Sammy was understandably curious why.

Shaking my head at him, I said, "I haven't a fucking clue, Sammy. I didn't even want the case. From the beginning, I made it clear I would only pursue the truth."

Sammy watched me through a curling tendril of smoke. "So you made no . . . agreement?"

I glowered at him. He knew me better than that.

"Burt, please. They went to a lot of trouble to bring you in. They must have had a reason—"

"Sure. They probably realized Brannigan isn't smart enough to handle this thing."

Sammy appeared less than convinced. I couldn't blame him; I didn't really swallow my own argument either. It still didn't take a genius to whitewash evidence.

"Look," I said, "maybe it's my connection to Chun. Maybe he's the killer and pulled strings to get me assigned—"

"You're reaching, Burt."

"Dammit, Sammy. You said yourself Chun has connections—"

"*Local* connections. Chun wouldn't have any influence with your government. Besides, he didn't even know you were on the case until I told him."

"And you believed him?" I said dryly.

"He had no reason to lie, Burt."

I eyed him. "Now it sounds like you're ruling out Chun as the killer."

Sammy thoughtfully flicked ash from his cigarette. "Anything's possible, but I doubt it's Chun. When we spoke, he had no interest in talking about the murder."

"Huh? Then why the hell did he come here?"

"Money."

I gave him a blank look.

From his jacket, Sammy removed a folded paper and a penlight. He rolled the paper tightly and pushed it through the fence. As I unrolled it, he shone the light so I could read.

A faxed copy of a standard military Subject-To letter, with the 7th Air Force header printed across the top. The letter was dated today and written in alternating lines of English and Korean. It had been sent by General Muller to the Song-tan Business Council.

There were only two cryptic sentences in the body. General Muller was following protocol and informing the Song-tan Business Council that, as of 0600 hours tomorrow morning, the base would be sealed off until further notice. Muller cited the reason as a military exercise and apologized for the short notice and any inconvenience.

I'd expected this eventuality, just not this soon. Whenever tensions heightened, overseas military installations turned into bunkers. Depending on how long the base was locked up, Chun and the rest of the Ville businessmen could lose thousands, possibly millions.

As I slid the page back to Sammy, I said, "I take it Chun was pushing you to solve the case quickly."

A tight smile. "He gave me two days."

"He threatened you?"

"No. He just said I had two days."

"Or . . ."

Sammy shrugged, flicking the cigarette over his shoulder. His tight-lipped expression told me he was worried. I was, too. With all the political heat, the last thing we needed was a wild card like Chun hanging around in the background.

I had to get going, but there was one final item I wanted to clear up. Sammy's initial concerns over my role still didn't explain why he'd lied about Soon-ri's photograph.

When I asked, Sammy said, "I had to be careful, Burt. My superiors were very angry about the appearance of the reporters. They were convinced there was a leak within the police. They demanded I find out who had reported the killing. That wasn't impossible."

"Why? Susan said it was probably a neighbor."

"It wasn't a neighbor. No one on Soon-ri's floor was home during the killing. And the police initially justified their presence by claiming there had been a burglary."

"So what? Someone still could have overheard something or perhaps even . . ." I trailed off, frowning. Sammy had an odd smile. "Son of a bitch," I murmured. "It was you. You were the leak."

"I had no choice, Burt. It was the only way to make sure the truth gets out. But I had to play it . . . cool because of Ko. He knew I often visited Soon-ri. Once Ko figures out no one in the building made the call, he might start thinking it was me. If he asks, I can say I didn't identify her until after the reporters showed. Maybe he buys it. And if not . . ." He shrugged.

"Ko would turn you in to your superiors?" To me this was ludicrous because of their close relationship.

Sammy shrugged. "I don't want to put him in the position to decide. Sergeant Ko's got three kids. Another on the way."

I understood now. If Sammy got burned, he wanted to make sure he went down alone. At that moment, any lingering concerns over his relationship with Soon-ri faded. Whatever happened between them, I knew there couldn't possibly be a connection to her death.

"So," Sammy said tentatively, "we okay now?"

When I nodded, he grinned and held a hand over the fence. "High-five? Seal the deal?"

I shook my head at the offer, suppressing a smile.

Sammy's eyes drifted past me toward Susan's car. "She used to have blond hair, right? Cut real short?"

I nodded slowly. "About a year ago. When she first arrived."

"Do me a favor, huh? Tell her I'm an okay guy. Tell her I apologize."

"Apologize for what?"

"Too much So-ju." He winked, stuck his hands in his pockets, and sauntered away.

So-ju was Korea's version of Everclear, which meant Sammy was apologizing for being drunk. Now the question was, why would Susan care?

★ As I walked toward Susan's car, my resentment toward Ray returned. It wasn't just that he must have known about Brannigan and had conveniently neglected to tell me, or the fact that my participation in the case had never been necessary. Rather, it was the nagging feeling I was being set up, for reasons I had yet to understand.

I sighed. Even though Ray and I had drifted apart these past few months, I still couldn't convince myself that he would ever hang me out to dry. A little ass-kissing to get ahead was one thing, but to knowingly set me—

And then a thought occurred to me.

Maybe that was it. Maybe Ray was also being kept out of the loop.

I took out my phone, not to confront him, but to tell him I'd swing by later. I wanted to hash this out face-to-face, where he would have a harder time dismissing my concerns. When the answering machine in his BOQ picked up, I tried his office. I was mystified as I ended the call.

I'll be in the office or at home, Ray had said. So where the hell was he?

★ The moment I opened the passenger door, the Sebring's engine roared to life. Folding myself into the seat, I saw Susan bent forward, intently listening to her cell phone. From her grim-faced expression, I thought something might be wrong with her son, David. Then she began speaking, and I realized she was again conversing with Sergeant Barnette of the Security Police. Susan became increasingly agitated. She kept interrupting Barnette, barking out questions. There seemed to be a problem with an Airman named Theresa Collins. Apparently she never arrived—

It suddenly became clear why Susan was so upset. I was incredulous. I told myself that I was jumping to conclusions, that they couldn't be this bold. But moments later, Susan removed any doubt when she announced sarcastically, "Yeah. He's here, Sergeant. He'll be thrilled when I tell him your emergency dispatcher is missing."

★ Susan darted through the evening traffic like Jeff Gordon at Daytona as she filled me in on the details. Per my earlier instructions that she'd relayed, Sergeant Barnette had ordered Airman Theresa Collins to appear at the Security Squadron by 2100 hours, so we could question her. When Collins was a no-show by 2115, Sergeant Barnette got on the horn to the women's barracks and spoke to Airman Collins's roommate. Upon hearing her story, he'd immediately called Susan with the bad news.

"A trip?" I said, interrupting Susan. "What kind of trip?"

"The roommate didn't know, Burt. Airman Collins packed a couple of suitcases and told her roomie she'd be gone for a couple of weeks. Collins wouldn't tell her why or where. Around twenty-thirty, two men showed up and escorted Collins to a car."

"Were these men Americans or—"

"A black guy and a white guy. Mid-thirties or so. Apparently they were very polite, but didn't say much. One thing that struck the roommate was the way the men were dressed. They wore business suits instead of military uniforms." Susan gave me a knowing look.

I followed up on her inference by asking whether the men showed any ID. Susan said the roommate hadn't noticed. It didn't really matter. The men's presence on the base meant they were connected with the government. The civilian clothing suggested either FBI or CIA or possibly State Department security. Since the latter two organizations had operatives permanently assigned to the Seoul embassy, it was a good bet that the men had been sent by Ambassador Gregson. I shook my head, recalling Ray's earlier assurances. *Gregson was after the truth, my ass.*

"Okay," I grunted. "Now we know what we're up against."

A nod as Susan made a tire-squealing turn.

I said, "At least Collins's disappearance proves one thing . . ."

She looked over.

". . . the voice she heard belonged to an American."

"That's what I thought, Burt. But if that's true, why didn't they take the tape of the call?"

I glanced at her in surprise. "They *didn't?*"

"Not according to Sergeant Barnette. That's where we're headed now. He's holding it for us."

I slumped back, trying to figure this. Why put Airman Collins on ice and leave the tape? The only possible explanation was that they hadn't had a chance to pick it up yet. And if not—

I checked my watch. The way Susan was driving, we'd be at Osan in ten minutes. Maybe less. The question was whether we would be in time or—

"Burt . . ."

When I turned, Susan was hunched over the wheel. Without bothering to look at me, she said, "Thought you should know I tried calling Major Sean Wilson again. When he didn't answer, I had him paged at the O-Club. He wasn't there."

Her statement hung in the air. I said, "Maybe the F-16s are night-flying—"

"They aren't. I checked with the command post."

"Let's not get ahead of ourselves. The men might not even be aware that Major Wilson was Soon-ri's boyfriend."

Susan gunned the engine as we merged onto the highway. "But if they are . . ."

I didn't respond. She already knew the answer.

After a minute, she asked softly, "Do we have a chance without Wilson?"

She was talking about solving the case. Before replying, I considered the two scenarios, first assuming that Major Wilson was the killer, and then assuming that he was only a witness who had stumbled upon the body. Either way, the conclusion came out the same.

I gave Susan what I hoped was a reassuring smile. "We always have a chance."

So I lied.

13

During the remainder of the ride to Osan, I brought Susan up to speed on my conversation with Sammy, explaining that he'd lied about Soon-ri's photo because he'd been covering for his call to the press. I also briefed her about his meeting with Chun, ending with Sammy's belief that he wasn't involved in the murder.

"How can he say that?" Susan said. "Chun's a goddamn crook."

I shrugged. I wasn't going to argue.

"Chun speak English?" she asked.

"Yeah, but not well enough to be taken for an American."

"Still might not mean anything, Burt. A guy like Chun wouldn't have done his own dirty work."

"True, but I doubt he employs many killers who speak fluent English."

She hesitated, then nodded grudgingly.

We blew by the Daewoo plant. Susan put on the brakes so we wouldn't plow into the line of cars ahead. Over a slight rise, we could see the

Y-shaped intersection adjacent to the Osan main entrance, the bright glow of the Ville visible off to the right. Less than a minute out now.

Susan said, "Sammy is right about one thing. Your selection to replace Brannigan makes no sense."

"No . . ."

"Who actually chose you, anyway? General Muller?"

I gave her a quick-and-dirty on how things happened, that in a roundabout way I'd ultimately been selected by Ambassador Gregson.

Approaching the intersection, Susan stopped at a red light and toggled the blinker. It was almost 10 P.M., the witching hour when the Ville kicked into high gear. Everywhere we looked, cars and people swirled around us. On the curb to our right, middle-aged women, in preparation for the late-night crowd, were lining up a gauntlet of food carts, which hawked everything from dried squid to "hambugees." The flow of military personnel was particularly heavy for a weekday evening. I suspected most were reacting to the impending base closure and were out for a final binge.

"Any chance Ambassador Gregson might not want this thing covered up?" Susan asked.

I eyed her skeptically. "Who do you think sent the two feds to baby-sit Collins?"

"It's still possible Gregson didn't give the order. I mean we don't actually know who the men were—"

"You know damn well they wouldn't have interfered without a nod from Gregson. Or General Muller."

She sighed. "I guess you're right. It was a long shot, anyway."

"What's a long shot?"

"It's probably nothing. But everyone knows that you're a straight shooter, Burt. So I was thinking maybe that's why you were chosen. You know, because someone actually wanted you to find out the truth." She glanced over. "Crazy, huh?"

Actually, I wondered if it was. I pointed. "The light's green."

★ A big metal sign on the concrete island in front of the gatehouse said, WELCOME TO OSAN AIR BASE. And below, hanging from hooks, a smaller one: INCREASED SECURITY ALERT. 100% ID CHECK. NO EXCEPTIONS.

We came to a stop, and Susan offered her military ID to one of the security cops who came forward. Before he took it, he glanced to me, then immediately popped to attention and snapped off a spring-loaded salute. As we drove through, a female cop stepped into the gatehouse and picked up a phone. She stared at us as we went by, hurriedly punching in a number.

"Looks like you were expected, Burt," Susan said.

For some reason, that worried me.

★ Osan is a small, picturesque base, less than four square miles in area, with most of that occupied by the runway and a nine-hole golf course. With its manicured lawns and rows of neat, cream-colored buildings, it resembled any stateside military installation with the exception that the more strategically important facilities—the hospital and the various intelligence and command centers—were bunkered or hardened to withstand bomb blasts. Two more subtle differences from the norm were the Korean Air Force compound tucked away on the northern end and the camouflaged antiaircraft batteries that surrounded the base's perimeter.

The Security Police Squadron was located up a small hill across from the 51st Wing Headquarters Building, about a mile from the gate. With a posted speed limit of twenty-five, it should have taken us a little over two minutes. Susan kept the pedal to the metal and made it in half that.

As we squealed to a stop out front and hurried inside, I checked my watch. Less than ten minutes since Susan had spoken to Sergeant Barnette. She had put the odds at 70–30, while I called them 90–10. The bottom line was we were both convinced it was inconceivable that Sergeant Barnette would still have the tape.

But as we went into his office, he rose from his desk and held out a small cardboard evidence box. I removed the lid and peered inside.

I still couldn't believe it.

★ Out of sight, out of mind.

While most stateside bases had joined the twenty-first century and installed computers to digitally record emergency calls, the Air Force, citing budget constraints, had delayed the upgrade for overseas installations like Osan. As a result, the Security Police still relied on an antiquated voice-activated cassette system that look suspiciously like an oversized answering machine. But at least the thing usually worked.

Sergeant Barnette was a small, compact man with nervous eyes and a blond mustache that you had to squint to see. While I looked over the cassette, he kept glancing at Susan, as if expecting her to chew him out again. After he confirmed the tape was wound up, I asked him for a cassette player. He led Susan and me to another office down the hall, across from the holding cells. Once Barnette left, I shut the door, popped in the cassette, and punched Play.

A hiss followed by an automated canned voice, noting the date and time of the call. Six July, 1323 hours.

Then a woman came on: "Osan Air Base Security Police. Is this an emergency?"

A man, hesitantly: "Yes. A woman's been hurt."

"Can I have your name, sir?"

"There isn't time. She's bleeding badly. You . . . you must hurry."

"Sir, I'll need your name before we can—"

"She's at the twelve-ten Sochan Road. The Chosun Apartments. Room Six-G."

"Sir, that's off base. You need to notify the Provincial Police."

"She's dying. You must hurry."

"Sir, I told you we can't respond to—"

A loud click.

"Sir? Are you there? Sir? Hey, Sergeant Givens, we might have a problem. Call the ROKs and tell them to send over a—"

I clicked off the player and glanced at Susan leaning against the door. The disappointment on her face told me she had reached the same conclusion I had.

"The guy had a hell of an accent, Burt," she said quietly. "No way Airman Collins would have mistaken him for an American."

"No . . ." I removed the cassette from the player, studied it for a moment, then slipped it into my jacket pocket.

Watching me, Susan said, "At least we know why that was still here, waiting for us. They wanted us to think the killer was Korean."

I nodded. "C'mon. Maybe Sergeant Barnette can shed some light on who switched the tapes."

★ Normally, I would have handled the questioning, but I wanted answers fast and Susan had a particular talent for intimidation that went way beyond mine. While I had to consciously force myself to come across as hardass, with her it was instinctual. An ability she'd been forced to develop as a kid just to survive.

Susan barged into Barnette's office without knocking. Within thirty seconds, she had him shaking. Within a minute, he was practically crying. He swore he didn't know anything about the tape being altered. According to Barnette, Lieutenant Colonel Carl Reemer, the Security Police commander, had kept the tape in his possession most of the day, only turning it over to Barnette when he came on duty at 1800 hours. When Susan pressed him, Barnette called the staff sergeant who had manned the duty desk during the day shift. After a brief conversation, Barnette told us that the staff sergeant did recall that two civilians had met with Colonel Reemer earlier that afternoon.

A black guy and a white guy.

Wearing suits.

"Those Feds get around," Susan said gloomily, as we climbed into her car. "*Dammit*, this is frustrating."

"Don't be discouraged."

"I'm trying, but it's hard not to be. Whatever we try, they cut us off at the knees."

I tried to come up with something reassuring, but drew a blank. No matter what I said, Susan would know I was just talking.

She gave me a long look. "You still want to check out Major Wilson's place?"

"Of course."

"He's probably long gone."

"His car might not be."

She started the engine.

★ Another unique characteristic of Osan was the fact that the majority of the personnel assigned here were without their families. Years earlier, when a second Korean war was considered a real possibility, preventing military members from bringing their wives and kids made sense. Now, with the North and South engaged in a political love-fest, the Air Force had continued the policy because they had no choice; Osan simply didn't have the infrastructure to support large numbers of dependents.

People on accompanied tours, like Susan, resided in one of two high-rises near the DOD school. The rest lived in either enlisted dorms or what I called the Officer Ghetto—a series of cookie-cutter, two-story BOQ buildings that terraced up a steep hillside across from the Officers' Club. As a general rule, the more senior the officer, the higher up the hill he or she lived.

Major Sean Wilson's building was the second from the top, which happened to be the same one I'd lived in before marrying Chung-hee. We parked against the curb behind a Humvee caked with mud. After we got out, we checked the cars sitting along the street, most of which were visible in the glow of the streetlights. I counted seven civilian vehicles, two of which were Hyundai sedans. Neither was gold.

"Strike two," Susan said.

We headed up the concrete walkway toward the glassed-in entrance of Wilson's BOQ building, less than thirty yards away. After a half-dozen steps, we saw the doors open and two men emerge, followed by a third. For a few moments they were in partial shadow, then they came out into the glow of a nearby streetlight.

Susan stopped dead in her tracks, and so did I.

Though none were black, the two men in the lead wore suits. My eyes immediately focused on the third man, who was dressed casually in tan slacks and a pullover Izod shirt. I automatically checked off Yata's description of Soon-ri's boyfriend: blond hair, seventy kilograms, two meters in height. Not that I needed to. The knapsack slung over Major Sean Wilson's shoulder and the suitcase in his hand had confirmed his identity.

The two Feds slowed, squinting at us. One was tall, lanky, with close-clipped thinning hair going gray. The other was shorter, with a muscular build and a head that went straight into his shoulders. An instant later, the tall man's eyes widened in recognition and his narrow face spread into a grin. "Hell, is that you, Burt?"

"Hello, Roger."

Ignoring Susan's stare, I continued up the walk.

14

At the American Embassy in Seoul, Roger Gentry's official title was assistant protocol officer. In reality, he was the CIA's deputy station chief for Korea. On the espionage case I worked last year, it was Roger who first tipped me off to the Air Force major's spying activities.

Roger broadened his smile as Susan and I walked up. But charming affability had always been Roger's particular talent, which was a major reason why he'd risen so rapidly up the spook promotion ladder. He could come off as your best buddy right up until the moment he stuck a knife in your back, and never give it a second thought. As the three of us shook hands, Roger didn't bother to introduce his partner or Major Wilson. Not that I'd expected him to. Roger knew why I was here, and he knew that I knew. His goal was to get rid of me with as little fuss as possible.

"So, Burt," he said, "the stuff I heard about you true? You actually bailed out from the Air Force to run a jewelry store?"

I nodded. "It belongs to my wife."

"Hey, that's right. You got married. Congratulations." And Roger, of course, sounded as if he meant it.

I reciprocated by asking about his two kids, and we spent maybe a minute making small talk. As we spoke, I could almost see the gears turning in his head as Roger worked out his next move. I casually stole a couple of glances at Major Wilson. He'd put down his suitcase and was doing an antsy two-step, trying to decide whether he should be worried about Susan and me.

Finally, Roger said to his partner, "Say, Fred, why don't you two go on to the car. I'll be along in a minute."

Susan tensed; she knew this was something we couldn't allow. As Fred started to walk by me, I casually stepped in front of him. "What's the hurry, Fred?"

Fred and Wilson gave me startled looks. Fred squinted at me, uncertainty in his eyes.

Roger said amiably, "What the hell are you doing, Burt?"

"My job." I smiled pleasantly. "I need to talk to Major Wilson about a murder."

Wilson stiffened, his eyes darting between Roger and me. A tongue ran nervously over his lips.

Roger sighed. "Jesus Christ, Burt. What is this shit? Didn't you get the word?"

"Word?"

"You're working for us."

"Really? The CIA?"

"Don't be a smart-ass. You know what I mean. You signed the goddamn contract."

I made like I was thinking. "Sorry, Roger. As I recall, the CIA wasn't anywhere on it." I gave him another smile.

Roger had always had something of a temper. He finally lost it then, his face twisting into a snarl. "*Goddammit, I said you're working for us!*"

I shrugged.

Fred puffed up, flexing his muscles in case I hadn't noticed. He grunted, "Screw this guy, Rog. I can take him."

"Try it, asshole," Susan shot back.

I gave her a hard look. That kind of help I didn't need.

For the next five seconds, we all stood there, looking at one another. I felt like a boxer in a stare-down before a fight.

"You're way out of line, Burt," Roger finally said, his voice thick.

"Probably so."

"I'm going to have your ass for this, so help me."

"Be gentle."

Susan giggled, then caught herself.

With a withering glare at her, Roger stepped back toward the building to make a call on his cell phone. I'd anticipated this move, but there was nothing I could do about it. Roger lowered his voice, but I overheard enough to know he was describing the confrontation. He came forward and shoved the phone in my face. "See if you think this is funny, asshole."

I hesitated, then took the phone.

Anticipating Ambassador Gregson's high-pitched voice, I was surprised to be greeted by a familiar rasping baritone. Instead of sounding ticked off, Lieutenant General Harry Muller's voice was quiet, almost resigned.

"Burt, do me a favor. Keep this CIA prick happy and act as if I'm chewing you out."

★ Roger and Fred were staring at me. I stood there, the phone to my ear, trying not to tip them off to the sudden confusion I felt. General Muller spoke less than a minute. I threw in two "But, sir"s, four head bobs, and attempted to look appropriately chastised. Afterward, I passed the phone back to Roger.

"We understand each other?" he said coolly.

"Yeah. You were right. I was out of line."

"*What?*" Susan said.

I flashed her a look of warning.

She disregarded it, saying, "You can't be serious, Burt. We can't let Wilson just walk."

"That's enough, Susan."

"Dammit. He's a wit—"

"*Enough*, Susan."

She stuck her hands on her hips, glowering at me.

Watching our exchange, Roger and Fred relaxed into amused smiles. Major Wilson was back doing his anxious two-step. To me, Roger said, "Hell, I'm glad we got this all worked out. I figured it was just a misunderstanding. Tell you what. Next time I'm in town, I'll stop by your store. Maybe pick up a ring for the wife."

"That'll be fine, Roger."

"This thing has everybody acting crazy. I'm glad we got everything straightened out. See you around, Burt."

"Good night, Roger."

I moved onto the grass so they could get by. Susan hesitated, then reluctantly followed. As we watched the three men go down the walkway, she said, "You son of a bitch."

I sighed, explaining that I really had no choice. That we couldn't have prevented them from leaving with Wilson.

"Spare me. You sold out, Burt."

"Now just a minute—"

"You rolled over because General Muller yanked your chain."

"Muller had nothing to do with my decision."

"Give me a break, Burt. I heard you sucking up—"

"*That* was for the benefit of Roger." I quickly filled her in.

Afterward, Susan slowly shook her head, looking mystified. "An act? Why would Muller want you to put on an act?"

"He didn't say." Roger, Fred, and Major Wilson were walking up to a silver Chevy Lumina. Before getting in, Roger turned and threw up a hand. I responded with a halfhearted wave.

"Friendly thing, isn't he," Susan said sarcastically.

As their car drove away, we started down the walkway. Susan said, "Still doesn't figure, Burt. The way I see it, General Muller was feeding you a line to get you to back off. You said yourself he has to be part of the cover-up."

"He still might be."

We continued without speaking. It was a quiet night, and we could hear a smattering of voices from the crowd emerging from the theater across the street. To the west, past the hangars, we could see the glow of the airfield lights and the silhouette of the control tower, a half mile away.

"Mind if I ask a question?" Susan asked.

"You want to know why I went along with Muller's request?"

"Sure. You're not in the military anymore. Besides, I thought you hated the guy."

"A couple of reasons. Initially, I was more curious than anything. Muller didn't order me to comply. Instead, he told me he needed a favor."

"Muller?"

I nodded.

To understand Susan's surprise, you had to know General Muller. As a three-star with a better than even chance to get a fourth, he was one of the military's anointed and acted like it. Gruff and dictatorial, he seemed to get off on abusing subordinates simply because he could. In the year since he'd taken command of the 7th Air Force, Muller had fired two-thirds of his staff and half of the various unit commanders, most for minor infractions known only to him. Curiously, Ray was the one person who had thrived under Muller, and not just because he sucked up to him. A few months back, Ray had made the comment that Muller owed him. For what exactly, Ray would never tell me.

Anyway, the point is that a guy with Muller's ego would never *ask* a subordinate to do anything. Certainly not a former major whom he probably despised. But he had.

We were almost to the car. Susan split off to the driver's side while I continued around. She said, "You mentioned a second reason . . ."

"Yes. General Muller assured me he'd explain everything."

Susan looked at me over the top of the car. "He will? When?"

"Now. He's expecting us." As I reached for the passenger door, I stepped back, remembering a call I had to make. An important one.

"Give me a minute, Susan."

★ I leaned against the hood of the car as the phone rang. I'd phoned the jewelry store because, like most businesses in the Ville, we stayed open until midnight. When Chung-hee answered, the voices in the background told me she had customers.

In the middle of my apology to her, Chung-hee interrupted me. "Don't, Burt. It was my fault. I don't know why but . . . but I just seem to . . . to react. Take it out on you."

I was tempted to ask if someone had insulted her, but knew I'd be wasting my time. Chung-hee never revealed the names because she didn't want me confronting the person. She reasoned that my involvement would only make things worse, possibly escalate things. I said sympathetically, "You're under a lot of stress. With running the store and—"

"It's not that. It's . . . it's this *place*."

"Then let's leave. Sell out and go back to the States like you want. Get you started on your career."

In light of the way she's been treated, most of our acquaintances are mystified by Chung-hee's desire to return to the United States. But as she tells them, the bias she's been subjected to here has less to do with her being Asian than her association with the Ville. That statement, while true, only partly explains her desire to leave. Her college experience forever changed her, unlocking an ambition she never knew she had. Since returning, she has found it increasingly difficult to accept the constraints that Korean society places upon women. She knew that if she remained, she would never realize her potential, never be anything but a shopkeeper. That was a future she couldn't and wouldn't accept.

She said, "But the price is too low—"

"Forget the price." Since quitting the military, I'd been trying to get her to accept any reasonable offer, while she insisted on holding out for the quarter mil the store was worth. With the depressed Korean economy and the political uncertainty surrounding the future of the base, it could be years until we got her asking price, if ever. Ironically, I liked living in Korea and could handle the wait; she didn't and couldn't.

She asked hesitantly: "What about my mother?"

"Whatever she decides is fine with me."

A long silence. I said, "Honey . . ."

"I'm here, Burt. My . . . my mother wants to come with us to America."

Up to now, her mother had never actually voiced a preference, probably because she wasn't in the greatest health and didn't want to be a burden. "Good. I was going to suggest it."

"You really mean it?"

I got a warm and fuzzy feeling at the excitement in her voice. "Of course. Besides, she's the only one who knows how to cook."

She giggled. "God, I love you."

"I love you, too."

After telling her I'd be a few more hours, I hung up and got into the car.

"What have you got to be so happy about?" Susan asked.

★ Lieutenant General Harry Muller lived at the top of the hill, in a sprawling five-bedroom ranch-style house that overlooked the air base and the rice fields beyond. As Susan and I drove up, we passed the four duplexes where the colonels resided. Ray's building was the second from the end. The drapes over his living-room window were drawn, but I could still see lights on.

Susan parked in Muller's driveway, behind his staff car that Ray had been driving earlier. We followed the winding stone pathway past the colorful flower beds toward the front steps. As we went up to the front porch, I asked Susan if she'd ever met General Muller before.

"Seen him around a bunch of times. Never actually spoke to him."

I rang the doorbell. "Might be better if I did the talking, then."

"Why? You think I can't handle him?"

I sighed, looking at her. "Of course not. But I've dealt with him before and know how he—" I saw her eyes glaze over. "Fine. You ask the questions, then. But you'd better know the ground rules first."

"Ground rules?"

"Don't introduce yourself to General Muller unless he initiates it. Don't say anything unless he specifically asks you. And then only respond to the question. Do not add or embellish anything. And never engage in pleasantries."

"I heard he was a jerk, but—"

"He also likes to play mind games with people he doesn't know. Press their buttons to see how they'll react. Remain professional and don't let him get under your skin." At the sound of approaching footsteps from within the house, I faced the door. "And when you question him, he'll try to intimidate you. He'll appear angry, so it's important not to get rattled—"

"I've changed my mind, Burt. He's all yours."

Finally.

The door swung open.

15

A black-jacketed Korean man with slicked-back hair and a pleasant face stood in the doorway. Even though I'd never met him, I knew he had to be Mr. Kim, General Muller's houseman and sometime driver. In book-proper English, Mr. Kim asked for our names, then led us down a tiled hallway to a set of French doors across from an elegant living room. From somewhere toward the back, we could hear a TV playing.

Mr. Kim knocked once, entered at a grunted reply, then announced us and stepped aside.

Susan and I walked into an overwhelmingly masculine study of dark paneling, mahogany furnishings, and red carpeting fully three inches thick. Two entire walls were filled with photographs and mementos of General Muller's career, while a third was reserved for a built-in wet bar bracketed by gold-framed paintings of military aircraft, most of which Muller had probably flown. Notably absent were pictures or reminders of his wife or three grown children, which spoke volumes about Muller's priorities.

As Mr. Kim closed the door behind us, Susan and I stopped in the middle of the room. I'd anticipated that Ray might be here, but the only other person in the room was a balding, heavyset man with intense dark eyes, who was camped behind a desk the size of a pool table, looking over the contents of a folder.

General Muller made no move to acknowledge our presence, which was typical. I'd once cooled my heels before him for five minutes, waiting to be noticed. He was still dressed in his class-A military uniform, with the rows of embroidered medals and the three stars glittering on each shoulder. Considering the hour, I couldn't help but wonder if he'd put it on specifically for this meeting, to ratchet up the intimidation level.

Muller finally looked up, his eyes glossing over Susan to focus on me. "Thank you for coming, Burt."

I nodded, struck by his words and manner. Like on the phone, he was uncharacteristically polite and subdued.

General Muller motioned us to two nearby chairs, which was also a first. In my previous meetings with him, I'd never once been invited to sit.

As Susan and I took our seats, Muller's ruddy face looked me over coolly. "Let's clear up a few things first, Burt. Would it be fair to say that you think I'm a horse's ass?"

I tried not to show my surprise and failed.

He seemed to smile at my reaction. "It's a simple question. A yes or no will suffice."

The mind games were starting early. I gazed back calmly as I tried to figure out his angle. "Yes, sir," I said finally.

"And you, Lieutenant Torres?"

The safe response would be a denial. Instead, Susan said cautiously, "You have that . . . reputation, sir."

Another vague smile. To me again: "Now, would you say that I am a liar?"

What the hell is this? I shook my head.

"Dishonest?" he asked.

"No, sir."

"Corrupt? Perhaps immoral?"

"No, sir."

He tented his fingers, watching me. "So my problem is that I'm basically an egotistical prick?"

I slowly nodded. And as I did, I finally realized what he was attempting to do.

Muller abruptly lowered his hands. "One final question, and I want a straight answer. No bullshit. What if . . ." He paused for effect, his eyes boring into mine. "What if I told you that I would never cover for a murderer, would you believe me?"

Neatly done. He thought he had me cornered. "Depends, sir."

He scowled disapprovingly. "Sorry, Burt. You can't have it both ways. Now, either I'm a liar or—"

"There's a third option, sir."

"Oh . . ."

"You could be mistaken over someone's guilt. Believe he's innocent when he's not."

His voice hardened, matching his eyes. "There's no goddamn mistake. Major Sean Wilson never killed that girl."

"How do you know, sir?"

"Any number of reasons. His father and I went through flight school together. I've known Sean . . . Major Wilson . . . since he was a child. I can vouch for his upbringing and character."

I said, "That's hardly proof of—"

"Then there's this." General Muller slid over the folder he'd been looking at earlier. "Take a look."

As I plucked it from the desk, Susan leaned over to see. Inside were two Xeroxed pages. The first was a copy from an aircraft maintenance log, commonly known as a Form 781. I immediately focused on the entry under the pilot block. Wilson, S. A., Major, followed by a Social Security number. Dated today.

Susan pointed to the takeoff and landing times. I nodded, then flipped to the second page. Three typed names. Two lieutenants and a captain.

Next to each was a phone number, Osan BOQ address, and unit affiliation. They were all pilots with the 36th FS.

I closed the folder.

"Satisfied?" Muller said. "The seven eighty-one proves Major Wilson was flying at the time of the murder."

I met his gaze. "It could be a forgery, sir."

General Muller's face reddened, and I braced for the explosion. Instead, he said tersely, "Major Wilson flew a four-ship formation. The second page lists the other pilots. Major Wilson was also seen getting into the jet by at least a dozen maintenance personnel. There are the people who worked the tower, heard his voice on the radio. Now, unless you think everyone is lying . . ." He dropped the ball over to my side of the net.

I had no argument, and he knew it. Even in an institution as rigid as the military, it was highly unlikely that so many people could be pressured into lying. I said, "If Major Wilson is innocent, sir, then why the hide-and-seek game tonight?"

Muller kicked back in his chair. His tone was low, almost professorial. "When Ambassador Gregson found out that the press was tipped off to the murder, he decided he had no choice. The goddamn bleeding hearts in the ROK government are pushing President Rhee hard to request a U.S. troop withdrawal. The only reason Rhee's been able to stall them as long as he has is because the Korean public still supports our presence. Not by much, but the margin is still there. Mostly it's the older Koreans who still appreciate what we did during the war and the businessmen who want our dollars. But I got to tell you that rape incident really hurt. If an American gets linked to this killing, that could be the ball game for us in Korea. With the Japanese talking about throwing us out of Okinawa, that means there could be no U.S. military presence in the Pacific to keep the goddamn Chinese in check. The bottom line is our government simply can't allow any suspicion to fall on Major Wilson."

"Colonel Johnson explained the political concerns, sir," I said. "What I want to know is why we were prevented from interviewing Major Wilson this evening." I tapped the folder on my lap. "This would have cleared him, sir."

"Would it?" he said quietly.

I frowned, then understood. Witnesses or not, the Korean public would never believe the Air Force hadn't doctored the maintenance log to exonerate Wilson.

Even though I knew the answer, I had to give it a shot. "Sir, it still would help if we could talk to Major Wilson. He might be able to shed some light on—"

"I'm afraid that's not possible, Burt. But maybe I can answer some of your questions.

"*You*, sir?" I said.

"I sat in on most of the CIA's interrogation of Major Wilson, which was something Ambassador Gregson insisted on beforehand. To clear up his concerns."

My brow furrowed. "His concerns? You mean in regard to Major Wilson's guilt?"

He smiled thinly. "Despite how it looks, Ambassador Gregson would never had shielded Major Wilson if he thought he might be guilty." He gave me a long look. "And neither would I."

His tone and manner came across as truthful, but I couldn't bring myself to believe him. Not with what I knew was at stake.

I made a writing motion to Susan. As she dug out her notepad, I asked General Muller if Major Wilson knew why someone would have wanted to kill the victim.

"He said he didn't."

"No one at all, sir? An ex-boyfriend or . . ."

Head shake.

". . . perhaps a Mr. Chun?"

He squinted. "Chun?"

I got off most of a sentence before Muller cut me off, saying, "Didn't make the connection at first, Burt. Hell, I know Chun. He's the son of a bitch who runs the Song-tan Business Council. He called about an hour ago and read me the riot act for shutting down the base. Said how much money the merchants were going to lose and demanded I tell him how long the closure would last."

Which backed up Sammy's story that Chun's appearance at the apartment building had been motivated by money.

Susan was madly scribbling away. When she finally caught up, I asked Muller about Major Wilson's relationship to the victim.

A shrug. "He said he knew her only casually."

Susan's head popped up, but I managed to keep my face expressionless. I said, "So they were just friends? Nothing more?"

"I know what you're thinking, and the CIA pressed him on that point, believe me. But Wilson was insistent that he and the girl were never . . . romantically involved."

I paused, waiting for Muller to expand upon the obvious, that Wilson had to be lying. When he didn't, I asked, "Did you believe him, sir?"

"Does it matter, Burt? We know he didn't kill her."

Which was the response I expected. When I'd dated Chung-hee, Muller had raked me over the coals, putting our relationship in the worst possible light. But now he was apparently willing to give Major Wilson a pass. Nothing like a little favoritism among friends.

Still, I was curious that Wilson would have the balls to lie to a couple CIA types, knowing they would never swallow his story. I asked Muller if Major Wilson was married or engaged and got negative responses to both. Of course, Wilson might simply have been trying to protect his professional reputation. Or perhaps he was worried that Muller might tell his parents that he'd been banging a stripper. The latter was a stretch, but you never knew.

Susan tapped my leg. When I glanced down, I saw a circled word on her notepad. *Toothbrush?* I nodded and asked General Muller if Major Wilson had visited the victim earlier today, before his flight.

"That would've been impossible," he said. "Major Wilson was the morning SOF at the squadron."

SOF stood for Supervisor Of Flying. I said, "And he came on duty at . . ."

"Zero six hundred this morning. Worked straight through until his flight."

Switching gears, I asked, "Did Major Wilson say anything about a disagreement with the victim in the last few days, sir? Perhaps mention why he removed his personal effects?"

"What personal effects?" His tone suddenly suspicious.

"Toiletries. Possibly some clothing—"

"Aren't you listening? They were *friends*. Period. Major Wilson wouldn't have had any reason to keep personal items there."

"General, there are indications that some toiletries might have been removed—"

"Not by Major Wilson." He ended the comment with a glare.

I was uncertain as to how to proceed. Even though Muller couldn't possibly believe Wilson's denial about being involved with Soon-ri, he was acting as if he did. The question now was whether I was willing to press the issue. I gathered myself together and said, "Sir, I think it's clear Major Wilson and the victim were lovers—"

"For chrissakes, Burt. Wilson denies it and you have no proof—"

"I might, sir."

An icy stare.

"The baby," I said.

He blinked, confused.

After I explained, he sagged back in his chair, slowly shaking his head. "You're certain the girl was alive when—"

"Yes, sir." Susan backed me up with a head bob.

"But *dammit*, the baby couldn't have been Major Wilson's. I specifically *asked* him. He swore to me that he had no relations with her."

Susan frowned. Like me, she found it curious that Muller genuinely appeared to have bought Wilson's denial. "We still don't actually know if it's his, sir," I admitted.

Muller didn't seem to hear. He closed his eyes as if taking in the horror of what I'd told him. This was a side of him that I'd never have guessed existed. But being a hard-nosed general didn't make him any less human.

Muller's eyes cracked open. "A genetic test would prove paternity."

"Yes, sir." I added, "We'll need Major Wilson's cooperation."

"You'll get it," he growled.

He dug through a Rolodex, then picked up a phone. As he thumbed in a number, we saw the anger build in his face. Maybe that's what was bothering him all along. The realization that Major Wilson had lied to him.

"Agent Gentry, this is General Muller. I want to speak to Major Wilson. *Now.*"

16

For the next three minutes, General Muller went at Major Wilson like a cop, peppering off questions. Even under the onslaught, Wilson appeared to stick to his story. Twice I asked if I could speak to him, but Muller ignored me. When he hung up, he shook his head grimly. "He still denies any relationship, Burt."

"And a blood test . . ."

"He agreed. Says there's no way in hell he's the father."

"Did he resist taking one?"

"No. In fact, he insisted on it. The sooner the better."

A point in Wilson's favor. "Did he know the victim was pregnant?" I'd heard Muller ask the question.

"He swears he didn't. How far along was she?"

"Only a few months. She wouldn't have been showing."

Muller gazed at me evenly and began massaging the back of his neck. "What else you want to know, Burt?"

Another tap on the leg as Susan passed on a second message. One I'd intended to ask Wilson. "General," I asked, "is Major Wilson well off financially?"

He stopped rubbing. "Not even close. Why?"

I told him about the hundred grand or so it took to buy out Soon-ri's contract from Chun and set her up in the apartment.

He almost laughed. "A hundred grand? You're dreaming, Burt. Major Wilson went through a nasty divorce a few years ago. Spent a bundle on lawyers, and his ex still took him to the cleaners. Hell, he's only now getting his head above water."

"What about his family—"

"Martin . . . Major Wilson's father . . . retired from the Air Force as a light bird and now works for the FAA. Midlevel administrator. He couldn't . . . wouldn't have given that kind of money to Sean."

Susan's head swiveled sharply toward me. I knew what she was thinking. First Wilson doesn't balk at a blood test and now we learn he's no Bill Gates. Had we jumped the gun?

Maybe we had. Maybe Major Wilson wasn't Soon-ri's sugar daddy or the father of her baby. And maybe he had no idea who killed her or why.

I *was* sure about one thing.

There was no way a red-blooded male like Wilson could have resisted sleeping with a woman as beautiful as Soon-ri.

A leg tap. The third one.

This was getting ridiculous. The reason I'd wanted to question Muller was to protect Susan. If she'd come on too strongly, he could have retaliated and ruined her career. But that concern seemed moot now, considering Muller's cooperative manner, which I still wasn't sure I understood.

"General," I said, glancing at Susan, "Lieutenant Torres has a few questions."

She looked startled. She recovered, slowly shifting her attention to Muller, who was gazing at her with a vaguely amused expression.

"Relax, Lieutenant," he said. "I'll try not to bite."

Susan smiled back nervously, but when she spoke, her voice was calm.

"Sir, I was wondering about the tape of the emergency call. If you've heard it— You have?"

Muller was nodding. "Agent Gentry played it for me."

She asked him if the voice belonged to an American or a Korean.

"A Korean male."

He'd hesitated fractionally before answering. Normally that suggested a lie, but the CIA, by definition, always played things very close to the vest. And knowing how Roger Gentry operated, it's conceivable he had played Muller the altered version.

"Sir," Susan said. "That's not what we were initially led to believe—"

"I know. The dispatcher, Airman Collins, was apparently mistaken. The tape should be in the SP squadron. You can judge for yourselves."

I wondered if Susan would tell him that we'd already listened to that tape and reveal our suspicions that it had been switched. Instead, she asked, "Is there any chance we might speak to Airman Collins, sir?"

"You're aware she's . . . unavailable."

Susan nodded.

He started to comment, then thought better of it. He checked his watch and gave her an expectant look.

Taking the hint, Susan said, "Sir, I only have two final questions . . ."

"Fine . . ."

"First, I don't understand how you . . . the CIA . . . learned of Major Wilson's connection to the victim." She glanced at me. "We only learned that within the past hour."

Great question.

But not one Muller wanted to hear. He pursed his lips and shook his head. "Sorry. I can't say."

"By can't, you mean—"

"Just that, Lieutenant. I can't. What I will tell you is *how* we learned of the connection has absolutely nothing to do with the murder."

For an instant, Susan seemed tempted to press him. She wisely backed off, asking, "Sir, I was wondering about Major Wilson's car."

"What about it?"

"It's a gold Hyundai and—"

"I'm familiar with it. I want to know why you're interested in it."

"The victim was seen in it on more than one occasion, and we understand it was often parked at her apartment building. A forensic analysis of the vehicle might suggest who else from the base she'd been in contact with."

"Meaning the killer could be an acquaintance of Wilson's?"

"It's a possibility, sir."

Muller thought for a moment, then shrugged and reached for his phone. "Agent Gentry was searching for somewhere to store the car for a few weeks until this mess blows over. He was going to have it driven to Seoul, but I intervened, knowing it might be a hassle for Sean to get it back. I told Gentry I'd take care of it."

Susan and I exchanged glances. She said, "Sir, are you telling us . . ."

"It's sitting in my garage," Muller said. "Kim will show it to you."

He placed the phone to his ear and pressed the intercom button.

★ Thirty seconds later, Mr. Kim appeared at the door. As Susan and I started to rise, General Muller said, "Burt, hang around for a minute."

I eased back down. Susan glanced back quizzically, then left with Kim. After the door closed, Muller said hesitantly, "I've done a great deal of soul-searching. For what it's worth, I want you to know I . . . I was wrong, Burt."

"Sir?"

"About you. Your marriage. When you confronted me, I overreacted. I downgraded your evaluation without cause. My actions were unprofessional and I . . . apologize."

I couldn't believe what I was hearing. I sat frozen, making no attempt to hide my shock.

"Just wanted to clear the air, Burt." He gave me a little smile.

I tried to draw upon my old resentment toward him, get angry. But nothing I could say now would restore my military career, and lashing out seemed somehow pointless. Besides, I knew how difficult it was for someone like him to apologize. "Thank you, sir."

He nodded and bent forward, forearms on the desk. "I had another reason for wanting to speak to you privately. There are a few items about this case I didn't mention. I need your word you won't reveal the source."

It took me less than a second. "Agreed."

"The tape. I almost told you the truth earlier. Without my approval, Gentry altered the original version."

I eased out a breath. "So the caller was an American?"

"I couldn't swear to it, but he sounded like one. Gentry seemed convinced, which was why he asked Major Wilson if he knew of another American who was close to the victim. Wilson said there were a number in her past, but none she'd seen recently. The problem was he couldn't provide names."

I said, "By recently . . ."

"Two months. Since she quit dancing."

"We can check at the Studio 99 Club, sir. Some of the other dancers may know the names of her old boyfriends. They should also be able to tell us who bought out her contract."

Muller nodded, glancing at the phone on his desk. "Ambassador Gregson also called before you arrived. He was pretty upset over your confrontation with Gentry. He said if you pulled a stunt like that again, he would hold Ray and me personally responsible."

I frowned. "You and Ray, sir? Why would Ambassador Gregson—"

But Muller was already telling me. He said, "Ambassador Gregson's pissed because we recommended you to handle this case instead of Colonel Brannigan." Muller saw I was about to interrupt and went on quickly, "I know, I know. Ray told you it was Gregson's idea to bring you on board. It wasn't. I knew you'd never have agreed to assist if you thought the request had come from me."

I could only stare at him.

"Don't look so surprised, Burt. You're the best investigator around. Brannigan would have sat on this thing. Let the case die. I wasn't about to let that happen."

I was still reeling. I said, "Sir, you actually *want* the murder solved?"

"Goddamn right," he said. "Want to know why? Might be a little hard to believe."

I edged toward him. "Try me, sir."

"Not without a drink. Join me?" He stood and gave me a questioning look as he went over to the wet bar. I shook my head at the offer. A minute later he returned with glass of Chivas, neat. He sat down heavily, took a large swallow, then settled back, chin to his chest.

When he spoke his voice was quiet, but with an undercurrent of emotion. "It ties into one of the reasons I resented you, Burt. You had the balls to say fuck your career. Face up to the pressure and follow through on your marriage. In a way I suppose I was . . . a little envious. But it was more complicated than that. It was because you reminded me of what I should have done. Sometimes, even now, I think that was a . . ."

He drifted off and sat very still, staring at his glass. As if remembering.

I watched him, saying nothing.

His eyes flicked once, and he abruptly began talking again. "Her name was Mi-yong. A dancer at one of the clubs. She wasn't the prettiest girl, but there was something about her. An innocence. She was running away from an abusive family and had only been working for a week when we met. We . . . connected." He shrugged, looking at up me. "Anyway, you asked why I wanted this case solved. She's it. She's the reason."

I was silent, frowning.

He sipped his drink, watching me over the rim of his glass. "You still don't get it, huh?"

I shook my head.

"Life," he said, with a trace of sadness, "is all about choices, Burt. Forks in the road you never anticipate taking." He paused, his voice turning bitter. "Twenty years ago I found myself faced with a decision similar to yours. My commanders hounded me about how I was going to destroy my career if I continued my relationship with Mi-yong. God knows I tried to resist. In the end, I gave in. I let them convince me to walk away from the one woman I ever really—"

He broke off; he couldn't say the word.

Instead, he raised his glass and angrily drained it in two swallows.

★ From somewhere above me air hummed softly through a vent. Muller was hunched forward at his desk, eyes again on the glass he'd just refilled. For almost a minute, he never moved. I watched the walls, thinking I should probably leave. But you don't walk out on a three-star general.

So I just sat there, waiting.

Finally, he glanced up at me. "Now you know."

I hesitated. "Sir, you're telling me you're pursuing this case because of a girl you once—" I almost said "loved."

"It's the truth, Burt."

"Sir, that was a long time ago."

"I told you it wouldn't make much sense. Hell, I'm not even sure why it's important to me. Call it guilt. Call it anything you want. But I've never forgotten Mi-yong. Maybe in some screwy way I'm trying to make amends to her. All I can tell you is I want the murder solved."

I studied him. Again he came off as sincere, and I found myself slipping to his side of the fence. Yet . . .

"Sir, the tape of the call suggests the killer is someone from the base—"

"I'm aware of that."

"If I'm successful in identifying him, Ambassador Gregson . . . the military . . . will almost certainly hold you responsible for the political fallout." Because that was the military way. Any time a unit had a problem—a plane crash, a scandal, anything—the commander was usually the first one sacrificed to the gods.

"We don't know how Gregson will react. He's a straight guy. If push comes to shove, I doubt he'd cover for a killer."

"It might not be his decision, sir."

He shrugged. "So I retire a little early."

An hour ago hearing him say this would have floored me. I found my concerns toward him fading. I said, "Agent Gentry could pose a problem, sir. If he finds out I'm focusing on someone from the base—"

"I'll handle him. You just solve this damn thing. Get me a name, and I'll take it from there."

I hesitated.

He looked right at me. "You're going to have to trust me on this, Burt."

He was right; I was. But before signing on, I wanted to clear up one confusing point. I asked him why he was willing to go after an American now.

"I just told you," he said, with a trace of irritation.

"I'm not questioning your rationale, sir. My confusion is over the reversal of your position. When I took on the case, I was told to target a Korean. Yet now you're telling me—"

"What the hell are you talking about? I never changed my position."

I stared at him. "You didn't, sir? But Ray made it clear I was to target—"

"I don't care what Ray said. I made it known from the beginning that I wanted the killer found. Korean or American, I didn't give a damn."

I frowned. "And Ray knew how you felt?"

"Hell, yes. He was with me when Gentry played the tape. That's when I made my feelings known. Whatever Ray told you, he wasn't speaking for me."

But that's precisely what was throwing me. One reason Ray was the perfect executive officer was that he never did anything on his own. A running joke among the base's elite was that Ray wouldn't take a piss without Muller's okay. He hadn't even come to my wedding because Muller hadn't given his blessing.

"So," Muller said, "you going to provide me with the name or not?"

I nodded slowly. "Sir, the Koreans will have criminal jurisdiction—"

"We'll cross that bridge when we come to it. Now, if you've got nothing else, we can—"

He looked past me as someone began fumbling with the door handle. A woman began calling out to him. Her speech was slurred, and she sounded very drunk.

Muller swore.

17

I twisted around in my chair as a dowdy woman with a pile of bleached-blond hair finally managed to open one of the French doors. She wore a bright pink bathrobe that barely covered her ample frame. She stood in the doorway, swaying, holding on to a cocktail glass rimmed with lipstick smears. She didn't appear to notice me.

"You coming to bed, Harry?" Her voice was nasal, whiny.

"In few minutes, Lorna."

"Now, Harry. I'm tired."

Looking at Mrs. Muller, I made no attempt to hide my disgust. She'd been one of the women who'd been particularly rude toward Chung-hee. When Chung-hee attended her first and only Officers' Wives Club meeting, Mrs. Muller had humiliated her in front of everyone by asking her to leave.

"Please, Lorna," General Muller said. "I'm busy. I'll be along in—"

In an instant, Lorna's expression twisted into a snarl. She spat, "Busy. You're always too goddamn busy for me, Harry. What's the matter? Don't I do it for you anymore?"

"Lorna, you're drunk. You should go to—"

A harsh, sloppy laugh. "Hell, yes, I'm drunk. That's the only way I can take you. Take living in this goddamn country. Take this joke of a marriage—"

She stopped, staring at me as if suddenly aware of my presence. She squinted hard, trying to focus. "Do I know you?"

I nodded.

Her eyes slowly widened. She took a step toward me, stumbled, and spilled some of her drink on the floor. She didn't seem to notice. "Sure, I remember now. You're the one who married that—"

"Don't say it, Lorna," Muller said.

She turned on him, her voice rising shrilly. "Screw you, Harry. You may not like it, but I'm your goddamn wife. I can say anything I damn well—"

"Shut up, Lorna."

"No, I won't shut up. You can't make me shut—"

"I said shut up!"

That finally did it. She stared at him, her face a mixture of hurt and shock. Her shoulders sagged and tears began welling in her eyes. She wiped at them with a sleeve. "You son of a bitch. You never loved me. I tried. God knows . . ." She began to cry.

General Muller said, "Lorna. Please. I didn't mean . . ."

But she turned and was shuffling out the door. We heard her footsteps fade down the hallway.

Muller and I sat in an uncomfortable silence. He avoided looking at me, and I took the hint. As I rose to leave, I asked him how to get to the garage. After he told me, his eyes remained on mine. At that moment, I didn't notice his medaled uniform or the stars on his shoulders. I only saw a man who looked old and worn, as if the weight of the world were on his shoulders.

"Remember what I said, Burt," he said softly. "Life is about choices. When you make the wrong one, you can never go back."

I nodded.

"Your wife's name is Chung-hee?"

"Yes, sir."

"Tell her I'm sorry for the way she was treated."

"I will, sir."

"Good night, Burt."

"Good night, sir."

As I left, General Muller was back at the wet bar, making another drink.

★ "Find anything?" I asked Susan, as I entered the immaculate, two-car garage. She was bent at the waist, peering inside the trunk of the gold Hyundai, which was parked next to the blue Lincoln Town Car that Mrs. Muller usually drove. Mr. Kim wasn't anywhere to be seen.

Susan straightened and shut the trunk as I walked up. "Not a thing. Car's clean as a whistle."

"Major Wilson could be a neat freak."

She shook her head as she adjusted the latex gloves on her hands. "No one's that neat. I looked under the floor pads and pulled up the rear seats. Didn't even find so much as a gum wrapper or a dust ball. And take a look at this." She stepped around, opened a rear passenger door, then gestured to the carpeting on the floor.

I immediately noticed the streaks. "Vacuumed recently."

"Yeah. Had to be Gentry's men. He didn't want us to uncover hair or clothing fibers that would tie Soon-ri to Major Wilson."

"Fingerprints, too," I added, noticing how the interior shone wetly, as if it had been recently wiped down with Armor All.

She closed the door. "Thorough fella, your buddy Gentry. So, you still want me to have a forensics crew sent over?"

Her tone indicated it would be a waste of time, and I agreed. Besides, the last thing I wanted was for the word to get back to Gentry and have him go ballistic over the possibility that I was still interested in Major Wilson.

"Forget it," I said.

Susan snapped off her gloves and pointed to a small door next to the garage door. "Kim says we can go out that way."

As we exited onto the driveway, I glanced down the street to check if Ray's living-room light was still on. It was.

"*Well?*" Susan said.

Since I'd given my word, I couldn't reveal that Muller had heard the original tape. Not that it mattered. She already knew the caller had to be someone from the base. I began by telling her that Muller was the one who had selected me for the case, and not Ambassador Gregson. When we arrived at her car, I hit her with the zinger that Muller once had a Korean girlfriend twenty years ago.

She gave me a bug-eyed look. "*Muller?* You gotta be kidding me. He really shacked up with some— Where are you going, Burt?"

I kept walking by her toward the sidewalk. "To talk to Ray."

When she scooted up to me, I continued filling her in on Muller's love affair with the bar girl, Mi-yong. Afterward, Susan still appeared amazed. "So General Muller was actually going to marry this girl?"

"Sounded like it."

"What a hypocrite. He nails you to the wall when he almost did the same thing."

"Don't spread it around," I said. "It would be embarrassing for him."

"You serious? After what he did to you?"

I shrugged. "He apologized. Besides, he didn't have to tell me about the relationship."

"Why did he, then?"

Ray's duplex was just ahead, on the other side of the street. As we crossed over toward it, I explained Muller's reason.

"Man," she said, "this just gets better and better. You're telling me he wants the case solved because of guilt?"

It did sound a little ridiculous, hearing her say it. "You had to have been there. Seen his face when he talked about her. He really loved her."

"So what? That's ancient history. And it's not like the victim was his old squeeze. Now, that I could maybe understand. But you and I both know General Muller would never put his career on the line for some bar girl he doesn't even know."

I shrugged.

We turned up the concrete walkway toward Ray's front door. Stepping onto the small portico, we heard music playing.

As I rang the doorbell, Susan asked what I wanted to talk to Ray about. After I told her she said, "That's easy. The reason Colonel Johnson wanted you to concentrate on Korean suspects was because he was following General Muller's orders."

"Muller denied giving him such orders."

"Big surprise," she said dryly.

I pressed the doorbell again. After a few seconds, I began knocking and checked the handle. Locked.

"He must be out," Susan said.

I took out my cell phone. Moments later, we could hear ringing from within the house. When Ray's answering machine picked up, I hung up and called the only other place he might be this time of night. He wasn't at his office.

"He could be in the Ville," Susan said.

"Ray doesn't troll the bars," I said, stepping off the portico. I cut across the lawn toward the living-room window. The drapes were closed except for a two-inch slit. I peered inside, blinking against the brightness of the light. I was looking at Ray's dinette table. Beyond, I could see the back of an armchair and most of a sofa. I pressed up against the glass and glanced to the right.

I saw Ray then. At least part of him.

His legs were splayed out on his leather recliner. From my angle, I could see only to his waist. He still wore his uniform pants, but no socks or shoes. And lying nearby on the white carpet I spotted an empty bourbon bottle. I rapped sharply on the glass. No movement. I shook my head and was about to step away when something on the floor caught my eye.

A long, cylindrical object, partially hidden by a chair leg. My mouth went dry when I realized what it was.

Fighting a sense of panic, I turned to run and stumbled on a bush. I swore.

"What is it, Burt? What's wrong?"

"Ray's been drinking, and he's got a gun."

She read the fear on my face. "Don't tell me you really think he might—"

But I was already kicking open the front door.

★ Susan and I stood over Ray, watching his chest rise and fall. On the stereo, the local Armed Forces Network radio station was playing a John Denver tune. I leaned over the recliner and shook Ray gently. He reeked of booze. When he didn't stir, I tried again, more vigorously.

He rolled over on his side, smacked his lips, and began to snore.

"Passed out," Susan said, picking up the empty bourbon bottle and placing it on the coffee table. "I didn't know he was a big drinker."

"He isn't normally."

"He'll be pissed about his door."

Like I cared. I picked up the shotgun, which was a twelve-gauge pump. On the butt was an MWR stamp, indicating it had been signed out from the base Morale, Welfare, and Recreation Office. I checked the breech. Empty. I glanced around, looking for a box of shells; didn't see one.

"So," Susan said, "want to tell me why you thought he might waste himself?"

I held up the shotgun.

"So what's that prove, Burt? Colonel Johnson could have been doing a little shooting at the Rod and Gun Club."

"He doesn't shoot." Glancing to Ray, I added, "And the only time he drinks is when he's under stress, and even then, it's rarely more than a glass or two. The last time I saw him passed out was during our senior year in college, after an argument with his father."

Susan was silent, but the look on her face told me she knew there had to be more.

I said, "Ray went through a divorce a while back. His wife wanted it, not him. He's been flying back to the States two, three times a year to see her and his two kids. I think he always held out hope that maybe they'd get back together. He recently found out his ex is getting remarried, and he took the news pretty hard."

This was a reason Susan could understand. Her expression turned sympathetic. "That's rough."

I told her to get a blanket from the bedroom. When she returned a minute later, I'd turned off the stereo and most of the lights. After we covered him up, I paused to gaze down at Ray's sleeping form. I tried to decide whether I believed he could ever kill himself.

I honestly didn't, but that didn't mean much. Ray was someone who always kept everything bottled up inside, and went off into his own private corner when he was hurting. If something was eating at him, odds were no one would ever guess the extent until it was too late. Like the problems with his father back at school. Sure he'd finally told me about it, but it took him almost four years and as many drinks.

In the end, I decided I had no choice. As I held the door open for Susan, she glanced at the shotgun in my hand. "Aren't you carrying this concern a little bit too far?"

"Probably."

"I suppose you'll want the shells, too?"

"Shells?"

"There's a box in his bedroom. On the bureau."

I gave her a look of annoyance as I turned for the hallway.

"Hey," she called out after me, "it's not like you *asked*."

18

As Susan and I retraced our path toward General Muller's house, she began throwing out names of possible suspects and checking for my response. To make sure we were on the same page.

I shook my head at Major Wilson, and gave her a possible but unlikely at Chun. I didn't comment at Sammy's name, because I knew she was mentioning him to get a rise out of me.

The fourth person she mentioned took me by surprise because I never saw it coming. I told her she was crazy.

"Hear me out, Burt. I'm not saying General Muller killed her. I'm just saying it's possible he might have had something going with her on the side. That would explain why Soon-ri was so secretive about who her boyfriend was. And if anyone on the base could afford to shell out a hundred Gs, he'd be the guy."

I sighed. "Give me a break. General Muller's too well known around Song-tan. If he'd been seeing Soon-ri, someone would have spotted them together. Said something by now."

"Maybe not. There aren't a lot of people living in the apartment building. He could have visited her late at night. Come in the service door—"

"He's *married*. His wife would wonder why he was gone."

"Not necessarily. It's no secret Muller and his wife don't get along. Hell, maybe that's part of it. If he's screwing around, that could explain their marital problems."

"You think Mrs. Muller knows about Soon-ri?"

"Suspects, anyway. And if Muller *was* sleeping with Soon-ri, that tells us why he's pushing so hard to get this case solved."

There it was, the basis of her entire argument. Until she answered this one particular question to her satisfaction, she wasn't going to let go of her suspicions toward Muller.

I said, "Let me get this straight. You *don't* think Muller killed Soon-ri because he wants the killer found—"

"Right."

"Yet that's the very justification you have for thinking Muller might have been involved with Soon-ri."

She nodded.

I continued, "And according to your scenario, the motive for the killing would be . . ."

"Same as before. The fetus."

"With Muller as the father? No?"

She was energetically shaking her head. "I suppose he could be. But what makes more sense is that we're back to the jealousy angle. You know, sorta like what we thought with Major Wilson."

"Meaning someone killed Soon-ri because she was cheating on him with General Muller?"

"Something like that."

"And the father of the baby is the killer?"

"Sure. That might even be what drove him to kill. The thought that the mother of his child is screwing some other guy. And if you think about it, that could also explain why he removed the fetus while she was still alive."

Her last statement came out of left field. I asked what she meant by it.

"The killing," she said, "struck me as almost ritualistic. The killer might have considered the fetus a symbol of his union with Soon-ri. Removing it broke the connection between them. And by committing the act while she was alive, the killer made sure she suffered for her betrayal."

Susan had earned her bachelor's degree in psychology, and my first reaction was that she was either spouting off a bunch of psychobabble or had seen *The Silence of the Lambs* too many times. But as I digested her comments, I realized they contained an odd logic. Still, I couldn't accept her premise about General Muller and told her so.

"It's a *theory*, not the Ten Commandments. So maybe I'm wrong about Muller screwing Soon-ri. One thing I *am* certain about is that Muller isn't interested in this case just because of some old girlfriend."

I would have argued the point except for one thing: I'd been receptive to Muller's story because he touched me emotionally. The bottom line was his explanation didn't pass the smell test. But what other reason could General Muller have that would cause him to risk a shot at a fourth star—

"Burt," Susan said, "your phone's ringing."

★ When I answered it, Susan and I were less than thirty yards from General Muller's house. I heard a man's voice on the other end, but couldn't make out his words because of the blaring rock music in the background. Moments later, the music became muffled, as if the man had closed a door. "Hey, Burt? You hear me now? Burt?"

It was Sammy. I slowed my pace but kept walking. "Loud and clear, Sammy. Where are you?"

Susan scowled at the mention of Sammy's name.

"The Studio 99 Club," Sammy said. "I came to interview one of the dancers. A friend of Soon-ri's called in to the station, saying she might know who the killer is."

I frowned at the skepticism in his voice. "You don't sound exactly thrilled."

"I'm not. This is a bullshit call. A setup."

"A setup? Why?"

This piqued Susan's interest, and her head tilted toward me. I stopped walking and held the phone out so she could hear.

"Since when do bar girls call cops? And how does this girl even know Soon-ri is dead? Only way she could is if that son of a bitch pulled a double cross—"

The rest of Sammy's response was drowned out by a blast of music, as if the door had suddenly been reopened. The music died off, and we could hear him conversing with someone in Korean. He came back and said the girl he was to question was almost finished with her set.

"Who's a son of a bitch?" I asked.

A long pause.

"Can't talk?" I said.

"I'm with the club manager. In his office."

That clued me in to the name he didn't want to mention. After telling Sammy we were on our way, I passed on that Major Wilson seemed to be a dead end and briefly explained why. I was about to hang up when Sammy asked, "Is Susan there, Burt?"

She shook her head and stepped away from me. "She's here," I said, as she shot me a dirty look.

"Put her on."

I cupped the phone and offered it to Susan. "Sammy wants to talk to you."

She gazed at it, but made no move to take it. "Why?"

"He didn't say." I added, "If it means anything, I was supposed to tell you earlier that he's sorry and apologizes."

Her expression thawed a little. "He really said he was sorry, huh?"

I nodded. "He didn't recognize you at first because you'd changed your hair. He also said something about drinking too much."

A hint of a smile. When I saw it, my earlier suspicion became a certainty. Susan took the phone, then looked at me. "Uh, Burt, you mind . . ."

"Hmm. Oh, sure."

I slung the shotgun over my shoulder and continued to the car. As I walked, I thought about the person who Sammy suspected had put the girl up to identifying a killer. The timing ticked me off as much as his interference in a murder investigation. Two days was how long he'd given Sammy. Now he'd gone back on his word.

Like Sammy said, Uncle Chun could be a son of a bitch.

★ I'd been leaning against the driver's door of Susan's car for less than three minutes when she strolled up. As she handed me the phone I tried to read her face, but she wasn't giving anything away. Still, I'd seen her smile at least twice during her conversation. Once, I thought I'd even heard a laugh.

I said, "You two friends now?"

She hesitated, then nodded. "We cleared up a little misunderstanding." She took out her car keys and motioned me to step away from the door. I remained where I was, gazing at her expectantly.

She gave me an amused smile. "I take it Sammy still hasn't told you how we met?"

"No."

"And it's killing you. Not knowing."

"I could go homicidal any second."

"It's really none of your business."

"True."

"I suppose you'll keep bugging me if I don't talk?"

"Constantly. And I'll pester Sammy."

"He might not tell you."

"Eventually, he will."

She sighed. "Fine. Get in. I'll tell you on the way."

★ When Susan finished her account, we'd just passed through the main gate and were now stuck in the Ville's bumper-to-bumper traffic, which would continue until the 2 A.M. curfew. I said, "That's it, huh? You just met him the one time?"

"That's it. A grand total of maybe four hours. You look disappointed, Burt."

I was a little, though I'm not sure what I really expected. Something spicier.

Susan had met Sammy shortly after she'd arrived in Korea last year, at the annual dinner between ROK Provincial Detectives and the Osan OSI. Ostensibly, the purpose of the get-together was purely professional—a forum to promote the exchange of investigative techniques and to enhance cooperation on both sides. In reality, the dinner usually turned into a drinking competition, with a lot of cheering and backslapping as the Americans and Koreans bonded by trading shots of So-ju.

Susan had first noticed Sammy when they were both slugging down shots. They bailed out before the end, and Sammy came over to talk to her. Sammy must have really poured on the charm, because when the dinner broke up, Susan accompanied him to a quiet bar across the street. They remained until closing, and afterward, made a dinner date for the following weekend.

Susan arrived at the restaurant promptly at seven, in a dress she'd bought for the occasion. She sat nursing a drink at a table for over an hour.

Sammy never showed.

He never called.

She never heard from him again.

Until tonight.

When Susan saw Sammy at the crime scene, she decided not to say anything. She was determined to play it cool. Let him sweat a little, wondering when she was going to confront him. But there was a problem with her plan that she never anticipated. Initially, she figured Sammy was putting on an act. He had to be putting on an act. He couldn't have forgotten her.

But he had.

That realization understandably ticked her off more than being stood up.

Yet now, after their phone conversation, apparently all was forgiven. I was curious what excuse Sammy had come up with for skipping out on their date, and asked her.

"He got called out at the last minute to work a case in Inchon. He was going to phone me, but lost my number and was too hungover to remember my name in order to contact me."

"Ah. The So-ju defense."

"Hey, it's possible. We were both pretty wasted. I thought my head was going to explode for two days afterward."

I gave her a sideways glance. "He could have tracked you down."

A shrug. "He was gone for over a month. By the time he returned, he was too embarrassed to call."

I was amused by the way she was sticking up for him, even though I had to admit that Sammy's excuse was certainly plausible. So-ju was potent as hell and could not only affect one's memory, but, in mass quantities, had been known to paralyze the optic nerve. While the Koreans were aware of the nasty side effects, So-ju still remained the country's most popular alcoholic drink. Go figure.

I gazed out the window as we crawled past an endless line of flashing neon. After a few moments, Susan began quizzing me about Sammy. How well I knew him, the cases we'd worked on, how long he'd been a cop. That sort of thing. I played along for a while, then casually asked about her sudden interest in him.

"We're working with him, and I figure I should know a little about him."

"Admit it. You're attracted to the guy. That's why you let him off the hook."

A frosty glare. "You're crazy."

"When are you two going out?"

"Oh, grow up, Burt."

"Planning on a big wedding or maybe something a little more intimate? Chung-hee and I got married in the mountains. If you want, I can make a few calls—"

"You're such an ass." She hunched over the wheel, ignoring me.

I grinned and settled back in my seat. Susan's problem was she could dish it out but couldn't take it. We were coming up on the jewelry store, which put us about two blocks from the Studio 99 Club. I was curious to see Chun's limo again parked against the curb out front. But maybe he was intentionally avoiding the Studio 99 Club, so he couldn't be accused of compromising the investigation.

As we rolled by the store, I spotted Chung-hee at the counter. She was waiting on a male customer—

I swore, my head swiveling around.

"*Now* what's the matter?" Susan asked, noticing.

I faced front, thinking hard. "I'm not sure. I just saw Chun talking with Chung-hee."

"So? He's her uncle, right?"

"Chun rarely visits Chung-hee because he knows she doesn't like him. Yet he decides to drop by tonight."

"And you're worried because you think he's talking to her about the case?"

I hesitated. "No. About me."

Her brow furrowed. "Why? To see if he can use her to get information on the investigation from you?"

"Possibly."

"I thought Sammy said Chun didn't question him about the case?"

"True, but—"

"I dunno, Burt. It seems that if Chun wanted information, he'd come to you first before going through your wife."

Logic I couldn't refute. I sighed. "You're right. I'm probably reading too much into it."

Still, I was tempted to call Chung-hee to find out what Chun wanted. But moments later, Susan made a quick right into an alleyway adjacent to a gleaming black, two-story building covered with ribbons of pulsating red neon. The renovated warehouse that was now the largest and gaudiest nightclub in the Ville.

The Studio 99 Club.

19

Cars lined the dimly lit alleyway, and Susan had to cruise for about a block before finding a space across from a shabby building that housed one of the more low-rent brothels. Two women in bathrobes were squatting on the crumbling stone steps outside, smoking cigarettes. As Susan and I got out of the car, one woman rose and gave me a come-on wave. I smiled politely and shook my head. Out of the corner of my eye, I noticed Susan wiping the bottom of her shoe on the pavement.

"Something wrong?" I asked.

"I think I just stepped in puke."

I fought off a smile. After she took a few more swipes, we headed toward the glitter of the main street. A group of young GIs appeared under a streetlight, unsteadily trailing an elderly Korean woman with a stooped back. They approached us talking loudly, slurring their words as they bickered with the woman over the price of a girl. As they went by, one of the men hollered out to Susan, "Hey, round-eye, how much you charge?" His buddies slapped him on the back and laughed. "Nice tits," someone else shouted. More drunken laughter.

Shit. I knew what was going to happen. I reached for Susan to try to stop her, because I didn't want to waste time screwing around. But she'd twirled on her, heel and was gone, striding after them.

"All right, assholes," she said, flipping her OSI credentials in their faces. "I'm Agent Torres, and I want to see some identification *now*."

The GIs suddenly became sober as they regarded her in shock. Susan barked once more and they fell all over themselves trying to dig out their military ID cards. The old woman tugged at Susan's sleeve and began babbling hysterically in Korean. Susan told her to beat it and began inspecting the ID cards with a penlight. As she did, she began ticking off a list of charges, including sexual harassment, conduct unbecoming, and public intoxication. One of the GIs tried to interrupt, and she told him to shut up. Once she got their names down, she passed back their cards and informed them their commanders would be notified of the charges and that they should consider seeking legal counsel from the JAG office.

"Questions?" she asked.

They all appeared dazed. No one made a sound.

She smiled sweetly. "Have a nice night, fellas."

"Feel better?" I asked, as she came over to me.

She grinned. "Much."

"You really going to turn them in?"

"Hell, no. Too much paperwork. I just wanted them to wet their pants a little so they'd learn some manners. Besides, they were right, you know."

"Right about what?"

She winked. "I got great boobs."

★ We made a left down the sidewalk, ignoring the phalanx of street vendors who kept calling out to us, hawking everything from pirated CDs to eel-skin wallets. As we approached the club entrance, I finished telling Susan about Sammy's suspicion that Chun had put the girl up to identifying the killer.

"Why?" she asked. "To keep General Muller from keeping the base closed?"

"Sure. The sooner the base is reopened, the less money he loses."

"Nice guy. He'd actually frame someone, huh?"

"In a heartbeat."

"That means the girl will finger a Korean?"

A rhetorical statement. I nodded anyway. We arrived at the frosted double doors, each one etched with the life-sized figure of a nude woman. As I stepped around to open a door, Susan turned to say something, but her words were drowned out by a wall of sound. Still I understood her. Another rhetorical question.

"Wonder who the poor bastard is?" she asked me.

We went inside the Studio 99 Club to find out.

★ We paused in the entryway, letting our eyes adjust to the smoky darkness and the dizzying light-saber strobes. Before us was an enormous open room designed to resemble a giant brothel. The walls were all red felt, the ceilings mirrored, and there were statues of nudes everywhere. A heart-shaped chrome-and-glass stage with the prerequisite brass pole sat in the center of the sunken main floor, surrounded by maybe a hundred tables that fanned outward in a circle. Three additional dancing platforms were strategically placed throughout to ensure that the clientele got an up-close-and-personal view of each girl as she rotated through her set. To our left was a twenty-foot-long bar, and beyond it, the glass-enclosed DJ booth. I did a slow pan around the room, pausing on each of the bikini-clad dancers as she gyrated to a grunting hip-hop number. Most of the women, including the miniskirted waitresses, were young, in their late teens to early twenties. That was the attraction of the larger clubs like Studio 99; they always got first dibs on the freshest girls. After a few years, when the girls became worn, they were relegated to seedier establishments . . . or worse.

"Not quite as crowded as usual," Susan said into my ear.

I nodded. The place was maybe two-thirds full. A few months back, when Soon-ri was headlining, the club would have been completely jammed. No wonder Chun hadn't been happy about losing his star attraction.

"Where's the manager's office?" Susan asked.

I pointed to a door over to the right, near where a heavyset Korean guy was straddling a stool. I vaguely recognized him as a bouncer and sometime pimp. He rose and held out his hand as we approached. When I mentioned Sammy's name, he backed off with a grudging head bob and opened the door.

Both Susan and I did double takes as we went inside. From what Sammy had said on the phone, we expected him to be here with one girl. Instead, I counted seven scantily clad women packed into the cramped office, along with a greasy-haired guy in a suit parked behind the desk, whom I took to be the manager. Chun, I decided, obviously figured the more witnesses the merrier.

Sammy glanced at Susan and me, flashed a tight smile, then resumed questioning the women. He went on for another five minutes, his manner low-key, almost pleasant. Turning to the manager, he nodded at the door and asked him to leave. When the man hesitated, Sammy repeated the request more firmly. The manager reluctantly rose and shuffled toward Susan and me. I played doorman and ushered him out.

The moment he was gone, Sammy's manner became harsh, almost brutal. He walked up within inches of the women, screaming in their faces like a Marine DI. Even though I couldn't follow much of what he was saying, it was clear Sammy was trying to get them to change their story and intimidate them into admitting they were lying.

And the first part worked; he was scaring the hell out of them. Three or four were literally quivering in their bikinis. Two broke into tears. But as he continued his tirade, they still seemed to stick to their story. Regardless of how many times Sammy asked, they repeated the same line. It sounded almost like a chant.

"*Mr. Su ga Soon-ri reul ju-gyeot-sseo.*"

"Mr. Su killed Soon-ri."

Finally, Sammy angrily drew back, signaling he'd had enough. He abruptly motioned to the door, and the women practically ran over Susan and me to escape. I closed the door behind them and gazed at Sammy expectantly.

He parked on the edge of the desk, lit a cigarette, and took a deep drag. He slowly looked over, his eyes going first to me before pausing on Susan. He acknowledged her with a weary smile, saying, "They're accusing Mr. Su of killing Soon-ri."

Susan said, "And Su is . . ."

"A muscle guy who used to work here at the club. He had a big-time thing for Soon-ri. An obsession. He constantly harassed her. Followed her around and tried to get her to go out with him. The manager finally had him removed from the club when someone broke into Soon-ri's apartment and raped her. Even though the attacker wore a mask, everyone figured it had to be Su."

He fell silent, thoughtfully tapping his cigarette against an overflowing ashtray. We waited for him to conclude that the accusations were all fabrications. When he didn't, Susan asked, "Couldn't the women be lying about Su to set him up for a frame job?"

Sammy shrugged. "That's the problem. I'm not sure they are."

Susan appeared puzzled. I said, "What do you mean you're not sure?"

He considered us for a moment. "You saw their reactions when I came down on them. Threatened them with arrest if they were lying—"

I said, "Sure, but—"

"They were plenty scared. But no matter how hard I pushed, they kept insisting that Su had to be the killer."

"Sammy," I said. "This has to be a setup orchestrated by Chun. Hell, you know his reputation. The girls were probably a lot more afraid of him than a cop."

"I'm not assuming Su is guilty just because of their accusations, Burt."

"No, then why—"

"The rape happened. Soon-ri told me about it two months ago."

I didn't have a response. Susan slowly shook her head.

We now understood Sammy's concern. Since the women *hadn't* fabricated the rape accusation, they might also be telling the truth about their suspicions of Su.

Susan asked Sammy, "Did Soon-ri ever mention to you that she suspected Su of the rape?"

"No."

"Did she say he'd harassed her?"

A head shake.

"Did the police ever uncover any evidence linking Su to the rape?"

"She never reported it officially to the police. She knew it would be a waste of time."

Susan seemed to study him. "I see. So she only told you about it, huh?" It came out like an accusation.

Sammy gazed at her as if perplexed by the comment. He shrugged, casually blew a smoke ring, and looked away.

For a few moments no one spoke. We were all wondering if it could be this easy. Could Soon-ri's murder simply be explained away by a guy with an obsession?

My eyes went to Susan, who was still fixated on Sammy. It was obvious she was again concerned about his relationship with Soon-ri. This time, I wondered if her interest was more personal than professional.

Susan noticed me looking and said, "Hell, I guess it could happen, Burt. This guy Su sounds pretty damned unstable. If he raped Soon-ri, then later found out she was pregnant with his kid and shacked up with an American—"

"I disagree. This is too damned convenient. Chun obviously found out about Su's obsession with Soon-ri and figured he'd be a perfect fall guy." That got a nod from Sammy. I continued, "And even if Su did rape her, that still doesn't prove he killed—"

Sammy abruptly swore in Korean. He angrily crushed out his cigarette in the ashtray, his eyes going to me. "I must be tired, Burt. You're right. Su couldn't have killed Soon-ri."

I said, "Okay . . ."

"Why?" Susan asked.

He smiled grimly. "Think back. Why did we assume the killer knew Soon-ri?"

She thought. "The fetus?"

"No. Before we knew about that."

"Well, there were no signs of forced entry—"

"Exactly. Neither to the building nor to her apartment. That means Soon-ri either let the killer in or gave him a key . . ."

"Which she wouldn't have done for Su," I finished. I added, "That clinches it. We can scratch Su from the list and concentrate on finding— What, Sammy?"

He was looking uneasy. "It won't be that simple. The tip that came in mentioned Su by name. My superiors know about the accusations."

I realized what he was really saying. So did Susan, because she said, "You mean you're expected to arrest him?"

"Not expected. I was *ordered* to arrest him."

No surprise there. Once Su had been arrested, the case would be over. Guilty or not, there would be a confession, which would be released to the press. With a Korean national tagged as the killer, Soon-ri's murder would be forgotten. From Washington to Seoul, politicians would be breathing easier at the gift-wrapped solution that had fallen into their laps.

Sammy, of course, knew all this. He also knew that if he didn't pick up Su, he'd be replaced by someone who would.

Susan suggested, "Maybe you could say you couldn't locate Su."

Sammy shook his head. "Chun would never allow it."

"Chun?" she said.

He gave her a knowing look. "The manager said Chun banned Su from having contact with Soon-ri, but still kept him on. Now that Chun's set Su up for the killing, he'll expect us to arrest him quickly. If we don't, Chun will no doubt turn him in on his own."

"The bastard isn't taking chances, is he?" Susan said sarcastically.

Chun wouldn't, I thought. In a way I had to hand it him. He'd come up with a plan we couldn't get around.

"What I need," Sammy said, "is evidence to convince my superiors to give me more time. If I could identify the baby's father, show he had a motive—"

"Forget it, Sammy," I said. "Your boss will never go along unless you hand him another Korean. Even then, it's unlikely—"

I stopped talking because Sammy wasn't listening to me. His eyes were blankly locked on the wall. He'd slipped into one of his zones, searching for a solution. Susan started to speak, and I put a finger to my lips. An interruption could cause Sammy to lose the thread he was following.

Seconds passed. Then a minute. Through the door, we could hear the pulsing beat of Donna Summer's "Hot Stuff." I tapped my foot along while Susan shifted impatiently. In the middle of the song's chorus, Sammy pushed away from the desk. His face told me he had something. Before I asked, he was by me and out the door. He reappeared moments later, followed by the manager and the bouncer who'd been camped outside.

Sammy began questioning them. They were discussing a girl. Another dancer. The men seemed reluctant to say much, and I could tell Sammy was getting irritated. Finally, he turned to Susan and me and told us to leave.

"Why?" Susan asked.

A vaguely apologetic smile. "I don't want you to see this."

Susan frowned. Before she could press him for an explanation, I took her firmly by the arm and led her outside.

Five minutes later, Sammy emerged. He was breathing hard and his hair was mussed. As he closed the office door, Susan and I caught a glimpse of the bouncer kneeling over the manager, who was writhing on the floor in pain. Susan stared at Sammy as if she were seeing him for the first time. Her reaction surprised me, since I assumed she knew this was the way things were done in Korea. But maybe she hadn't expected Sammy to get physical.

Sammy drew us off to the side, speaking loudly so we could hear. He told us Soon-ri had once mentioned another dancer at the club, a close friend whom she'd considered almost a sister. If anyone might know who bought out Soon-ri's contract and fathered her child, it would be this girl.

"So where is she?" I asked, looking around.

Even with the music blaring around us, we could hear the anger in Sammy's voice.

"Chun owns a whorehouse," he said.

20

We exited the club and made a right down the sidewalk, returning the way Susan and I had come. Once we turned into the quiet of the alley, Sammy filled us in on what else he'd learned from the manager. As Susan had suspected, Chun had been enraged over Soon-ri's departure. Not so much at her actually leaving, but because she'd outmaneuvered him in the negotiation. Made him lose face.

Chun had wanted to retaliate against Soon-ri, but since she was out of his control, he went after the person closest to her. A young dancer Soon-ri had taken under her wing.

Her name was Mi-nah. Chun had her beaten badly, then had photographs taken and delivered to Soon-ri. When Mi-nah's bruises healed, he forced her to work in his filthiest brothel. She was seventeen.

Something welled up inside me. I knew it was hate. "That *bastard*," Susan snarled savagely.

"And that's not the worst of it," Sammy went on. "Chun also made her a *geom-dungi sae-kki chang-nyeo*."

I nodded grimly, but Susan looked puzzled.

Sammy hesitated. "She does the black GIs."

"I see," Susan said. But her face made it clear she still didn't understand the true implication.

Sammy glanced at me to pass the ball, the Korean in him uncomfortable with explaining this to a woman.

I told Susan that the girls who slept with the black soldiers were considered the lowest of the low and were often harshly treated by the rest of the women in the brothel. I added, "Chun did it to completely humiliate her. Destroy what little dignity the girl had left."

Susan was too furious to speak. I heard her take a few ragged breaths as she tried to rein in her emotions. Finally, in a strained voice, she said to Sammy, "You must be wrong about Chun. The bastard obviously hated Soon-ri enough to kill her."

"Except he didn't," Sammy said. "The manager told me that after Soon-ri received the pictures, she begged Chun to let her buy out Mi-nah's contract. Chun gave Soon-ri a price of ten million won. Five times what Mi-nah's contract is worth. Soon-ri promised to raise the money."

Susan swore, realizing that Sammy's assessment was probably correct. With Chun, everything came down to money. Even if he wanted Soon-ri dead, his greed would have prevented him from acting before he got paid.

We walked along, wrapped up in our own thoughts. Even though Sammy hadn't told us where we were going, I knew there were at least four brothels in the alley. It made sense that Chun would own at least one of them, so he would have a convenient place for his turned-on customers to go once they left the Studio 99 Club.

Sammy brought up Major Wilson, and I responded with a rundown of what we'd learned on base, highlighting our encounter with Gentry, our suspicions that the CIA had altered the emergency tape to implicate a Korean, the meeting with General Muller, and Major Wilson's alibi at the time of the killing. I finished by explaining why I was inclined to believe General Muller's assurances about wanting to find the killer.

Afterward, Sammy asked if I was also convinced that Major Wilson had nothing to do with the murder.

"Pretty sure," I said.

"He could have paid someone to kill her."

"True."

"And General Muller still bothers me. I'm not sure I'm willing to trust— That's the whorehouse just ahead."

Sammy angled toward the building with the crumbling stone steps.

★ The two women smoking outside were gone.

Like the steps, the rest of the single-story, wooden building was in disrepair. Paint peeled from the walls, and the entire structure bowed inward as if on the verge of collapse. No signs or markings out front indicated the place was a brothel, which was typical. While prostitution wasn't illegal in Korea, it also wasn't openly condoned.

The front door suddenly flew open and a chubby man with blond hair emerged, tucking in his shirt. He looked at us in surprise, tossed Susan an embarrassed smile, then took off down the alley.

Sammy went up the steps. Susan was about to follow when I suggested she wait outside. She stared at me like she'd been slapped, then began protesting.

"This isn't a debate," I said. "I don't want you losing control again." Because nothing upset Susan more than seeing how the prostitutes were treated. Three months earlier, she and I had gone into a brothel to check out the alibi of a sergeant accused of a burglary. We were about to leave when Susan saw one of the operators slapping around a girl. I had to physically restrain her from going after the guy. But that was the rule. As OSI investigators, we had no legal right to interfere with the Koreans.

She said, "It just happened that one time—"

"My concern is it doesn't happen again."

She glowered at me, then threw up her hands. "Fine. You got my word. I'll behave."

"Not so fast. You don't say or do anything without my okay."

"Sure. Whatever." But her eyes were firing darts into me as she spoke.

"No shooting off your mouth," I continued. "No getting into anyone's face. You only observe. That's the deal."

She sighed. "Got it, Burt. I'll be a Girl Scout."

I studied her. "All right."

From the top of the steps, Sammy was watching us with a bemused smile. As we started toward him, my cell phone rang. It was Chung-hee, and she sounded excited.

"Uncle Chun's here, Burt. He says he wants to buy the store."

I immediately knew why.

★ I hung up a minute or so later, after telling Chung-hee to close up early and I'd call her later at home. I needed time to gather my thoughts, and I didn't want to say anything to Chung-hee with Chun still there.

As I tucked the phone away, I noticed Sammy and Susan staring at me. From their grim expressions, I knew they'd overheard enough to figure out what had just happened.

"How much did Chun offer?" Sammy asked me.

"Roughly two hundred thousand dollars."

"Lot of money," Susan said.

"Store's worth it," I said. But we all knew Chun wasn't only buying the store. Now that he'd set up Su for the Korean cops, he was also purchasing insurance to ensure that the American military ended their investigation.

"So," Susan said, "what are you going to do?"

The decision was obvious. Still, I hesitated because I was thinking of Chung-hee, and her disappointment when I told her the reason behind Chun's offer. I felt suddenly angry at being put in this position.

"What the hell do you think?" I growled at Susan.

Sammy bowed deeply, showing me respect, then turned and opened the door of the brothel.

★ We entered a darkened, airless hallway that smelled of old socks and something else I couldn't place. The only light came from a couple of red bulbs that dangled from wires in the ceiling. Roughly a half dozen rooms lined both sides, a few with their doors opened, most not. Through the plywood walls, we could hear occasional voices interspersed with grunts of passion. Maybe ten feet away, two men in tank tops were sitting in fold-out chairs next to a card table with a metal cash box on it. One looked about fifty and was extremely fat, with a fleshy face that reminded me of Jabba the Hut. The other was stocky and in his early thirties. Both gazed at us with suspicion, because they either recognized Sammy or were bothered by the presence of Susan.

As we approached them, Sammy leaned close to Susan. "I apologize for my behavior, but it's necessary."

"Your behavior?" she said.

But Sammy's attention was back on the men. This time he didn't bother with any preliminaries. He showed them his badge and asked which room was Mi-nah's. When he didn't get an immediate response, he grabbed the fat guy by the throat hard enough to make him cough. The second guy made a guttural sound and jumped up. With a flick of his wrist, Sammy caught him by the neck and sent him sprawling to the floor. The guy started to rise again. By then Sammy had his pistol out and pointed at him.

The guy slowly sat back down.

Sammy casually looked at the fat guy, who was gasping as he tried to breathe through Sammy's grip. His eyes were fixed wide in terror. Sammy loosened his hold and repeated the question. This time he got an answer.

Sammy stepped back and calmly put his gun away.

As we followed him down the hallway, Susan murmured in my ear, "*Jesus*. And you were worried about me."

Sammy walked up to the last room on the left. The door was closed, and we could hear moans coming from within.

We went in anyway.

21

A wiry young black man was lying on top of the girl, pumping away. He never knew we were there until Sammy tapped him on the shoulder. He spun around and looked at us in horror. He had a baby face and I put him at nineteen, tops.

He threw himself off the girl and scrambled to cover himself with his hands. "*Goddamn!* What is this shit! What the hell are you doing—"

"OSI," I barked as Susan flipped out her ID.

He swallowed hard, his eyes flying around wildly. He sputtered more than spoke. "Oh, *God*. Sir, I . . . I was just having some fun. I didn't mean to do nuthin' wrong—"

"Relax, son," I said. "You're not in any trouble. What's your name?"

"Harris. Senior Airman Harris."

"Fine, Airman Harris. I want you to get your clothes on and get out of here."

He stared at me as if he didn't believe what I was saying.

"*Move*."

Harris shot off the bed and lunged for his clothes on a chair. He frantically began throwing them on. He still wore a rubber and didn't stop to remove it. Susan didn't bother to look away as he dressed.

I turned my attention to the frightened girl still lying on the bed, which was just a mattress thrown on the floor. She sat up slowly, watching us with fearful eyes, a sheet clutched to her chest. She was pretty the way a doll is pretty. A tiny, frail girl who was more child than woman.

I stood there thinking how young she was and what she'd been through in her short life. The familiar sense of helplessness returned, the same feeling I always got when I encountered girls like her. A conflict between wanting to help them and knowing you can't.

Sammy knelt beside the girl and began speaking reassuringly. Even though I could understand only the occasional word, I knew he was telling her not to be frightened. That everything would be all right.

But of course everything wouldn't be all right. Not for her. Ever.

"Sir, can I . . . can I go now?"

I looked at Harris, who was standing, spring-loaded, by the door. I barely nodded before he bolted. Susan closed the door behind him and came over to me.

Sammy was still talking quietly. The girl, Mi-nah, continued to gaze at him fearfully. We heard Sammy mention Soon-ri's name. Mi-nah's face registered surprise. Sammy went on talking, and we saw her eyes mist over. She covered her face with her small hands and began to cry. Deep, wailing sobs. The intensity of her anguish suggested she was grieving not only for Soon-ri but also for herself. The realization that her one chance of leaving the brothel had died with her friend.

Sammy watched her, shaking his head pityingly. This was one of the reasons I liked Sammy. While most Korean cops say they're bothered by the treatment of the girls, I knew they were just talking, unlike Sammy, whose compassion was genuine. But like he often reminded me, I shouldn't judge the Korean people too harshly. After all, without the American military, there would be no sex trade.

"Burt, please . . ."

Turning, I saw Susan's eyes were shiny. I knew what she was asking. I nodded, since I was on the verge of doing the same thing myself.

Susan went over and put her arm around Mi-nah, trying to comfort her. After a few minutes, Mi-nah's crying quieted. Sammy handed her a silk handkerchief to dry her eyes. He gave her a few moments, then began asking questions. The girl clung to Susan. She had difficulty speaking more than a few words before breaking down. I tried to follow along, but many of her responses were barely decipherable and Sammy had to lean close to hear. After almost ten minutes Sammy finally rose, indicating he was finished. Reading his face, I knew he had bad news.

"Mi-nah," he said, "had no clue Soon-ri was pregnant. She also didn't know the name of the rich boyfriend, because Soon-ri was careful not to tell her." He paused, looking at me. "But she can identify him. It's not good, Burt. It looks like General Muller lied to you about Major Wilson."

"Okay . . ."

"Three times, a man fitting Major Wilson's description visited Soon-ri at her room in the Ville, while Mi-nah was there. Each time, Soon-ri asked Mi-nah to leave. The same man appeared here last Tuesday, posing as a john. He gave Mi-nah a letter from Soon-ri. That's how she learned that Soon-ri was trying to buy out her contract from Chun."

"That still doesn't prove anything," I said. "We already know Wilson was friendly with Soon-ri and— Go on." Sammy seemed anxious to add something.

"The third visit," he said, "took place the morning before Soon-ri bought out her contract. Mi-nah remembers the man had an eel-skin briefcase with him. Later, after the man had gone, Mi-nah noticed the briefcase was still in Soon-ri's room." He kept looking at me, waiting for me to connect the dots.

I did an instant later. "Soon-ri," I said. "How did she pay for her contract?"

"Cash."

Susan's head snapped around to me, the I-told-you-so look in her eyes.

I responded with a nod to concede I'd been wrong about General Muller. And if he'd lied to us about Major Wilson's finances, maybe he'd also orchestrated the elaborate fabrication to make us think Wilson was flying. I stood there feeling gullible and foolish as I thought about how I'd let Muller sucker me with that story about an old girlfriend. My mistake was thinking he'd changed when he hadn't.

The son of a bitch wanted his fourth star after all.

"Two things," I said to Susan. "Stop by the base personnel office first thing in morning and get a photo of Wilson from his file to show to Mi-nah. Then we'll meet me at the JAG office and get a warrant to check Wilson's bank statements. Once we prove he provided Soon-ri with the money, we'll go after his alibi. Pressure the witnesses hard until someone talks."

She nodded thoughtfully. "General Muller will try to stop us."

"*Fuck* Muller. If we act fast enough, he might not catch on until—"

A phone rang. I automatically reached into my jacket before I realized it was Sammy's. His deferential tone told us he was speaking with one of his superiors. After less than ten seconds, he hung up. His face said it all, but he told us anyway.

"Chun wants to turn over Su," he said.

★ "What about Mi-nah?" Susan asked. She was still on the bed, an arm around Mi-nah, who was leaning against her, looking sad and scared and confused.

Sammy frowned at Susan. I said, "What about her?"

"We can't just leave her here."

I sighed. Susan was again putting on her social-worker hat. "I understand how you feel, but you know we can't just take her."

"Why the hell not?" she shot back.

"She's under contract to Chun. Legally, she has to stay—"

"Don't give me that crap, Burt. We . . . *you* have an obligation to protect her now." The last statement was directed at Sammy.

Sammy blinked. "I'm sorry—"

"Your stunt with those guys outside," she said. "The moment we leave, you know they'll take it out on her."

Sammy didn't reply; he knew Susan had a point. Mi-nah's eyes were darting nervously among the three of us, as if she knew we were discussing her fate. She settled on Sammy, her falsetto voice quivering with desperation.

"Jeol yeo-gi-du-go ga-ji-ma-ra-yo," she said.

Pleading with Sammy not to leave her.

I tried to block out the sudden compassion I felt. I'd been in this situation before. I tried to tell myself that she was just one of many. That it was impossible to help them all. That we couldn't . . . shouldn't get involved.

This time it didn't work.

Sammy swallowed hard, which told me he felt the guilt, too. He gazed at Susan. "What you're suggesting will be difficult—"

"Dammit, *look!*"

At that instant, Susan turned Mi-nah around by her shoulders, revealing her bare back. Sammy hissed sharply in shock. I stared, sickened.

Rows of pencil-thin scars. Too many to count. She'd not only been beaten, but whipped. I had to turn away.

Sammy's face chilled into a mask. When he spoke to Susan, his voice was low but coldly determined. "There is only one way to take her legally."

"The hell with legal. Let's just walk out with her—"

"Don't be a fool," he snapped. "Chun will only hunt her down."

Susan stared at him.

"Chun," Sammy went on, "has no choice. If he didn't, it would set the wrong example. Be bad for business."

"For chrissakes," Susan said, "she's not a *slave*."

"No, but she is an investment."

Susan gritted her teeth. "So you're saying what? That we have to buy out her contract?"

Sammy nodded.

"How much?" she asked.

Sammy shrugged. "Chun gave Soon-ri an inflated price. I can probably get him to accept a few thousand dollars."

Susan's shoulders sagged, her eyes heavy with disappointment. For a first lieutenant raising a child, that was a lot of money. And even if Sammy wanted to help, he couldn't. Not on his salary.

Of course I knew what I was going to do. What I had to do.

"I'll put up the money," I said.

★ Sammy and I went out into the hallway to clear things with the two men while Susan got Mi-nah dressed. Sammy figured it would be better if Chun thought he was the one interested in Mi-nah and not me. I agreed, because the last thing I wanted was Chun using the girl as leverage against me once he realized I would continue investigating Soon-ri's murder.

The men weren't exactly enthused about our strolling out with Mi-nah on the promise that we'd contact Chun. Not that we gave a damn.

When we returned to the room, Mi-nah was wearing a tattered dress about two sizes too big. Everything she owned fit in two plastic shopping bags. She moved around in a daze, as if she couldn't believe she was actually leaving. Sammy spent another few minutes talking to her, to soothe her concerns. If anything, Mi-nah seemed even more nervous afterward. Not an altogether surprising response, since bar girls had little reason to trust Korean cops.

The plan was for Susan to take Mi-nah to her apartment, where her maid would help look after her. In the meantime, Sammy and I would handle Su's arrest.

Before getting into her car, Susan impulsively squeezed my hand. "I appreciate this, Burt."

"Sure."

She nodded her thanks to Sammy, standing beside me. To me, she said, "Mind if I make a suggestion . . ."

"Shoot," I said.

"Contacting the JAG office might be a mistake. Odds are General Muller has a standing order disapproving any warrants concerning Major Wilson."

I'd considered this. "It's not like we have a choice."

"Actually, we might. One of the assistant bank managers lives in my building. She was a civilian cop before she got married. We're pretty tight. If I let her know what we're up against, she'd probably be willing to slide the rules."

I hesitated. "When will you know?"

"I'll talk to her tonight. If she says no, we can always try the JAG."

"All right. Call me either way. And let me have that rope remnant. . . ." When she passed it over, I told her I'd swing by base supply in the morning to see if it matched any of the base's stock.

"Anything else?" she asked.

I thought, then shook my head.

With a smile at Sammy, Susan climbed into the driver's seat. As she drove away, we saw Mi-nah in the passenger seat, looking at us. Her small hand in the window was waving good-bye.

We waved back.

When the car disappeared around the corner, Sammy turned to me and said quietly, "You know we'll both be off the case by tomorrow."

"I know."

"Anything we do after that will have to be unofficial."

"Yup."

"Even if Major Wilson is guilty, they'll never let us bring him in."

"Probably not."

"That's okay with you?"

I shrugged. "It's better than the other option."

"And that is . . ."

"Doing nothing."

Sammy smiled and patted me on the back, and we headed up the alley toward his car.

★ Sammy's unmarked Daewoo police cruiser was parked near the entrance to the alley. As we walked up to it, I decided to bring up something else that was nagging at me. Something that wasn't any of my business, but I couldn't let it go.

Facing Sammy, I said, "I think Susan likes you."

Sammy didn't react. For an instant, I wasn't sure he heard me. Then I saw him smile. "You're sure?"

I nodded, looking right at him.

His smile faded at my somber expression. "Something wrong?"

"I like her, Sammy. I don't want her hurt." He tried to interrupt, but I kept on talking. "That's a problem for me, because I also like you. If I have to choose, I want you to know I'm on her side."

He gave me a hurt look. "C'mon, Burt. You got me all wrong . . ."

"Uh-huh."

"So I date a lot of girls. It's a casual thing. You know, just for a few laughs. Have a good time. There's nothing wrong with that."

"Fine. Make sure Susan knows that before you ask her out. That you're just doing it for a few laughs."

He stared at me as if trying to determine if I was on the level. He must have decided I was, because he said, "Don't feed her any of my bullshit, huh?"

"Not unless you mean it."

He sighed unhappily. "Okay. I'll go along. But I'm telling you Susan is missing out. Girls tell me they *like* my bullshit." He said it with a completely straight face.

Brother, I thought.

As I swung around to the passenger door, my phone rang. I answered, figuring it was probably Chung-hee, letting me know she'd arrived home. Instead, Susan's anxious voice greeted me.

"Bad news, Burt. Chun's arranged a reception when you make the arrest."

22

It took Sammy less than three minutes to drive the block and a half to the bar next to Chung-hee's jewelry store, which was locked up tight, the metal shutters drawn over the windows. Chun's limo was still sitting out front, along with a black Provincial Police car, two uniformed cops pacing nervously beside it.

Not that I was really paying much attention to the cops or the three press vans parked farther down. Rather, I was focused on the sidewalk directly in front of the bar, where the crowd that Susan had warned us about was gathered. Other than a few curious Americans, the majority were obviously members of the Korean media. Many were either scribbling in notepads or talking into handheld cassette recorders. Two television cameras were set up nearby, the talking heads already giving a play-by-play. That Chun could generate this amount of media interest on such short notice confirmed his influence. The man had real power.

Sammy pulled a tire-squealing U-turn and double-parked beside the cop car. The reporters immediately surrounded us, faces and hands pressed against the glass. They began banging on the roof, shouting out Sammy's name. The uniformed cops hurried toward Sammy's door, yanking bodies out of the way as they went.

Ignoring the turmoil, Sammy closed his eyes, as if to prepare himself. As I took in the scene around us, the realization . . . the finality . . . of what we were about to do sank in. I said, "This is *crazy*. We're about to arrest an innocent man."

His eyes cracked open, looking at me.

"Forget it, Sammy," I grunted. "I don't think I can be a part of this."

"I see. And you think that will lessen your guilt?"

"Maybe."

"It won't."

"It might."

He shrugged. "Anything can happen, Burt. We could get lucky and catch a break. Find a way to free Su."

"You believe that?"

No response. His eyes returned to the window. We watched as the two cops cleared out a space by the driver's door. Without looking at me, Sammy said, "You want to come, it's up to you."

Then he drew in a deep breath and stepped outside. Questions erupted and cameras flashed. The cops began shoving the reporters aside as they escorted Sammy to the bar.

I shook my head, thinking I should just go home. Lick my wounds and hold Chung-hee close. That was my game plan when I finally emerged from the car.

But instead of flagging down a cab, I found myself following after Sammy.

★ Three burly bouncers were guarding the club entrance, including the guy in the red muscle shirt whom I'd seen earlier in the evening. They parted to let Sammy and the cops inside. I bulled my six-five frame through the crush of bodies and managed to get up to the door as the bouncers closed ranks. Someone shoved a camera in my face and took a picture. I staggered, almost blinded by the flash. I kept shouting above the clamor, trying to get Sammy's attention. Red T-shirt shot me a grin, grabbed my hand, and pulled.

I nodded my thanks as I stumbled past him into the gloom of the bar. He immediately slammed the door shut behind me.

It was cool and quiet.

I paused, blinking to clear my vision.

This bar was roughly a third the size of the Studio 99 Club and maybe two notches above a complete dive. Built in the seventies during the disco craze, the interior reflected almost thirty years of neglect. The checkerboard tables were scarred and shabby, the red tile floor cracked and chipped, and the mirrored walls flecked with fractures, entire sections missing. A glance confirmed the place was empty, the customers and bar girls having been cleared out. Sammy and the cops were weaving their way across the floor to a table by the stage, where four middle-aged men in suits and a younger guy in a blue pullover shirt were standing. The only person I recognized was Chun.

Chun grasped Sammy's hand warmly before stepping back and shaking his head regretfully. Instead of pointing to the guy in the pullover, who I assumed was Su because of his dress and age, Chun indicated something behind the table. Toward the floor.

As I started over, the other men began drifting back, making room for Sammy and the two cops. Chun hovered by Sammy's side, gesturing animatedly as he explained something. Sammy turned and barked out an order to the cops. They picked up the table and moved it back against the stage. As they did, they revealed a wet area that glistened on the tile. It was at least a foot wide. More of a smear that trailed across the floor as if—

The realization popped into my head like a jolt. *Son of a bitch*—

But when I looked at Sammy, he appeared calm, unconcerned.

For an instant, I was confused. Two strides later, I saw Sammy remove latex gloves from his pocket.

So did one of the cops.

And finally his partner.

I was seething. Not so much because Chun would do this, but because he thought he could get away with it.

By the time I reached Sammy, he was bent forward, eyes fixed on the floor. The cops began clearing chairs out of the way. Looking past Sammy's shoulder, I saw the body of a man. A large man, lying facedown in a pool of blood. His right hand still held a gun, while his left was raised over his head. As if crawling. Trying to get away.

Sammy crouched down and began prying the gun from the stiff fingers. As he did, my eyes went to the dead man's face. His profile.

I stared, amazed. The last thing in the world I'd expected was to recognize him, but I had.

It was Odd Job, the chauffeur.

★ "Ah, Burton, such a tragedy. I should have realized Su might react violently to his arrest. I blame myself."

Chun was looking up at me, speaking in remorseful tones as he lit a cigarette. He took a deep drag and slowly shook his head as he recounted a confession Su had made, admitting to having killed Soon-ri.

I tried to keep my cool, but this was too much. I took a step toward him, so furious I could spit. All I could think about was slapping the phony concern from his face. Tell him he could take the offer for the store and shove it up his—

"Burt," a voice said sharply, "take this to the car."

I blinked in surprise. Sammy had materialized in front of me and was now blocking my path to Chun. He held out the pistol, which was partially wrapped in his silk handkerchief.

"In a minute," I said, trying to get by him. "First, I want to tell—"

That was as far as I got, because Sammy jabbed the pistol against my chest hard enough to hurt. "*Now,* Burt," he said.

I started to argue. He shut me up with a cold look.

So I grudgingly backed off and took the gun. As I did, I became aware of the silence in the room. Looking up, I saw Chun scowling at me through a haze of smoke. The other men in the room were also staring at me with disapproval. They shook their heads and began whispering to one another. Chun made a guttural sound and started toward me, but Sammy intercepted him with a deep bow and began speaking rapidly in Korean. He repeatedly gestured to me as he spoke. His manner toward Chun was formal and deferential. Chun's face relaxed into a smile. He made a comment to the other men, and they all laughed. I was confused, because I knew the joke had something to do with me and Chung-hee.

Sammy and Chun conversed for a few more seconds. Chun reached into his jacket and produced another pistol. This one Sammy slipped into a coat pocket. He bowed again to Chun and asked if he could be excused. Chun nodded almost regally.

I took in the scene, getting angry again. Only this time, I was pissed at Sammy. Thirty minutes ago in the whorehouse, he had come across as if Chun was the scum of the earth. Now he was blatantly kissing up to him.

Sammy pivoted around to me and jerked his head toward the exit. As we walked toward it, he placed his hand against my back, pushing me along. I looked over in annoyance. "What the hell are you doing?"

"Trying to save your life."

23

Sammy wouldn't say anything more until we came to the exit. His brusque manner told me he wasn't happy with me. Instead of continuing outside into the bee's nest of reporters, he took my arm and led me into a filthy rest room. When he flipped on the light, a rat squealed and scurried over the urine-stained floor, disappearing into a crack in the wall.

Once Sammy shut the door, he took back Su's gun, confirming it was just an excuse to get me away from Chun. As he put it in his jacket pocket, he gave me a hard look. He rarely criticized me, but did so now. "You almost blew it back there, Burt."

"Why?" I snapped. "Just because I was going to get in Chun's face?"

"*That,*" he said, "would have been stupid as hell. You were about to embarrass Chun in front of his superiors."

I stared. "'Superiors'? You mean those men—"

"*Kkang-pae*. Members of the Seoul crime syndicate. High-ranking members. You notice the heavy guy in the brown pinstripe suit . . ."

I shook my head. I hadn't paid them much attention.

". . . that's Kun. The big boss. Probably came down from Seoul when he heard the base was closing. Find out what Chun was doing to protect the *kkang-pae*'s interests."

" '*Kkang-pae*'s interests'?"

"Chun," Sammy went on, "is Kun's front man in the Ville. Most of the businesses Chun manages are owned by the *kkang-pae*. The syndicate runs a lot of the bars outside every American base in Korea. Yong-san, Pusan, Taegu, the DMZ. You name it, the *kkang-pae* are there, raking in the bucks from the GIs."

Now I finally understood why Chun had gone to such lengths to produce a Korean killer. If the U.S. military installations in those locations were temporarily shut down—a given in the event of civil unrest—the financial hit to the *kkang-pae* would be significant, but nothing compared to the devastating losses if the United States was actually forced to pulled out.

Even though I knew Sammy's response, I wanted to hear him say it. I asked him if he was going to let Chun get away with killing Su.

"If it helps, Su probably raped Soon-ri."

A feel-good way of telling me yes. I said, "So because Su was a dirtbag he deserved to die?"

Sammy sighed. "What do you want from me? Even if I wanted to arrest Chun, I couldn't. The witnesses will swear Su drew the gun first and Chun shot him in self-defense."

"I can't believe this," I said. "Chun blatantly interferes in a murder investigation, frames a guy, then kills him after conveniently getting a confession, and we still have to let the bastard walk."

"He outsmarted us," Sammy said. "It happens."

"And that doesn't bother you?"

"Sure it bothers me. But that's life." He shrugged.

"That's a fucking cop-out, and you know it."

A flat smile. "Ah, I see the real problem here. You're upset that I didn't confront Chun."

"*Confront him?* Your lips were planted on his ass."

He slowly shook his head. "Burt . . . Burt . . ."

"What?"

"You're not thinking things through. I had to play up to Chun. Our only chance to solve this thing is if he believes he's won."

I said, "Why the hell should it matter—"

I clammed up. The light finally came on. I felt foolish. "Shit."

Sammy nodded.

"Chun," I said. "If he realizes we're still investigating, he'll try to stop us."

"Not only him," he said. "The entire syndicate."

I felt a chill. Sammy was telling me the *kkang-pae* wouldn't hesitate to kill a couple of cops to protect their interests. "Why the hell didn't you bring up your concerns earlier?"

Sammy looked right at me. "I didn't think it was necessary."

Translation: I should have been smart enough to figure it out myself. "That's why you hustled me out. So I wouldn't tip Chun off to our intentions . . ."

A nod.

"But when I turn down Chun's offer for the store, he'll know something's up."

"Not if you're respectful, Burt. We only need a few days. You could stall him, tell him you haven't made up your mind about wanting to leave Korea."

I grimaced at the thought of cozying up to Chun. "All right."

Sammy gave me a sympathetic smile. "You look beat. How about I call you in the morning?"

He was telling me it would be better if I went home. I wasn't about to argue. But before leaving, I mentioned something I was still curious about.

Sammy's face reddened. "Joke? What joke?"

"The one Chun told the other men. He mentioned my name and Chung-hee's."

"You're wrong. Chun never told any joke."

I frowned, taken aback. He was obviously trying to avoid telling me, but why? Before I could press him, he reached for the door. I slid over a foot to keep it from opening. He lowered his hand and reluctantly faced me.

"Cut the shit, Sammy. Why won't you tell me what Chun said?"

No response. He wouldn't look at me. He played with his tie, tugged on his lapel, then played with his tie some more. Stalling.

"Sammy . . ."

His eyes slowly focused on my face. "It's nothing, Burt. A meaningless comment about your children."

"Chung-hee and I don't have kids."

"That was the joke. Why you are childless."

"Let's hear it."

He sighed. "Please understand I had to tell Chun something to explain your aggression. The anger you were displaying. It had to be something believable that he could tell his boss and save face. I . . . I said you've been under great pressure because you hadn't had children yet."

I still didn't get it. I asked what the big deal was about not having kids.

"I told Chun you were . . . *seong-gi bul-gu-ja*."

"In English."

He turned away. After a few seconds, I figured he'd decided not to tell me. Finally, in a quietly embarrassed voice: "It means you can't get it up."

My jaw dropped. I didn't know whether to laugh or yell.

"You fucking asshole," I said.

★ Red T-shirt cracked open the bar door and nodded at me. I tipped him four thousand won—three bucks—then followed his bulk through a parting sea of reporters toward the curb where the cab was waiting. I barely noticed the flashing cameras or the flurry of questions in broken English. All I could think about was Chung-hee's reaction to the news that by tomorrow, everyone in her family was going to think I was a washout in the sack.

Her husband, the big strong American.

What a funny joke.

Ha, ha.

Chung-hee and I lived in a rented Western-style two-story stucco house surrounded by a security fence, less than a mile from the Ville. When the cab dropped me off in front of the electric gate, I automatically looked toward the carport to confirm that Chung-hee's Hyundai wagon was there. I found myself hoping Chung-hee would be asleep, but as I punched the gate code into the keypad, the light over the front door came on. As I strode across the spacious lawn toward the house, Chung-hee's silhouette appeared in the doorway.

When I stepped inside, she gave me a kiss, then handed me a beer. I took off my jacket, tossed it on a hook by the door, then sat down wearily on the couch in the family room. Chung-hee joined me, saying, "Sammy just called."

I sipped the beer, the local brand, OB, since I didn't have commissary privileges anymore and wasn't about to fork over black-market prices for Miller Lite. "Oh?"

Chung-hee covered her mouth with the back of her hand in the demure Korean way. She appeared to be fighting the urge to smile. "He called to apologize to me. He said you almost got into an argument with my uncle—"

And then she burst out laughing. She kept it up for almost a minute before finally regaining her composure. She shook her head and said, "*Seong-gi bul-gu-ja,*" which brought on another round of giggles.

This, off course, wasn't the reaction I'd anticipated, but then she wasn't the one who was going to be called the Korean equivalent of noodle dick. At least her humor made what I was going to say next easier. I said, "You through?"

She nodded, wiping her eyes.

I said, "You mention Chun's offer to your mother?"

"Hmm. No. She was upstairs asleep."

I paused. "Good. That way she won't be disappointed."

Her brow furrowed at the comment.

I set my beer down on the coffee table and took both her hands in mine. I shifted around to look into her beautiful eyes. "I love you."

"I love you, too." But as she said it, I could see she sensed that something was wrong.

I set the stage by telling her about Soon-ri's murder, describing how she was killed and our suspicions as to who and why. After detailing the politics involved, I brought up Chun's interference, including his subsequent frame job and murder of Su. I also told her about Mi-nah and Chun's brutality toward her. I'd saved this part for last, to help her make the decision I hoped she would.

When I finished, Chung-hee was slumped back against the sofa, staring dully at her manicured hands clenched tightly in her lap. She closed her eyes briefly, and when they opened, she looked both horrified and saddened. "That poor girl . . ."

I nodded.

"When . . . when will you need the money for the contract?"

"Not for a few days. Sammy will let us know."

She swallowed hard. "I knew her, Burt."

"Mi-nah?" I said, surprised.

"No. Soon-ri. I . . . I sold her some earrings a few months ago. And a silver tennis bracelet." She paused. "She . . . she was very beautiful. The customers spoke of her often. For her to die like that . . ." She trailed off, her voice breaking slightly.

We sat without speaking. I finished my beer and got another from the kitchen. When I returned, she was fidgeting with her hands. Trying to decide. I'd made up my mind not to pressure her. The way I saw it, it was her store and ultimately her decision. She knew what acceptance of Chun's offer meant.

She looked at me, and I saw her eyes misting over. "No one will make an offer now. Not if they know Chun is interested."

I nodded. I'd suspected as much.

"This is difficult, Burt. I . . . I feel guilty. I want you to find the killer, but . . . I don't know how much more I can take. Staying here."

"Who says we have to?"

"But the store . . ."

"Dump it. Sign it over to one of your cousins."

She appeared shocked. "You can't be serious?"

"Absolutely. The important thing is for you . . . us . . . to be happy." I gave her a smile. "Besides, I've got some savings. Enough to get by on until we're established."

She came to me then, collapsing in arms. I began stroking her hair. Slowly the tension left her body. I felt wetness against my cheek and realized she was crying. She murmured, "When can we leave?"

"I'd like to finish the case first."

"Can . . . will you find the killer?"

"I don't know."

She looked at me and wiped the moisture from her eyes, smearing her mascara. "I don't think my uncle killed her."

"How do you know?"

"Because Soon-ri would have disappeared. In the past, that's what happened to . . . to people he didn't like."

"Other girls?"

"Mostly businessmen. His competition. I . . . I suppose it's possible he's killed women." She added with feeling, "I hate him."

"You won't have to worry about him much longer."

She suddenly lifted her head, threw her arms around my neck, and kissed me hard. As she did, I gently picked her up and carried her up the creaking staircase to bed.

★ We crawled into bed around 1 A.M., wrapped in each other's arms. Once I was sure Chung-hee was asleep, I slowly uncoiled. For the next hour, I lay awake, trying to block out the questions dancing in my head. But they kept coming.

Major Wilson. Was his alibi a fabrication? If not, did he hire someone—a man or men—to kill Soon-ri? If so, were they Korean or American? Did General Muller know of or only suspect Major Wilson's guilt? If Muller was covering for Wilson, why the song-and-dance about wanting the case solved when he could have ordered me to back off? Even more puzzling: Why did he tell me the voice on the emergency tape was made by an American?

As the case played out in my mind, I kept returning to that singular revelation. General Muller must have had a reason for telling me, but what?

When I finally drifted off, only one answer remotely made sense.

Was it possible he'd told me the truth about wanting the case solved?

Not a chance.

24

WEDNESDAY

I'd barely fallen asleep when I heard the shrill of the alarm. I groggily banged on the cutoff button, wondering how I could have screwed up setting the time. The alarm kept ringing. I banged harder.

Then Chung-hee's sleepy voice: "It's the phone, honey."

I muttered, "Who the hell calls in the middle of the night?"

"It's almost morning."

When I opened my eyes, the alarm clock said six-ten and the reddish glow of first light was peeking between the drapes. I groaned and picked up the phone.

It was Sammy, calling from his car. His voice sounded tense and anxious. "We need to talk, Burt. I found something important."

"We're talking now."

"In person. I'm on my way."

I lay back against the pillow, feeling drugged. I massaged my forehead, trying to jump-start my brain cells.

Sammy: "Burt . . ."

"Still here. So what did you find out?"

"Sergeant Ko located Soon-ri's phone bills. Someone else on base knew her besides Major Wilson."

I sat up, suddenly awake. Chung-hee rolled over in annoyance, wrapping a pillow around her head. "Who?" I asked Sammy.

"Not over the phone, Burt."

"C'mon, Sammy—"

But he'd hung up.

I cradled the receiver, my mind racing. But I had no idea who the person could be. As I swung my legs out of the bed, I heard the sound of squealing tires, followed by the blare of a car horn.

I threw on a robe and hurried downstairs to open the gate for Sammy.

★ Sammy sat at the kitchen table as I pressed the ON button for the coffeemaker, which Chung-hee had set up last night on the counter. Once it began to drip, I camped out in the chair across from Sammy. As usual, he was immaculately dressed, this time in a lavender suit with a matching silk tie. His hair was damp from a recent shower and perfectly combed, and his eyes were bright and clear, showing no evidence of the fact that he'd had even less sleep than I.

I drummed the table with two fingers, waiting for him to reveal the person Soon-ri had called. Curiously, Sammy suddenly seemed in no hurry to talk. He yawned and continued to gaze out the window at our tiny backyard.

I gave a suggestive cough. When he looked at me, I asked, "What's the guy's name?"

"We're still tracking him down. The bills contained only phone numbers and locations. Sergeant Ko has requested a printout from the phone company."

"The number have a base prefix?"

"Local calls weren't listed on the bill. But we know it was to a cell phone."

Now I was confused, since there was no way to tell where a cell phone was located. I asked how he knew the caller was someone from the base.

He hesitated, giving me an odd look. "I recognized the number."

"You *know* the guy?"

A vague nod. He appeared troubled. "This isn't easy, Burt."

"What isn't easy?"

He gave me a sad smile. "I'm sorry. I truly am. I'm sure this is a misunderstanding and you have an explanation."

For a moment, I wasn't sure I'd heard him right. "*I* have an explanation. For what? What the hell are you talking about?"

Sammy didn't reply. He took out his cell phone and notepad. He consulted the pad and carefully punched in a number.

An instant later, I turned in disbelief toward the living room.

A phone was ringing.

The next thing I knew, I was on my feet, following the sound. Past the silent phone on the end table beside the couch. Up the two short steps into the entryway. I looked at the clothing hooks by the front door. My jacket was hanging where I'd left it last night.

It rang again.

★ The ringing stopped. I stood there, my heart pounding, looking at the jacket. I became aware of Sammy, coming up behind me. He was talking, but I wasn't really listening. I was trying to convince myself that the man I knew wasn't a killer. That Ray would never commit murder to protect his career.

But twenty years of history flooded back. From our first day in school. The way he'd pushed himself and the choices he'd made. Always his drive to succeed had won out.

Over his happiness.

Over his marriage.

Over our friendship.

Everything.

Things I didn't understand earlier suddenly began to make sense.

My selection to the case, which Ray probably talked Muller into, so he could influence me.

Ray's insistence last night that I concentrate on a Korean killer.

General Muller's confusion: *I don't care what Ray said. I made it known from the beginning that I wanted the killer found. Korean or American, I didn't give a damn.*

And the way we found Ray last night in his BOQ.

Passed out.

With the gun.

No. Ray would never kill himself over a failed marriage. But if he'd been racked with guilt over a murder—

A hand touched my arm. Then Sammy's voice, asking if I could explain the phone. This time I gave him an answer.

"I can," I said.

★ Sammy removed the cell phone from my jacket and we returned to the kitchen. As I poured out two coffees, I told Sammy how Ray had lent it to me. I couldn't bring myself to express the rest of my concerns yet. Not until I talked with Ray.

When I passed Sammy his coffee cup, he looked visibly relieved. "I knew it had to be something like that."

"Right," I grunted, with more than a trace of sarcasm.

A wry smile as he placed Ray's cell phone on the counter. "Give me a break, Burt. What was I supposed to think when the number matched the one you gave me?"

I let it go, because I was wrestling with a similar decision. Trying to resist jumping to conclusions because of a phone number. As we took our seats at the table, I said, "All the phone call means is Ray knew her. Not that he killed her. Hell, Soon-ri probably knew a hundred guys from the base."

"They aren't on her phone bill."

"Not yet maybe. But you can bet there'll be other Osan numbers when you get the printout of her local calls. Including Major Wilson's."

He shrugged, then almost reluctantly reached into his jacket and handed me an envelope. "Better take a look," he advised.

I did. Inside were two faxed pages of phone bills. Even though the writing was in Korean, they obviously belonged to Soon-ri. My eyes went down the columns, focusing on the phone numbers. Sammy had highlighted in yellow the ones made to Ray's cellular. And at the bottom, he'd noted the total for each month.

She'd called Ray fourteen times in May. Seventeen times in June.

Almost every other day.

Something twisted in my stomach. I closed my eyes, recalling the drive to Soon-ri's apartment last night. How Ray knew the way and his explanation: *I've driven General Muller here a couple of times to visit General Pak. A retired Korean four-star who lives nearby.*

My eyes popped open. I had to know. Two minutes later, Sammy had the answer after calling his precinct. He gave me an address I didn't recognize.

"How far does General Pak live from Soon-ri's apartment?" I asked.

"The other side of town."

There it was. Another lie. I felt numb. When I picked up my cup, my hand shook and hot coffee spilled on my fingers.

I never felt a thing.

25

"I'm sorry, Burt." Sammy was watching me over the rim of his cup.

"Yeah . . ." He'd heard me talk about Ray before and knew we were close.

We sipped in silence. I knew I should eat, but didn't feel hungry. From the living room a clock chimed once. Six-thirty A.M.

Sammy said, "I understand how you feel. I went through the same thing. Wondering if I could bring you in."

"You obviously decided you could."

"I'm a cop," he said quietly. "And so are you."

I looked at the table. Avoiding his gaze and the message that went with it.

"It's your decision," he went on. "I was notified last night that Soon-ri's murder is officially closed. You walk away now, and there's nothing I can do. Your friend Ray will be in the clear."

"Sammy," I snapped, "we don't *know* he killed her!"

"Burt, please . . ."

"So they knew each other? So what? I know Ray. He's not a killer."

Sammy didn't say anything. He reached into his jacket, removed another envelope, thicker than the first. He opened the flap and began sliding over a series of photographs. One after another. Pictures of Soon-ri's body, taken from various angles. Including close-ups of the wound.

After I turned away from the gore, the photos kept coming. I said, "You son of a bitch."

He finally put down the envelope. "I need your help."

"Fuck you."

"Burt . . ."

"No!"

I could see the disappointment in his eyes. He rose and slowly gathered up the phone bills and photos. All except one, which he placed in front of me. Without a word, he turned for the door. I glanced down at the picture, which was larger than the others. Instead of Soon-ri's corpse, I was looking at the photograph, now removed from its gold frame, that Sammy had taken from her dresser. The one in which Soon-ri and her mother were standing on the unpaved street of the village. Again I was struck by the sadness in their eyes, as if they'd known what the future held.

I felt a tightness in my chest. I mentally flipped a coin, knowing beforehand how it would land.

"Wait, Sammy," I said.

★ So I spelled out my suspicions about Ray. I didn't hold anything back. Sammy listened without interruption, writing in his notepad.

"And his finances?" he asked when I finished.

"Ray's not as well-off as he used to be because of his divorce."

"You know what I mean."

"He's always been frugal. I know he's invested regularly for years."

"So he might have been able to swing a hundred-grand payout?"

"Maybe. Probably."

"I take it he never mentioned to you that he knew Soon-ri?"

"No." Which was another inference I couldn't get around. Still, I was holding a couple of cards that favored Ray, and I played the first one now. "Anyone in the apartment mention seeing a black man with Soon-ri?"

A head shake.

"Then that tells me he's not her sugar daddy."

"Depends when he came by. If he was careful, visited late at night . . ."

"Someone would still have noticed a six-two black guy, Sammy."

He shrugged. "If that's the case, why wasn't anyone except Major Wilson seen with her?"

A valid point, if we went with the assumption that Wilson wasn't the seemingly invisible Mr. Moneybags. I played my second card. "Ray also doesn't have his own car, and he wouldn't have risked using a military vehicle to visit Soon-ri. It would have been hard for him to get rides to her apartment."

"He could have used base taxis."

"That would still have been risky. The drivers on base know him. They would have wondered why a bird colonel was making a bunch of late-night visits to a downtown apartment house."

"He could always have borrowed a vehicle."

"That would still have been inconvenient; he could never have counted on being able to use it. And again he would have had to explain why he needed the car."

Sammy closed his notepad, looking at me. An unspoken moment passed between us. He casually slid over his cell phone. Telling me we had to have an explanation for all those calls.

I picked up the phone.

When Ray answered, his disjointed voice told me he was still feeling the effects of his bender. I told him I was coming over, explaining that there was a major break in the case I wanted to discuss.

"I heard. General Muller just called, said he was opening the base back up. Told me the killer was some Korean chauffeur."

Instead of sounding relieved, Ray's tone was curiously indifferent. But maybe it was the hangover. I told him I'd give him the details when I got there.

I was about to hang up when he said irritably, "You also going to let me know why you busted in my door?"

I sighed. I hadn't wanted to get into this over the phone. "How did you know it was me?"

"General Muller mentioned you two spoke last night. I figured you must have stopped by afterward. What the hell's your problem, Burt?"

I fessed up, explaining my actions. Afterward there was a long silence. Then: "You've got to be shitting me. You actually thought I might shoot myself. *Me?*" Ray burst out laughing. "Man, you are some detective, buddy." And he laughed even harder.

But to me his reaction was over the top. Forced. As the laughter died off, I said, "You finished?"

"Hey, don't get sore, Burt. You have to admit, it's funny as hell. Better give me back that shotgun if you don't want Muller jumping on your ass."

"Muller?"

"Sure. I checked it out for him. He's shooting trap this afternoon with a couple of ROK Army generals at the Rod and Gun Club. Been practicing all week so he doesn't get embarrassed."

I wanted to believe him, but— "This is straight?"

A sigh of irritation. "Man, what's with you? First you think I'm a head case and now you're calling me a liar."

"No, Ray, I just—"

"*Ask* Muller." And he hung up with a bang.

When I handed Sammy his phone, I tried to remind myself that this was necessary and our relationship would recover. That I wasn't really setting Ray up.

"He still might be innocent," Sammy said.

"Sure."

As I went upstairs, I felt the need for a shower.

★ By six forty-five, I was dressed in a tan summer blazer and Dockers slacks. After running a comb through my hair, I reset the alarm for eight, which was when Chung-hee and I normally awoke, so we could have a leisurely breakfast before opening the store at ten. I paused, looking down at her beautiful face in the semidarkness, debating whether to awaken her. Ask her if I was doing the right thing.

I quietly withdrew, because I was only seeking reassurance for an answer I already knew. The question was whether I could live with it.

I walked out into the hall and gently closed the door. The bedroom door at the far end was open, and I could hear my mother-in-law snoring. Through the window came the faint chirping of birds and the yapping of my neighbor's dog. The familiar sounds that greeted me every morning. But of course this morning was different. This was the day I might have to accuse my best friend of murder.

★ When I went downstairs, Sammy was nowhere to be found. Then I heard his voice and followed it to the small sitting room at the back of the house, which Chung-hee and I had turned into an office. Sammy was seated behind the desk, staring at the computer monitor and speaking into his cell phone. He ended the call as I entered and gave me a gloomy head shake. "That was Dr. Yee, the deputy coroner. Your choice, Burt. You want the good news or the bad news first?"

I hesitated. "The good news."

"Yee was right about Soon-ri being drugged. It was ether."

I slowly nodded. Ether was short lasting, which explained why Soon-ri had regained consciousness so quickly. I said softly, "And the bad . . ."

"Yee just got the word to wrap up his forensics testing on Soon-ri."

"So the DNA results are out?" Because they took at least a week to complete.

"Yeah . . ." Sammy sat back and shrugged. "But we might still catch a break, because the case was such a high priority. Once Dr. Yee finished the autopsy last night, the tissue, blood, and fluid samples were flown to Seoul, in an attempt to get a quick determination on the race of the man who fathered the fetus. Dr. Yee's expecting some results in the next few hours. He'll try to hold off on his final report until they come in."

Since DNA testing was out, determining race would be a difficult task. It came down to the presence or absence of specific genetic markers in the blood, which might suggest the person who impregnated Soon-ri was an Asian or American. The latter really being an AWG—Average White Guy.

I asked Sammy if Dr. Yee had determined Soon-ri's blood type.

"O positive."

"I think Ray's is A," I said. I added, "And I'll try to find out Major Wilson's."

He made a notation on his notepad. Once we had the results of the fetus's blood type, we could at least rule out suspects, since certain blood combinations are impossible. For instance, if the baby was B, Ray couldn't be the father.

I asked how long Soon-ri had actually been pregnant.

"Between six and eight weeks." He put his notepad away. "And the cause of death was as we figured—heart failure brought on by loss of blood. Dr. Yee said it could have taken up to twenty minutes, depending on her heart rate. How much it was slowed by the ether and how much she struggled."

My jaw tightened at the image of Soon-ri thrashing against the ropes, as the life drained from her. At that moment, I felt a surge of determination to hold the killer accountable, no matter who he was.

Sammy's eyes dropped to the computer monitor. "After you left, Chun spoke with the reporters."

"What did he say?"

He rose and offered me the chair. "Have a look."

I went around the desk and glanced at the screen. Scrawled across the top was the banner for the Web page of the *Korean Herald*, an English-language daily. And below, an article titled HEROIC SONG-TAN BUSINESSMAN KILLS MURDERER OF BAR GIRL.

"Chun's publicity stunt worked," I grunted. "General Muller opened up the base."

Sammy nodded without comment. When he saw I wasn't interested in reading the article, he bent down and began shutting off the computer. With a final click, he straightened, saying, "I offered Chun a million won."

I frowned, then understood. The price for Mi-nah's contract. I said, "That's less than a thousand dollars."

He shrugged. "He was in a good mood last night. I'm thinking he might take it."

I refrained from saying what was on my mind. I spent the next few minutes making copies of the phone records on my fax machine. As we were about to leave, the office phone rang. I had my suspicions about who'd be calling this early and why.

Instead of General Muller, the annoyingly perky voice on the other end belonged to Major Helen Davis, his aide-de-camp. She told me to be at Muller's office in the 7th Air Force Headquarters building promptly at 0900 hours. Helen said she'd already passed the word to Susan. And no, she didn't know why Muller wanted to meet with us.

"We've got about two hours until my services are terminated," I told Sammy.

"Then we'll have to act fast."

★ On our way out, I detoured by the kitchen to pick up Ray's cell phone and to jot down a quick note to Chung-hee, saying I'd call her at the store.

When I reentered the family room, I saw Sammy standing by the edge of the front window, peering through a gap in the drapes. He turned to me, and I saw the worry in his eyes.

"We have company," he said.

There were only two possibilities.

I went over to take a look.

26

I peered over Sammy's shoulder as he held back the drapes about an inch. Through the iron grillwork of the fence, we saw a shiny black sedan parked in the street, almost blocking my gate. Rather than CIA types, I could make out two Korean men sitting in the front seat, smoking cigarettes. Both appeared young.

"Chun's men," I murmured.

Sammy nodded.

"Not very subtle, are they?"

"They want to be seen. Chun obviously didn't believe my story last night about your behavior. He's sending you a message to play ball."

"And if I don't . . ."

Sammy hesitated. "You recognize the driver?"

I squinted, finally realizing he was one of the men with Chun's group in the bar last night. The guy in the pullover shirt. "Yeah."

"His name is Chi. He's an enforcer for the *kkang-pae*."

I let out a breath. "By 'enforcer,' you mean . . ."

Sammy stepped away from the window, looking at me. "He kills people. He's probably the one who really shot Su."

It took all my self-control to remain calm. "We knew this could happen. That Chun would try to intimidate us. Or worse."

"It's more serious than that, Burt. By sending Chi to your house, Chun's making it clear what you're risking."

For a moment I was unsure of what he was trying to say. Then Sammy slowly tilted his head back and looked up at the ceiling in an ominous way. I said, "Oh, Lord . . ."

He nodded.

I tried to speak and coughed. Me being a target was one thing, but *this*—

I said, "You mean Chun would go after Chung-hee . . ."

Sammy nodded.

"For chrissakes, she's his *niece*."

"It may not be Chun's decision. Kun . . . his boss . . . could be calling the shots."

My knees felt weak. I tried to fight off a growing sense of panic. All I could think about was where to take Chung-hee and my mother-in-law. To keep them safe until I could figure out—

And then the answer came to me in a sudden moment of clarity. Exactly what I had to do.

I started to explain my idea to Sammy, but he was already taking out his phone, thumbing in a number from his notepad. Once he began speaking, I realized that he'd come up with the same solution. I wasn't surprised. After all, that was the only place where Chun couldn't touch them.

I spun around and raced up the stairs two at a time.

★ Two minutes later, we were all standing in the living room. Chung-hee and my mother-in-law were dressed in their bathrobes, blinking sleepily as Sammy ran through the plan in Korean. There was a flickering of fear in Chung-hee's eyes as she finally grasped was going on. Moments later, my mother-in-law's face shifted from confusion to a smoldering anger. Like her daughter, she was tall and thin, with a mass of silver hair that she wore rolled into a bun. At the mention of Chun's name, she loosed a litany of harsh invective, a testament to her hatred toward her brother-in-law.

Sammy nodded at me when he finished. I went over and gave my mother-in-law a hug, then kissed Chung-hee on the lips.

"Be careful," she said softly.

"I will."

She gave my hand a final squeeze and guided her mother upstairs, to get ready. As Sammy waited by the front door, I returned to my office for the spare gate remote, the Velcro leg holster I used for undercover work, and the 9mm pistol that I was no longer authorized to carry. When I returned, Sammy was gone. I opened the front door and saw him sitting in his car, the engine running.

I took a deep breath and stepped outside, the weight of the pistol heavy against my leg.

★ The morning was cool, but I was already beginning to sweat. The men were still sitting in the sedan, and I could feel their eyes on me as I walked toward Sammy's car. When I opened the passenger door, loud rock music greeted me. Meatloaf's "Paradise by the Dashboard Light," which was the informal anthem of the Ville's bars. Sammy was listening with his eyes closed, one hand tapping the beat against his leg. As I started to buckle up, Sammy glanced over and shook his head. I understood. If the fireworks went off, we wanted to be able to get out fast. Sammy removed his pistol, chambered a round, and placed it in his lap. I did the same.

Sammy listened to the music for a few more moments before reluctantly punching out the CD. He smiled. "Great song."

I nodded.

"First time I got laid, it was to this song."

"Congratulations."

The smile faded. "I'll take Chi. You have the driver."

I nodded again and keyed the remote.

As the gate began to open, we slowly rolled toward it. The black sedan started up, a puff of smoke coming from its exhaust. Getting ready to tail us, which was what we wanted.

We rolled through the gate. We could see the driver, Chi, smiling at us. Sammy's eyes glossed over him and checked the traffic. He started to pull out into the street.

At that instant, the sedan shot forward in a squeal of tires, blocking our path.

Sammy swore, jamming on the brakes. We rocked forward.

In a single motion, Sammy threw the car into reverse and went for his gun. Mine was already coming up. Car doors slammed as the men hopped out of the sedan. I aimed at the passenger, body tense, waiting for Sammy to back up.

Nothing happened. When I looked over, Sammy was just sitting there, his gun on Chi, his foot poised over the accelerator. I was incredulous.

"*Dammit,* Sammy . . ."

"They're unarmed, Burt. They seem to want to talk."

Which was true. The men were standing by their car, giving us wide smiles. They held out their hands, to show they weren't carrying. I said, "It could be a trick. It has to be a trick."

But Sammy was silent, trying to figure out how to play it. Chi and the passenger patted their trousers and shirts, again to prove they didn't have a weapon. They began calling out to Sammy.

He remained still, watching them. Seconds passed. A finger of sweat ran down my eyelid. I blinked it away.

Finally Sammy rolled down his window and began speaking to Chi. As they conversed, I was struck by the way Chi kept looking toward me, occasionally saying my name. At a gesture from Sammy, Chi reached into the sedan. My finger tightened on the trigger. But when Chi turned around, I saw he held a small red box.

Sammy motioned again and Chi came toward my door.

"Roll down your window, Burt," Sammy said.

I did. Chi gave a little bow and held out the box to me. "*Seon-mul.*" A gift for you.

I took the box.

27

The black sedan backed up just enough to let us by, then waited against the curb with the engine running. I looked down at the box, which was covered with red felt. It was maybe four inches square and two inches deep, with a heavy cardboard lid.

"From Chun," Sammy said.

I nodded, figuring as much.

"Pretty light," I said. "Couple of ounces. Can't be a bomb." I was only half kidding.

Sammy rolled out onto the street and gave a satisfied nod when the sedan followed. I pried open the lid. Inside, nestled in cotton, was a glass vial containing a white powder. A gummed label with Korean writing was stuck to the side.

I inspected the vial, then held it out so Sammy could read the label. After a second glance, he surprised me with a laugh.

"What's so funny?" I asked.

"Chun is paying you back for being a jerk last night. He gave you *nogyong*."

I gave him a blank look.

"Ground deer horn. You never heard of it, huh? No?" He grinned. "It's to help you . . . perform."

I felt my ears redden. I said irritably, "This is all your fault."

He gazed back innocently.

I glared at him, then rolled down the window and began to unscrew the cap of the vial.

"Hey," Sammy said, "you're not throwing that away? That stuff isn't cheap."

"Why? You want it?"

"Better than letting it go to waste." He winked. "Besides, you never know when it will come in handy."

I rolled my eyes and passed him the vial.

We rode along for a few moments. Casually, I said, "What if you're wrong?"

"Wrong?"

"About what's in the vial. Maybe it's not deer horn."

No response. He kept glancing down at the vial. Twice he started to place it in his jacket pocket, but reconsidered. Finally, he made a face and muttered to himself in Korean. As we rounded a corner, he cracked open his window, threw out the vial, then reached down to slide in the Meatloaf CD.

"You know," I said helpfully, "you could always try Viagra. I hear the stuff is effective for . . ."

Sammy cranked up the volume and drowned me out.

I gazed outside so he wouldn't see me smile.

★ We cruised through the Ville toward the Osan main gate. At this time of the morning, the main street resembled a ghost town, the stores and bars all closed. In the harsh daylight, the shabbiness of the place was revealed. The sidewalks were dirty and piled with uncollected garbage, the buildings were decrepit and colorless, and there was an unpleasant odor in the air. But once darkness returned, reality would again be transformed by the glitter of dizzying lights, and perception altered by the flow of booze. Gazing out the window, I shook my head, thinking I was tired of all this. Maybe Chung-hee was right; it was time to leave.

If we could.

Approaching the Osan main gate, we could see a small crane already lifting the concrete berms onto a flatbed truck, confirming the downgrade of the base's security status. Sammy tapped the brakes, responding to an enlisted flagman, who was signaling us to stop.

As we waited for the crane to clear the lane, Sammy turned down the music and glanced around. "You see her?"

I was busy scanning the street. Looking over my shoulder, I spotted the Chrysler Sebring, partially hidden in a nearby alley, its front end poking out. "Bingo," I said, taking out my cell phone. "The street next to Mr. Oh's tailor shop."

Sammy looked and nodded.

Chung-hee picked up on the first ring. She and her mother were dressed and in the process of packing. No, she didn't think anyone else was watching the house. I described the Sebring and told her it'd be another ten minutes, then hung up and immediately placed another call.

"You want me to wait or go?" Susan asked.

I checked the side-view mirror. The sedan was still brazenly planted on our bumper. "Hang loose until we know what these guys are going to do."

"Rog."

A few seconds later, the crane moved aside and Sammy drove up to the gate.

I watched as the black sedan pulled a U-turn and parked against the opposite curb. Chi waved, and I waved back. Pleasant sort. The type of guy who'd probably give you a cheerful smile even as he put a bullet in your brain.

"Take off," I said to Susan.

The Sebring slowly drove away.

★ Again I got the star treatment at the gate, which meant I was still on the A-list. Even though Sammy showed his badge, according to Air Force regs, he should have been required to sign in. Like last night, we were immediately waved through.

We rolled to a stop in front of Ray's duplex at ten after seven. As we got out, a four-ship of F-16s screamed across our heads in a thunderous roar, heading toward the Yellow Sea to play tag.

At Ray's door, Sammy gazed at the splintered lock, then gave me a tiny smile. I said, "I'd like to handle the questioning."

"You're sure?"

"I'm sure."

"We'll need a confession."

"I know."

I stepped forward and rang the bell.

★ Ray looked like hell, not that I'd dare say anything. His normally chiseled face was puffy and haggard, his bloodshot eyes resembled a road map with a couple of car wrecks, and he blinked constantly as if suddenly sensitive to light.

He'd met us at the door in uniform trousers and a T-shirt, his hair damp from a shower. As Sammy and I went inside, I immediately checked out the living room. The empty liquor bottle and the blanket I'd covered him with last night were gone, and the couch cushions had been fluffed up, showing no sign that Ray had slept on them. Not that I expected anything less from Ray. At school, he'd always been a fanatic about order, as if neatness too was a competition.

After I introduced Sammy, we followed Ray into his equally immaculate bedroom so he could finish dressing. On his dresser, a half dozen silver-framed photos of his two boys were displayed, mostly family shots that included his ex-wife, Linda, proving he still had a tough time accepting the divorce.

Sitting on the edge of his bed to put on his socks, Ray said, "You guys did a good job, Burt. According to General Muller, Ambassador Gregson is pretty ecstatic at the outcome. Mentioned something about Gregson possibly sending you a letter of commendation."

As Ray talked, he never once looked at me or Sammy. And his voice had a wooden quality, as if he was going through the motions, throwing out a compliment because it was expected. I wondered if my confrontation with him earlier had tipped him off to the real reason we were here.

Ray swallowed a yawn and pointed to his closet. "Mind handing me my shoes, Burt?"

I stepped back and picked up the pair of spit-shined black low-quarters, sitting just inside the closet door. As I handed them over, Ray wriggled his toes in one, saying, "Guess everyone got riled up over nothing. I mean who'd have figured it would be this easy, that some chauffeur would turn out to be the killer?"

The opening I was waiting for. Still, I had to nudge myself to take it. "Not us," I said.

Ray began looping a knot. "Oh?"

"In fact, we're pretty sure the guy was framed, then killed so he couldn't deny his guilt." I glanced to Sammy as I spoke. He nodded his agreement, then drifted over to the closet, trying not to be overly obvious as he peered inside.

Ray's hands froze before completing the knot. He sat up slowly. "General Muller said he confessed."

"Supposedly. In the presence of at least five men."

"And you still don't buy it?"

"Do you?"

A bleary-eyed squint. "That crack supposed to mean something?"

"I'm just asking if you think the chauffeur killed Soon-ri."

"How the hell should I know? You're the cop." But his blink rate had shifted into high gear, and not because of his hangover.

"Actually, Ray," I said, "you have an insight that could be helpful."

"Insight? What kind of insight?" His tone was wary now.

I looked right at him. "I'm not the one who knew the victim, Ray."

It took maybe a second for his synapses to make the connection. He shot me a look of disbelief. "You're fucking crazy."

"Am I?" I reached into my jacket.

"She was a *bar* girl. You know damn well I don't go downtown. How the hell would I have even met—"

He stopped.

He stared at the phone bills in my hand.

To the highlighted lines where I was pointing.

Ray had always been a quick study. His mouth twitched and his shoulders sagged. He took a ragged breath and seemed to deflate a little. When he looked up, his face was resigned. "I knew you'd find out eventually. I kept hoping, you know, that if you solved the case quickly, maybe . . . somehow none of this would . . ." He trailed off, looking at the floor.

I gave him a moment before moving in for the kill. I said, "I need the truth now. An innocent man is dead because— What the hell do you mean no?" I was dumbfounded to see Ray shaking his head. "Dammit, Ray. You could be in a lot of trouble. Your only chance now is to tell me exactly—"

"Can't, Burt," he interrupted. "Sorry."

"Ray, I'll help you any way I can. You've got my word. But I need you to talk to me—"

He waved me off. "You don't understand. It's not my call."

"Not *your* call? Then whose the hell is it? General Muller's? Ambassador Gregson's?" Because Ray had always been Mr. Military, someone who obeyed orders without question.

Ray seemed suddenly uncomfortable, as if he'd let something slip. He changed the subject, saying, "Look, this thing is complicated. There are certain aspects I'm simply not allowed to discuss."

"This is a murder investigation."

He gave me a look of annoyance, then went on quietly, "What I can confirm is that I knew Soon-ri. I can also tell you I was trying to help her . . ."

"So you bought out her contract?"

He ignored me and kept on talking. ". . . and that neither I nor Major Wilson had anything to do with her murder. I can also confirm that General Muller and I both pushed for you to be assigned to the case because *we wanted the murder solved.*"

He'd emphasized the last statement in an obvious attempt to convince me of his sincerity. I wasn't buying it and bluntly told him why.

He responded slowly, choosing his words. "I had certain . . . reasons for wanting you to focus on a Korean perpetrator. Reasons that had nothing to do with the politics."

"For example . . ."

"Can't say."

"General Muller acknowledges the killer could be an American."

"He's mistaken."

It was like talking to a wall. "I see. So what you're really saying is you know who the killer is?"

He looked me in the eye. "If I did, don't you think I'd have told you?"

Which wasn't exactly a denial. I rephrased my earlier question. "Are you withholding information on orders from General Muller?"

A flat smile. He finished tying his shoes, then stood and walked past me into the closet. A moment later, he reappeared, throwing on a starched uniform shirt already adorned with his name tag, command pilot wings, and colonel epaulets.

I said, "We're not finished, Ray."

He kept on buttoning his shirt.

I said, "I could bring you in for questioning."

Ray snorted. "On what grounds? The case is officially closed. And if you took me in because of a few damned phone calls, I guarantee that General Muller would have me re—"

He sucked in his final word. He realized he'd just made another mistake.

"Released?" I finished quietly. "Are you saying General Muller wouldn't care that his executive officer called a murder victim thirty-one times?"

There was nothing he could say, so he didn't. He returned to buttoning his shirt.

I said, "That means General Muller must have been aware you had something going with Soon-ri."

Ray didn't reply. He went over to a chest-high armoire and yanked out a tie.

By now Sammy was over by the dresser. He mouthed a word to remind me of a question. One Ray would have to answer.

After I asked him, Ray glanced up from knotting the tie. He managed to sound both weary and aggravated. "My alibi? Get fucking real, Burt. You of all people should know I'd never kill anyone. Especially not a woman. Christ, when I think about what happened to Soon-ri . . . how she was cut open like some animal . . ." He trailed off as something flickered across his face. A sadness. After a few moments, he became aware of Sammy and me staring at him. Without a word, he turned and disappeared into the bathroom.

Sammy shot me a knowing glance. I nodded, to let him know I understood. Ray's reaction seemed to verify what the phone records suggested, that he had had more than a casual relationship with Soon-ri.

Still, I couldn't quite accept that someone with Ray's ambition would risk his career over an affair with a bar girl, no matter how beautiful she was. This was a guy who defined his life by his promotions, who had sacrificed everything to make the next rank. And even if he had been dinking Soon-ri on the side, the last person in the world he'd tell would be General Muller. Yet Ray's comments clearly indicated that Muller was at the very least aware of some kind of relationship—

Ray popped out from the bathroom, cinching the tie around his neck. He smelled of cologne. I said, "I still need an answer. Where were you between thirteen hundred and fifteen hundred hours yesterday afternoon?"

He eyed me coolly. "I didn't kill her."

"Ray, just answer the—"

"The office," he snapped. "I was in it most of the afternoon, working on an exercise briefing. General Muller saw me. So did Penelope. Probably one or two others." Penelope was Penelope Diaz, General Muller's secretary. Ray added, "Now, if there's nothing else . . ."

His icy tone made it clear he didn't care if I had anything else. I answered with a head shake. Out of the corner of my eye, I noticed Sammy had worked his way over to the armoire and was now staring with interest into the small waste can beside it.

"Good," Ray grunted to me. "Now where's the shotgun? Of course, I could always tell him what happened, that you busted in my door, destroyed government property, and stole the fucking thing because—"

"That won't be necessary. I'll have Susan drop it by your office when she shows up for the meeting with General Muller."

A grudging nod. His hand shot out. "I'd also like my phone back."

I fished into my jacket and handed it over, telling him I'd drop off the spare battery later. Ray immediately brushed past me toward the bedroom door. As I started to follow, Sammy said, "Colonel Johnson—"

When Ray turned around, Sammy flashed an apologetic smile. "I was wondering if I might use your rest room."

Ray threw out a hand. "Knock yourself out."

As Ray and I continued into the living room, I looked back at Sammy. His handkerchief was in his hand. He suddenly bent down and reached into the trash can. His body blocked my view, but when he stood, I could tell he'd removed something. Casually, he slid the object into his right trouser pocket, tucked the handkerchief into his breast pocket, and stepped into the bathroom.

28

Ray and I waited for Sammy in a strained silence by the front door. An all-too-familiar occurrence in recent months. I was about to say screw this and wait outside when Ray cleared his throat. "Look, Burt, I'm sorry I got you mixed up in all this. I'll admit I've been acting like a horse's ass. I know you're only trying to do your job. I want you to know that if I could tell you more, I would. No hard feelings, huh?"

An olive branch I wasn't quite prepared to embrace. I met him halfway with a cautious "I'll survive."

He attempted a smile. "About those phone calls. I know it looks pretty bad. But I swear to God I had nothing to do with Soon-ri's death. I never would have hurt her." His eyes searched mine, looking for a sign that I believed him.

I went with my gut. "I know you didn't."

He seemed to relax slightly, then threw me another curve by saying, "You know, a lot of this is my fault."

"Oh?"

A nod. "If I'd been straight with you in the beginning, maybe you would have had a chance of solving this thing. And I wanted to tell you. Lord knows. But . . ." He hunted for a word.

"It's still not too late."

"It is, Burt," he said quietly. "And you and I both know it. By next week, no one will even remember Soon-ri. Or care."

I didn't argue, because what he was saying was true. In the scheme of things, a dead bar girl didn't amount to much.

We stood there looking at each other. I said, "You sound like you care."

He drew in a deep breath and nodded. The sadness returned to his eyes again, followed by a tight-lipped look of determination. Abruptly, he said, "Let it go, Burt."

I frowned.

"The case. Drop it."

"Like I have a choice. In case you didn't get the word, General Muller's about to make the decision for me."

"Don't give me that crap. The fact that you're here, grilling me, tells me you're not about to quit. Hell, that's the main reason I pushed Muller to select you in the first place. Because I knew you'd see it through."

"And now you've changed your mind?"

He nodded.

"Want to tell me why?"

He turned away as if he wasn't going to respond. Then softly: "Because it's really my responsibility."

"Your responsibility?"

He didn't say anything more.

★ Sammy sauntered up moments later. Ray opened the door, and we all went outside. As we headed across the front walkway, Ray seemed preoccupied. I had to say his name twice before he finally glanced my way. I asked him if he wanted a ride to 7th Air Force Headquarters, which was at the other end of the base.

"I'll pass. I need the walk to clear my head."

At the sidewalk, he shook Sammy's hand, then mine. Our eyes met and he said, "You're going to stick with this case, aren't you?"

"Probably."

"If you identify the killer, what then?"

"I don't know. If the evidence is strong enough, maybe we could contact the local press—"

"Try again," Ray said. "The ROK government will never allow the story to get printed." He glanced at Sammy. "Am I right?"

Sammy nodded.

"She was murdered, Ray," I said. "Someone needs to be held accountable."

"That's just it. No matter what you do, the killer is going to get off. My advice is to bail out now before you cause yourself problems."

I frowned. "What kind of problems? I'm a civilian. What can anybody do to me?"

"Don't be too confident, Burt. Muller told me Gentry was plenty pissed over that confrontation with Major Wilson last night. Who knows what he'll do if he finds out you're still working the case."

"What are you saying? Did Gentry threaten me somehow?"

A head shake. "All I'm saying is he could cause you grief. You've worked with him. You know how he operates. He's a fucking spook, for chrissakes."

I felt oddly relieved by this statement. Not because I doubted what Ray was telling me, but because I now understood his comment about feeling responsible.

I said, "That's why you want me to back off? Because of what Gentry might do?"

He sighed, worry in his eyes. "I got you into this mess, Burt. Anything happens to you—"

"It won't. I can handle Gentry."

A resigned shrug. "Fine. Do it your way."

I smiled to let him know I appreciated his concern. "Do me a favor. Don't mention our intentions to pursue the case to anyone."

"I won't have to. You keep digging, the word will get out eventually."

"I know. But we need to buy some time."

"I'll have to tell General Muller."

Sammy gave me a slight head shake. "No one," I said.

Ray appeared uneasy, and I knew he was trying to figure out the ramifications if General Muller learned that Ray had kept him in the dark.

"It's important, Ray."

"All right. I'll keep quiet. But we never had this conversation."

"What conversation?"

A grudging nod. With a mock salute, he started down the hill. As Sammy and I watched him go, his head bent and his shoulders dropped. As if an enormous weight was bearing down on him.

"Ray didn't have anything to do with the murder," I said, anticipating an argument from Sammy.

"I agree."

I gazed at him suspiciously. "You believe he still wants the case solved?"

He nodded. "His concern for you also seemed real."

"And his alibi?" Because Ray's reluctance to volunteer one had given me doubts.

"No way. Only reason he came up with an alibi was because you pushed him. My guess is it will fall apart, once we begin digging." Noticing my puzzled expression, he went on, "What convinced me of his innocence was the same thing that probably convinced you. Ray's reaction when he talked about Soon-ri. He had a thing for her. Maybe even loved her. And that confuses me."

"Because he wouldn't tell us what he knows?"

"Not only that. From the beginning, I always thought the killer would turn out to be Soon-ri's boyfriend. The guy who knocked her up. Who else could it be? But now I'm thinking that guy might be Ray, and that surprises me. I'd never guessed Soon-ri would go for a guy like him."

"Like him?" Then I caught on. "You mean because he's black."

A cautious nod. "No offense, huh?"

"No." Sammy was only telling it like it was. Because of the Korean cultural bias against other races, particularly blacks, it was a bit unusual that someone as beautiful and popular as Soon-ri, who could have had her pick of most men, would have chosen Ray. Still, maybe . . . probably . . . her decision came down to money; the realization that Ray was her ticket out of the Ville.

Or maybe she actually loved him.

When I mentioned the latter possibility, Sammy immediately shot it down. The conviction in his voice irritated me. I told him he was wrong to dismiss the basis of their relationship because Ray happened to be black.

He shrugged. "You'd make the same conclusion if we were in the States. Korea is no different. Asian girl falling for a black man doesn't happen. Same thing the other way around. A black girl and an Asian guy."

"Sure it happens," I insisted.

"Not much."

"More often than you'd think. Race isn't as big a deal in America as it is in Korea." The moment I finished the sentence, I knew I'd touched a nerve.

Sammy's jaw muscles knotted. "Not as *big* a deal?"

Uh-oh. "Sammy, what I meant was—"

Too late. He cut me off angrily. "The hell it isn't a big deal, Burt. I watch CNN. What about those riots in Cleveland last year? The inner-city ghettos? How come everyone living in those is black or brown or yellow? How come *white* people don't live there?"

"Sammy . . ."

"Shit, man, race is what America is about. It's how the system works. Judges people. *Defines* people. Tell you what, let's talk about the goddamn American cops. The bastards who think it's no big deal when a black or Asian gets wasted . . ."

He was practically yelling in my face now. I'd never seen him this worked up. Out of the corner of my eye, I spotted a woman in a maid's uniform, watching us from the doorway of a nearby duplex. Two female majors in BDUs were also staring at us from the sidewalk. I said, "Sammy, hold it down—"

"*Fuck*, hold it down! You think Korea is *more* racist than America? I got news for you, buddy. I *know* what it's like in America. I *know* what it's like when a relative is killed and for no one to give a damn. I *know* what it's like when—"

"Sammy, *shut up!*"

His mouth hung open in shock. Almost instantly, the tension left his face, as if a switch had been turned off. He slowly closed his mouth and backed away from me.

Where did that come from? My eyes went to the maid, who noticed me looking and hurriedly shut the door. I tossed out a casual wave to the two officers, to let them know there wasn't a problem. I was relieved when they resumed their walk.

When I returned to Sammy, his breathing was deep and measured. In a stilted, formal voice, he said, "I am ashamed, Burt. My outburst was unprofessional and rude."

"Want to tell me about it?" I asked.

There was a long pause. He said guardedly, "I reacted without thinking. I thought you were . . . calling Korea a racist society."

Of course, I knew there had to be more. Sammy was someone who prided himself on keeping his cool. No way he'd have jumped down my throat because I'd said something insensitive. Nevertheless, I played along. "If I've offended you, that wasn't my intention. I'm sorry."

A curt nod. He shifted around to watch Ray, who was now halfway down the hill. I told Sammy I wanted to go to the base supply to check on whether the rope remnant matched anything in their stock.

"Let's wait a few minutes, Burt."

"Why?"

He shrugged.

So we kept standing there, gazing down at Ray and taking in the view. Spread out below us was the base's social center—the Officers' and NCO

Clubs, and the Base Exchange, gymnasium, and movie theater. Looking toward the runway, we could see the various command-and-control and intelligence installations, and the miscellaneous support facilities like billeting, finance, and personnel. Ray's destination, 7th Air Force HQ, was a rectangular two-story building situated on top of another smaller hill, roughly two miles away. As expected for this time of morning, the sidewalks teemed with mostly green-suited figures who were making their commute to work. To the west was the expanse of the golf course and the newly renovated clubhouse. I could just make out a couple of golfers walking up to the first tee. The first guy hooked his drive wildly into the trees and slammed his club to the ground. Temper, temper.

Turning to Sammy, I said casually, "I didn't know you'd lived in the States."

"Who says I did?"

"You did. You implied it."

A long pause. "It was a long time ago."

"And this relative who was killed—"

"A cousin. I really don't want to talk about it."

I sighed. This was turning into a morning of butting heads with friends. "Sammy, you know damn well I wasn't trying to knock Korea."

"Let's just drop it, Burt."

"No. This is a subject you obviously feel strongly about, and I want to clear the air." Sammy looked at me blandly. I continued, "For starters, I wasn't denying that America has racial problems—"

He made a derisive, sucking noise. "You better believe America has problems. Sure blacks and Asians and whites can live together. Get along. But only up to a point. For most people there are still boundaries. Racial lines they won't cross. Falling in love, maybe getting married and having a kid together. That's what people have trouble accepting. That's what *society* has trouble accepting. Korea, America, it doesn't matter."

"That's not true—"

"Come off it, Burt. Look what happened to you and Chung-hee. Her family didn't want her marrying a white guy, and your military friends thought you were crazy to marry a local girl. *That's* reality."

"Then reality is wrong."

"Sure it's wrong. All I'm saying is that's how the world works. Everyone's a little prejudiced. That's human nature. People have to have somebody they look down on. Soon-ri did. When she worked at the bar, she usually avoided the black and Mexican guys. Can you blame her? She never *saw* a black or Mexican before she went to the Ville."

"She obviously hooked up with Ray later."

"But not because she had feelings for him."

I resisted the impulse to respond. There were holes in his argument, but now wasn't the time to solve the world's racial problems.

Sammy watched me, shaking his head.

"What?" I said, annoyed.

"The look on your face. The fact that what I'm saying bothers you. You telling me you aren't even a little prejudiced?"

"I'm not."

"So you'd marry a black woman."

"Sure. If I loved her."

"And your parents wouldn't mind?"

I hesitated, caught off guard.

Sammy leaned in close, his voice low, insistent. "The truth, now."

"I'd like to think they wouldn't care either way."

His tongue clicked in satisfaction. "Ah, but you don't know. Or maybe you do. Even if they didn't say anything, you know they really wouldn't approve."

"I suppose not." I added, "They don't know many black people." Even to me, that excuse sounded lame.

"But you wouldn't call them racists."

"Of course not."

"Same thing with us Koreans. We're uncomfortable with other races because we have no history of living with them. For over four thousand years, we kept to ourselves. Our society developed in isolation. Westerners called us the Hermit Kingdom, and it was true. Up until the Korean war, most of us never dealt with a white man, much less a black or brown one. Acceptance . . . integration . . . takes time. Eventually, it will happen, but gradually. Look how difficult the process has been on you Americans, and you've been going at it for what, over a hundred years."

"We're making progress."

"So are we." He still sounded defensive.

We fell silent. I was relieved when Sammy seemed to lose interest in continuing the conversation, now that he'd made his point.

A door slammed shut. We watched the maid I'd seen earlier shoot us a couple of worried glances as she scurried over to another duplex. Sammy said, "Anyway, I was being straight with you about Ray. I don't see him as Soon-ri's killer." He gazed at me evenly. "But I got twenty bucks that says he was at her apartment shortly after she was murdered."

"The emergency phone call," I said, making the connection. "You figure Ray found Soon-ri's body? Called in the report?"

"It had to be him, Burt. In his bathroom, I noticed two toothbrushes in his holder. One green and one blue. Got me really curious when I realized they were both almost new." He gave me a knowing look.

A reference to Susan's theory that someone had removed a toothbrush from Soon-ri's bathroom. Still, I wondered how Ray had managed to get in and out of the apartment house in the middle of the day without being seen. I mentioned this.

"Sure he was seen. Maybe not by someone in the apartment building if he came up the back way, but by people on the street or someone who drove by. Last night we were in a tough position when it came to finding witnesses. We weren't allowed to put the word out that we were looking for an American."

I looked down at Sammy's right pants pocket, which bulged out under the hem of his jacket. "Want to tell me about that?"

For the third time in the past two minutes, he gazed down the hill. Ray was almost to the bottom, turning the corner. When he disappeared behind the retaining wall surrounding the Officers' Club, Sammy reached in his pocket and carefully withdrew his hand.

A familiar-looking gold picture frame glinted in the morning sun. The glass was intact, and there was no photograph inside.

I frowned. "What gives, Sammy? That looks like the frame from the picture of Soon-ri you showed me earlier."

"You're wrong, Burt. That one is in my briefcase in the car."

29

I insisted on being absolutely sure.

Sammy humored me by setting his briefcase on the hood of his car and popping the latches. He handed me a second picture frame, which I compared to the one he'd removed from Ray's trash can. They matched.

I passed them back, shaking my head. "Wonder why Ray took it? You'd think if he and Soon-ri were an item, he'd have pictures of her stashed away."

"Maybe Ray wanted one of Soon-ri as a child."

"Why?"

Silence. Sammy had turned and was staring toward Ray's duplex. At the front door with the busted lock.

That's when I realized why he'd wanted to hang around. I said, "Don't even think about it, Sammy."

But Sammy was already closing the briefcase. He tossed it in the backseat and shut the car door. "Wait here. I'll be back in a few minutes."

"No. You're talking about breaking and entering."

"You want to solve this case or not?"

"Of course, but—"

"Then we have to do this. If we find the picture, we might understand why Ray took it. And his financial records will tell us whether he bought out her contract."

"That's not the fucking point—"

"Hey, hey, relax, huh? Besides, we'd only be guilty of entering. You already took care of the breaking part." He grinned and took off toward the duplex.

I swore and glanced around. The surrounding sidewalks were empty, and the maid was nowhere to be seen. General Muller's staff car was also gone from his driveway.

As I hurried after Sammy, I tried to recall what the penalty was for a first-offense B & E charge. Not that Sammy would be the least bit concerned.

★ Ray's compulsive neatness and the fact that most of his belongings were in storage back in the States made the search go quickly. Sammy took the master bedroom while I concentrated on the smaller second room, which Ray used as a study. I immediately headed for the built-in bookshelves, where Ray kept his bulging photo album. As the neatly printed labels indicated, most of the family pictures inside were of his ex-wife Linda and his two boys, with a few shots of Ray's mother and sister thrown in. Notably absent were any pictures of his father.

One addition that surprised me was a glossy eight-by-ten of Ray and me in our mess dress uniforms, taken twelve years earlier, at his wedding reception. I'd been the best man and was at the dais toasting him. Something about love and friendship lasting forever. Hokey, I know, but that was the way I looked at life, back when I was young and naive and had more hair.

When I flipped to the last page, I came across a dozen or so pictures of a teenaged Ray sitting in a variety of small sailboats, sometimes alone or with a crew. To prepare him for his future as a naval officer, Ray's father had taught him to sail almost before he could walk. When Ray went to the Citadel, it was with the understanding that he would accept a commission in the Navy upon graduation. Instead, Ray, without telling his father, chose the Air Force. When his father showed up at Ray's commissioning ceremony, he took one look at Ray's blue uniform and walked out. That night, I remembered asking Ray if he hated his father.

I never got an answer.

I sighed and returned the album to the shelf, then went over to Ray's oversized rolltop desk—a standard-issue item for full colonels and above—where he kept his investment records and bank statements. The only problem was that the desk cover and drawers were locked, a point I found curious since Ray lived alone and didn't shell out for maid service. My second option was to check out the Quicken program on his laptop computer. I did a slow three-sixty. No computer, which meant it had to be at his office.

Moving on, I targeted the small closet, which contained Ray's luggage, formal and winter uniforms, civilian suits, and assorted sports equipment, including the Ping golf clubs he'd bought last year and never used. His spare gym bag was on the top shelf. Empty. Of course, he could have used something else to carry his personal items from Soon-ri's apartment or, knowing Ray, had already put everything away.

I was shutting the closet's clamshell doors when Sammy entered, saying he hadn't found anything. "Likewise," I grunted.

He said, "But you were right about the toilet rim. No stains."

Which was what I'd expected. A neat freak like Ray probably always wiped the rim when he missed. I said, "Odds are it was one of the killers who used the bathroom at Soon-ri's."

"Unless Ray was in a hurry." He was staring thoughtfully at Ray's desk.

"It's locked," I said.

He gave me a questioning look, which I met with a determined head shake. Busting into the desk was a line I wasn't about to cross. I said, "I'll tell Ray we know he took a picture from Soon-ri's."

"He'll deny it."

"We have the frame."

"So what? We can't prove it actually belonged to Soon-ri."

We went around this for a while. Finally, Sammy gave in with a frustrated grimace and walked out. As a Korean cop, he never had to worry about annoying little things like the Fourth Amendment.

We teamed up for a fruitless search of the living room and kitchen, then continued through the sliding glass door onto the back patio, where Ray's trash can was sitting. We waded through the contents using our latex gloves. No pictures of Soon-ri or anything else to suggest he knew her, but we did find three empty bourbon bottles.

Sammy picked one up by the neck, squinted at it in the sunlight, then gave it a sniff. "Strong stuff. I thought you said Ray wasn't much of a drinker."

I shrugged. "He didn't used to be— Where are you going?" Sammy was disappearing inside the house, gingerly carrying the bottle. I frowned as I trailed him into the kitchen. When I saw him remove a grocery bag from a drawer and carefully place the bottle inside, I finally realized what he had in mind.

★ As we left the duplex, I said, "There's something else I don't understand . . ."

Sammy gave me a sideways glance.

". . . the only reason for Ray to throw out the frame is because he thinks it might be incriminating. But that seems senseless since he kept the picture."

"How do you know he kept it?"

"Why take it in the first place if he was going to throw it away?"

Sammy's brow knitted. After a few steps, he tossed out, "Could be there's something in the photo he didn't want anyone to see."

"I've considered that. But what could be in a picture from Soon-ri's childhood— You got something?"

Sammy had stopped walking so suddenly, I'd gone past him. When I faced him, I caught a glimmer of excitement in his eyes.

"What?" I asked.

He focused on me, but his mind was elsewhere, thinking. "The picture. What if it wasn't like the others? What if it wasn't from Soon-ri's past?"

"Okay . . ." Then I saw where he was going. "Sure. Soon-ri and Ray. That has to be it. Ray took the picture because it showed them together."

"Actually, I'm considering another explanation, Burt."

I frowned.

Sammy spoke very rapidly, as if trying to keep up with his thoughts. "When you asked Ray if he knew who the killer was, he played it cute. Not really denying it. Now, maybe he was screwing with you and maybe not. But if he did know who the killer was, why not tell us?"

"He told us it was a Korean."

"How could he know that?"

I thought. "The obvious answer is Soon-ri. She could have told him about some old boyfriend who had threatened her. Someone who was jealous about her and Ray—" I grew annoyed at the way Sammy kept shaking his head. "Look, if there's something on your mind, spit it out."

"Your theory doesn't tell us why he wouldn't reveal the identity of the killer. And it doesn't give him a motive for removing the picture from Soon-ri's apartment."

"We just discussed this. If the picture shows Ray and Soon-ri together—"

"Ah. But what if it doesn't?"

I stared at him.

"You see, Burt, I think it's possible those two events are connected. The removal of the picture *and* why Ray won't tell us who the killer is. One explanation is that Ray is the murderer and took the picture because it could incriminate him. But neither of us thinks he killed her—"

"He didn't."

"So we go with a second explanation. That Ray took the photograph to protect someone else. Someone he thinks or knows is the killer."

I tensed in anticipation. “You know who that person is, don’t you?”

“I think so.”

“And . . .”

Sammy turned away from me, looking toward the house across the street. The large one with all the pretty flowers and the three-star placard planted in the front yard.

30

Sammy and I stood there, side by side, staring at General Muller's house. Overhead, the four-ship of F-16s returned, flew over the runway, then pitched out, one by one, rolling in for the landing.

When the engine noise died off, I calmly turned to Sammy. "You think General Muller was in the picture Ray took? That he was the one who had an affair with Soon-ri?"

"It's a possibility."

"And the phone calls to Ray's cell number?"

He studied me. "You notice how long the calls lasted? No? Most took only a few minutes. Some less than that. I'd wondered why such a short time. Now it makes sense that those calls were part of an arrangement. Ray could have been the middleman. When Soon-ri wanted to talk to the general, she called Ray to pass the word."

"What about Major Wilson's role? You think Soon-ri was seeing him and General Muller?"

He thought. "You said Major Wilson and General Muller are close—"

"Family friends."

"Then it fits. Major Wilson could also have been helping Muller keep the affair quiet."

"And the toothbrush? If it belongs to Muller, why would Ray have it in his bathroom?"

Sammy didn't have an answer. Like a lot of his investigative scenarios, he'd worry about the details later. Of course, one explanation could simply be that both toothbrushes were Ray's and that he'd already disposed of the one from Soon-ri's apartment. I said, "I still think you're wrong about General Muller."

Sammy shrugged.

I said, "You're forgetting that General Muller wanted me to continue the investigation."

"He *told* you he wanted you to continue, Burt. There's a difference."

I shrugged. He was right. All I had was Muller's word, supported by Ray. Still, I would have argued my position except that I recalled the angry scene last night between Muller and his wife. And of course Susan's earlier comments: *It's no secret Muller and his wife don't get along. Hell, maybe that's part of it. If he is screwing around, that would explain their marital problems.*

Plus there was another fact I couldn't ignore. The one I wrestled with last night in bed.

This was Korea, where it was common practice for rich and powerful men to have a public mistress whom they squired to social events while the wife stayed home with the kids. Possibly Muller was somehow influenced by this practice. Saw other ROK generals with mistresses and gave in to temptation, figuring he could get away with—"

"Burt . . ."

Sammy was looking at me. He said, "The knots tell us there were at least two killers . . ."

"Yes."

"I'm not accusing Ray. A man in Muller's position could easily enlist others to commit the murder . . ."

"Not easily."

"He's a general—"

"Not a *Korean* general. His authority isn't as absolute." Korean general officers wielded an almost godlike authority over their subordinates. One U.S. army officer I knew once witnessed an ROK general almost beat a soldier to death for falling asleep on guard duty. The chilling thing was that if the man had died, no one would have said a word.

Sammy's puzzled expression told me he didn't see the difference. To him, a general was a general. He continued, "What I have to know is whether Ray would protect General Muller?"

I took my time before responding. I looked toward the runway as another fighter roared into the sky. Beyond the antiaircraft-gun batteries lining the perimeter fence, I could see farmers slogging through the rice fields. There was a slight breeze and I thought I could detect the faint scent of manure, but maybe it was my imagination. The sun was already a third of the way above the horizon, and it was getting warm.

When I returned to Sammy, his cell phone began ringing. He made no move to answer it. He kept looking at me. Waiting.

"Ray might," I said quietly.

As I turned for the car, he finally answered his phone.

★ *It's who you know and who you blow.*

In a nutshell, that little ditty defined the military promotion system. To make rank, an ambitious junior officer needed a sponsor who could push his or her career. The higher the rank of the sponsor, the better. As the sponsor moved up the chain, the theory was that the junior officer would ride along on his coattails.

Ray had come to Korea specifically to latch onto General Muller. He knew if Muller got his fourth star, he'd be guaranteed at least one or two. Ray also knew the converse was true: If Muller fell from grace, especially from a scandal or worse, Ray would be damned by association and his own career would go right down the crapper.

Would Ray cover up a murder for General Muller?

He'd have no choice.

The realization was upsetting, and I tried not to dwell on it.

From the passenger seat, I watched as Sammy slowly approached the car, the cell phone to his ear. He leaned against the driver's door for another thirty seconds before ending the call. Climbing behind the wheel, he said, "That was Sergeant Ko. Soon-ri's family doesn't have a phone, so he drove out to Chun-ye this morning to interview them and inform them of Soon-ri's death."

Chun-ye was the village where Soon-ri had been raised. The place in the pictures. I said, "And . . ."

"Nothing. They couldn't think of anyone who might have wanted Soon-ri dead and had no idea she was pregnant." Eyeing me, he added, "Soon-ri's uncle also made it clear he didn't want the body."

Not surprising, considering how much the family despised her. I grunted. "Sounds to me like the uncle would be a good suspect."

Sammy started the engine, then fiddled with the air conditioner, which was blowing out hot air. "I don't see a farmer being able to cut out the fetus so cleanly."

"A lot of farmers have experience butchering animals. If he studied up—"

He looked at me.

"Hey," I said. "It's possible. I mean he hated Soon-ri, right?"

"The family all had alibis. They were working in the fields."

"I'll bet."

He sighed, still looking at me. "One question, Burt. Why would the family even care about removing the fetus? The uncle certainly wouldn't be the father."

"True, but—"

"Then there's the aunt . . ."

"Aunt?"

He returned to fiddling with the air conditioner. "Soon-ri's mother's sister. She is married to the uncle who treated Soon-ri and her mother badly.

Soon-ri told me her aunt often tried to protect her and her mother from her uncle's anger. Soon-ri said they were very close. That the aunt considered her almost a daughter."

Again I was struck that Soon-ri would confide all this to him. "So you think that if the uncle had been involved in the killing, the aunt would have told Sergeant Ko?"

"Or made an anonymous call to the police. Something." He held his hand over a vent, then nodded in satisfaction at the cold air.

I didn't see a rural Korean woman turning in her husband and told him so.

"For most things," he said, "you'd probably be right. But we're talking about the murder of her niece. For something that serious she would talk."

I frowned at the certainty in his voice. "How can you be so sure?"

He gave me a little smile. "I know how women like her think. To them family is everything. I was born in a small village not far from here. Spent a lot of years busting my ass in the rice fields." Noticing my surprised expression, he said, "You didn't know, huh?"

I shook my head. I'd always assumed he'd grown up in the city.

Sammy was about to pull out into the street when he got another call on his cell phone. He grimaced in annoyance as he answered it. He was speaking to another detective named Kwan. Sammy seemed to tense up. He kept repeating the phrase *hal-meo-ni*. I was curious about his interest in an old woman.

And then I remembered.

★ It had been right after I arrived at Soon-ri's apartment. As Susan and I were going up the back stairs, she'd mentioned that the Provincial cops who'd first responded had noticed a distraught old woman standing on the curb outside. Later, when they went down to interview her, the woman had disappeared.

Sammy punched off his call with a pensive look.

I said, "I take it the woman wasn't someone who lived or worked in the building?"

"Hmm. No. Detective Kwan interviewed the building's janitor and he didn't recognize her description. The woman's clothes were also very shabby. We think she might have been a beggar."

I eyed him. "Seems a little coincidental. Her being so upset right after the murder."

"I've considered that she might have seen something. But if so, why didn't she mention it to the police?"

"They *spoke* to her?"

"Briefly. When they first arrived. To make sure she was all right."

His description of the woman's clothing had triggered another possibility, which I mentioned.

Sammy smiled, eyes on a Humvee that was approaching. "Way ahead of you. I also wondered if the woman could have been someone from Soon-ri's family. Possibly even her aunt. That's why I had Detective Kwan check her description. The old woman was thin with gray hair. Soon-ri's aunt is stockier and she's got black hair."

"Okay," I said. "I guess we can rule out the family."

Sammy nodded. "The important thing now is to find out if our suspicions about General Muller and Soon-ri are correct." The Humvee rolled by, and he made a U-turn. "Where to now? Base supply?"

I checked my watch. Twenty to nine. We'd run out of time.

We drove to General Muller's office at 7th Air Force Headquarters.

★ As we rolled down the hill, I used Sammy's phone to call Susan's cellular. She was at her apartment. In the background, I heard women's voices, speaking Korean.

I said, "I take it everything went okay."

"Yeah," she said. "Didn't notice a tail. Only hiccup was the men who followed you were still hanging out by the main gate. They took a good look at us when we drove by. They know what Chung-hee looks like?"

"They might."

"Could be they recognized her, then."

"Doesn't matter. They can't touch her on base." I hesitated. "I appreciate this, Susan."

"Hey, the more the merrier. Be like the slumber party I never had as a kid."

I smiled at the image. "How's Mi-nah holding up?"

"Better. Poor thing's been in kind of a shell, but seems to be opening up now, talking to Chung-hee."

Sammy braked behind a line of cars at the intersection past the O-Club. A security cop was blocking traffic so a slow-moving convoy of trucks could cross. Sammy kicked back in his seat and yawned. I asked Susan if she'd contacted her friend at the bank.

"Jenny Swanson? Yeah. Last night. Didn't take much convincing for her to go along. She still thinks like a cop. The way I figure it, whoever shelled out the bucks for Soon-ri must have had the money transferred to his base bank account, but probably not in one lump sum. I told Jenny we were interested in anyone who made large deposits or withdrawals of more than five grand. Jenny's also going to check out the accounts of Major Wilson and Colonel Johnson."

"When will she have the information?"

"Pretty soon. Jenny was hot to get started. She's already at the bank running a computer search of the records. She'll call me when she's finished."

"Better tell her to add another account—"

"Whose?"

"General Muller's."

A pause. "I'll be . . . You mean I was right about him?"

"Maybe." I outlined Sammy's theory about Muller, then told her about the picture frame we'd found at Ray's. By the time I finished, the convoy had passed by and we were moving. I told Susan to bring Ray's shotgun to the meeting with Muller.

"I take it Colonel Johnson had no intention of killing himself?"

"No. The gun was for General Muller. He's shooting later today."

"So I was right *twice?*"

I sighed. "Yeah. And I was wrong . . . twice."

She laughed. "Want me get off the line and put your wife on?"

"Please."

"Hang on."

★ When Chung-hee came to the phone, her voice was understandably subdued. I said gently, "Honey, I know this has been stressful. It shouldn't be more than a day or two before—"

"That's not my concern, Burt. I've been talking with Mi-nah. She showed me the scars. That Chun could do something so horrible . . ."

"Don't think about him. You'll only get more upset."

"How can I *not* think about him? How can I *ever* forget?"

I was silent. There was nothing I could say.

Someone called out Chung-hee's name. She turned away from the phone, speaking Korean. When she returned to me, she said, "Mi-nah is scared, Burt. She just asked my mother what's going to happen to her now."

"I don't know. I assumed she'd probably want to return to her home."

The sudden shrillness in Chung-hee's voice caught me by surprise. "That's just *it*. She *can't*. She's terrified of her father. He's the one who forced her to work in the bars and made her send him money. She says he'll only throw her out."

I heard her breathing into the phone. Waiting for my response.

Frankly, I was puzzled by her reaction. Chung-hee had grown up around the Ville's sex trade. Knew how it worked and the kind of life the women led. Maybe not the beatings, but the rest of it. Then it occurred to me that

Chung-hee had probably never really gotten to know any of the bar girls. Not that she consciously avoided them, but as the daughter of a successful businessman, she lived in a privileged world they could only dream about. Anyway, maybe that was it. Maybe Chung-hee now saw Mi-nah as a real person.

We were on the north side of the base, working our way west. I pointed out the 7th Air Force Headquarters building to Sammy, and he made a left up the hill. To Chung-hee, I said, "I've got to go, honey. Try not to worry Mi-nah. We'll help her get back on her feet."

"But what can we do, Burt? We're leaving Korea in a few weeks."

"We'll think of something. I promise."

As I ended the call, I knew Chung-hee thought I was only telling her what she wanted to hear. And I suppose I was. Our options to assist Mi-nah were limited. She was a girl with no training, skills, or education. In my heart, I knew that once she was left on her own, she would invariably be sucked back into the life of the bars. A dismal prospect, but that was how these situations usually played out. The truth was girls like Mi-nah and Soon-ri had no future and never did.

When I gave him his phone, Sammy read my face and said softly, "*Sseul-mo-eom-neun nyeon.*"

I gave him a blank look.

"Throwaway girl." He smiled sadly. "You had it all wrong, Burt. Korea's problem isn't racism. It's the way we treat women."

We continued up the hill in silence.

31

When we rolled into a visitors' slot at the front of the 7th AF Headquarters Building, I noticed Roger Gentry and his no-necked sidekick, Fred, hurrying up the sidewalk toward the chrome-and-glass entrance. When I pointed them out, Sammy appeared puzzled by their appearance. I told him that Gentry probably wanted to ensure that I was out of the picture before allowing Major Wilson or the Security Police dispatcher, Airman Collins, to return.

"I understand that, Burt," Sammy said. "I'm wondering why he's bothering to show up at all. Drive down from Seoul. It's not necessary. The case is finished, and you're about to be removed."

"Gentry's a cautious guy and—" Then it clicked what he was driving at. "Sure. Gentry must know that the chauffeur Yee wasn't the real killer. That's why he wants to make sure I drop the investigation."

Sammy nodded.

"The killer," I said, following the thread. "Hell, Gentry might even know who it is."

"Or at least suspect." And he looked at me in a meaningful way.

I nodded. Another affirmation that the killer was someone from the base.

As I reached for the door, I was curious when Sammy suddenly killed the engine. "You're coming in?"

"No. Figure I'll keep you company. Wait for Susan." He pointed to the clock on the dash. "Still got twelve minutes."

I told him I didn't want to be late.

He reclined his seat. "Relax, Burt. Hang out for a few minutes. Take a breather."

He obviously had some reason for wanting me to stay. I eased back, waiting for him to tell me why. Instead, Sammy cracked his door for some air and began drumming on the dashboard with a finger. After a few moments, I said, "So what are you going to do now?"

The drumming stopped. "We need evidence. I'm going to Dr. Yee's office, wait for the test results." He paused, then added, "And I want to send a few men around Soon-ri's neighborhood, see if they can get a lead on the old woman."

Meaning he hadn't totally discounted the possibility that she'd seen something.

From his jacket, he removed a glassine packet. When he held it up to me, I saw it contained an intact knot that had been cut from Soon-ri's bindings.

"This," he said gloomily, "is driving me crazy. Why were the knots so complicated? Why only use *one* square knot?" He looked at me.

"It's puzzling," I admitted. Logically, it made sense that one person would have tied Soon-ri down while the other guy or guys restrained her. Unless they'd switched places, all the knots should have been the same. And if a second person had tied the square knot, why didn't he do more than the one on her right hand—

A suggestive cough. Sammy offered his cell phone to me. "Maybe you should call someone at base supply. Tell them I'll be dropping off the rope."

"You want to go there now?"

"The sooner, the better."

I understood his concern. Once Susan and I were off the case, we'd have no official sanction to investigate, thereby making further inquiries difficult.

So I called Chief Master Sergeant Lucille Ritter, the 51st Supply Squadron noncommissioned officer in charge. Chief Ritter was tough, smart, and, as the ranking enlisted person, had the authority to get me an answer fast. Besides, Ritter owed me a few favors. During her watch, I'd personally solved two cases of theft from the supply warehouse.

"Tell your friend I'll be outside in fifteen minutes," Chief Ritter said cheerfully, after I told her what I wanted.

I passed on Susan's cellular number and told Chief Ritter to call when she had something. Handing Sammy his cell phone, I relayed Ritter's message, then pointed him to the four-story supply warehouse, which was visible along the flight-line road.

Sammy nodded, pocketing his phone. "We'll identify the knot and rope pretty soon. Sergeant Ko is driving to Seoul to check with our forensics people." He gave me a tired smile. "How about you ask General Muller whether he was a Boy Scout?"

He was joking, since we knew Muller probably wasn't one of the actual killers. I glanced at the grocery bag containing the bourbon bottle, which was sitting on the backseat. "When will you get the results from that?" Sammy had taken the bottle because it had Ray's fingerprints, which he intended to compare with ones lifted from Soon-ri's apartment.

"Not long. Maybe an hour."

"Call Susan if you get a match."

He nodded. "Be nice if we had a sample of General Muller's prints and blood type. Major Wilson's, too."

"I can check with the hospital—" Sammy shook me off. I went on, "I agree. That would send up too many red flags." I considered a few possibilities, then said, "I'll see what I can come up with. I'll also try to find out where General Muller was during the murder."

"He'll have an alibi."

"Probably."

Sammy kept throwing me glances like he was still bugged about something. When he still didn't say anything, I told him I needed to get going.

As I opened the passenger door, he said, "Burt, about the reason I lost my cool earlier . . ."

I looked over. "What about it?"

He hesitated. "I didn't tell you the truth. Not all of it. It wasn't really what you said. Your comment about Koreans being racist."

"Forget it, Sammy. You don't owe me an explanation—"

He held up a hand. "Please, Burt. I . . . I need to do this."

As he spoke, I was struck by the emotion in his voice and the quiet pain in his eyes. That's when I knew.

I sat back, waiting for him to tell me about his cousin's murder.

★ Sammy spoke slowly, pausing often as if reliving the memory was difficult for him.

"When I was a kid, I spent a few years in the States. My cousin sent for me, needed someone to help him. He had a small grocery store in New York City. An Asian market on Canal Street, in Chinatown. My cousin got tired of paying protection to the Tongs . . . the Chinese gangs. He got this crazy idea . . . this plan . . . to organize the Asian business owners. He figured if everyone stopped paying protection, the Tongs would have to back off. He knew what he was doing was dangerous, but he . . . he was just tired of it. Figured someone had to take a stand. And for a while . . . the first few months . . . he seemed to be making progress. Got a couple of hundred people to sign up. Quit paying. There was this big meeting with the Tongs . . . to tell them how things were. My cousin made the pitch. The Tongs . . . their leader . . . a guy named Chen . . . never said a word. Never made any threats. And I think that was part of it. The success of the meeting made my cousin . . . made *everyone* think, you know, that everything would be okay."

Sammy paused to lower his window and dig out a cigarette. His hand shook slightly as he lit it. "It was a Saturday. I was working the register, and a guy came into the store. Looking for my cousin. He said he wanted to discuss some business. An older guy. He had on a nice suit, a gray pinstripe number. Shiny black briefcase and a gold Rolex. Classy, you know. So I thought he was okay. I mean he *looked* okay. I . . . I told him my cousin was in the storeroom. A few minutes later . . . maybe five minutes . . . the guy left. The store was so busy that I never had a chance to . . . I should have . . . But it never occurred to me . . ."

Sammy drifted off, watching the smoke curl from the end of his cigarette. For only a few seconds, but it seemed longer. He began speaking again. "I went back into the storeroom about an hour later. That's when I found my cousin. At his desk. Dead. A head shot. Blood on the walls. I . . . I never heard a thing. He was only twenty-seven. Growing up, he used to send me money, help me out."

Sammy took a drag and looked out the window. His upper lip quivered. I said, "It wasn't your fault."

Sammy didn't respond. He just sat there, smoking quietly. I didn't try to say anything more. Finally, he asked me, "You know what the police did?"

I shook my head, even though he wasn't looking my way.

"Not a fucking thing. Two detectives showed up. For maybe a couple of days, they went around the neighborhood, asking questions. That's it. They wrote it off as another gang killing. Asian killing Asian. They said they couldn't find any leads. People were too scared. Nobody would talk. They said that's usually the way it was with Tong murders and they were sorry. *Sorry.*" His voice turned bitter. "Such bullshit. The real reason was the cops had another case to worry about. A case people cared about. A girl was murdered in Central Park the same day." He looked right at me. "A pretty *white* girl."

I didn't know what to say. "I'm sorry."

"Yeah . . ." He sucked hard on the cigarette. "Like I told you, that's how the world works. Equality is all crap. Some people aren't considered important. My cousin wasn't important."

"How old were you?"

"Fifteen, sixteen."

"They never caught your cousin's killer?"

A single head shake.

I said softly, "I'm surprised you don't resent Americans."

He shrugged. "Why? The system in America is no different than Korea. Some people matter and others don't. Fact of fucking life." He looked over. "Besides, I've done that same thing."

My eyebrows went up.

"It's true. That bar girl who was run over last year. In front of the Golden Dragon Night Club. You remember?"

I nodded. It had been a big story locally. "The hit-and-run."

"I found the car. Belonged to a Japanese businessman named Minori. Rich guy with plenty of connections who was looking to invest big bucks in Korea. Before I could make the arrest, I was ordered to close the case. Walk away. So . . . I did." He shook his head. "Koreans protecting a Japanese. Crazy fucking world." Like most of his countrymen, Sammy still resented the Japanese for their brutal, forty-year occupation of Korea.

We sat without speaking until he finished his cigarette. People walked by the car, giving us curious looks. One major I knew flashed an uncertain smile, which I acknowledged with a nod. As Sammy crushed out the cigarette in the ashtray, he said, "Anyway, I thought you should know."

"Thank you for telling me."

"Sure."

After I got out of the car, I looked down on him. "I think Soon-ri was important."

He seemed to smile.

Watching Sammy drive away, I realized I finally understood him. Why he'd become a cop, his determination to solve Soon-ri's murder. All of it. My concern now was whether he'd blame himself if Soon-ri's killer wasn't found. I hoped not.

Going up the steps, I checked my watch. A minute until the meeting, and no Susan.

I was almost to the entrance when I heard the squeal of tires behind me.

32

More squealing brakes and screeching rubber as the Chrysler Sebring swerved wildly into a parking space. In a flash, Susan was out of the car and jogging towards me, a leather fanny pack and paper sack in one hand, the shotgun in the other. A burly senior master sergeant who'd just emerged from the building took one look at her and did a head-snapping double take. I knew he wasn't reacting to the gun.

Susan's normally conservative dress hadn't done her figure justice. She was wearing a white silk blouse that clung to her curves and flowed seamlessly over her hips into dark slacks. With each step, her breasts bounced provocatively as if straining to break free. The sergeant couldn't take his eyes off her, and I was having trouble myself.

She came up to me panting slightly. She had on more makeup than usual and smelled of perfume. The sergeant was still staring at her. I shot him a look of annoyance. He flashed a loopy grin and hurried down the steps.

"Susan," I said, trying not to lower my eyes below hers. "What the hell were you thinking? We're meeting with General Muller."

She batted her eyes innocently. "What do you mean?"

"Your clothes."

"What about them? They're within regulations."

"It's your . . . blouse."

"My blouse?"

For the love of— "You want me to come right out and say it?"

"Say what?" But she was smiling now.

I let it go. She was screwing with me, and it wasn't like there was time for her to change.

She handed me the shotgun and the paper sack, which contained the box of shells. When I stepped around to open the door, she said, "I guess Sammy took off, huh?" She sounded disappointed.

I chewed my tongue to keep from responding.

As we went inside, she said coyly, "So you want to know why I'm late?"

"Putting on makeup?"

A chilly stare. She stopped at the staircase, cinched on her fanny pack, then unzipped it and removed a folded paper. "I was waiting for a fax from Jenny."

Her friend at the bank. Susan unfolded the page and passed it over.

A list of bank deposits and withdrawals over the previous two months. The withdrawals totaled well over ninety grand. My body tingled as I stared at the name on the account. Suspicion was one thing, but seeing the name in black and white—

"Looks like Sammy was right," she said.

I nodded and pocketed the page. "Nothing unusual on the other two accounts?"

Susan shook her head. "Except that Major Wilson is broke. His account never showed more than five hundred dollars."

We hurried up the steps.

★ The office of the commanding general for 7th Air Force took up almost a third of the second floor. Susan and I hustled down the hallway and pushed through the heavy oak door close to two minutes late. The anteroom was large and plush, the paneled walls lined with somber-faced paintings of the twenty-plus previous 7th AF commanders. As the executive officer, Ray's desk was situated within yards of the entryway, so he could play gatekeeper for the general. At the moment it was empty, which meant Ray was probably in the meeting. As Susan and I went over to drop off the shotgun and the paper sack containing the box of shells, a harried voice said, "Thank God you're here, Burt . . ."

I pivoted toward the matronly woman sitting at a corner desk by the window, a petite female second lieutenant standing before her with an armful of files. Instead of her usual welcoming smile, Penelope Diaz, General Muller's civilian secretary, was gazing at me anxiously. Snaring her phone, she said, "Colonel Johnson said to leave the gun on the desk. The general's been calling for you. I'll let him know you're here."

She hung up seconds later and gestured down the hallway to our left. "Everyone's in the conference room. I'd better warn you, he's in one of his moods."

"That bad, huh?" I said.

She made a face. "In twenty years, I've worked for nine generals and three admirals, and he's the worst. Always on the rag. One of these days, I swear I'm going to spike the man's coffee with Midol." She said it without a smile, but the lieutenant giggled.

I grinned. I'd always liked Penelope. "Oh, one question, Pen. Yesterday Colonel Johnson and I got our wires crossed. I tried to phone yesterday for a late lunch. Around one-thirty. I was told he wasn't in, but he says he was."

"You know whom you talked to?" Penelope asked.

I shook my head. "It was a woman."

She looked at the butter-bar second lieutenant. The butter-bar shook her head.

"Wait," Penelope said, sitting back with a frown. "You sure it wasn't a little later, Burt? Closer to two?"

"Might have been."

"That was probably it. Colonel Johnson was in the conference room, working on a briefing. I dropped by to have him sign some papers, but he'd stepped out for a while."

I could have asked how long Ray was gone, but that would be pushing Penelope's curiosity button. And I wasn't about to question her about General Muller. "Thanks, Pen."

★ Susan and I headed down the carpeted hallway. More paintings on the walls, this time depicting the various military aircraft that had been based at Osan since the Korean war. Glancing over at me, Susan said softly, "So Colonel Johnson doesn't have an alibi?"

"Doesn't look like it."

Two steps later, I said, "Don't mention the bank statement yet."

She nodded.

We passed by General Muller's private office and were approaching the double doors of the conference room at the far end. "Who is everyone, anyway?" Susan asked.

She was referring to Penelope's comment. "Roger Gentry and his partner are here."

"Ooh, the CIA. Lucky us."

As we arrived at the doors, we could hear angry voices emanating from within. I listened, but the words were too garbled to make out. I thought I heard my name.

"Wonder what they're pissed off about now?" Susan said. "The case is finished. You'd think they'd be happy."

"You'd think." I rapped on the door. "Try not to take any deep breaths, Susan."

"I get it. Ha ha."

The voices inside went mute. I knocked once more, and someone hollered to come in. It sounded like General Muller.

Susan and I had gone maybe two steps inside the conference room when I pulled up short. Behind me, I heard Susan inhale sharply. She wasn't jerking my chain over my earlier comment, but was reacting to the presence of two uniformed figures in the room.

What the hell are they doing here? I wondered.

★ The briefing room was silent.

From the gleaming conference table, ten pairs of eyes stared at Susan and me. General Muller was seated at the head of the table. To his left were Roger Gentry, his partner, Fred, and a pudgy, red-haired man in a gray suit whom I didn't recognize. As usual, Ray was sitting to Muller's immediate right.

At the moment, my attention was focused toward the back wall, where two muscular Security Policemen were standing ominously. Both were young staff sergeants and could have been twins. The taller of the two, Sergeant Riley, I'd spoken with a few times. He met my gaze without a flicker of recognition. Not good.

For an instant, I thought that my illegal search of Ray's quarters had been discovered. But how? No one saw Sammy and me enter his house. And even if someone did, he couldn't know we were acting illegally—

General Muller cleared his throat. Like last night, he was dressed to the nines in his class-A service coat with three shiny stars on each shoulder and a nest of pretty medals on his chest. Unlike last night, his face was locked in an ominous scowl, looking nothing like the man who'd confessed to me his closest secret. Now my pucker meter went way up. I tried to read him, hoping to figure out how much trouble I was in.

He flashed a tight smile. "Thank you both for coming."

Susan and I nodded warily. I glanced at Ray, who was sliding an opened binder in front of Muller. Across from him, Roger Gentry and Fred No Neck were gazing at us without expression. That was rule number one in the CIA. Never tip your hand. Beside them, the red-haired man appraised us with a sour expression.

General Muller flicked a hand toward two chairs, which were side by side at the opposite end of the table. "Have a seat, Burt. You, too, Lieutenant."

Susan and I eased over and sat down, peering back at the faces. I felt like a condemned man about to face a trial where the outcome had been decided. Now, what was my crime?

Muller's head swiveled to the right. "I think you know agents Gentry and Markle . . ."

Roger gave me a nod. Fred broke his CIA training with an arrogant grin.

". . . and this is Mr. David Olsen from the American Embassy."

The red-haired man bent forward to look at Susan and me. He was pushing fifty, with a pudgy face, and at least two more chins than he had been born with. He fixed us with a superior gaze and settled back.

Muller's eyes shifted to the two security cops. He gave them a barely perceptible nod. They wordlessly marched to the door and left. Susan gave me a knowing look, which I understood. At the very least, the SPs had been here to crank up the intimidation factor.

As the door clicked shut, Muller said, "I asked you both here to pass on my appreciation for your assistance in solving the murder. You should be commended. You helped prevent what could have been a politically unviable situation."

"Thank you, sir," I said. Susan nodded, but said nothing.

"But," Muller continued, focusing on me, "I have to tell you that I'm quite concerned over a rumor I've recently heard. I understand that you have misgivings over the guilt of the alleged killer. This chauffeur, Mr. . . ." His eyes flicked to the binder. ". . . Mr. Su. Frankly, I don't understand why you would persist in pursuing the case since . . ."

Concerned over a rumor? Misgivings over the guilt? I felt like I'd been kicked in the stomach. Muller kept talking, but all I could think about was the source of the rumor. The person who had told Muller that I was still investigating the case. I'll keep quiet, he'd said.

When I looked at Ray, his eyes were locked straight ahead. Ignoring me.

My teeth clenched. It was more than the sense of betrayal that pissed me off. It was the fact that I'd fallen for Ray's phony line about being concerned about my welfare. By now I should have realized that the only person Ray gave a damn about was himself—

Susan nudged me sharply in the ribs. I became aware of a silence in the room. Muller was glaring at me. So was everyone else. Except, of course, Ray.

"What the hell is the matter with you, Burt?" Muller demanded.

I blinked. "Sir?"

"I asked you a question. Do you believe that this chauffeur killed the bar girl?"

An outright denial was out because of Ray. I began, "Sir, I think the evidence as to his guilt is questionable—"

"He confessed."

"I'm aware of that, sir, but—"

Muller talked over me. "Can you tell me *who* really murdered the girl?"

"No, sir."

"Surely, you must have your suspicions."

"Yes, sir."

"And . . ."

"I think it's someone from the base."

"Who?"

"I'd rather not say."

Tiny veins appeared above his temples. His voice was like ice. "*Who is it!*"

I gazed back, saying nothing.

Gentry edge forward in his chair and cleared his throat. "General, if I may . . ."

Muller fired him a hard look, irritated by the interruption.

But Gentry was already swinging his eyes to me. When he spoke, his manner was relaxed, friendly. "C'mon, Burt. You're not being smart about this. We're all on the same side. What's the harm in telling us who your suspect is?"

Our eyes met. Gentry squeaked out his plastic smile. I ignored it and returned to General Muller, who was now staring intently at Susan. No mystery what he was thinking.

"So," Gentry said, "how about it, Burt? Tell us the name."

I took a deep breath. Let it out. Seconds passed. No one spoke. They were all waiting for my response.

I finally looked at Gentry and shook my head.

Gentry swore and almost came out of his chair. Fred glowered at me in disgust while the embassy man, Olsen, muttered under his breath. My eyes went to Ray. He continued to sit like a mannequin, eyes fixed straight ahead.

"What the fuck are you trying to pull, Burt?" Gentry said, his voice thick. "You're working for us on this case. We have a right to know who the hell you think murdered that—"

He stopped when Muller leaned over to him and whispered in his ear. Gentry listened, nodded, and eased back.

General Muller focused on Susan. "Lieutenant, I'm giving you an order. I want to know the name of your suspect."

Susan hesitated.

I said, "She doesn't know, General."

Muller eyed me coldly. "One more interruption, and you will be removed from this room. I'm waiting, Lieutenant . . ." He was looking at Susan again.

Susan's voice was quiet, almost a whisper. "I don't know, sir."

Muller appeared stunned, as did the other faces in the room. A defiant former major with a bad attitude was one thing, but lieutenants didn't disobey orders from general officers.

"*Goddamnit*, Lieutenant!" Muller exploded, "I gave you a direct order. Now, unless you want to find yourself court-martialed, I suggest you *tell me the fucking name*."

Susan was silent, her face retreating into a defensive mask. But glancing at her, I saw the fear in her eyes. She knew she was playing a game she could only lose. While I admired her resolve, I realized any further resistance was pointless. If the bastard wanted to know, I was going to give it to him.

By now, Muller was shouting for the SPs. An instant later, Sergeant Riley and his clone popped through the door. Gesturing at Susan, Muller ordered, "I want you to arrest Lieutenant Torres on a charge of disobeying a direct—"

I jumped in then. "You win, General. Call off the dogs."

His hand froze in midair as he appraised me warily. For the first time, I realized Ray was also looking my way. "The name?" Muller breathed.

"You're not going to like it, sir."

"Dammit, Burt—"

"You're the prime suspect, General."

Muller's jaw dropped and stayed there. The room fell into a stunned silence. An instant later, the protests of indignation erupted.

"He's crazy."

"You son of a bitch, Burt."

"He's lying, General. He doesn't know what he's talking about."

Among the belligerent faces and gesturing arms, Ray continued to sit quietly. At my statement, he hadn't even batted an eye, which meant he already knew.

I rose to my feet. "Let's go, Susan."

33

Susan remained seated and looked up at me like I was crazy to try and leave. Maybe I was, but I wasn't about to hang around for another grill-and-intimidation session. I also wanted to get her alone. Talk to her.

Grabbing her by the arm, I pulled her upright and hustled her toward the door. The SPs eyed us with uncertainty as we brushed past them into the hallway.

Then came Gentry's voice, shouting for us to stop. Muller joined in the chorus, an octave higher.

Susan said nervously, "Uh, Burt . . ."

I tilted my head toward her and picked up the pace. More shouts. I spoke rapidly, keeping my voice low. "Listen up. You've got to go into damage control. Think about your career. Whatever happens, you stick to your story that you weren't aware of my suspicions of Muller. You also don't know anything about Ray's role. You were only following my orders—"

"They'll know I'm lying."

"So what? They won't be able to prove a damn thing."

We were almost to the front office. From her desk, Penelope watched our approach with a mixture of alarm and confusion. I threw her a grim smile and yanked open the door. Behind us came the sound of rapid footsteps.

"Stop, Major!"

Susan and I froze, looking back.

The two Security cops were nervously pointing pistols at us. I gave Sergeant Riley a big smile and nodded toward his weapon. "Your safety's still on, Sergeant."

Sergeant Riley glanced down, his face reddening. His partner rolled his eyes and motioned with his gun.

Susan and I stepped away from the door.

Shit.

★ Divide and conquer.

That's the approach Gentry and General Muller settled upon when the questioning resumed. While Susan was hustled off to the briefing room, I was deposited in the tiny copier room next door. I took out the fax of General Muller's bank account and studied it. Most of the money, almost eighty thousand, had been withdrawn two months earlier, within a span of a few days—the payment to Chun. A week later, another five thousand dollars—the cost of setting up Soon-ri in the apartment. Since then, between a thousand to fifteen hundred dollars had been taken out every ten days to two weeks. In addition to the withdrawals, the only other thing worth noting was that the account was in Muller's name only, which made sense since he didn't want his wife to know he'd probably cashed in their savings and investments.

To be safe, I made five copies and tucked them in various file cabinets, mostly in folders filled with rarely used forms. I also ripped out a half dozen pages from my notepad and lined them inside my shoes. The big question was what to do with my pistol. Hiding it seemed out of the question, since it would probably be discovered long before I ever had a chance to retrieve it. Besides, if they found it on me, so what? My fate was already decided.

For the next twenty minutes, I watched the walls until Sergeant Riley poked his head inside and beckoned me into the hallway.

I exited just as Susan was emerging from the conference room, accompanied by Ray. He wouldn't make eye contact, which meant I wasted the fuck-you look I gave him. As Susan walked by, she responded to my raised eyebrows with a slight nod, letting me know she'd stuck to her story of being kept in the dark. Frankly, I was relieved. Considering Susan's ego, I wasn't sure she could pull off the yes-sir, yes-sir, three-bags-full, sir, dumb-lieutenant routine.

There were three people remaining in the conference room when I entered: General Muller, Roger Gentry, and Fred Markle. I was again pointed toward the chairs at the end of the table.

The moment I sat down, Gentry launched into me, demanding to know why I suspected Muller of the killing.

"No comment," I said.

His thin face pinched in a glare. "You have any evidence linking him to the crime?"

"No comment."

"Witnesses, fingerprints. Anything?"

"No comment."

"Fucking smart-ass," Markle grunted, proving he could string at least two words together.

Gentry joined in with another withering gaze. "You don't have any damned evidence, do you?"

I tried to think of how to say "no comment" in Korean. Couldn't. "No comment."

Gentry took a deep breath, working to keep his cool. "You going to say anything but no comment?"

"No comment." And I gave him a smile.

"You think this is funny, asshole?" Gentry shot back. "Well, keep screwing with me and you'll buy yourself more trouble than you can handle."

I kept my face neutral, but his threat was unsettling. Earlier, I'd dismissed Ray's concerns over what Gentry might do because the guy was a rarity, a spook who usually played within the rules. Still, if I pissed him off enough—"

Gentry abruptly turned to General Muller. "We're wasting our time with him, sir. He hasn't got any evidence. He's guessing. Trying to make a case when there isn't any."

"He can still make accusations," Muller said.

"You told me he has a grudge against you—"

"Yes. I recommended he be passed over for promotion."

"Fine. Then even if he shoots off his mouth, you can put out the word that he's a disgruntled former officer. Shouldn't be a problem."

As I listened to their discussion, I was reminded of Sammy's hunch about Gentry. That he knew or suspected who the killer was. To stir things up, I said, "Ask him, Roger."

Gentry blinked, surprised I'd spoken.

"Go on," I said. "Ask the general if he knew the victim."

Muller snarled, "Why, you slanderous son of a bitch. You say that again and I'll sue you for everything—"

"I know about the ninety grand, General."

Muller froze. The blood drained from his face, and something flickered in his eyes. Not fear exactly, but close. He sagged back in his chair.

Gentry turned on me, gripping the edge of the table so hard I thought he might break it. "Get it through your fucking head. The case is *over*. Your investigation is *over*. End of story. You repeat a word of this to anyone . . . the press . . . a politician . . . the fucking man on the moon, so help me, I'll bury you."

Looking in his eyes, I knew he probably would. Maybe I should have been worried, but all I could think about was an omission in his tirade. The fact that he hadn't asked what I *meant* by the ninety grand.

Thinking back, it made sense that Gentry must have been aware of General Muller's and Soon-ri's relationship from the beginning. More than anything, that singular fact explained the Chicken Little response by the American and Korean governments and the extent of the cover-up. If an enlisted man or a junior officer had been linked to the killing, the subsequent political firestorm might have been survivable. But if the murderer was a three-star general—

A phone buzzed. Muller's hand shook slightly as he picked up an extension that was recessed into the tabletop. He listened, then said, "Tell Ambassador Gregson I'll call him in five minutes." He glanced at Gentry as he hung up.

Taking the hint, Gentry said, "I'm done, sir." He gave me a hard look. "I'm through screwing with you, Burt. You understand what I'm telling you? I don't want any more problems." Markle put on his tough-guy face and nodded along.

I was tempted to tell them both to go to hell, but knew that would be stupid. I nodded.

Generally Muller eased forward, gazing at me. "You're wrong about me, Burt," he said quietly.

I shrugged.

He continued, "You will be escorted off base. If you try to gain entry, you will be arrested. I have ordered Lieutenant Torres not to have any further contact with you. If she does, I will have her court-martialed. And if that Korean police lieutenant . . ." He looked at Gentry.

"Lieutenant Son-yon Sam," Gentry said.

". . . and if Lieutenant Sam persists in his investigation, I'll call the Provincial police chief and have him demoted and reassigned. Sergeant!"

The door opened and the SPs reentered, immediately coming toward me.

"Cuff him, first," Muller ordered.

Prick.

34

The opening scene of the sixties TV show *Branded*, starring Chuck Connors.

That's what my departure from the building reminded me of, except without the music and no one tore the buttons off my jacket or broke a saber.

Thanks to my earlier incident with the SPs, the building's grapevine had obviously spread the word that the ex-chief of the OSI was in trouble. When I was paraded though the hallway with my hands cuffed behind my back, at least thirty people poked their heads out of offices to watch. Roughly a quarter I knew and another quarter I recognized, which heightened the embarrassment. I didn't see either Susan or Ray, and once outside, I noticed Susan's car was gone.

The cops placed me in the back of a Security Police cruiser. Sergeant Riley got in the passenger seat and his buddy drove. They never said a word to me. As we headed toward the gate, Gentry and Markle followed in their sedan. They weren't taking any chances; they wanted to be sure I was deposited out of the promised land with no way to get back in.

I settled in the seat and tried to figure out my next move. Whether I even had one.

General Muller was Soon-ri's sugar daddy and almost certainly the father of her child. While that gave him a helluva motive for murder, it didn't prove guilt. For that we needed evidence that would be almost impossible to gather with Susan and me on ice. Even if Sammy wanted to disregard General Muller's threats and press on, he couldn't. Not without the help of someone from the base. I tried to come up with an investigator with the OSI who might be willing to stick his or her neck out, but I had to accept that no one would dare. Not now. Not once the word got out about what had happened to me. And not with what was going to happen to Susan.

Even with the blame laid on me, Susan's career was probably over. At the very least, Muller would ensure she was given a stinging LOR—a letter of reprimand—and nail her on her annual performance evaluation. The combination would effectively end her chances for promotion.

Gradually, it sank in that we'd come up against a wall we simply couldn't get over.

The realization left me drained, not so much physically as emotionally. In my mind I kept seeing Soon-ri's brutalized body and couldn't shake the feeling that I'd failed her. What bothered me almost as much as the actual killing was the knowledge that if Soon-ri had been an American, the U.S. government would probably have pulled out all the stops to find her killer.

I felt myself getting angry. The frustrated anger of someone who is desperate for justice but has nowhere to turn. Sammy had said equality was all crap, that some people weren't considered important, and he was right.

At least if you're a *sseul-mo-eom-neun nyeon*. A throwaway girl.

★ At the Osan main gate, the SP cruiser continued through the intersection into Song-tan, while Gentry's sedan swung left to pick up the highway toward Seoul. Chun's men were still sitting in their car outside the gate, so I ducked down as we went by. I figured I would be driven home, but a few blocks later, the car pulled over in front of the jewelry store. Instead of releasing me, both Sergeant Riley and the driver just sat there. After a few seconds, the driver checked his watch, then flipped on the radio. A military forecaster was rattling off the local weather. Ninety degrees and humid. Next came some local interservice softball scores; the Osan base team had lost a squeaker to the Yong-san Army all-stars five to four. A Garth Brooks number followed.

I cleared my throat. "Uh, anytime, fellas."

No reaction. Sergeant Riley casually scratched an ear.

I tried again. "Anything in particular we're waiting for?"

The only response was the music.

I gave up and sat back against my hands.

Finally, two songs and a public-service announcement later, the car phone rang. Sergeant Riley picked up, said a single "yes, sir," and hung up. Climbing out, he opened the rear door, then motioned me outside and unlocked my cuffs. Without a word, he got back into the car. As the cruiser drove away, I shook my head.

What was that about?

Ignoring the curious stares of a few passersby who probably thought of me as the Korean equivalent of John Dillinger, I dug out my keys and started to unlock the jewelry store. I had two calls to make: first to Sammy to let him know he was on his own, and then to Chung-hee—

Someone honked.

When I turned, I was astonished to see a familiar car rolling to a stop against the curb. A hand waved: "Hey, Burt! Burt!"

I went over as Susan pushed open the passenger door. I said, "You crazy? You heard General Muller. We're not supposed to have any contact. None."

"Get in. It's okay."

"What do you mean it's *okay?*"

"Penelope. She called. Told me the Security cops would be dropping you off here and I was to pick you up. She said Colonel Johnson wants to meet with us."

My eyes widened. "You mean he changed his mind about cooperating?"

"All I know is he's waiting for us in a hotel. Now, you coming or not?"

★ The Han House was one of two modest hotels used to house officers during major military exercises, when on-base billeting wasn't available. It was located just off the main drag, less than a quarter mile from the Osan front gate. We parked on a street a block away and approached the hotel from the rear to avoid being seen by Chun's men, who had a view of the entrance. As we cut across an asphalt parking area toward a side door of the hotel, Susan grew increasingly irritated. Wiping perspiration from her forehead, she said, "This is bullshit, Burt. We've got to do something about those two assholes watching the gate."

"I'm open to suggestions."

"What about you calling Chun? If he knew you'd been fired, he might figure you aren't a threat and pull them off."

"Never work. He'd be suspicious of anything coming from me."

"What if someone else called?"

"Like who? He wouldn't trust anyone from the base."

As we passed through a side door into the hotel, I felt guardedly optimistic. The only reason Ray would choose to talk to us here was to keep General Muller from finding out.

A short hallway led us into a small lobby with scuffed wooden floors and dingy, yellowing walls. It was deserted except for an elderly Korean man camped in a chair, smoking and hacking wetly as he thumbed a newspaper. A bored-looking clerk sat at the reception desk, flipping through a magazine with Madonna on the cover. As we went by him, the clerk glanced up and I tossed him a smile. He yawned, showing more metal than teeth, and returned to the magazine.

Susan and I stepped into the ancient elevator. As she punched the button for the fifth floor, she eyed me. "You think Colonel Johnson will really tell us what he knows?"

"We can hope."

The elevator doors rattled closed.

★ Room 532 was located at the corner of the L-shaped hallway. From experience, I knew these rooms were suites, usually reserved for visiting lieutenant colonels and above. I stood at the door, listening. Nothing.

"There a problem?" Susan asked.

"Ray's no big spender."

"Okay . . ."

"I'm wondering why he'd shell out the bucks for a suite. And I'm a little curious about why he didn't call you personally to tell you about the meeting."

"You think this may be a setup?"

I shrugged.

"Gentry?"

"Possibly. Or some of his men."

"What would Gentry or the CIA have to gain? We're off the case."

"True—"

"And it sure as hell can't be Chun who had Penelope call me."

Point taken. I was being paranoid. Still . . .

I rapped on the door.

Moments later, we heard footsteps. When the door opened, Susan inhaled sharply and I stared in astonishment.

Him?

35

General Muller was standing in the doorway, looking amused by our reaction. Instead of his uniform, he wore a navy blue collared shirt and dark slacks, his ever-present cell phone clipped to his belt. He was perspiring heavily, as if he'd just come in from the heat. At that moment, I understood the reason why I'd been delayed in the car. To give him time.

Muller stepped aside, eyes on me. "Come on in, Burt. Sorry for the subterfuge."

Susan and I didn't move. I returned to life first, saying, "I take it Colonel Johnson isn't here?"

"No. After our confrontation, I knew you probably wouldn't come if I'd asked so—"

I didn't bother to listen to the rest. I turned and began walking away. Susan started to follow, then stopped dead as if aware of what she was doing. I understood. Muller was a general and she was still in the military.

General Muller called out, "Burt, wait. It's not what you think."

I kept walking.

"Goddammit! At least let me explain."

I quickened my pace.

By the time I reached the elevator, I could hear Muller talking to Susan. As I punched the DOWN button, I heard the click of a door closing. Glancing over, I was surprised to see Susan still in the hallway. She began walking toward me.

As she approached, she said, "General Muller wants us to stay on the case. He says he can prove he had nothing to do with Soon-ri's murder."

"He just fired us. Remember?"

"He says he had no choice. It was the only way to get Gentry to back off and quit interfering."

I snorted. "To appear *convincing?* That was why he had me handcuffed and humiliated?" I shook my head. "No fucking way. I told him I knew about the money he'd given Soon-ri. This is a ploy to find out what else we've got on him."

Susan was silent, her big eyes looking at me.

"Don't tell me you actually believe him?" I said. "Hell, you're the one who first thought he was mixed up in the murder."

"Actually, I said he was probably screwing her—" She saw I was about to interrupt. "Just hear me out. What Muller is saying now . . . it fits with what Colonel Johnson told me. Colonel Johnson said he urged General Muller to come down hard on you because he was concerned about Gentry. This morning Gentry made threats to him about what he was going to do if you kept pursuing the case."

I was watching the blinking indicator lights as the elevator crawled toward us. I grunted, "Give me a break. Now I'm supposed to believe Ray sold me out to protect me."

She hesitated. "Not just you."

My head snapped around at the implication. "Gentry threatened Chung-hee?"

Susan nodded. "Gentry realized there wasn't much he could do to you. He told Colonel Johnson that if you didn't back off, he'd go after Chung-hee. Make some calls, get the ROKs to revoke her passport. Or possibly get U.S. immigration to screw up her citizenship paperwork."

"Jesus." But I knew what she was saying could be true. When Gentry and I had worked together, I'd told him about Chung-hee. How she'd been educated in the States and how much she wanted to return. And now, thinking that maybe she'd have to remain here because of—

The elevator dinged. I stood there, watching the doors open.

Susan said, "If it helps, General Muller told me he didn't tell Colonel Johnson about this meeting. He knew Colonel Johnson would be against it. Bringing you back."

I was silent.

Susan sighed and squeezed my arm. "Look, you do what you have to do. I told General Muller I'd hear him out."

"He order you?" I asked, without looking over.

"Actually, no. He asked." She turned and walked away.

I didn't move. I just kept standing there, staring into the empty elevator.

Moments later, from down the hallway, Susan said, "Uh, Burt, you do realize the doors just closed."

"Yes."

"Thought I'd mention it."

"Thank you."

After two deep breaths and three head shakes, I finally walked over to her.

★ The suite had a musty quality and smelled vaguely like an old shoe. General Muller waved Susan and me to a futonlike couch, while he took a straight-backed armchair across from us. Next to the chair was a small leather briefcase embossed with three silver stars and Muller's name. I remained standing, gazing toward the bedroom door, which was closed. Walking over, I pushed it open; empty. I looked in the closet, then checked out the bathroom. Returning to the sitting area, I went over to the sliding glass door and pushed back the drapes, revealing a small balcony that overlooked the Ville's main street. I about-faced and, ignoring Muller's mildly contemptuous gaze, continued to the front door. After locking the dead bolt, I slipped on the chain and rejoined Susan on the couch.

General Muller eyed me cynically. "Going a little overboard, aren't you, Burt?"

And I was. But I wanted him to know I was tired of being jerked around. I reached under my pant leg, removed my gun, and set it beside me on the couch.

Susan watched me in disbelief.

Muller said, "What the hell do you think you're doing?"

I just looked at him.

"Put that damn thing away," he ordered.

"General," I said calmly, "from the beginning you've used us and lied to us. You had me arrested and handcuffed . . ."

"Didn't Lieutenant Torres explain—"

I waved a hand around and kept on talking. ". . . and for all I know, this room could be bugged. Or Gentry's men could be waiting to break in and haul us away. Or maybe the men who you hired to kill Soon-ri could be waiting—"

"That's a goddamn lie. I'd never hurt her."

"No? You bought out her contract, got her an apartment, made her your mistress . . ."

"That's enough, Burt." His general's baritone voice rose in warning.

". . . and when you found out she was pregnant, you knew you had a big-time problem. What happened, sir? She decide to use the kid to blackmail you, threaten to go public unless you coughed up more mon—"

"*Shut the fuck up!*"

Muller had almost come out of his chair. His face was purple and his hands were clenched into fists. For a moment, I thought he might actually try to take a poke at me. Slowly his hands relaxed and he sank back down. "You son of a bitch. You have no right. You don't know what you're saying."

I was smart enough to keep quiet.

Muller sat for a moment, taking deep breaths as he tried to ratchet down his anger below the homicidal level. "If you knew how much I loved her. Tried to help her . . ."

"Tell us now, sir," Susan said softly.

Muller shifted to her. He didn't seem to understand.

Susan said, "You mentioned you had proof . . ."

A nod. He picked up the briefcase beside his chair and opened it on his lap. He removed a photograph and handed it to Susan.

Susan held the picture toward me so I could see.

For a moment I was mystified. I'd expected to see an incriminating image of Soon-ri and General Muller together—the one Ray had removed from the apartment. Instead we were looking at Soon-ri's mother standing arm in arm with a slender American man—

My heart began to thump against my chest. The man was twenty years younger and thirty pounds lighter, and his hair was dark and full. Still, we recognized him.

The picture trembled in Susan's hand. We both looked at General Muller.

"Soon-ri was my daughter," he said.

36

From the hallway outside, we heard the creaking wheels of a maid's cart. Then footsteps and a murmur of female voices speaking Korean. Someone laughed. The voices and footsteps trailed off, and it was quiet again. Susan still seemed dazed as she handed General Muller back the picture.

For almost a minute, he gazed at it, then shook his head pityingly. "When I think about the life Mi-yong led. If only I'd realized . . . After I left Korea, some friends wrote me that Mi-yong was trying to contact me . . . tell me she was pregnant. I . . . convinced myself she was just trying to get me back . . . A desperate fabrication. All these years . . ." He swallowed, struggling with his composure. "But of course Mi-yong hadn't been lying. She had been pregnant. And she passed away before I could tell her how I felt . . . how sorry I was for . . ."

He looked at us, blinking rapidly. "Jesus, this is hard."

Susan and I nodded sympathetically.

Muller took a final look at the photograph, then opened his briefcase and carefully placed the picture inside. Afterward, he focused on me with dull eyes. "I never would have harmed her."

He was talking about Soon-ri now. I nodded.

"She was my daughter. I was trying to protect her. That's why I wanted her out of the club."

"Sir," I said quietly, "I'd like to apologize."

Our eyes met. He managed a tight line that passed for a smile. "We both made mistakes. I should have told you the truth from the beginning."

"We'll need the truth now, sir," Susan said.

Muller nodded.

She said, "How you and Soon-ri were reunited, who helped keep your relationship quiet, everything, sir."

Another nod.

By the time Susan and I dug out our notepads, he was already talking.

★ Muller spoke in a somber monotone, hesitating occasionally to gather in his emotions: "When I was reassigned to Korea, I never planned on seeing Mi-yong. Twenty years is a long time; she'd have another life. But as the months went by I couldn't get her out of my mind. Part of it . . . most of it . . . was guilt I felt over abandoning her. Anyway, it became almost an obsession. Wondering how she was . . . if she was all right. And at the back of my mind was her story about her child. Our child. Whether that was true. Finally, I couldn't take it anymore. Not knowing.

"So I asked Major Wilson to track her down. Check out the clubs, see if any of the old *ajumas* might remember her. It took him a couple of weeks before he got a lead. One of the older barmaids told him Mi-yong had had a daughter who was now a dancer. When Wilson realized the girl was the Tiger Lady—an Amerasian—he put two and two together and notified me.

"For another few weeks I didn't do anything. I was worried about my career. What a scandal would mean, how the Korean media would play it up, all that. And of course my wife, Lorna's, reaction. Things haven't been going well between us for years and . . . But that's not really the truth. Not entirely. A lot of it was the fact that I was scared. Two hundred missions over Vietnam and this scared the hell out of me. But what do you say to a child you abandoned? What can you say?

"I finally gave Major Wilson the okay to set up the meeting. Just him and Soon-ri. I told him to play it cool, feel her out about who her dad was. They met at her apartment in the Ville. Filthy place she shared with two other girls. And right away she asks him, Did my father send you? Easy as that. Hell, she'd known I was her old man all along. Seen my picture in the papers and, of course, knew my name. Funny thing was, she didn't want anything to do with me. Hated me, in fact. She told Major Wilson her mother was dead and blamed me. Said it was my fault for walking out on her. She talked about the shame her mother had had to live with, having a bastard child by an American. How hard life had been for them.

"So anyway, that's how it all started. It took me another three months to gain her trust and for her to agree to accept my help. Not that we ever got very close. Soon-ri was still resentful, but who could blame her? Maybe with time, things would have changed. But it turns out we didn't have time. Only a few months . . . Not even that really . . ." He trailed off, staring at his hands. Susan and I watched him, saying nothing.

After a few moments, he resumed talking, filling us in on the rest.

As we suspected, it was Major Wilson who'd served as the front man to buy out Soon-ri's contract from Chun, set her up in the apartment, and provide living expenses. The apartment had been selected because it was in a new building with few tenants. That fact coupled with the location of Soon-ri's unit near the rear stairwell allowed Muller to make evening visits without much risk of being seen. Because of the demands of his schedule, he visited Soon-ri infrequently, not more than three or four times a month. He tried to talk to her on the phone daily, hoping to break down the wall between them. And his efforts seemed to be working. Recently, Soon-ri had seemed less resentful and appeared to welcome his calls.

At this point General Muller fell silent again. He sat very still, slumped in his chair. When I realized he was through talking, I said, "Sir, wasn't Colonel Johnson also involved in keeping your relationship with Soon-ri quiet?"

Muller nodded.

I said, "When Soon-ri wanted to talk to you, she called Colonel Johnson first?"

He looked up dully. "Her phone records?"

"Yes, sir." I removed the copies I'd made and held them out.

He nodded again. "Colonel Johnson would relay her messages, and I'd call her back."

"Sir," Susan asked, "whose clothing or toiletries did Colonel Johnson remove from her apartment, if it wasn't yours?"

Good question.

Muller sighed and rubbed his jowls. "I don't know. If Colonel Johnson removed those items, he certainly didn't tell me." He glanced at his briefcase. "The only thing I knew that he took was the photograph."

Susan said, "So you do acknowledge that he was at her apartment yesterday, sir?"

"Yes. Soon-ri had phoned him. She was upset and insisted on seeing me. I was in a meeting with the ROK air staff and couldn't break away. Neither could Major Wilson, since he was flying. So Ray went. He took Major Wilson's car and . . . found her."

I was looking at the page that showed the calls Soon-ri had made yesterday. I frowned at Muller. "What time did she call Ray, sir?"

He thought. "A little after noon."

I held out the page to him and indicated the line. "And the second call? The one at thirteen-twenty."

He looked. "She might have been getting impatient. Ray got tied up and couldn't leave right away."

Plausible, but . . . "Was she often impatient, sir?"

"Not really. She . . . knew I had to be discreet."

Susan and I exchanged glances. *Was Soon-ri's anxiety connected to her murder?* I followed up by asking Muller if he knew why Soon-ri was upset; he didn't. I said, "When Colonel Johnson found her, she was still alive?"

"He thought she'd . . . expired. She didn't seem to be breathing."

"So he made the emergency call to the security police . . ."

"Yes."

". . . and also phoned you?"

"Yes."

"And you called Ambassador Gregson?"

"Ambassador Gregson wasn't in. I spoke to Mr. Olsen."

Pudgy Face from the meeting in Muller's office. I said, "You told Mr. Olsen about your relationship with Soon-ri and that an investigation might implicate you."

"Yes. My intention was to hold a press conference and reveal that she was my daughter before that came out in the investigation. Olsen contacted the ambassador, who ordered me to remain silent."

Another mystery solved. Now Susan and I understood how everyone up the chain had known who Soon-ri was even before Sammy had officially identified her.

Susan asked, "Sir, to enter Soon-ri's apartment, Colonel Johnson must have had a key?"

"He borrowed mine. I had keys for the security door and her apartment."

"Who else had a key, General?" she asked.

"Soon-ri, of course. And Major Wilson. He's the one who usually responded if she had a problem. Needed money. If Major Wilson was TDY, he usually left her his car so she could get around. She rarely used it. She'd only recently gotten her license and was uncomfortable driving."

"So the items Colonel Johnson removed, could they have been Major Wilson's?"

He thought. "I don't know. I suppose . . . I suppose it's possible. She is . . . was . . . very beautiful."

A change from last night, when he dismissed any relationship between

Major Wilson and Soon-ri outright. Susan asked him if he now thought Major Wilson had anything to do with Soon-ri's murder.

"Don't be ridiculous, Lieutenant."

"Sir, he had a key—"

"I don't give a damn. He wouldn't have killed Soon-ri. He wouldn't have had a reason."

"Even if he made her pregnant, sir. Knew you'd be angry—"

"No." And he gave her a hard look, telling her to drop the subject.

So she did, glancing my way to see if I wanted to take over. I asked Muller if he knew of anyone else who could have fathered her baby.

"No. I didn't even know she was pregnant."

My surprised expression matched Susan's.

Noticing our reactions, Muller said, "I honestly had no idea. And I'm sure Major Wilson and Colonel Johnson didn't or they would have told me."

A naive response born out of Muller's loyalty to Major Wilson and Ray. The reality was that if either man had knocked up Soon-ri, the last person they'd have told would have been Muller. "Sir," I asked, "do you know anyone who might have wanted her dead? Perhaps a jealous former boyfriend or—"

"I know she despised her uncle. Apparently he was a real son of a bitch. Cruel as hell to both Soon-ri and Mi-yong. Soon-ri was also afraid of the bar owner, Chun." He paused, thinking. "And the only boyfriend I'm aware of is the Korean man she was dating when she left the club. But you know about him."

I blinked. So did Susan. I said, "Boyfriend, sir?"

Muller appeared puzzled. "You didn't get the word? I had Gentry call the Provincial Police chief to list him as a possible suspect. Soon-ri said the man became very angry when he thought she was moving in with Major Wilson."

"You have a name—no?"

Muller was shaking his head. "She never told me. Major Wilson and Colonel Johnson said they didn't know either."

"This boyfriend," I said. "Was he the reason Ray was trying to get me to go after a Korean suspect?"

"Possibly." He added, "Or he might have thought he was protecting me."

"General," I said, "other than Major Wilson and Colonel Johnson, who else on base knew of your relationship with Soon-ri?"

"Only Mr. Kim. He sometimes drove me to Soon-ri's apartment."

I hesitated, torn whether to go with the obvious follow-up. It had to be asked. "And your wife, General?"

"Lorna hasn't said anything, but . . . I think she might. We've been arguing more lately, and whenever I'm away, she's begun calling, checking up on me."

Scanning my notes for items I'd missed, I asked Muller when Major Wilson would be back on base.

"This afternoon. Gentry's keeping him and Airman Anderson in a hotel in Seoul."

"I'll want to talk to them both, sir."

"I'll notify you when they arrive."

I looked at Susan to see if she had any additional questions and got a head shake. I wrapped up by asking Muller to notify the Osan commanders that Susan and I were to have full cooperation, and to emphasize that my arrest was a misunderstanding. I also told him to contact Ray and order him to tell us everything he knows.

"That it?" Muller said.

"Yes, sir."

He held Susan and me in an even gaze. "What I said last night still goes. When you find the bastard, you come to me with his name. No one else. I've got contacts in the press and government. Both Korean and American. Important people who can get the story out, force the ROKs to reopen the case."

Susan and I signed on. What Muller was proposing would end his career.

Muller checked his watch. "Give me thirty minutes to get the word out on your status. And Colonel Johnson and I have a lunch meeting with a visiting congressional delegation. He probably won't be free until after two."

"That will be fine, sir," I said.

Motioning us to keep seated, he rose and picked up his briefcase. He stood for a moment, looking down upon us, his expression softening. "I'd . . . I'd like to arrange for Soon-ri's burial. I was wondering about the procedure for requesting her body . . . whom I should call . . ."

"I'll check, sir," I said.

"Thank you, Burt."

As Muller turned to go, his shoulders drooped and his head tilted down, making him look small and old. Susan shook her head, which told me she was feeling the same thing I was.

Pity.

★ As Muller's footsteps faded away down the hall, Susan stood and went over to the sliding glass door. Moments later, I heard her say, "Bastards are still there." Glancing at me, she added, "Probably should have said something to General Muller. With his horsepower, he might be able to— Did I say something, Burt?"

She had. I shot upright in my chair at a sudden possibility. Just maybe . . .

I sprang to my feet and headed for the door. Susan hurried after me, saying, "What is it? What did I say?"

"You're right. Muller can help. He can call Public Affairs."

" '*Public Affairs*'?"

By then I'd thrown open the door and was jogging down the hallway. Muller was just stepping into the elevator.

"Sir!"

37

Ten minutes later, I was back on the sofa, looking over my notes as I tried to digest Muller's account. Behind me, Susan was pacing in front of the sliding glass door, simultaneously monitoring Chun's men while she spoke on her cell phone, briefing Sammy on the meeting with General Muller. Occasionally she'd revert to an annoying little-girl voice, and it was all I could do not to make gagging sounds.

Ending the call, she slipped the phone in her fanny pack and told me that Sammy wanted to meet for a noontime lunch at a nearby restaurant to discuss some of the forensics evidence that had come in.

"Fine with me." My eyes still on my notes, I started humming the "Wedding March."

"Oh, fuck off, Burt."

"Look," I said, glancing up, "if you like him, why don't you ask him out?"

"I want him to ask me."

"Since when did you become a traditionalist?"

Her eyes turned chilly, like I'd touched a nerve. "You really don't get it, do you?"

"Get what?"

"Why I'm playing up to him. Coming on to him?"

I squinted, taken aback by the question.

"Never mind." She turned away, gazing out the window.

I said, "What are you trying to say? You *don't* like him?"

A silence.

I sighed, thinking I would never understand women. Switching topics, I said, "So what did Sammy say about the Korean boyfriend?"

She looked back. "He's got no clue. This was the first he'd heard of the guy. But if we're assuming General Muller was telling the truth . . ."

"He was."

"Agreed. So why didn't the chief of police pass on the information to Sammy? Doesn't figure."

"No . . ." Politically, a Korean boyfriend would have been the ideal suspect. At the very least he should have been checked out and cleared. The more I thought about it, the more this omission bothered me. *Why hadn't the chief of police divulged his existence to Sammy?*

I motioned Susan to toss me her phone, so I could call the one person who might know the boyfriend's name.

Chung-hee answered on the third ring, the tinny sound of a television in the background. Mi-nah was taking a bath. She would ask her about the boyfriend, but wouldn't promise anything. You see, there was a problem . . .

"Mi-nah was starting to open up to me," Chung-hee said. "Then I made the mistake of mentioning Soon-ri, and she withdrew into her shell and wouldn't say anything more."

"Try, honey. It could be important." Then I told her there was a chance she and her mother could return home today.

A long pause. The phone hissed in my ear.

I said, "Chung-hee . . ."

"Burt, I was thinking. I don't think it's a good idea for her to keep staying with Susan."

"You don't?"

"Susan's place is so small. Two bedrooms. Even after we leave, Mi-nah will still have to sleep on the couch. And there's really no one for her to talk to."

"It's only temporary until . . ." I stopped. I should have seen this coming. "You want Mi-nah to stay with us?"

"It makes more sense. Susan doesn't speak Korean, and we have more room. And Mi-nah could help us out in the store."

It was my turn to be silent.

"Burt?"

"I thought we were going back to the States in a few weeks."

"We will. It's only until I can teach her some skills. So she could get a job. Have some kind of chance."

Which could take months. I said, "This is that important to you?"

"Yes. I'm not sure why, but . . . I have to do this."

I smiled into the phone. "I know you do."

She said tentatively, "Then you don't mind?"

"I don't mind." Truthfully, I felt a little ashamed. For a few moments, I'd misplaced my priorities. Forgotten that Mi-nah was a terrified young girl who needed help.

"*An-nyeon-hi-ga-se-yov,* Burt," Chung-hee said softly.

"Good-bye."

When I hung up, Susan was giving me a dewy-eyed look, telling me she'd followed the conversation. "You're doing a good thing."

"It's Chung-hee's idea."

Her pretty face spread into an affectionate smile. "You keep this up, and you'll ruin me for other men. You really will."

My ears reddened. I was relieved when the phone rang, saving me from a response. I snared it and shoved it to my ear.

It was Major Kathy Baker of the Wing Public Affairs Office.

★ As the chief of public affairs, Kathy served as the base's primary liaison to the Song-tan city government and the local press and media. She also had a well-deserved rep as a gossip hound, which was probably why she was so good at her job. She said, "I don't suppose you want to tell me what this is about, Burt."

"Can't, Kat. Sorry."

"First, I hear that you're back working a part-time gig for His Highness the general. Then I found out that the general had you hauled out of his office in cuffs like a scene out of *COPS*. And now you got *him* playing messenger boy."

"We kissed and made up."

She sighed. "You're killing me, here, Burt. You really are. Anyway, I got in touch with my contact on the Song-tan business council. Assured him there was no danger of the base closing. Hinted that it had something to do with the murder that was solved. That got his curiosity working overtime. Once he began asking questions, I let it drop that the base's chief investigator pissed off General Muller, who reacted very general-like by having the investigator arrested and thrown off the base. I laid this part on thick. Even said you had to be pepper-sprayed."

There was a rumor that Kathy had once worked for the *Enquirer*, and I believed it. I said, "You mention me by name?"

"Didn't have to. It seems you're one very popular fellow. He already knew about you. So, that what you wanted?"

"Yeah. Thanks, Kat."

A pause. I could almost see Kathy's red-painted nails drumming on her desktop. Finally: "C'mon, Burt. Drop me a bone. Something."

"Sorry, Kat."

She shifted to her hurt voice. "Well, you can't blame a girl for trying. And Burt, next time you need something from me, don't bother. You, I'm starting not to like."

I smiled, listening to the dial tone.

"Uh, Burt . . ."

When I looked up, Susan was gazing out the sliding glass door. "The black car's leaving," she said.

When I peeked outside, the car was rolling by the hotel. Two blocks later, it turned a corner and disappeared.

On our way out the door, I called Chung-hee and told her to catch a cab home.

★ We emerged from the side entrance of the Han House into the brightness of the midday sun. The heat radiating up from the asphalt felt like a steam bath turned on high. I removed my jacket and threw it over my shoulder as if that might actually make a difference. As we made a left toward a narrow alleyway, Susan said, "With General Muller out as a suspect, that leaves Major Wilson, Colonel Johnson, or someone still unknown. As for Koreans, I think Chun is still a player as well as this mystery boyfriend."

Recalling Muller's comment about the uncle, I added, "And don't forget Soon-ri's family is still a possibility."

She nodded. We stepped across a concrete culvert into the alley. Two scantily clad, big-haired bar girls strolled by and gave me a long look. I smiled, and they tittered. Susan made a face like she had gas, but refrained from comment.

I asked her whom she considered the prime suspect.

She hesitated. "You really want to know?"

"Ray?"

She nodded. "He was there, and he had a motive for killing her and the baby."

"He called the Security cops."

"He had to. General Muller knew Colonel Johnson had gone over there."

"But that's precisely what bothers me. Why kill her when he could be placed at the scene? Why not wait until later, maybe try to establish an alibi first?"

"Again, because he had to. He was desperate to shut her up."

I frowned, then understood. "What Soon-ri was upset about . . . you think she was going to tell General Muller she was pregnant with Ray's child?"

"Timing fits." After a few steps, she added, "I forgot to tell you that Chief Dryke called. The rope matched stock she had in the warehouse."

"I see." But while suggestive, I didn't share Susan's view that this was completely damning. One of the realities of life here was that almost anything on base could be purchased on the Song-tan black market.

Leaving the alley, we turned left onto a busy street. A few blocks away was a bustling outdoor market, where you could buy anything from Daewoo big-screen TVs to knockoff designer gowns. I resisted the urge to take a swing through, to see if we could find any of the rope for sale. Susan's car was just ahead, parked in front of a small grocery. I asked her, "Do you *believe* Ray killed her?"

"To be honest, not really. Colonel Johnson's always struck me as a stand-up guy. When we spoke after the meeting, he sounded genuinely concerned for you. But I guess that could have been a line. I mean he is the one who pushed General Muller to get you to back off, right?"

"He's also the one who wanted me on the case in the beginning."

"Yeah . . ." She had no response.

We were almost to her car. As I swung around to the passenger door, Susan got another call from Sammy. She barely got out three words when she froze, listening intently. Her face told me the news wasn't good. She said we'd head right over and hung up, shaking her head.

"The Provincial Police chief just suspended Sammy," she said.

★ As we drove down the street, away from the market, I asked Susan what had happened.

"The police chief," she explained, "happened to show at the morgue when Sammy was talking to Dr. Yee. Once the chief realized Sammy was still working the case, he read Sammy the riot act and suspended him indefinitely."

An eventuality I had expected, but not this soon. I frowned when Susan made a left at the next light. I jabbed a thumb and told her the restaurant was the other way.

"Sammy wants to meet at a different place." She described a location near Soon-ri's apartment building.

"Why does he want to meet there?"

She shrugged. "All I know is what he told me."

"And that is . . ."

"The food is better."

38

The Jong-soo Restaurant was located a half block north of the alley we'd parked in the previous night. We stepped inside a little after noon, pausing by the cash register to look for Sammy even though we hadn't noticed his car outside. The place was cafe sized and no-frills, with unadorned white-painted walls and a dozen or so cheap Formica-topped tables. Except for a group of matronly women sitting near the front, the patrons were exclusively dark-suited business types—office workers or local shop proprietors in for a quick bite. I became aware of a lull in the conversations and realized every eye in the place was on us. Or rather, Susan.

A pretty waitress who looked maybe seventeen shyly pointed us to a table at the back, and as we walked toward it, the eyes followed us. A couple of men flashed Susan appreciative grins. As we passed a crowded table, a beefy guy made a comment and his friends laughed.

Susan immediately shot the offender a frosty look. He gave her a suggestive wink. More laughter.

"Easy, Susan," I said, nudging her along. "He just said you were attractive."

"My face or my boobs?"

But she continued to the table.

We sat with our backs to the wall so we could watch the door and the large, plate-glass window that looked out onto the curb. Susan ordered the spicy pork noodle soup and I had Kim-bob, Korean sushi. When we finished eating thirty minutes later, Susan got about a hundred more glances, but there was still no Sammy.

"One thing we know," Susan said, pushing her half-full bowl away, "whatever reason Sammy wanted to meet here, it sure wasn't the food."

"No kidding," I said dryly.

Checking her watch, she said, "Maybe he's not coming."

"He would have phoned."

She snorted.

"Call him," I said. "Ask him where he is."

"I got a better idea. Let's just leave."

I kicked back in my chair, eyeing her. "All right. Want to tell me what you're up to?"

She looked at me.

I said, "Why are you coming on to him if you don't like him?"

"Guess."

A moment later, the light finally flickered on. "You mean this is payback?"

She tapped her nose. "Bingo."

"You want him to ask you out so you can stand him up?"

"Damn right. What he did showed me complete disrespect. I sat in the restaurant with my thumb up my ass for over an hour. *An hour.* I bought a new dress—"

"For chrissakes, Susan. He was called out on a case."

"*He didn't even remember me.*"

"Well . . ."

"I dated a lot of guys like him, growing up. In my neighborhood, they were all like Sammy. Smooth talkers who are out for a good time and a quick feel. Turn on the charm until they get what they want. After that, you never hear from them again. Like the bastard who knocked me up. As soon as he found out I was pregnant, he took off. He never even called to ask about the baby. *His* baby."

She was furious, the words spilling out. She snatched up a glass of Coke and spilled some on the table. She swore.

"Susan," I said. "Be fair. Sammy's not like that."

She set the glass down hard, spilling more Coke. "Oh *no?* You know he's dated women from the base . . ."

"Sure."

"Well, he's got a reputation for being a complete jerk. Captain Merrilee Mann over in Maintenance went out with him for a couple of months. Merrilee told me in the beginning he was all charm, but became controlling as hell. Wanted to know where she was all the time, who she was seeing—"

"He's a Korean male." I nodded toward the man who made the comment to her earlier. "They're all a little controlling. That's their culture."

"So that gives them a free pass to harass women?"

"Now, Susan—"

"When Merrilee tried to break it off, Sammy got pretty damned upset. Accused her of being a racist. A couple of times he even followed her when she went off base."

"Sammy?"

She shrugged.

I wasn't sure I was buying all this. I said, "Is that why you questioned his relationship to Soon-ri?"

She gave me a long look. "The only English he was teaching Soon-ri took place in the sack."

"How do you know?"

"Oh, come on, Burt."

"And if he was sleeping with her, what does it have to do with the case?"

"Well, he lied to us, for one thing."

"Did he? I don't remember asking him."

"You know what I mean."

"Look, you want to know so badly, why don't you just ask him?"

She stuck out her jaw. "Maybe I will."

I ended the argument with a glance toward the window. "Here's your chance. He's walking up now."

We watched as Sammy strolled across the sidewalk toward the door, a white evidence box tucked under his arm. As he entered the restaurant, Susan and I both were both stunned by his appearance.

"Jeez," she said, "I hope he got the number of the truck."

★ Sammy was a handsome man, but he didn't look handsome now.

There was a large red welt over his right cheek, and his left eye was puffy and starting to discolor. As he checked out the patrons, I threw up a wave. He nodded, but instead of heading our way, paused to talk to the young waitress.

"Good," he grunted when he finally came over, "Mr. Choo hasn't arrived yet."

"Who's Mr. Choo?" I asked.

"The owner of the restaurant. He has something for me." As he sat down, he seemed tense and edgy. He placed the box on the edge of the table, lit a cigarette, and kept looking at the door.

"Well?" Susan said.

He frowned at her, then carefully touched his cheek. "Oh? You mean this? My fault. I should have known better. I got in the chief's face for not telling me about the mayor's son. Not smart, pissing off the chief." He gave her a smile. "Looking good, Susan. I like the blouse."

She ignored the compliment, saying, "You mean your chief's the one who hit you?"

"I questioned his authority and made him angry. It happens." He shrugged, taking a drag from his cigarette.

The waitress appeared and handed Sammy a bottle of orange Fanta. When she asked if he wanted anything to eat, he shook his head.

As the waitress left, I asked Sammy why he'd questioned the chief about the mayor's son.

"Because," he said, after another look toward the door, "it turns out the mayor's son was Soon-ri's ex-boyfriend. A playboy type who liked to cruise the Ville and throw around money. He dated Soon-ri on the sly for a while until she dumped him."

Susan said, "So there's a chance this guy could—"

"No chance." Sammy gingerly sipped from the bottle. "He left for school in England a few days after they split up." He gazed at her for a moment, then added, "Besides, I think I already know who killed Soon-ri."

"You do?" Susan said.

"Who?" I asked.

A vaguely enigmatic smile as he took a last drag and crushed out his cigarette. Removing the lid from the evidence box, he began clearing a space in the middle of the table. "I managed to get some of the evidence before the chief arrived. To me there's not much doubt, but I'll let you decide."

With that he turned the box over and at least two dozen glassine bags spilled out into a pile. Sammy immediately began picking through them. Most appeared to contain dark fiber samples, though a number were the knot remnants cut from the rope used to bind Soon-ri.

Sammy tossed a packet between Susan and me. I pressed the plastic against the contents to see better. Short dark hairs, tightly curled. I knew at once they were head hairs from a black man.

Sammy handed me another bag. Then a third, fourth. All contained hairs from Ray, probably taken from various areas of the apartment. Susan gave me a puzzled look. I shrugged. To Sammy, I said, "This tells us nothing. We know Ray was at Soon-ri's apartment. You must have also found his fingerprints . . ." Sammy nodded, still sorting. I went on, "So the fact that Ray's hairs were recovered doesn't prove anything other than that he visited—"

I never finished my statement, because Sammy suddenly passed me a fifth packet. This time he sat back expectantly. Waiting.

More black hairs. Only much longer and less tightly curled. My mouth turned to sand when I realized what they were.

Pubic hairs.

★ Around me I could hear the murmur of conversation. From a nearby table came the clink of glasses. Then soft laughter and a scraping of chairs.

I slowly placed the bag on the table and focused on Sammy, who was still staring at me. I said, "These came from Soon-ri's bed?"

He nodded. "We also found semen stains on the sheets."

"What about Major Wilson?"

Sammy picked up two more bags and passed them over. Both contained light hairs. Straight and blond.

"From the living room and kitchen, Burt. None from Soon-ri's bedroom."

"You didn't recover any of Major Wilson's pubic hairs?"

"No. Only Ray's and Soon-ri's."

I hesitated. "This still doesn't prove Ray fathered her child."

"It had to be him. Nobody else was fucking her." He looked at Susan for support. She nodded.

I said to Sammy, "You don't *know* that. She could have had other lovers. Someone we still don't know about. Someone who . . ." I trailed off. Sammy and Susan were shaking their heads in unison.

I sighed. They were right; I was in denial. Reaching for something that wasn't there. If Sammy had any evidence someone else had been sleeping with Soon-ri, he'd have said something.

There was an awkward silence. Sammy and Susan watched me sympathetically. Clearing his throat, Sammy said, "I'm sorry, Burt."

I nodded. "What about blood-test results on the fetus?"

Sammy shook his head. "Bad timing. The results came in right after the chief showed. After chewing me out, he ordered Dr. Yee to seal them. I slipped one of Dr. Yee's assistants twenty thousand won to try to get a look at the report, give me a call. Maybe he does, maybe he doesn't." His eyes lingered on me. "You want the rest of it, Burt?"

Meaning he had more evidence against Ray. I nodded.

He picked up another bag containing one of the knots. This time he just held it up for a few seconds before dropping it back on the pile. "Sergeant Ko identified the knot. *Ok-mae-deup*. In English it's called a bowline."

Susan said, "So?"

But Sammy was still focused on me. "Burt, you remember what you told me about Ray. How he grew up as a Navy kid. Got to be a pretty good at sailing . . ."

I nodded, knowing where he was headed. I looked down at the knot on the pile. "It's used by sailors."

"Yeah." He paused, then added, "*Mi-an-hae-yo.*" Again apologizing.

"Any leads on the second man?" Susan asked.

Sammy shrugged. "Could be there was no second man. Ray's a big guy. He could have handled Soon-ri alone."

"Then how do you explain the square knot?" Susan asked.

"I've been thinking about that," he said. "Ray could have been trying to throw us off, make us think there were two people."

She gazed back doubtfully, and so did I.

"Picture this, then," Sammy said. "Soon-ri was struggling, fighting him. Ray uses the square knot first because it's quicker. Once he ties her hand, he has more control. Now he can take his time— Problem?" He'd noticed Susan's sudden frown.

"Been a lot simpler to use all square knots," she said.

"Bowline is more secure," Sammy answered. "Square knot would be riskier, possibly come loose."

So maybe that was the explanation. When she was being sliced open, Soon-ri would have thrashed violently. Still, even now, the thought that Ray could be capable of . . .

"Still not convinced, Burt?" Sammy said.

"It's not that so much that . . . It's your evidence. It's all circumstantial. Nothing actually proves Ray killed her." I braced myself for an argument.

"I agree, Burt."

"You do?" I said.

"What's *this?*" Susan said, edging forward in her chair. "Aren't you boys forgetting something? Colonel Johnson was at the crime scene. He's the one with a motive. *His pubic hairs were in her bed.*"

"No, Susan," Sammy said. "Burt's correct. In court Ray could explain everything away as coincidence. We need something more conclusive. Maybe a witness who saw the killing. Or the murder weapon with Ray's prints. Possibly even—"

He broke off, looking toward the door. A fat man wearing thick glasses and an ill-fitting cotton suit had just entered, carrying a small paper sack. Sammy sprang to his feet and smiled tightly at Susan. "Maybe we just got lucky."

"How?"

But Sammy was already weaving past the tables toward the fat man who I took to be Mr. Choo, the restaurant owner. They spoke briefly, and Sammy showed Mr. Choo his police ID. Choo studied it then, satisfied, handed Sammy the paper sack. Using his handkerchief, Sammy reached inside and slowly drew his hand back. As he did, something glinted in the sunlight streaming through the window. Before I could see any more, Sammy turned his back to us, shielding our view.

"I'll be damned," Susan murmured.

"What?" I said. "You see what it was?"

"I think it's a knife."

39

When Sammy turned toward us moments later, he was holding the sack at his side, his expression grim. After tucking his handkerchief into his breast pocket, he and Mr. Choo angled past our table, their heads bent in conversation. Before disappearing through the swinging double doors into the kitchen, Sammy looked at Susan and me and motioned.

Susan and I started throwing the glassine bags into the box. When we finished, I jammed on the lid and stuck the box under my arm. I was almost to the kitchen doors before I realized Susan wasn't with me. Glancing back, I saw her pick up a glassine bag that had fallen to the floor. She paused, frowning at the contents.

I had to call her name twice before she pocketed the bag and hurried over. We pushed through a door into the smell of garlic.

★ The kitchen was surprisingly tiny, not much larger than a small travel trailer. A couple of T-shirted cooks were busy at the gas stoves, stirring large vats of soup while tossing in cloves of garlic. A third man rinsed a mountain of dishes in a sink. To the right, two girls were furiously chopping vegetables on a wooden cutting board. Everyone appeared young, late teens to early twenties. Even with an overhead fan circulating air, the temperature had to be well over a hundred degrees.

When Susan and I entered, we saw no sign of Sammy or Mr. Choo. Then one of the girls gave us a nervous smile and jabbed a knife toward the screened rear door.

"*Go-ma-wo-yo, a-ga-ssi,*" I said.

Susan and I passed through the door into the alleyway adjacent to Soon-ri's apartment building. Sammy and Choo's bulk were about five yards to our left, standing near a line of trash cans that swarmed with flies. Sammy was bobbing along as Mr. Choo explained something. As we approached, Mr. Choo stepped back from Sammy and gave a short bow. With a bland smile at Susan and me, he went by us into the kitchen.

Sammy motioned us away from the trash cans, a scowl on his squinty-eyed Popeye face. "Stinks like hell."

After about ten feet, he stopped and began putting on latex gloves, deftly shifting the paper sack between his hands as he did. Speaking quickly, he said, "This morning one of the cooks came out here to take out the trash and found the cans knocked over and crap spread everywhere. Probably by dogs. As the cook was cleaning up the mess, he found the knife. Knew it wasn't one from the restaurant. The cook kept it and mentioned it to Choo. Choo took the knife, thinking he'd give it to his son. When he drove to meet a supplier later, Choo heard the story about Soon-ri's murder on his car radio. He began wondering if maybe the knife might have been tossed in his trash can by the killer. Anyway, he called the local police, and they put him in contact with me."

I frowned, bothered by something in Sammy's story. Before I could say anything, Sammy removed the knife from the sack and held it out for our inspection.

The blade was close to seven inches long, and, looking closely, I could make out tiny coppery flecks of dried blood. But what got my attention was the distinctive design of the plain wooden handle. The way it was made to fold back against itself to expose the blade—

I looked away, a twisting sensation in my stomach.

"Hey," Susan said, "it's a butterfly knife."

Sammy nodded. "Big in the Philippines. Called a ballysong. Don't see many in Korea. That's why Choo wanted it for his kid." Glancing at me, he asked, "Ray ever been to the Philippines?"

"No," I said.

Sammy seemed taken aback.

"Then maybe it isn't his," Susan said.

"It's his," I said.

They both frowned at me.

I said, "Unlatch the handle, Sammy."

He hesitated, then did. The lower half of the handle swung down, dangling perpendicular to the blade. I crouched, pointing to markings visible on the upper part of the handle, an inch from the end. "See those initials."

Sammy squinted, turning his head: "C-L-J."

Susan said, "J could be Johnson . . ."

"Charles," I said, "is the name of Ray's father. He was stationed at Subic Bay in the Philippines."

"Now, Burt?" Sammy said quietly.

I checked my watch, knowing what he was asking. Almost one.

"All right," I said, handing him his evidence box. "We'll go question Ray."

★ As Sammy and Susan passed through the screen door into the kitchen I hung back, gazing up and down the alley. Then I went over to the trash cans and picked up the lids, swiping at the flies as I looked over the contents. Afterward, I carefully scanned the ground in a five-yard radius. Slowly a troubling suspicion began to form.

Digging out my Korean-English dictionary, I went inside to talk to the cooks.

★ When I returned to the dining room, Susan was at the cash register, receiving change from the waitress. Through the window, I could see Sammy already sitting in his car, which was parked a few spaces behind Susan's Sebring.

"You owe me three thousand won," Susan said as I walked up.

As we went outside, I handed her the money. After we got in her car, she asked, "So what kept you, anyway?"

I clicked on my seat belt. "Anything seem a little odd about the knife being in the trash can?"

She shrugged, checked traffic, and drove away from the curb. "Not really. Obviously Colonel Johnson—" She caught herself. "Obviously the *killer* must have parked in the alley. As he was about to leave, he spotted the trash cans and figured it was as good a place as any to ditch the murder weapon."

Glancing at the side-view mirror, I saw Sammy stuck on our tail. "I'm talking about the *way* the knife was found."

"What about it? Dogs knock down garbage cans all the—"

"No dog shit in the alley," I interrupted. "And none of the trash was chewed up."

She gave me a blank look.

I said, "This is Korea, remember?"

"So?"

And then her head snapped around to me.

"Yeah," I said. "When was the last time you saw a pack of dogs running around?"

"Hold on a sec," Susan said. "Not all Koreans eat dogs."

"No. It's a delicacy enjoyed by relatively few. And some Koreans have them for pets."

She tapped the brakes, stopping at a red light. "So it *could* have been dogs who knocked over the trash cans."

"Uh-huh. Dogs running around on their own don't last long." I looked out the window. "Besides, this is an upscale neighborhood. When I asked the cooks, they told me they'd never seen dogs loose around here."

"So what are you saying? That someone is trying to *frame* Colonel Johnson?" Her voice rose as if she questioned my sanity.

"Possibly."

"Who? And how would they get his knife?"

"Obviously it was someone with access to his house."

Sammy honked loudly, letting us know that the light had turned green. Susan glared at the rearview mirror, then made a right toward the highway. "But that would mean it would have to be someone close to Colonel Johnson. Either Major Wilson or General Muller or—"

"They wouldn't have anything to gain by framing him."

"Then who? It's got to be the killer, right?"

I hesitated. "Not necessarily."

A one-count later I caught a nod of understanding. She sat with her brow furrowed, dissecting this possibility. Susan had been around Korean cops long enough to become familiar with their methods. She knew that sometimes they weren't above fabricating evidence when they considered a suspect guilty. From their perspective, the ROK cops weren't doing anything wrong; they were merely helping the wheels of justice along.

She looked over. "You think Sammy could do something like this?"

"He hasn't in the past that I'm aware of, but . . . he has a lot riding on this investigation. Both personally and professionally. He also probably feels the case against Ray has to be airtight to have any chance of getting justice."

She eyed me cryptically. "He's right about that."

"Probably."

"You still believe Colonel Johnson is the killer?" she asked bluntly.

I hesitated. "I agree he's the most . . . likely."

"I think he's guilty as sin."

"So fabricating a little evidence is okay?"

"Of course not. It's just . . . I mean if Colonel Johnson is really guilty—"

"That's not part of the equation. We're cops. Our job is to play by the rules."

Susan put on the blinker, and we merged on the highway. For the next few minutes, neither of us said anything. Despite her expressed antipathy toward Sammy, I knew she was trying to decide whether I was laying the blame on him in order to explain away the damning evidence against Ray.

Abruptly, she asked, "If Sammy did plant the knife, how did he get it?"

I told her my theory.

"And who dropped off the rope at base supply?"

"Sammy. Why?"

Instead of replying, she took out her phone and made a call. From the bits and pieces I caught, I realized she was talking to Chief Master Sergeant Lucille Ritter at base supply. When Susan hung up, her face was troubled. "When Chief Ritter told me the rope matched, I never thought to ask her what kind of rope it was."

"Okay . . ."

"Parachute cord." She twisted in her seat and began unzipping her fanny pack.

I stared at her. "That's impossible. Chief Ritter is mistaken. There's no way the rope could be parachute— What's this for?" Susan was holding out a wadded glassine bag, which contained an unknotted length of rope.

"*That,*" she said, "is what I picked up off the floor of the restaurant."

Smoothing the plastic, I could see the rope was shiny skinned and narrower than the one used to tie Soon-ri. I slowly shook my head. I now understood what had led to Chief Ritter's mistaken identification.

"Looks like you were right about Sammy," Susan said quietly.

"Yeah . . ." I slowly pocketed the bag.

Susan said, "Makes sense Sammy would have made up two bags containing parachute cord. One to be tested by us, and one for Korean forensics. What I don't understand is how he was going to explain the difference between the two *types* of rope?"

I thought. "Sammy could say both were used. Remember, we only inspected the ones on Soon-ri's hands."

We rode along in silence, trying to decide our next move. Susan exited the highway toward the Ville, Sammy following right behind. "So what now?" she asked. "You going to confront him?"

I looked back at Sammy. His face was barely discernible behind the glare on the windshield. Shifting around, I told Susan to swing by Ray's BOQ.

"Why?"

"Let's make sure Sammy took the knife."

40

I tried to stay angry at Sammy but couldn't keep it up. As strange as it sounds, I realized his actions had been motivated by a sense of justice, a desire to do the right thing. With all the political heat on us to keep the killer from being an American and with the case now officially closed, he knew our only chance to nail Ray was to have undeniable evidence of his guilt. So when the opportunity came to pad the evidence, he took it. Was he wrong to do this? Of course. But I understood and, in some odd way, even sympathized.

The moment we turned up the hill toward Ray's BOQ, Sammy blared his horn. Looking back, I saw him gesturing for us to pull over. I tried to dispel his concerns with an exaggerated shrug. He hunched forward, glowering at me.

Two base civil engineer technicians were repairing Ray's front door when Susan rolled to a stop behind their van, parked out front. She and I were barely out of the car before Sammy's driver door slammed and he was on us.

"Why are we coming here?" he demanded, blocking our path to the house.

"We need to check on something," I said.

"Check on what?"

Susan and I went around him. I said, "This won't take long, Sammy."

"*What* won't take long? Dammit, Burt, if you're trying to stall or—"

Susan and I hurried up the walkway. Sammy trailed us, snorting angrily. Susan flashed her OSI ID at the two enlisted CE technicians and got a pair of why-do-we-care stares. She jabbed a thumb, and they stepped aside to let us by.

Ray usually kept the knife in the second drawer of his rolltop desk, along with a set of numchuks from his tae-kwon-do days. As we entered the spare bedroom, I fully expected to see splintered wood or evidence that the drawer had been forced.

But there were no marks on the wood. Not even scratches around the lock, which might indicate whether it had been picked. I checked a couple of drawers. Still locked.

"Guess we were wrong," Susan murmured to me.

I nodded, stepping back.

"Wrong about what?" Sammy asked. "What were you looking for?"

I pointed to the second drawer. "Ray usually kept the knife in there."

"So?"

I shrugged. "I was just wondering if someone might have taken it."

Sammy's face went cold. He gazed at me, growing quietly furious. "Meaning me?" he said softly. "You think I came back here?"

I was silent. If I denied it, he would know I was lying.

He kept his voice low, but there was no mistaking the anger. "Ray killed her, Burt. No one else. He cut her open and watched her die. I know you're still trying to understand why he wanted you put on the case. For me the reason is clear. Ray knew he would be the main suspect and knew you would be sympathetic toward him. Unwilling to believe in his guilt." He paused, his eyes boring accusingly into mine, then abruptly pivoted for the door.

I said, "Sammy."

He kept going.

"*Sammy.*"

He reluctantly turned around. "*Now* what do you—"

His hand flashed up, snaring the glassine bag I'd tossed at him. The one Susan had found in the restaurant.

I had to admire Sammy's self-control; he was Mr. Cool. He had to be surprised by the contents of the bag, but gave no sign. His face remained completely expressionless as he focused on the rope. His eyes returned to Susan and me. He almost sounded amused. "What do you want me to say, Burt?"

"I want to know how that got in your evidence box."

"Don't you know?"

"I think so."

"Then there's no point." He tossed the bag back to me.

"I don't want you questioning Ray," I said.

"You're the boss." He smiled coolly. "We've wasted enough time here. I'll be waiting outside." And he left.

"What a jerk," Susan said.

"Except that he's right," I said.

She frowned.

"I am too close to Ray. I shouldn't be the one who interviews him." I left the statement hanging, not wanting to order her. As a lieutenant, she might not feel comfortable questioning a full colonel.

"Not a problem," Susan said.

★ "No, the general can't talk to you, miss. No. I'm sorry. I told you before that's— I said *no!*" Penelope hung up with an exasperated head shake. Her eyes went to Susan, Sammy, and me as we approached her desk in General Muller's anteroom. She frowned quizzically at Sammy's bruised face, then gave me a wry smile. "*You* I thought I would never see."

"Neither did I." After introducing Sammy, I nodded at Ray's empty desk. "Colonel Johnson around?"

"He's in with General Muller. They're on a conference call to the Pentagon." She waved to the sitting area. "Have a seat. Be a few minutes."

Susan and I took the couch while Sammy sat down in a leather armchair. As Penelope clicked away at her computer, she kept firing me curious glances, and I knew she was wondering how I'd gotten back into Muller's good graces. But she hadn't survived twenty-plus years as a secretary to general officers by being nosy.

I settled back, watching Sammy, who was sitting with his knees squeezed together, the white evidence box and paper sack containing the knife balanced on his lap. His eyes darted around the room, looking everywhere but at me. Since our arrival, he'd given me the silent treatment and I was torn about how to resolve the tension between us. But dammit, if anyone should apologize, it shouldn't be me.

As we cooled our heels, a constant procession of people came and went through the hallway door. Mostly junior staff officers or admin types, picking up or dropping off various files as part of the endless paper shuffle that defined a military headquarters. Then Mr. Kim, General Muller's chauffeur, entered, carrying a couple of hangers with civilian clothing, including an Air Force–blue shooting vest stitched with Muller's name and rank.

"I'll take those, Mr. Kim," Penelope said, rising from her keyboard.

Mr. Kim obediently came forward and passed her the hangers. He gave a little bow, then pirouetted smoothly, tossed Susan and me a smile of recognition, and left. Penelope hung the hangers on a wooden clothes tree behind her desk. The shotgun was now propped up behind it, leaning against the wall.

As she returned to her desk, I asked Penelope what time General

Muller was shooting this afternoon. Partly out of curiosity, but mostly to be sure Ray hadn't been feeding me a line.

"At three," Penelope answered. "He's got a hundred-dollar bet riding on a round of trap with two ROK generals. That's why he's been practicing so much this past week. He actually thinks he has a chance to win."

"And he doesn't?" Susan asked.

Penelope gave her a slow blink. "They're *Army* generals."

"Oh?"

Penelope's phone jingled. She answered it and made a face. "Miss, I told you not to call back. I'm sorry, that's quite impossible. The general is very busy and—"

She cupped the mouthpiece, her eyes seeking out Sammy. "Lieutenant, there's a Korean woman who keeps asking to talk to the general. She doesn't speak English very well, and I was wondering if you would mind telling her not to call anymore."

Sammy smiled graciously and placed the box and paper sack on the floor. "Of course." He went over, took the phone, and curtly identified himself. Moments later, he frowned into the receiver, then shrugged and handed it back to Penelope. "She hung up when I identified myself as a police officer."

Penelope smiled in satisfaction. "Good. Maybe she won't call back."

As Sammy returned to his chair, he made eye contact with Susan but ignored me.

I sighed, told Susan I'd be back in a minute, and went down the hallway into the copier room. I was digging through a file cabinet, retrieving the last of the pages I'd hidden away earlier, when I heard the door close behind me.

Glancing back, I saw Sammy gazing at me, the box and sack under an arm. Instead of appearing confrontational, he looked solemn and a little sad. His eyes dropped to the floor and he shook his head regretfully.

"I am so ashamed, Burt," he said.

★ For a few seconds, neither of us spoke. Sammy kept staring at the floor. When he finally began speaking, his head remained bent in contrition. In quiet, deferential tones, he admitted he'd turned over the parachute cord to Chief Ritter. He told me he'd purchased it this morning, from a black-market vendor he knew. He said it was wrong and that he was sorry. He asked me to forgive him.

I took my time, weighing the sincerity of his mea culpa. "You saying you didn't act on impulse? That you planned on incriminating Ray all along?"

He finally raised his eyes, looking right at me. "I was willing to do whatever was necessary, yes."

"Dammit, Sammy."

"You don't understand, Burt. I've known since last night that Ray was probably the killer."

I was incredulous. "How could you know that?"

"Mi-nah."

I blinked.

"It's true," he said. "When I questioned her in the brothel, she told me there was one man who scared Soon-ri. Someone who had once beaten her."

"Mi-nah *told* you it was Ray?"

"Not by name. But she knew it was a black man."

My head was spinning, trying to understand. "Hold on. Ray didn't even know Soon-ri until after she quit working at the Studio 99 Club. And we know Soon-ri and Mi-nah had no contact since then, which means Mi-nah couldn't possible have known about Ray—" I broke off when I saw Sammy about to interrupt.

"Twice," he said, "Chun allowed Soon-ri to see Mi-nah. Chun wanted Soon-ri to know how much Mi-nah was suffering."

"Why didn't you tell me all this?"

He shrugged. "I'm telling you now."

"I meant before," I snapped.

He looked at me blandly. I knew what his silence meant; he hadn't trusted me. I turned away from him before I said something I might regret. Sure, Sammy had reason to be suspicious of my closeness to Ray, but to keep me out of the loop because—

"I was wrong, Burt. I overreacted. I was worried you might let it slip to Ray that we had a witness. I'm sorry."

I was silent, glowering at him.

A rap on the door, and Susan poked her head inside. "Let's go, guys. Colonel Johnson is waiting for—"

She stopped, her eyes shifting uncertainly from Sammy to me. "Am I interrupting something?"

"Where is Ray now?" I asked.

"Waiting in the briefing room."

As I started to follow her out, Sammy stepped in front of me and held out his hand. Reminding me that I was obligated to accept his apology. If I didn't, I would be insulting him.

I looked him in the eye. "Anything else you haven't told me?"

"No."

"Did you have a relationship with Soon-ri?"

"I never slept with her."

"Uh-huh."

"I didn't think of her in that way."

"Sammy . . ."

"She was a friend. That's all." Seeing I still wasn't convinced, he added simply, "I don't screw bar girls."

Now, this I could maybe swallow, since Sammy often remarked that he'd never lower himself to sleep with a prostitute. Besides, his taste was foreign women. "And you never took Ray's knife?"

"Of course not."

"You didn't do anything else to try to incriminate him?"

"No."

I studied him and decided he was either a helluva liar or telling me the truth. "All right."

His bruised face spread into a tiny smile. As I reached for his hand, he turned his palm upward. A further reminder of the contradiction he often posed. A Korean who acted more like a Westerner.

What the hell.

I low-fived him as I walked out.

41

No Spanish Inquisition setup this time.

When Sammy and I entered the briefing room, instead of Ray sitting on the hot seat at the end of the table, he was at his usual place to the right of Muller's empty chair. Susan was seated across from him, bent over her notepad. Noticing us, she shot us a look of warning, then glanced to our left.

When Sammy and I turned, we saw General Muller seated on one of the gallery chairs, tucked in the far corner. As if that made his presence and his three silver stars somehow less intrusive.

I shook my head. Muller should know better. One of the cardinal rules in the OSI was you never questioned a subordinate in front of his boss because of the intimidation factor.

As Sammy and I went over to him, I was struck by the change in Muller's appearance over the past few hours. His skin seemed to hang from his face, and there were deep bags under his eyes. At that moment, any lingering doubts about the love he felt for Soon-ri, a daughter he'd barely known, vanished.

When I politely suggested to Muller that he should leave, I got no response. He just stared at the table. I said, "Uh, General . . ."

"I heard you, Burt. I'm staying."

"Sir, I'm afraid I'll have to insist—"

A tight-lipped glare. I sighed, tucked my tail between my legs, and stepped back. I'd given it a shot. All I could hope for now was that he'd resist the impulse to interfere.

Sammy and I continued around the table. I took the chair next to Susan, Sammy beside me. Ray watched us coolly and appeared relaxed and unworried. He squinted at Sammy's face. "What happened to you?"

"Hmm. Oh, I walked into a door."

"Uh-huh."

Sammy set the evidence box and paper sack in front of me. When I pushed them over to Susan, his eyes narrowed. He caught on a moment later and nodded in approval.

Addressing Ray, I said, "General Muller tell you what this is about?"

"He said he filled you in about his relationship with Soon-ri and that I'm supposed to answer any questions you may have." Under his breath: "What the hell are you doing here, Burt?"

I noticed General Muller suddenly bend forward, trying to hear. "My job," I told Ray.

Ray looked at Susan. "You talk to him about Gentry?"

"Yes, sir," she said.

He shook his head at me, keeping his voice low. "Burt, this isn't worth it. Quit while you can. You don't fuck around with a guy like Gentry."

I didn't reply. I took out my notepad, flipped it open to Muller's interview, then sat back expectantly.

"Fine," Ray grunted. "It's your funeral. Don't say I didn't warn you."

I nodded to Susan. "Go ahead."

Susan's initial questions were benign, an attempt to relax Ray, get him in the mood to talk. Referring to her notes, she focused on the relationship between General Muller and Soon-ri, methodically confirming Muller's statements from the hotel. Satisfied, she moved on to Major Wilson, inquiring about his connection to Soon-ri, then pointedly asking whether he could have been romantically involved with her.

"No," Ray answered flatly.

"So he never slept with her, sir?"

"No."

"He spent a lot of time with her, sir. How can you be sure?"

"I'm sure."

"Could he have been involved in her murder?"

"Not a chance."

"Is there anyone on base who might have wanted Soon-ri dead, sir?"

"No."

"Did Soon-ri have any recent contact with any base personnel other than you, Major Wilson, or General Muller?"

Out of the corner of my eye, I could see Sammy squirming in his seat. He was getting impatient. He wanted Susan to confront Ray with the evidence. But Susan was playing it by the book. Once she confirmed what we knew, she would start centering the questions on Ray's role, hoping to catch him in a lie we could later use.

"Not to my knowledge," Ray answered, frowning at Sammy's antics.

Susan asked him, "Sir, you initially suspected the killer was probably a Korean. Any particular reason why?"

Up to now, Ray had responded without hesitation. This time there was a slight pause. Susan immediately jotted in her notepad; she'd noticed it. "A Korean killer was the most logical," Ray said.

"That's the only reason, sir?"

"Yes. I was convinced from the beginning the killer couldn't be an American."

"Sir," she said, edging forward, "I'm confused about how you could be so certain without having a specific reason."

Ray bristled at the inference. "I just know, Lieutenant. Let's leave it at that."

Susan immediately made another notation. Ray seemed increasingly unsettled by her writing, which was the idea. Switching topics, Susan asked, "When Soon-ri called you yesterday, did she say why she was upset?"

"No. She just said she had to talk General Muller. That it was important."

Susan glanced at me; my cue. I removed Soon-ri's phone bill and slid it in front of Ray. "What about the second call, sir?" she asked.

He barely looked at the bill. "She called to say she changed her mind. Wanted to talk to me instead of General Muller."

Susan's eyebrows went up, and so did mine. Even General Muller seemed surprised. "Bullshit," Sammy muttered.

I shot him a look of warning. He shrugged it off.

Ray addressed him coldly. "It's the truth. She told me to come over immediately. She didn't give me a reason."

"Oh, right," Sammy said sarcastically. "And we're supposed to believe that you dropped everything and went over without knowing why? Give me a break."

"She was anxious. I knew something was wrong."

Susan coughed. "Burt, if I could continue . . ."

"That's enough, Sammy," I said.

But Sammy saw his opportunity and was going for it. He focused on Ray, talking fast. "When you arrived at the apartment, was Soon-ri alive or dead?"

"I think she was dead," Ray said.

"You *think?*" Sammy said.

I was getting irritated now. I grabbed Sammy's arm above the elbow. "Sammy, I told you that's—"

He shook me off with surprising force. His eyes were shiny, and I recognized the look. He sensed blood and was moving in for the kill.

"Admit it, Colonel," he said, his voice rising. "She was alive when you got to her apartment. You attacked her, killed her because she was pregnant with your child . . ."

Ray stared at him in shock.

"*Dammit*, Sammy," I said.

But Sammy was on a roll, the words tumbling from his mouth. ". . . you tied her to the bed and cut out her fetus to prevent anyone from knowing you were the father. Afterward, you went around the apartment removing any evidence of your relationship—"

"*That's a goddamn lie!*" Ray roared. "You're lying. She was dead when I got there." He looked at me. "I swear to God, Burt. She was dead. Or close to it. That's why I called the SPs and General Muller. Why would I do that if I'd killed her?"

I tried to respond. Sammy cut me off, demanding, "Did you remove any incriminating items from her apartment?"

"Of course not."

"What about the photograph?"

Ray blinked, caught off balance. "Photograph?"

In a flash, Sammy was on his feet. Reaching across the table, he flipped the lid from the evidence box and removed a glassine packet containing a knot. He threw it in front of Ray. "And *this?* How do you explain *this?*"

Ray stared dumbly at the bag. General Muller rose from his chair and came over to take a look.

"Do you know what *kind* of knot that is?" Sammy demanded.

Ray hesitated, clearly rattled now. "No. Why should I?"

But the lack of conviction in his voice told us this was a lie.

Sammy started to reach across me for the paper bag. I grabbed his arm and squeezed. Hard. His head jerked toward me in surprise.

"Sit down, Sammy."

He gazed at me as if he didn't understand. His breathing was rapid, and I could see the excitement in his eyes.

"Sit *down!*"

Finally his eyes flickered and his face relaxed. He glanced around the table as if suddenly embarrassed. He forced a smile. "Sure, Burt."

I loosened my grip, and we all watched as Sammy meekly took his chair. I sighed, shaking my head. I glanced at General Muller, who was now standing a few feet behind Ray. I expected him to say something, express disapproval over Sammy's outburst. But he just stood there mute, his eyes fixed on the back of Ray's head.

"Burt," Ray protested, "this is all *nonsense*. You're making allegations without a shred of evidence. I had nothing to do with her murder. I found her and that's all. For chrissakes, I didn't even know she was pregnant or—"

"Stop lying, Ray," I said wearily.

"I'm not lying. I'm telling you—"

"Your pubic hairs were found in her bed," I said.

His mouth worked wordlessly, struggling for a response. He slumped heavily against his chair. "Oh, Jesus."

My eyes returned to Muller. *Now* I knew he would lose his legendary temper. Tear into Ray for betraying his trust and fucking his daughter.

But Muller remained silent, watching him with a steady gaze. He didn't even blink. It was a little creepy.

Susan tapped me on the shoulder. She pointed to the paper bag. I nodded. It was time to finish this.

She reached into her jacket and removed latex gloves. As she snapped them on, she said to Ray, "Colonel, we also found this near the crime scene."

Then she opened the sack and placed the knife on the table. "It has your father's initials."

Ray sat frozen, staring at the knife. Finally, his eyes sought out mine. Pleadingly. "You know I couldn't do this. Dammit, you *know*."

I kept silent. It wasn't easy.

Ray swallowed hard and began talking in a dazed voice as if he still couldn't accept what was happening. "I would never hurt Soon-ri. I couldn't. Our relationship was the best thing that's happened to me. Sure, I knew it was wrong. You don't know how hard I tried to resist her. Not get involved. But I . . . I was lonely. The divorce and . . . Hell, you've seen her, Burt. She was so damned beautiful. The thought that a girl like her . . . someone who looked like her . . . wanted me . . ." He trailed off, looking back at Muller. "Sir, don't listen to them. The knife doesn't mean anything. Soon-ri was scared. She wouldn't tell me why. I gave her the knife last week. So she could carry it around. Have something for protection."

Muller's expression never changed. His face was an ominous mask, fixed on Ray.

Ray slowly turned around and shook his head.

No one spoke. We all stared at Ray. Sammy's phone rang, sounding loud in the sudden quiet. Susan glared at him. Glancing at the face of his cell phone, he said, "I have to take this."

So we all waited as he had a brief conversation in Korean. After he hung up, he jotted something in his notepad, then tore out the page and slipped it to me.

I glanced at it and passed it to Susan.

She took a deep breath and looked at Ray. "You still say you didn't know Soon-ri was pregnant, sir?"

He was staring at the table, his smooth face the picture of misery. "I didn't . . . she never told me."

"What's your blood type, sir?"

He slowly raised his head. "A."

"So was the fetus's."

I saw the anguish in his eyes. He tried to speak and began coughing. In a strangled voice: "I didn't know. I swear to God, I didn't know . . ."

As he continued to protest his innocence, I looked at Muller because the next step was ultimately his decision. Not that there was any doubt about how he would respond. Noticing my raised eyebrows, he nodded once. Again, I expected him to say something, but he turned and wordlessly left the room.

★ The door softly clicked closed behind Muller.

I told Ray he was under arrest, and Susan read him his rights from a laminated card. Afterward, she asked him if he wanted to make a formal statement.

He gazed at her numbly, then shifted to me. "You want me to confess?"

"Yes, sir," Susan said.

But his eyes were on me. "I'm being framed, Burt."

Susan sighed and eased back in her chair. She was deferring to me, since I was obviously the one Ray wanted to talk to. I asked him, "Who is framing you?"

He started to reply, stopped. His eye twitched. "I don't know."

"What were you about to say?"

"Doesn't matter. Nothing matters. Not . . . anymore."

"What's that supposed to mean?"

A single head shake.

"Ray—"

"I don't know who is framing me."

"If you're innocent, why did you tell me this morning that you felt responsible for Soon-ri's death?"

"Because I am," he said simply.

"That doesn't make sense, Ray. How can you claim responsibility for her death but still deny involvement in her murder?"

A silence. He stared at the tabletop. I repeated my question, but he still wouldn't answer me. I looked at Sammy. His frustrated expression mirrored mine. Even now, Ray was holding back. Dancing around the edges, but unwilling to make an outright confession.

I said, "Is there anything else you would like to say concerning Soon-ri's murder?"

A slight head shake.

"Would you be willing to submit to a lie detector test?"

He paused as if actually considering my request. "I can't."

There it was, the final confirmation. I turned away. I suddenly couldn't look at him anymore. Up to this moment, I'd desperately clung to the belief that he could still be innocent. Now I had to accept the reality that he'd butchered a woman and ultimately his own child because—

"You hate me, Burt?" Ray asked.

I slowly faced him. "I feel sorry for you."

"Don't." He smiled sadly. "I've only myself to blame."

Another pseudo-confession. I nodded.

He sighed, shaking his head. In a quietly reflective voice, he said, "Don't ever want anything too much, Burt. It changes you. Corrupts you. Makes you . . . *forces* you . . . to do things you'll regret."

I didn't say anything. He was talking more to himself than to me. We sat in awkward silence. Even with what he'd done, I felt for him. I couldn't help it.

"So," Ray said, "are we about finished here?"

"That's up to you. We still have a number of unanswered questions."

A tired smile. "Later, Burt. After I have a chance to talk to the ADC."

The magic words. He was asking for a representation from the Area Defense Council, the Matlocks of the Air Force.

I turned to tell Susan to notify the SPs that we were on the way with a prisoner. I had gotten out maybe a sentence when I saw her eyes dart to my right, toward the door. Then I heard Sammy give a grunt of surprise. I looked over just as General Muller reentered the room, kicking the door closed behind him.

"You murdering son of a bitch," he said, pointing the shotgun at Ray.

42

We watched in horror as Muller walked purposefully toward Ray, who sprang out of his chair to face him. I jumped up, too, swearing, my knee banging painfully on the edge of the table. Susan said, "General, don't do this. He's not worth it."

But Muller kept going. His eyes were cold, dead. Susan kept calling out to him. Begging him to stop and think about what he was doing.

By now she and Sammy were also on their feet. My eyes went to Ray. I expected to see fear, but he was remarkably composed. He appeared completely unafraid as he watched Muller approach.

Muller stopped less than ten feet from Ray, staring at him with hate. "Why, Ray?" he spat. "Just to save your goddamn career?"

Ray looked right at him. Again, I saw no fear. "I didn't kill her, sir."

Sammy slowly began stepping off to the side. Working his way around the far end of the table as he slid out his gun, holding it low so Muller wouldn't see it. To distract Muller, I moved the other way, mouthing to Susan to keep talking. Susan followed me, saying, "General, this is crazy. This isn't the way to solve this. Put down the gun. Sir, I want you to . . ."

She kept up the chatter like an infielder in a Little League game, but Muller wasn't listening to her. "Don't lie to me," he snarled at Ray.

"I'm not, sir. I didn't have anything to do with—"

Muller suddenly stepped toward him. *"Don't lie to me!"*

Ray calmly looked at the gun barrel and fell silent.

"That's far enough, Burt," Muller grunted sharply.

I stopped walking. So did Susan. She said, "General, please. If you would put down the—"

"This doesn't concern you, Lieutenant," Muller growled.

"Sir, I'm afraid we can't allow you to—"

"Shut the hell up!"

Susan made the wise choice and did. Sammy was now positioned directly behind Muller, out of his line of sight. I could see him hesitate, trying to decide whether to jump him. I realized Muller's finger was curled tightly on the trigger. Any sudden jarring—

Sammy must have realized the risk, because he pointed his gun at the back of Muller's head, then looked toward me expectantly. Telling me it would be my call when to shoot.

Muller was again badgering Ray, demanding that he admit the killing. Saying he wanted to hear him say it. That he'd killed her and why. He also kept pressing him for the names of any accomplices. Ray wouldn't answer him, enraging Muller further. Any second, I expected the general to lose control and—

I took a deep breath and stepped forward. "General, he'll be court-martialed and convicted. Let the legal system handle this. You don't need to take matters into your own hands."

"*No!* The bastard could still get off."

"Not if we—"

He spun toward me, his eyes a little crazed. "The government will never let us have a trial. They *can't*."

I said, "Sir, you said if we publicize the case, show our evidence—"

"Stay out of this, Burt."

This came from Ray. I stared at him in disbelief.

But he was looking at Muller. *Smiling*. He said, "You want me to say it, sir? Okay. I killed her."

Muller blinked, flustered by the admission.

"You're right about me," Ray went on. "Right about everything. I killed her to protect my career. I had to. She was going to tell you about us. Our affair."

"Jesus," Susan murmured.

I knew what she was thinking. The scene last night in Ray's apartment. I'd been right after all.

Muller raised the barrel to Ray's head. "You sick, murdering bastard—"

"Don't do it, General," I said. "He wants you to shoot him. That's why he's confessing. The guilt is eating at him. He almost killed himself last night." As I spoke, I could still see Sammy poised, weapon pointed, waiting for my signal. Would he actually shoot Muller to protect Ray? I had my doubts. For the first time, I realized I might be getting through to Muller, because he suddenly turned to me, uncertainty in his eyes. Trying to decide if I was telling the truth or blowing smoke. I continued, "Dying is what Ray wants. It would be easier. He couldn't handle the shame of a trial or prison. By killing him, you'd be doing him a favor."

"Don't listen to him, General," Ray said. "I killed your daughter. I deserve to—"

And then Muller began to laugh.

Ray frowned at him, confused. Susan, Sammy, and I were also puzzled by Muller, who was continuing to laugh. A deep, sarcastic laugh, as if enjoying some private joke.

Shaking his head, he said to Ray, "You stupid son of a bitch. You really don't get it, do you?"

Ray ran a nervous tongue over his lips. He knew he should be worried, but didn't know why.

Still appearing amused, Muller motioned with the shotgun barrel and ordered Ray to sit down. As Ray cautiously did, Muller braced the butt of the gun against his hip and, freeing up a hand, reached into his shirt pocket. Glancing at me, he said, "See if we got it all, Burt."

"Got what, sir?"

Muller tossed me something small and black. I caught the object with both hands. When I opened my palms, my eyes widened.

Nestled between them was a tiny microcassette recorder.

★ Ray's voice sounded tinny on the tape, but his confession was all there.

Like Sammy, General Muller had realized that any case against Ray had to be airtight. To further that end, he'd orchestrated the crazed display of a vengeful father to force Ray into admitting his guilt. Whether the confession would hold up in court, even a more judicially lenient military court, was questionable, considering it had been coerced. Not that Muller gave a damn. As he saw it, the tape was primarily insurance against government pressure, both U.S. and South Korean. If either tried to interfere on Ray's behalf, the tape would immediately be released to every major media outlet in the world.

"Have the audiovisual lab make at least a dozen copies," Muller told me as I pocketed the tape and recorder.

"Yes, sir."

"You notify the SPs to pick up Ray?"

I told him Susan and I were planning on dropping him off.

He glanced at the wall clock. "Be quicker to have the SPs handle it. I want you two to draft up a report ASAP, detailing the evidence against Ray. I want to fax it to Ambassador Gregson by COB."

COB stood for Close Of Business. Muller obviously intended to send off the report as a preemptive strike. "Yes, sir," I said again, as Susan nodded along.

Muller turned to look at Sammy. "You're making me nervous, Lieutenant. In case you haven't figured it out, I'm not going to shoot the son of a bitch."

Sammy was still behind Muller, but had long since lowered his pistol. He holstered his weapon and came around the table to join Susan and me.

Ray was seated in his chair, looking shell-shocked. He seemed more shaken by the tape than when Muller had first barged in brandishing the shotgun.

Muller glared at Ray in disgust, the gun now crooked in his arm. He turned to go, then, almost as an afterthought, asked Ray if what I'd said was true: Had he really considered suicide last night?

Ray eased out a breath and nodded.

Muller shook his head and sounded disappointed. "Too bad you didn't have the fucking balls, Ray."

Then he leveled the shotgun at him and pulled the trigger.

43

The late-afternoon sun shone brightly on the whiteness of the runway. Heat waves rippled off the concrete as a C-141 military transport slowly taxied into takeoff position and ran up its engines to a piercing whine. The large plane bucked and rocked, straining to break free. The pilot released the brakes and the jet lurched forward, then rapidly picked up speed. Slowly the nose rose and the wings flexed and it rose awkwardly into the air. The plane banked toward the southwest, and the noise of the engines gradually faded. It finally disappeared into a line of billowing clouds, and I wondered if it was going to rain.

It was a little after 5 P.M., and I was standing in General Muller's spacious hilltop office, looking out the window. Because it was quitting time, the sidewalks were filled with green-suited figures hurrying to their Mustang Village apartments or BOQ rooms, or perhaps to their favorite bar in the Ville. Behind me, Susan was sitting in an armchair by the door, talking softly on her cell phone to her son about a homework assignment. General Muller had returned minutes earlier from his shooting match with the ROK Army generals, which he'd lost. Still wearing his civilian clothing with the blue shooting vest, he was bent forward at his mahogany desk, poring over the eight-page report that Susan and I had spent the past three hours drafting. It wasn't a literary masterpiece, but all the big stuff was there. All told, there were sixteen separate evidence items linking Ray to Soon-ri and, by extension, to the killing. I'd already bluntly told Muller that if he had any rewrites, he could do them himself. I was tired, depressed, and cultivating the beginnings of a headache. All I wanted now was to go home to Chung-hee, and self-medicate with a few beers and a couple of extra-strength Tylenols.

But mostly, I wanted to forget about the case. Forget about a good man who'd been corrupted by ambition and a beautiful girl who had to die because she got in the way. Forget about the tragic life she led and the grim reality that no one really cares when someone like her—someone considered disposable by society—dies.

Including me.

For the past hour, I'd wrestled with the question of whether I would have pursued the case if Sammy hadn't pushed me or Muller hadn't been involved. In my heart, I knew the answer.

After all, my first inclination when Soon-ri's friend Mi-nah needed help was to walk away. Looking back, I concluded I'd made the decision not solely based on the inconvenience that getting involved in her life would cause. Rather, I'd judged her a whore and therefore not worthy of the trouble. That realization tugged at me. I wasn't any different from the base elites who had treated Chung-hee harshly after our marriage. Like them, I also made choices about who mattered and who didn't.

I sighed, my eyes returning to the runway. As I watched a two-ship of F-16s land, I thought back to my conversation with Chung-hee. I'd called her when we were writing the report, to see if Mi-nah could shed any more light on what she'd told Sammy about the black man who had once beaten Soon-ri. I was hoping Mi-nah might have seen the guy and could provide a description. Something definitive. When I broke the news to Chung-hee that Ray was Soon-ri's killer, she'd reacted with understandable disbelief.

She asked me if I was sure of his guilt, and I said I was. She had difficulty accepting my conclusion, but then she'd always been fond of Ray.

I'd waited on the phone while she questioned Mi-nah about him. Initially, Mi-nah wouldn't admit she'd mentioned anything to Sammy. But Chung-hee kept pushing, and I finally heard Mi-nah give a tearful answer. Moments later, Chung-hee told me that all Mi-nah knew was that the man was black; she never saw him or heard his name. Then she added something which surprised me.

"I think Mi-nah might be lying, Burt."

"Oh? Why?"

"I don't understand why she was reluctant to tell me. I mean she already told Sammy about the man, right?"

I thought it over. "Who really knows? My guess is she's scared because Ray probably threatened her."

"But Mi-nah never met him."

"Ray could have had someone else pressure her or perhaps—"

"You're his *friend*. You believe he could really do this?"

"Honey, the evidence proves—"

But she was off and running with a theory that Ray was being framed. Someone had to be framing him. It was that person who must have put Mi-nah up to identifying Ray. If so, whatever evidence we'd gathered could be tainted or at the very least—

That's when I interrupted her, saying no one was framing Ray.

"You don't know that, Burt. If there is the possibility that he's innocent, you have a responsibility to—"

"Ray confessed, honey."

There was a stunned silence. Then she began to cry, finally accepting the unthinkable. I tried to think of something comforting, but there was nothing. I just sat there, listening to her grief. After a little while, she asked me how the person we knew could do something so horrible. I told her the truth; I didn't know.

I hung up without revealing how we'd gotten Ray's confession or what happened afterward, because Chung-hee would never have understood. She would have characterized Muller's actions as abusive and barbaric, and she would be right. Still, if I'd been in Muller's shoes and Soon-ri had been my daughter, I'd probably have done the same thing. At least been tempted.

Susan had been the first one to react when General Muller had pointed the gun at Ray. The moment he pulled the trigger, she had lunged toward him, screaming at him to stop. Then we heard the hammer click on an empty chamber. Ray had collapsed violently against the back of his chair, in anticipation of the impact. Susan, Sammy, and I stared at Muller, too stunned to speak. Muller never said a word to us or Ray. He just calmly lowered the shotgun, pivoted, and walked out of the room.

Afterward, when our heart rates recovered, Susan had called the SPs to pick up Ray. To avoid a replay of my arrest scene and to prevent the rumor mill from going into overdrive, we escorted Ray down the back stairs to the small parking area at the rear of the building. The cops arrived less than three minutes later. The driver was a female sergeant Susan knew, so Susan handed her the microcassette recorder, with instructions to get the copies of the tape made ASAP.

As the SPs drove Ray away, he'd turned and stared at me through the rear window. He never took his eyes off me until the car turned the corner. Sammy put his hand on my back and asked me if I was okay, and I said I was. A white lie, but I would be eventually.

"I didn't want it to be this way," Sammy said quietly. "When I first suspected Ray, I didn't tell you because I wanted to be sure. Soon-ri could have been seeing another black man. You understand?"

I told him I did.

"You want to grab a few beers tonight? Talk a little?" He glanced at Susan as he said it.

She declined, murmuring something about wanting to spend time with her son.

I said, "Some other time, Sammy."

A disappointed sigh. "Sure. Whenever. You guys call me. Let me know."

"I will." And I would call him, and soon. Despite how his headstrong antics often exasperated me, I still liked the guy. Besides, he was the one who had really solved the case. I told him that now.

For a guy with Sammy's ego, his response was unusually restrained. He looked away with a vaguely embarrassed smile. For a few moments, he had that same faraway look in his eyes I remembered from the car, when he'd told me about his cousin's killing. Watching him, it struck me then that he considered the cases connected. Not physically, but emotionally. By solving Soon-ri's murder, he was somehow making amends for his role in his cousin's murder.

We went back into the building, passed through the lobby toward the main entrance, then continued back outside toward his car. I asked Sammy how long he expected to be suspended.

"Not more than a couple days."

"That's all?" Susan said, surprised.

"It's no big deal. The chief will cool off by then. I'll make a big show about being sorry and throw in a couple of bottles of booze." He winked at her. "Usually works."

She suppressed a smile.

We came to his car. He faced Susan and me and held out his hand. After we shook, Sammy said, "Susan, can I talk to you?"

I took the hint and stepped away. They conversed for a few minutes, and I saw Sammy's face light up. He took out his card, gave it to her, then got in his car. Backing out of the parking space, he lit a cigarette and threw us a wave.

"You two have a date?" I asked Susan as we retraced our steps to the building.

A nod.

"You still going to stand him up?"

She just looked at me. Silly question.

Her phone rang. She answered it, spoke briefly. It was Jenny, her friend from the bank. Two steps later, Susan stopped so suddenly, I went right by her. Her tense expression immediately confirmed that something was wrong.

"What is it?" I asked her. "What's happened?"

But Susan was whirling around, the cell phone still pressed to her ear. She kept asking Jenny if she was sure. Something about money that had been transferred—

She took off across the parking lot, sprinting toward the exit, where Sammy was waiting to pull out. She waved an arm over her head, yelling at the top of her lungs.

"Sammy! Hey, Sammy . . ."

★ I turned away from the window when I heard General Muller call my name. He was frowning at me from his desk, holding up a page from the report.

"What the hell is this about Ray paying someone off?" he demanded.

I looked at Susan, to see if she wanted to take this since she knew more of the details. She was still on the phone to her son.

The report was in the format of a military staff summary package. Summary and conclusion pages toward the front followed by detailed explanations and finally attachments of supporting documentation. I told Muller to look at Attachment C. He hesitated, then began flipping through the pages.

"The last page, sir."

As he plucked it out, I walked over to his desk. He scanned the sheet, saying, "It's a fax of Ray's bank statement."

I nodded, pointing out the last entry. The one Susan's friend Jenny had called her about.

Muller's eyes followed my finger, and he gave a low whistle. "A ten-thousand-dollar bank transfer?"

"Yes, sir," I said. "Made at eleven-twelve this morning from Ray's account to an account at the Dong-chi Bank and Trust."

He looked up at me. "A local bank?"

"National. The transfer was made to the Song-tan branch."

"Whose account is it?"

"Don't know yet, sir. Lieutenant Sam is still trying to find out, but he's having trouble. The manager refuses to tell him."

Muller's eyebrows narrowed.

I nodded. "It's highly unusual that the manager wouldn't reveal the name. Lieutenant Sam said the manager was extremely nervous. Initially, he even tried to deny that the bank had an account with that number. The only thing we can figure is the person on the account must be someone important. Lieutenant Sam is still pursuing the matter. We might need your help if he's unsuccessful, sir."

"My help?"

"To lean on the Provincial Police chief or perhaps the mayor. Lieutenant Sam is going to meet with the police chief in the morning, hoping to convince him to pressure the manager."

"Why wait until tomorrow?"

I explained that the police chief had driven up to Seoul for a conference and wouldn't be back until this evening. Checking my watch, I added, "Besides, it doesn't really matter. The bank's already closed."

He glanced at the fax, and I heard the frustration in his voice. "Then the case isn't really over?"

"Not quite, sir. Ray obviously lied. His payment makes it clear he had at least one accomplice."

In one motion, Muller slapped the page to the desk and snared his phone. "What's the number for the SP squadron?"

"Sir, you're wasting your time. Susan and I drove over earlier and spoke with Ray. When we confronted him with the fax, he still insisted no one else was involved."

"How did he explain the money?"

"He didn't."

Muller gestured angrily at the box on his desk that contained the dozen cassettes that the audiovisual lab had made. *"But he confessed."*

"I know, sir—"

"Why the hell would he cover for someone else now? Especially some goddamn Korean?"

The million-dollar question. I shook my head. So did Susan, as she joined us at the desk after ending her call.

Muller glared at us, and we could almost see the steam coming from his ears. I started to count to ten.

He slammed down the receiver at four.

★ Of course, Muller had changes to the report. He was a general; they always did.

In this case, he wanted a paragraph added that specified who would receive the report should Ambassador Gregson not agree to his terms. All told, there were twenty-two separate agencies. Most were media sources, but there were also a number of the more liberal government watchdog groups.

After scrawling out the list, Muller held it out to me. I took it, then immediately passed it to Susan. I hadn't been kidding about not making changes. Besides, Susan was a lieutenant and I was a still a major. Sort of.

It took Susan less than five minutes to crank out the paragraph on the computer in the admin room down the hall. Normally, this kind of thing would have been handled by Penelope or one of the admin clerks, but Muller didn't want to risk the report's contents being leaked.

Yet.

Once he reread the paragraph, he picked up the phone to call Ambassador Gregson and inform him that the fax was on the way. He'd just punched in the number for the outside line when there was a knock on the door. "I said I didn't want to be disturbed," he barked when Penelope entered.

Ignoring him, Penelope said smoothly, "Sir, there's a Korean woman who keeps calling and asking for you."

He glowered at her. "Dammit, Penelope. You know I don't speak to local—"

As a tenured civil servant, Penelope was the one person on base who could get away with interrupting Muller without fear of repercussions. She did so now, saying matter-of-factly, "I've hung up on her four times today, General. This time I suggest you talk to her. She says she knows who killed the dead bar girl."

Muller gazed at her dubiously.

Susan and I were standing beside the desk. She leaned over and murmured in my ear. I nodded slowly. A long shot, but . . .

When Muller looked at me, I said, "Take the call, sir."

"Why?" he demanded.

After I told him, he still wasn't convinced. "Odds are this isn't the same woman who was seen outside Soon-ri's apartment."

"Only one way to find out, sir," I said.

"Line three, sir," Penelope said.

Muller hesitated, then grudgingly punched the extension that was blinking. "This is General Muller—"

The words died in his throat. His hand holding the receiver began to tremble and the blood drained from his face. "My God. It can't be . . ."

44

"There's the school," General Muller said, from the backseat of Susan's car. "Make the next left."

Susan was behind the wheel and I was sitting in the passenger seat, gazing out the window. It was almost 7 P.M. and we were slowly cruising down the potholed main street of Hong-tae, a small farming hamlet some forty-odd kilometers southeast of Song-tan. Most of the two dozen or so homes lining the roadway were made of mud with a few newer, wood-framed dwellings tossed in. All were topped by television antennas, and I shook my head at the apparent contradiction.

In the schoolyard, barefooted children scurried around a dirt field, kicking a soccer ball. We turned left down a dusty street and continued past a group of women washing clothes in earthen tubs. After a few hundred meters, we came to a row of dilapidated buildings. General Muller pointed to a two-story job with a pale yellow door and a sagging roof, which was sandwiched between a tailor shop and a dime-sized convenience store with a faded Coca-Cola sign.

We parked out front and slowly climbed out. Chickens squawked from a fenced enclosure across the street. Two elderly men playing Go, the Asian strategy game, roughly equivalent to chess, eyed us curiously from the sidewalk. I gave them a wave and asked Susan for her cell phone.

"You already tried Sammy twice," she said.

"We still need someone to interpret."

She scowled at my logic, but handed the phone over. As I made the call, Muller leaned against the car, tapping his foot impatiently.

This time Sammy answered. The loud music told me he was in a bar, which was what I'd suspected. A woman cooed his name, giggled, and cooed it again.

"Hey, hey, Burt," Sammy said. "You change your mind about grabbing a beer?" His slurred speech told me he'd already had a few.

When I told him about the old woman, he suddenly sounded sober. "Did she say Ray killed Soon-ri?"

"She wouldn't tell General Muller over the phone."

"Give me forty minutes."

Knowing Sammy, it would be closer to thirty. I punched off the call and handed Susan her phone. "On the way."

"Oh, goody."

General Muller was already walking up the small stoop, toward the yellow door. As we followed him, I noticed the building was unmarked, the windows shuttered tight. Muller rapped on the door, waited, and rapped again.

The lock finally clicked, and a white-haired man with stooped shoulders cracked the door tentatively. Seeing us, he flung it open wide and began rattling off staccato Korean. I heard him address Muller by rank and name. He motioned us inside, bobbing and grinning like we were long-lost friends.

After we entered, he closed the door behind us. We were in a cramped, dimly lit room that reeked of stale tobacco smoke. A wooden bar with a stack of glasses ran the length of one side. A half-dozen rickety tables filled up most of the floor space. Against the right wall was a velvet nude of a buxom blonde who bore a fair resemblance to Marilyn Monroe.

"So-ju bar," Susan murmured.

I nodded. So-ju bars were popular with working-class Korean men because they provided a cheap and quick way to get drunk.

The old man was still talking to Muller. He pointed the general toward a narrow hallway at the back. We could see plastic sixties-style beads covering what appeared to be a doorway. *"Jeo-gi-seo gi-da-ri-go-it-sseo-yo."*

Muller looked at me. I said, "She's waiting through there."

"Thank him for me," he said.

After I did, the man grinned and bobbed some more. He grabbed a bottle of So-ju from behind the bar and asked if we wanted drinks. I told him no.

Muller led the way down the hall. Pushing through the beads, we saw a staircase and, beyond, a closed door. From behind it, we could hear music playing. The melodic falsetto of Korean opera.

Muller suddenly appeared nervous. He paused to brush a hand over his thinning hair and appeared to suck in his gut. He knocked softly, and a voice in heavily accented English told us to come in.

So we did.

The bedroom was larger than I had expected. Maybe ten feet by twenty. The furnishings were simple and spartan: an old cot-sized wooden bed, three packing crates used to store clothing, a battered card table with an electric burner, a makeshift shelf in one corner topped with cooking utensils, toiletries, and an opened box of laundry detergent. The one thing that seemed out of place was a small refrigerator humming along the right wall; it looked shiny and new. Not that I was all that interested in the items in the room.

Like General Muller and Susan, I was focused on the thin woman with shoulder-length gray hair who was sitting on the edge of the bed, her back to us. She was wearing a blue *han-bok,* the traditional kimonolike Korean dress. It was tattered and faded, and seemed too large for her tiny frame. The music was coming from a palm-sized transistor radio lying beside her on the bed. I recognized the song as one Chung-hee had often played after the death of her father. She told me it was about an orphaned girl who was lamenting the cruelty of life.

The woman continued to stare at the wall, ignoring us. Muller attempted to speak.

"No talk," the woman said.

He frowned, puzzled. This wasn't the reception he'd expected. We stood, staring at the woman's back. Careful not to look at us, she picked up the radio and held it to her chest. As she did, I noticed her hands. Rough and callused. A laborer's hands.

The song ended. The woman clicked off the radio and placed it on the bed. She slowly ran a hand over her stringy hair. I thought she would finally face us, but she kept staring at the wall.

"Turn around," Muller said gently.

She shook her head. "No pretty."

"Doesn't matter," Muller said softly.

"You come. I . . . try . . . hard. Look good." She pulled at the sleeve of the *han-bok,* which was badly frayed. "Old. Like me."

"Turn around," Muller said again.

She shook her head stubbornly.

"Please."

She hid her face in her hands. Muller kept telling her to look at him. That he only wanted to see her. Slowly, hesitantly, she lowered her hands and shifted around to him.

Twenty years was a long time. The once roundly smooth face was now gaunt, the skin aged and weathered from countless hours under a hot sun. Not even fifty, she looked at least ten years older. Still, there were surprisingly few wrinkles, and I easily recognized her from the photographs on Soon-ri's dresser.

She really was Mi-yong, her mother.

The tears started streaming down Mi-yong's cheeks. Muller's eyes misted, watching her. He slowly moved toward her, removing a handkerchief from his pocket. "Mi-yong. I'm so sorry. God, I'm sorry. If I'd known . . ."

He took her in his arms and began gently drying her eyes. I felt a golf ball in my throat. It was a wrenching scene.

Susan tugged on my arm. She was blinking rapidly, struggling with her composure.

As we stepped out into the hallway, I could hear Mi-yong saying over and over, *u-ri-ttal*, *u-ri-ttal*. Our daughter, our daughter.

When I closed the door, Mi-yong's voice became even more anguished. She began repeating another phrase I didn't understand.

I paused in the hallway and flipped through my dictionary. "Curious."

"What is?" Susan asked.

"Mi-yong is asking General Muller to forgive her."

45

Twenty minutes later, Susan and I were sitting at a table in the tiny bar, sipping on bottled Cokes I'd purchased from the store next door. Above us on the second floor, we could hear the floorboards creaking as the old man walked around. His name was Yune. He spoke a few words of English, and with my rough Korean, I'd managed to get a few questions answered.

He was the bar owner. For the past six years, Soon-ri's mother had tended bar for him in exchange for a place to stay. Until two months ago, she'd also worked in the rice fields, but quit when her daughter gave her some money. Yune confirmed it was Soon-ri who also shelled out for the refrigerator. Yes, he knew Soon-ri had met a rich American, but didn't know that man was General Muller until today. Would I take a picture of him and the general together? When I said I would, Yune hopped up and bolted upstairs to find his camera.

"Burt . . ."

Susan and I turned to see Muller poking his head through the beads, his expression subdued. He said, "How much longer until Lieutenant Sam arrives?"

I checked my watch. "Fifteen, twenty minutes."

"You'd better come on back, then. Mi-yong is trying to tell me what happened on the day of the murder. It's going slow. She's forgotten most of the English I taught her."

Susan and I rose, draining our Cokes. Stepping around me, she placed the empty bottles on the bar. Watching her, Muller said, "Mi-yong confirmed she was at Soon-ri's apartment yesterday. She was supposed to be a surprise. My surprise."

Susan faced him quizzically. "Sir?"

"That's why Soon-ri was anxious for me to come over yesterday. I guess she'd finally decided to forgive me and was going to spring Mi-yong on me when I walked in. Mi-yong arrived only a few minutes before the murder happened."

Susan and I both started walking toward him. We slowed, fixated on him. Susan said, "Sir, are you saying she saw the whole thing and—"

"She *heard* it," Muller said. "Mi-yong was hiding in the bedroom closet. She says there were at least two killers." His eyes went to me. "Koreans."

I nodded. So Ray had more than one accomplice. "She's certain, sir?"

"Yes."

"Could she identify them?"

"No." He hesitated, then reluctantly added, "I'm not sure I believe her."

I squinted, curious. "You think she could be lying?"

He sighed. "It's nothing I can put my finger on. It's . . . it's the way she looked at me when she insisted she hadn't seen the killers. Almost like she was hoping I'd believe her, but didn't think I would."

"You think she's afraid to tell what she knows?"

"I don't know. Maybe."

I was silent, considering this possibility. I pictured Mi-yong cowering in the closet as Soon-ri was brutally murdered. Desperate to help her daughter, but helpless to do so. In my mind, Muller's suspicions didn't figure. Even frightened, a mother wouldn't protect the killers of her child. And certainly not if she'd witnessed the horror firsthand.

Still . . .

I went back to Mi-yong's odd comment about asking for forgiveness. Had she said it out of guilt, because she hadn't tried to prevent the killing? Or was there another reason?

Before I could question Muller about this, Susan said to him, "Did she know if Colonel Johnson was at the apartment during the murder, sir?"

"She says he wasn't."

"How can she be sure, sir?" Susan said. "I mean if she never saw the killers—"

"None of them spoke English."

Susan still seemed troubled. I suspected she was wondering about the same thing that was bugging me. Why would Ray have his accomplices commit the murder within minutes of his arrival, when he had no alibi? Had he been that desperate to silence her?

Ten thousand dollars suggested he probably was.

Muller gave me a long look. "When you question her, go easy. She's pretty raw emotionally."

I nodded. As he was about to pass back through the beads, I asked him about Mi-yong's forgiveness comment. His face went blank.

After I explained, he snorted, "Forgive *her?* I was the son of a bitch who screwed her over, remember? You must have misunderstood her, Burt."

"Yes, sir." But as Susan and I followed him through the beads, I knew I hadn't.

The bedroom door was closed. Muller reached for the knob, then looked over his shoulder at the sound of footsteps. The old man bounded down the staircase, grinning excitedly at him.

"Sa-jin jji-geo deu-ril-kka-yo?"

And he proudly thrust out an ancient Instamatic camera.

"He's asking to take a picture with you, sir," I said.

"No kidding."

After Yune handed me the camera, Muller motioned him over and put an arm around his shoulders. I carefully framed them in the viewfinder.

"Five bucks the flash doesn't work," Susan said.

I should have taken the bet.

★ Yune disappeared into the bar, whistling happily. Muller watched him go, his craggy face softening. He reached around to his back pocket, removed a wad of bills from his wallet, and held them out to Susan. "Give this to him when we leave."

Susan gave him a questioning look as she took the money.

He smiled faintly. "He saved Mi-yong's life. It took her six days to walk here from her village. He found her passed out in a rice field. He's been looking after her ever since."

I said, "Did she fake her death?"

He shook his head. "She just left. Walked away. Her brother-in-law probably made up the story about finding her body to save face. To explain her leaving." He paused, his voice breaking slightly. "The brother-in-law was forcing her to sleep with men from the village. Figured if she'd fucked Americans, it was no big deal. Beat her if she refused. She couldn't take the abuse anymore. Leaving Soon-ri behind was the hardest part. Her sister promised to look after her . . . as best she could. The only contact Mi-yong had with Soon-ri was through the few letters her sister could smuggle out." He swallowed hard, shaking his head. "Some goddamn life. When I think of what they went through because of me . . . because I didn't . . ."

He couldn't get it out. He fell silent, lost in self-recrimination.

"Bastard," Susan murmured.

She was talking about the brother-in-law, Soon-ri's uncle.

Finally, Muller took a ragged breath and looked at me. "Could be that was it, Burt. What she wanted forgiveness for. Leaving Soon-ri. But it's not like she had a choice. Am I right?"

I didn't reply; he wasn't expecting an answer.

We stood there gazing at each other. For a moment, I was tempted to throw an arm around his back, tell him that none of this was his fault. That he wasn't to blame. But he was a three-star general, and the familiarity would have been out of place.

At least that's what I told myself.

What really stopped me was the knowledge that I would be lying to him. The grim reality was it was his fault. At least partly.

"Remember," he cautioned me. "Go easy on her. She's suffered enough."

"I will, sir."

He opened the door.

★ Mi-yong was sitting on the bed, clutching Muller's handkerchief to her chest. She looked small and frail and scared. She watched us with red-rimmed eyes as we circled around her. Muller took her bony hand in his and held it reassuringly.

During the questioning, I stuck to basic Korean and English phrases, resorting to the dictionary or to drawing pictures in my notepad only as a last resort. Despite the language problem, I expected to fill in the slate on Soon-ri quickly, but that didn't happen. The problem was Mi-yong had had little contact with her daughter until two years earlier, when Soon-ri had left the village and begun working as a dancer. Since then, they'd visited only every few months, and on those occasions, Soon-ri rarely spoke of her private life. The end result was that Mi-yong didn't know about Soon-ri's relationship with Ray or anyone else, or even that she'd been pregnant.

Soon-ri had told her about Muller, but Mi-yong had resisted a meeting. He was an important man with a family and a wife; she assumed he had no desire to see her. And if he agreed to meet, it would be out of pity. Then there was her appearance. She'd wanted him to remember her the way she used to look . . . not like this.

In the end, she'd agreed to see Muller because Soon-ri insisted. Her daughter wanted them to be a *ga-jok*. A family. If only for a little while.

Mi-yong's voice trembled, talking about her daughter. She told me how she was a bad mother. How she had wanted to help her child when the bad men came, but couldn't. How she'd been scared. So scared . . .

And racked with guilt, she began to cry.

When I asked her about the killings, she became even more emotional, reliving the horror. A lot of the details I missed because I couldn't keep up with her ramblings. What I did learn was that she'd been in the bathroom when the men came. She heard them argue with Soon-ri and attack her. When they brought her to the bedroom, Mi-yong had run into the closet. She remembered Soon-ri screaming only once. After that, she heard only her muffled moans, then silence as Soon-ri was overcome by the effects of the ether. And the voices of the men. No, they never called each other by name. No, she didn't know why they wanted to hurt Soon-ri. Only that they did.

When the men left, Mi-yong remembered stumbling out of the closet and seeing Soon-ri lying on the bed. *Jeo-pi. Eom-cheong-nan pi-jom-bwa.* Blood. Much blood. She went over and touched Soon-ri's face. Pulled at her hand, but she didn't move.

Mi-yong had no memory of leaving the apartment. The next thing she knew she was standing outside on the sidewalk, begging people to help her. Telling them that her daughter was hurt. But everyone walked by. They just walked by.

It seemed a long time until the police came. She saw them hurry inside the apartment building. She knew they must be there to help Soon-ri. So she finally left.

I asked if she'd spoken with the police when they first arrived. She shook her head, which didn't mesh with what Sammy had told me. I asked her why she didn't wait to talk to them later.

"*Nal ja-ba-gal jji mol-la.*" They might arrest me.

"*Wae yo?*" Why?

"*Nan ga-nan-hae*." I am poor.

I flipped through the dictionary, searching. I stumbled through: "*Museun iri-ireo-nan-neun-ji bwat-ja-na*." But you saw what occurred.

She looked at Muller. "I call Hally." She was trying to say Harry.

Muller patted her hand.

I asked her a few more questions, but there was nothing helpful. I thanked her and stepped away. I felt a mixture of emotions about my next move, but I didn't see any way around it. Better it came from me than from Sammy, whose bedside manner would be less than sympathetic.

"Well?" Muller said.

"Can I talk with you outside, sir?"

Muller hesitated, then followed Susan and me out into the hallway.

"I'm afraid you're right, sir."

"Right about what?"

"I think she's lying."

46

I waited for General Muller to say something, but he just stared at me. Despite his own suspicions, he didn't want to accept this.

"I'll bite," Susan finally said to me. "Why?"

"The killers," I said, looking at her, "never planned on a witness. Yet Mi-yong insists they never referred to each other by name and never told Soon-ri *why* they were attacking her."

"Isn't it possible," Muller said slowly, "they were just being careful?"

"Why should they, sir?"

"He's right, sir," Susan said. "They'd have no reason."

"Look," Muller said testily. "It's obvious that Mi-yong loved Soon-ri. If she knew anything more, she'd tell you."

"General," I said. "You said yourself that you suspected—"

"I was wrong. As far as I'm concerned, this is unnecessary. Tomorrow you will find out the names of the accomplices from the bank. Or at least one of them. There's no need to put Mi-yong through any more—"

"One question, sir."

"I said no, Burt."

"Not for her. You."

He hesitated, suddenly suspicious. "Go on."

"Why did she leave before talking to the police, sir?"

"She was frightened. She'd been through a traumatic experience. She didn't know what she was doing."

"That still doesn't explain—"

"The hell it doesn't. You know how the local police treat women like her. It's understandable that she would feel compelled to leave—"

"Before knowing if her daughter had survived, sir?"

I had him. His mouth opened and closed a couple of times, searching for an explanation. Any explanation. But there wasn't one, and we both knew it.

He rubbed his face hard and sounded suddenly angry. "You win, Burt. How the hell do you want to handle it?"

I told him.

★ Three minutes later, I led Muller and Susan back into the bedroom. Susan and I went over to the bed while Muller hung back by the door. Glancing at the phrases I'd scribbled in my notepad, I again asked Mi-yong why she hadn't talked to the police. In the middle of her response, I cut her off.

"*Geo-jin-mal ha-ji-ma.*" Don't lie.

Her head jerked in astonishment. Her eyes darted to Muller.

I said sharply, "*Sa-si-rul mal hae. Dang-jang.*" The truth. Now.

She licked her cracked lips, looking pleadingly at Muller. "I no lie, Hally—"

I snarled in English, "He won't help you. He knows you are lying."

She began trembling, and I saw both confusion and fear in her eyes. She continued to insist she didn't know who the killers were.

I interrupted her again, demanding to know why she was lying to me.

She protested, "*Geo-jin-mal ha-neun-geo a-ni-e-yo.*"

"*Dang-jang mal-hae.*"

"*Mi-an-hae—*"

I suddenly stepped toward her. "*Dang-jang mal-hae!*"

"*Mal-hal-su eop-sseo-yo!*" I cannot tell you!

So there it was, a confirmation that she had knowledge of the killers. I was completely mystified. Why the hell was she reluctant to tell us what she knew?

Mi-yong was sobbing now. She seemed on the verge of collapse. I asked her one more time for the names. She shook me off and blew her nose.

I turned away, feeling ashamed. I couldn't bring myself to hurt her anymore. I looked at Muller and shook my head.

His face was pale. "Mi-yong, please. She was our daughter. If you know anything, tell us."

She stared at him, the tears rolling down her cheeks. She closed her eyes and began rocking back and forth, murmuring to herself. It took me a moment to realize she was praying.

She continued for almost a minute, then fell silent. Her eyes opened and she slowly rose from the bed, then went over to one of the wooden crates. She began digging through the clothing on top, searching for something. As she did, she gazed back at Muller. "*Yong-seo-hae ju-se-yo.*"

Again asking for his forgiveness.

We watched her dig. She finally stood, drawing back her hand. Her back was to us now, and we couldn't see what she'd found.

Then she turned and I saw she was holding a red cloth, folded into a rectangle. The cloth was obviously protecting something inside. Something rigid, fairly thin, and roughly six inches wide. A book?

Mi-yong held the cloth out to Muller with both hands and bowed deeply, offering it to him. As he came forward and took it, she apologized to him in Korean.

Muller placed the cloth on the edge of the bed and began unfolding the sides, which had been layered over the object. Even before he finished, I could make out a shiny gilded surface and knew it wasn't a book.

"A picture," Susan said.

★ Framed against the red cloth was a single five-by-seven photograph in a gold frame, similar to the ones on Soon-ri's dresser. It showed three people taken in front of a green meadow. Mi-yong stood to the right, and appeared to be in her late twenties. Soon-ri was on her left and looked no more than five or six. Next to her was a boy in his late teens. He was rail thin and handsome, with a square jaw and—

I stared at his face.

I felt numbed, dazed. I couldn't breathe. I blinked furiously, but the face was still there. Peering out at me.

I heard Susan inhale sharply in surprise. I heard General Muller asking me if it could really be he. I heard Mi-yong crying softly. I heard everything around me, but I wasn't really listening.

In my mind, the possibilities were swirling together. Slowly the pieces began to gel, forming an image. Hazy, but I could still tell what it was. What it had to be. I shook my head, sickened.

Muller and Susan beside him were fixated on the photograph, their faces bewildered. Trying to grasp the connection.

Susan's eyes went to me. "He grew up with Soon-ri . . ."

I nodded.

". . . which explains why he was so determined to solve the case. Because he did have a relationship with her."

"It's not the kind of relationship you think."

She and Muller both frowned.

"Ask yourselves," I said, looking at Mi-yong, "why she didn't want to show us this."

Susan said, "Okay . . ."

She trailed off, looking at me in growing horror. Noticing her reaction,

Muller finally understood. "My God, Burt. Do you know what you're suggesting?"

I did. To be certain, I asked Mi-yong. Saw her anguished nod of affirmation.

"She lied to protect her son," I told Muller. "And ironically that was the same reason she was afraid to talk to the police—"

Mi-yong cried out.

★ We immediately turned to her. She was staring at the door, her eyes wide with fear.

We knew then.

When Muller, Susan, and I spun around, he was standing in the doorway. His face had a red glow, like it always did after he'd had a few drinks. He said something to Mi-yong, calling her mother. She gazed at him, her body literally shaking. He shook his head sadly, then motioned to us with his gun.

"Better give me the picture, General," Sammy said.

47

Muller didn't move. He just glared at Sammy with naked hate. Susan said, "You sick son of a bitch. You killed your own sister."

"She left us no choice," Sammy said. "She wouldn't listen to reason. I tried, but she . . ." He trailed off, flashing me a tight smile. "It didn't have to end like this, Burt. You should have joined me for that drink."

If I could have reached my gun, I'd have shot him right then and there. "Fuck you."

He sighed, disappointed. He instructed Muller to place the picture on the floor and slide it over. Muller gazed back defiantly. While I admired his courage, he was being foolish now. I told him to do as Sammy asked.

No response. Muller stared into the barrel, as if daring him to shoot.

Now he decides to play John Wayne? I said sharply, "Dammit, General . . ."

Finally, Muller knelt down and pushed the picture across the floor. It came to rest against the wall. Sammy made no move to pick it up. He told Susan and me to kick over our guns. We did, one at a time. Sammy retrieved the pistols and jammed them into his belt. He seemed undecided about what to do next.

Of course, we all knew he had to kill us now. What we had to do was buy time. A few minutes. Until we could figure out some way to—

Sammy reached behind and shut the door.

"At least tell us why," Susan said. She was on the same wavelength, trying to stall. Get him talking.

"You wouldn't understand," he said.

I said, "It was the baby."

Everyone looked at me, including Sammy.

When he didn't saying anything, I went on, "All that stuff you were feeding me about racism and equality was a line, wasn't it? To keep me from suspecting you. Sammy, the cop who bucks the system and puts his career on the line for a dead bar girl because he's a good guy. And I swallowed it. How about that story about the murder of your cousin in America, the one you blamed yourself for? Did that even happen?"

A silence.

"So," I said, "the reality is you're as racist as they come. You couldn't live with the thought that your sister was going to have a black man's baby. You couldn't handle the shame if that ever got out. How'd it play out, Sammy? You try to talk her into an abortion and she wouldn't agree? Told you to fuck off, that it was none of your business. So you figured you'd teach her a lesson. Play doctor and cut her open and—"

"You're wrong, Burt. I never wanted this. Any of it."

"Like hell."

He shook his head, appearing hurt. "I said you would never understand."

"Try us." This was Susan. When I'd been talking, she had taken a small step forward. Trying to get close enough to rush him. "One person would never have a chance. But if we could time it so—"

"It was my duty," Sammy said. "An obligation."

Susan's face went blank. So did Muller's.

For a moment, I was also confused. Both by the statement and the look of regret in Sammy's eyes. I felt a chill at the possibility that he hadn't gone along with the killing willingly. That he had done so was a reflection of who he was and how he defined himself. In the past, I'd often regarded him as more American than Korean. A guy who'd long ago turned his back on the traditions with which he'd been raised.

That assumption, it seemed, had been a mistake.

Susan had moved another step toward him. Sammy finally noticed and shot her a look of warning. Before he could say anything to her, I said quickly, "Your uncle. Killing Soon-ri must have been his idea?"

He hesitated. "He's not my uncle."

"What do you mean he's not your uncle? How can he not—"

"It's not important, Burt." He shook his head sadly. "I'm truly sorry. I have to protect my family."

"You'll never get away with killing us," Muller said. "There will be an investigation. People saw you come in here—"

"General." His voice was quiet, resigned. "I expect to be caught."

This threw Muller. He swallowed hard, flustered. "But your mother—"

"She won't be harmed."

From behind us, Mi-yong spoke up, pleading with Sammy. He kept watching us, but I could tell he was listening to her.

Out of the corner of my eye, I saw Susan edge forward. My muscles tensed. When she made her move, I would go for his gun. Try to knock it—

"Don't try it, Lieutenant," Muller ordered.

Susan's head jerked around. She looked at him in shock.

I was outraged that Muller would do such a thing. Now our one chance to—

"This isn't necessary," Muller said to Sammy. "We can all walk away from this."

"A deal?" Sammy said.

Muller nodded. "I give you my word that I'll close the case."

Sammy shook his head dismissively. "General, you expect me to trust you—"

"I'll give you the tape."

Sammy's head shaking stopped. He squinted at Muller, as if uncertain if he'd heard him correctly. He looked at his mother, then returned to Muller. "You have it with you?"

"I can get it." Muller immediately reached for his cell phone clipped to his belt. Sammy watched him, but made no move to stop him.

It took Muller two calls. Sammy kept the gun pointed at Muller and listened intently to every word.

Afterward, Sammy sat with his back against the door, motioned his pistol downward, and lit a cigarette.

We all joined him on the floor to wait.

★ The minutes ticked by. The bedroom was thick with smoke, and my back ached from sitting on the floor. From the bar, we heard the faint sounds of conversation, as customers began arriving. Yune knocked on the door, but Sammy had his mother send him on his way. Twice I'd tried to get Sammy started in conversation, but he ignored me. He just sat there, quietly chain-smoking. Occasionally I caught him glancing down at the photograph, which was lying beside him against the wall. Finally, he reached down and turned it over, as if he couldn't bear to look at it.

An hour came and went. The noise from the bar became louder. Finally, a little after 8 P.M., we heard footsteps and another knock. It was Mr. Kim, General Muller's driver. Sammy crushed out his cigarette on the bottom of his shoe and told Kim to leave the package outside the door. When Kim left, Sammy cautiously peered out and retrieved a cardboard box, which was taped shut. He pushed it over to me and told me to open it.

I did, removing the tiny cassette player and the box of duplicates.

"Where's the original?" Sammy asked.

I held up the tape player and pushed the PLAY button. Ray's voice.

"Okay," Sammy said.

I clicked off the tape and tossed him the player. He also had me hand him two of the duplicates. He jammed the items into his coat and rose. He gazed at Mi-yong for a moment, then picked up the photograph from the floor. He told me to give it to her, and when I did, he spoke to her softly in Korean. She nodded back slowly.

Sammy carefully dusted his suit and straightened his cuffs. Still facing us, he reached behind and opened the door. We heard the clink of glasses and drunken laughter. Sammy paused, looking at me. "I didn't lie to you about what happened in America. Only the man who was murdered wasn't my cousin; he was my brother." He gave me a sad smile. "Now maybe you understand, huh?"

I hesitated. "I think so."

"I'm glad, Burt."

★ Sammy's footsteps faded rapidly down the hallway.

An instant later, Susan was on her feet and lunging for the door. I threw out an arm and managed to grab her leg. She yanked free, stumbled, and almost fell. She spun to me, her eyes flashing. "Goddammit, Burt—"

"He's armed."

"But he's not expecting anything. Maybe I could surprise him and—"

"Not a chance."

She gestured helplessly toward the door. "This is *crazy*. We can't just let him go. Not when we know that he . . . Oh, all right. *All right*." She glowered at me and stepped away from the door.

I shared her frustration, but the bottom line was there was nothing we could do. The tape was Sammy's get-out-of-jail-free card. The moment we tried to make a case against him and his uncle, all he had to do was play Ray's confession and scream that the big, bad Americans were engaged in a cover-up, then sit back and watch the fireworks.

I turned to Muller as I stretched out the kinks in my back. If anyone should be resentful about how the events had transpired, it should be

Muller. Instead, he appeared remarkably unconcerned. He was standing beside Mi-yong, quietly stroking her hair as she clutched the photograph to her breast. I gave a little cough, and when he glanced up, I told him I wanted to head back to the base and clear up the charges on Ray.

He nodded vaguely. "When you find out about the money and confession, call me at home."

"Yes, sir."

"And tell Kim I'll be out in a few minutes." He looked down at Mi-yong, signaling I was dismissed.

But I kept standing there. I said, "Sir, there are still a few items I'd like to clear up about the killing."

"It's finished, Burt."

"I'm also curious about Sammy's relationship to his uncle. Why he's so close to a guy who's supposed to be a real son of a bitch."

He hesitated; I'd tweaked his interest.

"I'll be brief, sir."

He still seemed reluctant. Finally, he nodded and moved aside.

I came forward and said gently, "Mi-yong . . ."

This was something else she didn't want to tell me. When she did, it became clear why; she'd been raped when she was fourteen and become pregnant. Because she was too young to raise a child, her sister had taken in the boy. Ironic considering the identity of the man who had attacked her.

Her sister's husband.

"So the uncle was really Sammy's father?" Muller said after I translated.

"Yes, sir."

I asked Mi-yong two final questions. Yes, Sammy had worked for an older half brother in New York who had been murdered. And yes, Sammy had argued with his "uncle," trying to stop him from going through with the killing of Soon-ri. "He good boy," she told me, sounding as if she still believed it.

But the key was that she never saw who actually cut Soon-ri.

As Susan and I left, I kept thinking back to what Sammy had told me this morning. *I don't see a farmer being able to cut the fetus out cleanly.* Then I recalled Sammy's job when he'd been a KATUSA, working with the American Army.

He'd been a medic.

48

It was raining heavily by the time we reached the Osan main gate. Despite the weather, there was a steady exodus of people heading downtown. During the forty-minute ride, Susan and I had gone over aspects of the case, filling in the holes as best we could.

The details of the actual murder were pretty straightforward. Sammy had probably called Soon-ri and said he was coming by. When she opened the door, he and his "uncle"—that's still how I thought of the son of a bitch—jumped her. Recognizing their voices, Mi-yong had hidden in the closet and overheard the entire brutal event. Initially, I suspected she thought they were there only to rough up Soon-ri a little, intimidate her so she would stop embarrassing the family. That judgment probably influenced Mi-yong's decision not to reveal herself; she was powerless to help her daughter, and there was no point in both of them being slapped around.

When the horror of what was really occurring sank in, she had no choice but to remain quiet. If her presence was discovered, she knew she would also be killed. Whether Sammy would have allowed that to happen was an open question. I'd like to think that was a line he wouldn't have crossed.

The motive had bothered Susan. That all this had occurred simply because Soon-ri was going to have a black child.

"What's so surprising about that?" I said. "People kill because of racism all the time. Read the paper."

"A member of their own family?"

So I told her how I'd worked things out during the hour we'd spent sitting on the floor.

Soon-ri had despised her uncle and family. She'd relished shaming them by shoving her profession in their faces. When she became pregnant with Ray's child, she saw an opportunity to humiliate them to the point where their reputations would never recover.

Once the village learned Soon-ri had had a black child, the backlash would have been swift. While no one would have done anything overt, the family would have been immediately cut off, treated as if they didn't exist. People would have gone out of their way to avoid contact with them, made hurtful jokes behind their backs. Financially, they would also have suffered because no one would have done business with them. Life would gradually have become intolerable, and eventually they would have been forced to leave.

"Shunned," Susan murmured.

"Pretty much."

"How do you know all this?"

"Chung-hee. Apparently, that's the treatment a lot of the bar girls receive when they return to their villages. That's why a lot of them end up returning to the Ville. It's the only place they have any acceptance. Among their own kind."

She got quiet, thinking about what I had said. After a few moments, she said, "The knots, the phone call to get Ray to show up, Sammy swapping the rope, that was all done because they needed someone convenient to take the fall?"

"It's more complicated than that. The fact that Sammy pursued Ray after the case was officially closed meant they wanted to punish him, exact a measure of revenge. My guess is the uncle was angry at Ray for knocking Soon-ri up and causing them so much trouble. Sammy also probably resented the hell out of Ray. He'd worked his ass off to get where he was, and because of Ray, could lose it all. His reputation would take a big hit once the word got out that his sister had had a black kid. No girl from a reputable family would ever marry him, because his bloodline would be tainted. Considered unclean. He'd also become the laughingstock of the department. Chances are, he'd be demoted or at the minimum reassigned. Can't have a detective lieutenant no one on the force respects," I thought, then added, "I also think General Muller figured into the picture. Why Sammy kept after Ray."

"Muller?"

"Yeah. Sammy was aware of Muller's rep as a hard-ass and knew he wouldn't be satisfied with Chun's clumsy frame job on the chauffeur. Sammy probably figured it was best to stick with the original plan and frame Ray with such overwhelming evidence that Muller would have to accept him as the killer. What he didn't count on was me. My involvement in the case. That worried him because of my closeness to Ray. Sammy knew he'd have to work to convince me of his guilt." I hesitated. "He obviously succeeded."

Susan said quietly, "We all thought it was Ray. Not just you."

"Yeah . . ." But we both knew it wasn't the same thing. I stared out the window.

Susan gave me a minute, then said, "I know Sammy must have forced Mi-nah to lie about Soon-ri having a black boyfriend who beat her . . ."

I faced her, nodding.

". . . but I'm curious when he did it. At the whorehouse?"

"Possibly. Remember when he spoke to Mi-nah right before we left? How she was so uptight afterwards? I think that was when he got the idea to use Mi-nah to pad his case against Ray a little more."

She passed a car and slid into the right lane. "How did Sammy and the uncle know Soon-ri was pregnant in the first place?"

"We know Sammy and Soon-ri had stayed in contact. She must have told him about the pregnancy, betting he'd pass the news on to his uncle. The why isn't too hard to understand. Soon-ri would want her uncle to sweat, knowing what was coming."

She was nodding along as I spoke. She said, "Sammy really couldn't tell his uncle . . . his father . . . no to the killing?"

"Not without shaming himself. He could also justify the murder because Soon-ri was a threat to the family's welfare. And don't forget the guilt Sammy carried with him over his brother's murder all these years. In his mind, Sammy had already let the family down once and couldn't do it again."

Susan nodded. "Even so, it still seems . . . well . . . crazy that he would go along."

And it was, but people had killed for a lot less.

When we rolled up to the intersection by the base, Susan asked me something I hadn't considered: Would the family's reaction have been different if Soon-ri had been a man? I told her I didn't know.

But as we drove through the gate, I recalled another of Sammy's comments from this morning. *The problem with Korea is the way we treat women.*

Prophetic, I thought, as I watched the rain come down.

★ *Why had Ray confessed, and whom did he pay the ten thousand dollars to?*

Those were the only questions we had left.

When Susan and I went into the Security Police Squadron, we thought Ray would finally give us the answers.

We were wrong.

★ "I told you," Ray said. "I confessed because I considered myself responsible for Soon-ri's death."

The clock on the wall of the interrogation room read 9:22. Susan was handling the questioning, which had been going on fruitlessly for ten minutes. She and I were sitting at a small metal table, watching Ray pace. He was dressed in blue uniform pants, black low-quarter shoes, and a white T-shirt.

Susan's face was a mask, hiding the exasperation she felt. I didn't get Ray's unresponsiveness either. Even now, he wouldn't tell us about the money or why he had confessed. And when we'd broken the news that Soon-ri's family had been responsible for her murder, he hadn't batted an eye. It was almost as if he'd known.

Yet, he *had* appeared surprised at Sammy's role and that he'd been Soon-ri's brother.

"So you didn't know they were related?" Susan had asked him.

"No. She never spoke of her family."

"Except her uncle."

"All she ever said was that she hated him. She never went into why, and I didn't ask."

Susan shifted gears and asked him about his confession. He responded with the canned line about feeling responsible for Soon-ri's death. On the question of the bank transfer, she got only silence.

"So," Ray said, continuing to pace, "I take it I'm free to go."

Ignoring him, Susan asked, "Colonel, did you feel responsible because you had made her pregnant?"

"I said she never told me she was pregnant."

"She told Sammy, sir."

"But not me."

"Why not, sir? You were the father. Was she afraid you would insist on an abortion?"

"That's a hypothetical, Lieutenant."

Susan's face darkened, but her manner remained calm. "Getting back to the money . . ."

"Sorry."

"Sir—"

"I won't discuss it."

She'd had enough. She pushed back her chair and rose from the table. "He's all yours, Burt. I'm going to fill out the missing-weapon report."

"Don't mention Sammy."

"I won't." But she didn't look happy about it.

Ray stopped pacing to watch her leave. To me, he said, "I'm not going to say anything different, Burt. Now, if there's nothing else, I'd like to get out of here."

"Ray," I said. "If this is about me . . . Your way of paying me back because I—"

"It isn't." His expression softened, matching his voice. "You did what you had to do. It's not like I made it easy for you. I should have been straight with you from the beginning."

"But you're not talking to me now."

"I will. Be patient."

"What's that supposed to mean?"

"I'll tell you tomorrow."

"Why tomorrow?"

He gave me an odd look but wouldn't say anything more.

49

While Ray went to retrieve his toiletries and put on his shirt, I used the duty sergeant's phone to call General Muller. He'd arrived home, and I could hear his wife's voice in the background, shrill and angry. Muller told me to hold on and cupped the mouthpiece. For several minutes, I drummed the desk, listening to the muffled voices of an argument. When Muller finally came back to me, it was quiet. I said, "Sir, I can call back—"

"You talk to Ray?" He was tense, speaking quickly.

"Yes, sir." I relayed the conversation.

"What's so special about tomorrow?"

"He won't say, sir. I can ask him again, but I doubt it will—"

I paused when I heard a loud banging sound. Like a door slamming against a wall. Then his wife screaming at him. Calling him a liar and a cheat.

Muller tried to talk over her, saying, "Honey, please. It was a long time ago. I swear to you I didn't . . . *For chrissakes, if you'd just listen—*"

He covered the phone again. More muffled sounds.

This time I hung up.

★ The rain was down to a light mist, and stars were beginning to peak through the clouds. Susan waited in the car while I walked Ray up to his door, which had been repaired. As he fit the key into the lock, I said, "I thought maybe I could come in and we could talk a little."

He glanced at me. "You never quit, do you?"

"We don't have to talk about the case."

"You still worried that I'm a little suicidal?" He sounded amused.

The look I gave him told him I didn't share his humor.

He sighed wearily. "Will you relax? You took the gun. Remember?"

We stood there, looking at each other in the semidarkness. Ray tried to reassure me with a smile, but I sensed a deep sadness. I told him that I didn't think he should be alone and that I wanted him to come over to the house. Spend the next few days with Chung-hee and me.

"She'd like to see you," I said.

"Tell you what, how about we grab dinner tomorrow?"

"Ray, I really think it's best if you—"

"Burt," he said, "last night was a bad moment. That's all. I'm past that now. I'll be fine. Now go on home and get some sleep, huh? And tell Chung-hee that I'm sorry for what I put you through." He squeezed my shoulder, stepped into the house, and closed the door.

I went back to the car wishing I could believe him.

★ "No wonder Muller's wife was pissed off," Susan said when I clicked on the seat belt.

Glancing up, I saw her staring intently across the street at General Muller's house, which was ablaze with light. His staff car was sitting in the driveway, and there didn't appear to be anyone around. I said, "I give up."

"Mi-yong," she said, pointing. "She's sitting in the staff car."

"She is?" I squinted, and from our angle, I could barely make out a dark form in the rear window. "You sure it's her?"

"It's her. Mr. Kim came out and talked to her." She shook her head. "I gotta hand it to Muller. He's got balls, bringing her here."

"Didn't have much choice. He obviously couldn't leave her alone, not in the state she was in."

"Yeah, but— Oh, oh."

Susan was reacting to Mrs. Muller's appearance at the front door. She turned as if talking to someone in the house, then went down the steps and walked across the lawn toward the staff car. At any moment, I expected the general to rush after her, but he never showed. Mrs. Muller had reached the car and was reaching for the door handle.

I felt myself getting angry. How could General Muller allow this to happen? I popped the seat belt and threw open the passenger door.

"What?" Susan said. "You're not going over there?"

"Damn right. If you think I'm going to sit by and let Mrs. Muller—"

"Better take another look first."

When I did, I couldn't believe what I was seeing.

Instead of raging at Mi-yong, Mrs. Muller was helping her out of the car and seemed all beaming attentiveness. Mi-yong gave her a bow and Mrs. Muller smiled back. They appeared to speak for a few moments, then Mrs. Muller put her arm around Mi-yong and led her toward the house.

I shook my head in amazement as I watched them disappear inside.

"Your problem, Burt," Susan said, suppressing a smile, "is that you don't understand women."

"Right. Like you expected this reaction."

"No, but I'm not completely surprised either. Mrs. Muller was reacting out of jealousy earlier. She thought her hubby was having an affair, and now she knows the truth. More important, she knows she has no reason to feel threatened by Mi-yong."

"Thanks for the lesson, Doctor," I said dryly.

She grinned, starting the engine. "Don't mention it."

As I eased back in the seat, I wondered if Mrs. Muller's being suspicious of her husband was one of the reasons for her harsh treatment of Chung-hee. If so, then perhaps I'd been overly critical—

"Uh, Burt. The door . . ."

"Oh, sure." I pulled it shut.

"Home?"

I nodded.

Except when I called, my mother-in-law said Chung-hee wasn't there.

★ Ten minutes later, we pulled alongside the curb in front of the jewelry store. Through the window, we could see Chung-hee and Mi-nah behind the glass display counter. Instead of the faded dress, Mi-nah was wearing a pink blouse and white slacks. With her face scrubbed free of makeup and her hair pulled back in a ponytail, she seemed even younger than I remembered. She was holding up a silver bracelet to the light, her eyes wide with wonderment. We saw her smile; it was a nice smile. A child's smile.

"Okay," Susan said quietly.

I glanced at her. "What's okay?"

She was still staring at the window. "I am. I'm okay with how the case turned out. We tried and things didn't work out." She paused. "What the hell. That's life."

"So the fact that Sammy—"

"*Screw* Sammy," she said with sudden emotion. "The important thing is Mi-nah. She has a chance now. That was all I ever needed. A chance."

And then she turned to me, and I saw her eyes were glistening. For the first time I truly understood how difficult it must have been for Susan to achieve what she had. Shake the welfare cycle and make something of her life. I told her she'd done well.

"So will Mi-nah, Burt. You'll see."

"I hope so."

As I opened the door, she touched my arm. "Mind if I come in? I'd like to tell Chung-hee she's doing a wonderful thing, giving her hope."

I smiled. "Sure. How about a beer?"

"I won't be staying that long."

Of course, I first had to tell Chung-hee about Ray and put up with her I-told-you-so's. I told her I'd give her the details later. She didn't care. Ray was innocent and all was right with her world. Afterward, while Susan chatted with Chung-hee, I went into the storeroom at the back and grabbed two OB beers from the fridge, betting on the come. When I returned, I saw what I had expected.

Chung-hee, Susan, and Mi-nah were all clustered behind the counter, talking and giggling like kids as they tried on an assortment of jewelry. I went over and handed Susan a beer, then parked myself on a stool, watching and sipping. What struck me was the joy on Mi-nah's face, the fact that she could even possess that emotion after the trauma she'd been through. At that moment, I began to believe she could make it, but only if there was someone there for her.

And Chung-hee realized this. She knew that once we took on Mi-nah, we would be committing ourselves long-term. The question now was whether Chung-hee could give up her ambitions long enough for—

I was aware of the sudden silence. I lowered the beer from my lips and looked at the counter.

Chung-hee was no longer smiling.

Neither was Susan.

And Mi-nah looked frightened.

I followed their eyes out the window. Two men were coming across the sidewalk toward the jewelry store. The man in front was small framed and wore a white suit. I swore.

Uncle Chun.

50

I rose from the stool, barking instructions. Chung-hee relayed them to Mi-nah and practically shoved her toward the back of the store. Mi-nah kept glancing back at her with panicked eyes as she darted past the counter for the staircase. It seemed to take forever until we finally heard her footsteps racing up the stairs.

The bell over the door jingled, and we all looked to the door.

Chun entered first, followed by Chi, the annoyingly friendly killer who'd been tailing me earlier today. Chi had upgraded his wardrobe from T-shirt and jeans to a cheap suit. I was curious to see he'd also accessorized by carrying an eel-skin briefcase. I checked his left armpit and saw the bulge. Ignoring my gaze, Chi casually locked the door and flipped over the Closed sign.

Still, I was calm. Chun would be crazy to try anything now. Not with all the people walking by outside.

Chun looked at Chung-hee, gave her a tight smile. As he walked up to me, he said smoothly, "Ah, Burton. You are looking well."

I nodded cautiously. "What do you want, Uncle Chun?"

Bad move. Chun's mouth twitched. He made a guttural comment in Korean, rebuking me for my rudeness. I knew better than to reply.

"Respect," he said, glaring at me, "is always important, Burton."

"Yes."

"This is something Americans do not always remember."

"Respect goes both ways, Uncle."

He appraised me coldly. I thought he was going to interpret my remark as further insolence. Instead, he shrugged it off and lit a cigarette, squinting at me through the curling smoke. "You should forget about what has occurred, Burton. It was business. Nothing more."

I nodded.

"We are family. We must have peace. You agree?"

I hesitated. "Yes."

He studied me as if judging my sincerity. Abruptly, his face relaxed, becoming almost friendly. "Good. We have an understanding. There will be no more talk of the past."

Keeping his eyes on me, he crooked a finger. Chi immediately sprang forward, placed the briefcase on the floor near my foot, then returned to his position by the door and folded his arms. I waited for him to toss me his trademark smile. He never did.

"My offer for the store," Chun explained, glancing down at the briefcase. "But the situation has changed, and I am afraid I cannot give you the original price."

"I see." Chung-hee was the owner, and he should be negotiating with her. That he wasn't doing so was because she was a woman. I looked at Chung-hee to she if she wanted to take over. She shook her head. She didn't want anything to do with Chun.

"How much, Uncle?" I asked him.

A scowl as if I'd said something distasteful. "The papers are inside, Burton. The price is final. You have until tomorrow to decide."

I nodded.

He turned and looked at Chung-hee expectantly. She hesitated; she did not want to do this. Chun's face remained a mask, waiting. Finally, Chung-hee lowered her head. "*Go-map-seum-ni-da, Sam-chon.*" Thank you, Uncle.

Chun nodded regally and pivoted for the door. Chi hurriedly unlocked it and held it open.

"Oh, Burton . . ." Chun paused at the doorway, looking back at me. "I will also want the check for five million won."

I said, "Check?"

Then I understood. This was a lot more than the price Sammy said Chun would accept for Mi-nah. Not that I was surprised. He was screwing me, putting me in my place. I told Chun he would have the money by tomorrow.

"Next time, Burton," he said quietly, "ask before you take."

"I will, Uncle."

He smiled coldly, flipped an ash from his cigarette, and strode out dramatically. Chi followed, drawing the door closed. We watched as they continued to the bar next door.

"Bastard," Chung-hee said, finally turning away.

"At least we have Mi-nah," I said.

Chung-hee didn't reply. She was staring at the floor, disgusted with what she'd been forced to do.

I said, "You had no choice, honey."

She sighed, finally looking at me. When she spoke, there was no bitterness—only a weary acceptance. "That's just it, Burt. I never will have a choice . . . here."

There was nothing I could say.

Susan caught my eye. "Sammy. He must have told Chun you had Mi-nah."

I nodded, bending for the briefcase. I froze as I picked it up. Glancing up, I saw Susan and Chung-hee frowning at me.

"It's too heavy for papers," I said.

★ Chun had no reason to kill us now. Not when we owed him money.

Still I wasn't about to take any chances. Chung-hee went upstairs to open the office window that overlooked the alley and to get Mi-nah. When they returned, I sent them outside to wait on the front curb. I didn't waste my time trying to convince Susan to join them.

After carrying the briefcase upstairs, I balanced it on the window frame while Susan carefully released the latches. We had to wait until a group of boisterous GIs walked by with a couple of bar girls.

I held the briefcase out the window as Susan waved a flashlight back and forth for a final look.

"Anytime, Burt," Susan said.

I let go.

★ The briefcase was lying on the ground less than six feet from the back door. The hinged lid had bounced open maybe three inches, and we could see the edge of something red poking out. Susan shone the flashlight down as I opened the lid all the way.

I removed a red folder, flipped through it to confirm it was probably the contract for the store, then passed it to Susan. The only other item in the case was a thick package wrapped in butcher paper, heavily taped and tied with string.

I removed it and tested the weight. Five or six pounds.

"Can you tell what's inside?" Susan asked.

I gently squeezed the sides. "Feels almost like small hand weights."

"Huh?"

We carried everything back into the store. As Susan and I placed the items on the counter, I motioned to Chun-hee and Mi-nah through the window. As they came inside, I told Chung-hee to lock the door while I pulled down the blinds.

Returning to the counter, I handed Chung-hee the contract, which contained a dozen or so pages written in Korean. As I dug out my pocketknife, I asked her, "How much?"

She flipped and read briefly. "Roughly half."

"Of what he was offering before?"

She nodded.

"That's still almost a hundred thousand dollars. It would set us up in the States."

"I know . . ."

She bit her lip, looking at Mi-nah, who gazed back blissfully unaware of her concerns.

As I cut away at the rope and tape, I saw that Susan was about to say something to Chung-hee. I shook her off; this wasn't any of her business. She locked me with a glare. I sighed and tore at the paper.

Now I was suddenly the bad guy. But, hell, what did Susan expect me to say? She'd witnessed the scene with Chun; she had to know the price Chung-hee would pay to remain in Korea. Regardless of how much I wanted to help Mi-nah, my first priority had to be for my wife. I didn't want Chung-hee to look back someday and regret having stayed simply because—

I frowned. I'd just ripped a large hole in the package and could see a dark metal cylinder, glinting in the light. Why in the world would—

I tore away at the remaining paper and tape. When I finished, I stepped back, shaking my head in confusion.

"Guns," Susan breathed.

I picked up the smaller one, popped the clip. Still loaded. "They're ours."

She inspected her pistol and gave me a searching look. "Why would Sammy give Chun our guns?"

I tried to think. "No clue."

"Could Chun have been involved in the murder with Sammy?"

"That still doesn't explain why Chun returned our guns to us."

There was a long silence as we tried to figure out this twist.

"What's that over there, Burt?" Chung-hee asked.

She was standing with an arm around Mi-nah, who was staring nervously at our guns. Chung-hee pointed my attention to the remaining butcher paper, still on the counter. I saw what appeared to be a business card poking out. I picked it up. Korean printing. I handed the card to Chung-hee.

"It's a junkyard north of town," she said, reading.

"Chun's?" I asked.

"Probably."

"The card might have been left by mistake," Susan said.

"It wasn't," Chung-hee said. She flipped over the card to reveal a blue-ink scrawl. It took me a moment to realize the words were in English.

"It's your name, Burt," Chung-hee said.

51

Chung-hee didn't want me to go; she thought it might be a trap. I agreed with her and stuck the card in my pocket. Normally we closed the store at midnight, but this was anything but a normal night. We were all physically and emotionally drained, and needed time to decompress. While Chung-hee and Mi-nah removed the jewelry from the display cases to lock in the upstairs safe, I called General Muller to resume our earlier conversation.

"Bad news," I told Chung-hee as I hung up the phone by the cash register. "General Muller wants Susan and me to come over and talk about the case."

She nodded in understanding, while Susan almost choked out the last of her beer in my face.

"Now?" Susan said.

"I'm afraid so," I said.

Susan swore, muttering under her breath.

Chung-hee watched her sympathetically. "How long?" she asked me.

"The general didn't say."

"I'll wait up."

"It could be at least an hour, honey."

She gave me a long look. "I'll wait. We need to talk."

Translation: She still hadn't made up her mind to accept Chun's offer. Frankly, I thought the decision was cut-and-dried. I went over and kissed her on the lips. She told me to hurry, and I said I would.

"An hour?" Susan said to me, as we walked out of the door. "What's Muller want to talk about for an hour?"

"Nothing."

She stopped on the sidewalk, squinting at me.

"I never called him." I gave her a smile.

The light clicked on then. She stared at me in disbelief. "You *crazy*? Jesus, the man *kills* people."

I nodded.

"Christ, Burt. You said yourself it could be a trap."

"It isn't."

"How the hell do you know that?"

"Because," I said, "Chun gave us our guns. The more I think about it, the more I'm convinced he did that so we *wouldn't* think this was a trap. Then there's the junkyard. That's pretty damned suggestive. Especially when you consider the banker's reluctance to tell Sammy the name on the account." I stepped off the curb and swung around to the passenger door.

Susan gazed at me over the roof. "What does the banker have to do with a junkyard?"

"Everything. Get in. I'll explain on the way."

"This," she said sarcastically, "I'm dying to hear."

But as she shifted the gearshift into drive, she suddenly turned to me. Her eyes were wide, the words spilling out excitedly as she tried to keep up with her thoughts. "Shit! The banker. He was *afraid*. That's why he wouldn't talk . . ."

"Yes."

"Chun. He owns the account. That means Ray paid him the ten grand—"

"Right . . ."

"Son of a bitch. It all fits. That's how Chun got our guns. *Sammy's at the junkyard.*"

★ The Sancho Junkyard was a fenced-in compound located in one of the older industrial zones in the north part of town, not far from the railroad station. Susan parked near the automatic gate and dug out her flashlight from the glove compartment. We got out and surveyed the area. There were a number of light poles interspersed within the perimeter, and we could see an assortment of junked vehicles strewn about or heaped in piles. From the center of the compound rose the silhouette of a crane arm, and over to the right, the peaked roof of a building was visible behind an enormous mound of tires.

"Doesn't seem to be anyone around," Susan said.

I hollered out, listened, then tried again. Only silence.

"No dogs either," Susan said, sounding relieved.

"None that we know of."

The gate was illuminated by a streetlight. We walked over to the left gatepost, which was affixed with an intercom. As I reached for the talk button, I froze.

The gate was already rumbling open.

"There," Susan said.

She was looking halfway up the light pole, at a small TV camera.

"They know we're here," she murmured.

I nodded.

We entered the compound, the gate closing behind us. I heard a soft click as Susan flipped off the safety on her gun. I fingered into my belt and did the same. We stood for a moment, scanning the shadows, ears straining. Still nothing.

We followed the asphalt roadway, which continued straight ahead. After maybe a hundred meters, it angled right into an open area. Everywhere we looked were piles of mangled metal, a number containing large blocks that had been crushed from vehicles—

Susan said tersely, "Burt . . ."

"I see him."

From the direction of the building we'd noticed earlier, we could see a man coming toward us. He was still in shadow, but we could make out the flare of his suit jacket as he walked. Susan and I tensed, hands on our pistols.

He stepped out into the light.

It was Chi, and this time he was smiling.

Chi stopped maybe ten feet away. He pointed off toward the crane and rattled off a few words in Korean. Then he gave us a friendly wave, turned, and casually strolled back the way he'd come.

"What did he say, Burt?"

"Something about a red car."

We headed for the crane, which had one of those big circular magnet assemblies dangling from the end of a cable. Thirty meters beyond, we could see an enormous, rectangular press used to crush metal into blocks. Near the base of the crane was a row of roughly a dozen vehicles. Most were heavily damaged, but one appeared completely unmarked.

A four-door sedan with a cherry red paint job.

We approached the sedan from the driver's side. Susan flipped on her flashlight and shone it through the window. Nothing.

Susan made a gagging sound. "The smell . . ."

I nodded. The overpowering odor of decomposing flesh.

We paused to put on the latex gloves. Susan held the light while I opened the door.

He was there.

★ He was lying faceup across the front seats, staring at us with unseeing eyes. He was in his late sixties and balding, a skinny little man with a laborer's weathered face. From the midchest up, he was bare, the remainder of his torso covered by a yellow blanket, which was dark with congealed blood.

"Move the light down a little," I told Susan.

When she did, I picked up the side of the blanket.

I dropped it fast.

"Jesus," Susan said, stepping back in shock. "They gutted him. The maggots . . ."

I nodded, following her.

We moved away from the car, taking deep breaths. The smell followed us. She said, "They did him like Soon-ri. Cut him wide open."

"That was the idea. It was a revenge killing."

"So he must be Sammy's father?"

"The age fits."

"He's been dead for a while. Certainly before we last saw Sammy."

I nodded. This was summer. For the maggots to appear, he had to have been dead for the good part of a day.

Susan gestured to the car. "I didn't see anyone in the backseat, but I didn't look down on the floorboards."

"I'll check."

Taking the flashlight, I walked over to the back door and shone the beam inside. It was empty except for some clothes wadded up on the floor. I picked them up. Pants and a shirt, wrapped around a pair of worn tennis shoes. No wallet or ID, but they would be careful about that.

I left the clothing and went back around to the driver's door, reached below the dash, then popped the release. Susan was already peering inside the trunk when I came around.

"The smell isn't as bad," she said.

★ Unlike his father, they hadn't bothered to cover Sammy with a blanket.

He was completely nude, curled up in the trunk in the fetal position. His eyes were closed and, at a glance, he appeared to be sleeping.

Except that most of his stomach and genitals were gone.

I shifted the light, located his clothes wadded toward the right front corner. I handed Susan the flashlight, leaned over, and grabbed the bundle with both hands.

"No maggots," Susan said, studying his wounds. "He hasn't been dead very long. Not much blood in the trunk, either. Killed him somewhere else and stuck him in here."

"Makes sense. They probably got his father to reveal who was in on the killing, then went after Sammy."

We were contemplative, staring at Sammy's face under the flashlight beam. In death, his facial muscles had relaxed, giving him a puffy look. Susan shook her head. "You know, I thought I hated him. But now, looking at him, I almost feel . . ."

"Sorry for him."

"A little. Crazy, huh?"

"Not really. I'm going to miss him."

She looked at me in surprise.

I shrugged. "He had a lot of good qualities. He was a good cop who usually tried to do the right thing. I think he just got caught up in a situation he couldn't handle. Got his priorities all balled up."

"Because he couldn't tell his father no."

"Something like that." I moved back and unfurled Sammy's clothes. Nothing dropped out. I checked out his pockets and handed the items to Susan, one by one. Cigarettes, a lighter, gum, car keys—

I removed a glassine packet from his inside jacket pocket. One of the knot remnants. The square knot. I stared at it under the beam of Susan's flashlight.

"Yeah," Susan said. "I'm wondering the same thing. Why the hell was Sammy so hot and bothered by the two types of knots? He was there when they were tied."

The answer was now obvious; Sammy and his uncle *hadn't* tied the square knot in the packet. I exhaled slowly, chilled at the implication.

"It had to have been Colonel Johnson," Susan said softly.

"I know . . ."

"When he walked into the apartment, Soon-ri must have been alive and able to talk. That's how he knew about the uncle."

"He didn't know about Sammy."

She thought. "She was probably in and out of consciousness from the pain and the ether. Maybe she passed out before she could tell Colonel Johnson about him. Or maybe Colonel Johnson figured out on his own that her family killed her. One thing's for sure, the square knot tells us he must have known he was the baby's father."

"Yeah . . ." I slowly pocketed the packet. *I'm responsible for her death,* Ray had said.

Now we finally knew why.

After Susan and I returned Sammy's clothing to the trunk, we stood for a moment, looking at him. Shaking her head, Susan said, "I still don't understand why Chun wanted you to see . . . this."

I shrugged. "It's a message."

"Message?"

"To warn me not to interfere again—"

Footsteps.

We spun and went for our guns.

52

We immediately relaxed, lowering our hands from our guns.

Instead of Chi or another of Chun's hoods, we saw a portly man in blue coveralls approaching the crane. He didn't acknowledge our presence in any way. He climbed up the steps into the cab, and we heard the rumble of the engine starting up.

Susan and I shut the trunk, popped off our gloves, and moved back about twenty meters to watch.

The magnet swung down and effortlessly picked up the red car by the roof, then deposited it between the clamshell-like hands of the giant press. Moments later came a high-pitched whine followed by the sound of shattering glass and the screech of tortured steel. It took less than a minute for the car to be reduced to an unrecognizable block, which the crane operator then dropped unceremoniously onto a mound with hundreds of similar cubes.

"Let's go," I said quietly.

As we walked toward the gate, I told Susan to call General Muller and tell him about Sammy.

She dug out her cell phone from her fanny pack. "And Colonel Johnson?"

"Not yet."

"We'll have to tell General Muller about him eventually."

We walked a few steps. "Not necessarily."

She sighed, shaking her head. "Sorry, Burt. I can't sit on this. Muller has a right to know about Colonel Johnson."

"Why?"

"*Why?* Colonel Johnson has to be held accountable—"

"You'll only hurt Ray's family."

"Burt, please . . ."

I stopped and faced her. "Call Ray first."

"Why?"

"Just call him." I told her the number.

She hesitated, then punched it in. Ray's machine answered. I gave her his cell phone, and she tried it with the same result. She shrugged. "He must have gone out."

"It's almost midnight," I said.

She frowned and started to reply. Then I saw a flicker of understanding in her eyes. She slowly returned her phone to her fanny pack.

"I guess General Muller can wait," she said.

★ I tried to keep my mind blank, but the images wouldn't let me go. They kept shuttering before me, one after another. Like the frames of an old sixteen-millimeter movie on a projector that was out of sync.

Ray removes the gag from Soon-ri as he leans over her on the bed. She has regained consciousness and tries to speak, her voice weak and barely audible. She struggles to form the words, tell him who did this and why. Ray's face is filled with horror as he begins to untie her. His only thought is to help her. Get her to a hospital.

As he loosens the first knot, it hits him what Muller's reaction will be and what this will mean for his career. Panic starts to set in. Ray tries to think clearly but can't. All he knows is that if he helps her, he'll lose everything.

He slowly picks up her hand and begins to retie it. Soon-ri's pain-filled eyes look at him in disbelief. She struggles to fight him, but has no strength. She tries to scream, but he gags her again. Ray avoids looking at her as he rushes around the room, removing anything incriminating: clothing, the photograph, his toothbrush. As he hurries to the door, his intention is to get away.

In my mind, the frame freezes. Ray's hand is on the door and he's looking back toward the bedroom.

He shakes his head.

He can't do it. He can't just let her die.

So Ray returns to the living room. He reaches for the phone and makes the call. He hangs up, takes a final look at the bedroom, then walks to the door.

As he leaves, the image fades.

Maybe that wasn't exactly what happened, but it wouldn't be far off. The only question was when had Ray actually made the call to the SPs. While Soon-ri was still alive?

Or had he stood by waiting for her to die?

I think I've known the answer all along.

I heard the click of the car blinker and felt the turn. Then Susan's voice, saying we'd arrived.

I sat up in the seat and opened my eyes.

★ Ray's BOQ was dark and silent. We rang the bell and banged on the door, but got no response. Susan tried his phone again and hung up when the machine came on. Finally, I motioned her aside. This time it took me two tries to splinter the lock.

As we went inside, I flipped on the light switch by the door and called out Ray's name. On the coffee table in the living room, we saw a half-empty bottle of bourbon. Susan looked at me and shook her head.

She took the spare bedroom while I checked out the master. Ray's bed hadn't been slept in, and his dirty uniform wasn't in the hamper. When I emerged, Susan was standing at the dining table, staring down at something.

I said, "Anything?"

She nodded, glancing at me somberly as I approached. She handed me three envelopes. The one on top was addressed to me; the second to Ray's ex-wife, Linda; and the third to General Muller. That was Ray. Mr. Organization.

Susan stepped back and said, "There's also a picture."

I looked at the table and picked up the photograph. It was the one of me toasting Ray at his wedding. On an index card paper-clipped to it, Ray had written simply: *Thought you might want this, Burt.*

My face felt hot, and I had to blink to see. I returned the picture to the table, then slid the envelopes into my jacket. "Ray's got to be here, somewhere," I managed.

"He is," Susan said.

When I looked at her, she was standing by the sliding glass door, gazing outside. She turned on the patio light and slid open the door. We heard a soft creaking sound.

As I followed her out, I finally saw him.

★ Ray was hanging from parachute cord that he'd looped around the wooden overhang. He was still wearing his uniform, his body swaying gently in the breeze. Below him was a metal folding chair, kicked over on its side. I held Ray up while Susan stood on the chair and removed the noose from his neck. We laid him faceup on the patio.

"Rigor is setting in," Susan said quietly. "He did this not long after we left him."

I swallowed hard, staring down at Ray's lifeless face. "You know I tried . . . I really tried. I wanted to help him. He wouldn't let me. I should have forced him to come with me. If only I'd—"

"He didn't want any help, Burt. He was going to end this his way. There was nothing you could have done. Nothing anyone could have done."

I felt the emotion well up inside me. I walked to the back edge of the patio and stared into the darkness.

"I can take it from here, Burt," Susan said, coming up behind me. "Handle the paperwork and brief General Muller." She paused, then added, "I'll do what I can to cover for Colonel Johnson."

I slowly faced her. "Forget what I said earlier." I reached into my jacket and removed the letter addressed to General Muller. "Give this to the general."

She took the letter with a puzzled look. "This is probably a confession."

"Ray wanted Muller to know."

I declined Susan's offer of her car keys, telling her I'd walk to the cabstand. That I needed to walk. On the way out, I took a last look at Ray, then retrieved the picture from the table and swung by his office for an envelope and a stamp. As I headed down the hill, it began to rain.

53

The rain was a light drizzle that felt cool on my face. The mile-long walk to the cabstand took me fifteen minutes. The ride home in the cab another twelve, because I had the driver swing by the post office so I could drop off the letter to Ray's wife in the box out front, along with a note of my own. Chung-hee was lying in bed reading the contract when I came home. She asked me if I wanted anything to eat, and I told her no.

She read my face and knew something was wrong. After I showered, toweled off, and changed into a robe, I made her get us both drinks before I told her. Later, we sat on the bed and read Ray's letter together. She cried, and for the first time since I could remember, so did I.

Ray's letter was three pages long, written in a sloppy scrawl, which told me he did it while he was feeling the bourbon. The opening paragraph was particularly difficult, because Ray talked at length of our friendship, what it had meant to him all these years. Next he discussed the regrets in his life, the fact that he'd misplaced his values along the way. He said he wished he'd been a better father and husband, and had spent more time enjoying life than just surviving it. He spoke with surprising eloquence of the dangers of an existence defined by ambition and achievement. "The problem," he said, "is you're never satisfied. Nothing is ever enough. Each time I was promoted, all I could think about was getting to the next rank."

Then he wrote of the pressure of being black in a white world, of how he'd been conditioned that he had to be better than anyone else to succeed. When he found out that wasn't true, at least in the military, he couldn't change. "Because I was too damned terrified of failure, Burt."

Ray wrapped up the letter with a brief account of his actions in Soon-ri's apartment. As Susan and I suspected, he'd found her barely conscious but alive. Ray said he'd reacted on impulse when he decided not to take her to the hospital. He'd regretted his actions almost immediately, but by then it was too late. He said the guilt had consumed him and now he was trying to make it up to Soon-ri in the only way he knew how.

"The bastards cut her because she was having a black kid. My kid. Helluva thing, huh? Her own family. Joke's on me. I'm the one who told my father that racism wasn't that big a deal anymore. Anyway, by the time you read this, they should be dead.

"Gotta go, Burt. Feeling the booze and don't want to pass out before I finish what I have to do. Tried to call my father. He wasn't in, but I left a message. I know I shouldn't ask, but do me a favor. Call him so he doesn't hear the news from someone else. Ask him to forgive me.

"I'm sorry for everything, buddy. I really am.

"Ray.

"P.S. Do something that's worth a damn with your life. I wish I had."

I had already finished reading and was watching Chung-hee. She blinked back tears and slowly lowered the letter to the bed. "I liked him," she said softly.

"I know."

"Did he really let Soon-ri die?"

I'd never lied to her and wasn't about to start now. "He didn't do anything to help her."

She gazed down at the letter, then picked it up and slowly rose from the bed.

I said, "I'll need the phone number at the bottom of the last page."

She tore out the number, then handed it to me. She took the rest of the letter into the bathroom. I heard the sounds of more paper tearing, followed by the flush of the toilet. She returned to the bed.

"We won't talk of this again."

"No."

After that we sat on the bed and sipped our drinks. I asked her about Chun's offer, and she started giving me a list of reasons why we should take it. She tried to come across as upbeat, but I could tell her heart wasn't really into what she was saying.

It took me a while to get her to admit she now wanted to stay. She told me that Mi-nah was only part of the reason she'd changed her mind. There were so many girls like her, and she had this idea that maybe she could do something to help them, set up a support program to get them out of the bars. She knew it would be difficult and that there would be a lot of resistance from the club owners, including her uncle. But someone had to do something, and she wanted to try.

Listening to the quiet passion in her voice, I found myself thinking of Soon-ri and her mother, Mi-yong, of the life they'd been forced to live and why. Then I thought about Mi-nah and the faces of the countless other girls I'd seen in the brothels. Finally, I thought about Ray, the tragedy of a life defined by ambition and little else, and how much I didn't want that to be me.

At that moment, I realized that this was one of the forks in the road that General Muller had mentioned, where you had one chance to make the right choice.

After I gave Chung-hee my answer, we held each other tight, and her tears felt warm on my skin. She kept asking me if I was sure, and I told her I had never been so certain of anything in my life.

Do something in your life that's worth a damn, Ray had said.

I'd try.

★ Chung-hee fell asleep in my arms with the light still on. Even though tomorrow would be a busy day, I was too jazzed up to sleep. Besides, I still had something important I had to do.

I eased out of bed, picked up the glasses and the contract, and took them downstairs. After I made another drink, I went to my office and wrote out a check for five million won—the payment for Mi-nah—and attached it to the contract with a letter to Chun saying we were declining his offer for the store.

Then I made notes on a page about the pitch I would give General Muller. How Chung-hee and I were starting a program for bar girls and needed the sponsorship of the base to keep the club owners from interfering. That Muller would go along wasn't a question, which was reassuring.

After that, I just sat for a while and stared at the number Chung-hee had torn from the letter. When I finally picked up the phone to call Ray's father, I still had no idea what to say—not that it really mattered.

I began by telling him Ray was my best friend. . . .

AUTHOR'S NOTE

★ I had two reasons for writing this story. First, I wanted to provide the reader with an entertaining murder thriller with more than the usual serving of plot twists. Second, I wanted the reader to gain some insight into the culture in which the story is based.

As the son of an American diplomat and a Chinese mother, I spent my formative years in Asia, primarily the Philippines, Thailand, and South Korea. Later, while serving in the military, I was stationed at a base in South Korea, which explains my familiarity with the red-light district I write about. Besides giving me a taste for bad beer and spicy food, my experiences taught me to appreciate the people in this part of the world: their incredibly strong work ethic, their inherent sense of integrity and loyalty, their concept of total selflessness, and their belief in placing the family unit above all else. The list of admirable qualities is endless, but as with any society, there is also a darker side.

At this point I'd like to mention that the judgments in this story are my own and are seen through the prism of an American's eyes. I'd like to think that my background as a half-Chinese kid growing up in Asia allows me some perspective, and I hope it's a fair one. My intent is not to cast stones at any one culture per se, but to point out an injustice within a segment of the population that is powerless to fight back.

In the red-light district, I've seen the shame in a young girl's eyes as she disappears down an alley with her third or fourth or tenth john of the night. I've met bar girls who dulled themselves senseless with booze and drugs to insulate themselves from that shame. I've talked to these same girls, and asked them why they didn't just quit and go home. The answer was always the same: They can't.

So night after night, they hustle for drinks, hoping the next American GI they meet will be their ticket out. It rarely happens, and when their looks begin to fade . . . Well, you can probably imagine the rest.

Anyway, I think a seedy bar scene is a good setting for a murder. As you read this, please know that my intent was not to embellish or disparage. I just thought the story of these girls and the life they're forced to lead is worth thinking about. Even for a little while.

PAT DAVIS